ST. MARTIN'S

MINOTAUR

MYSTERIES

OTHER TITLES FROM
ST. MARTIN'S **MINOTAUR** MYSTERIES

THE COMPANY OF CATS by Marian Babson
DEAD SOULS by Ian Rankin
A COMEDY OF HEIRS by Rett MacPherson
FAITHFUL UNTO DEATH by Caroline Graham
RUBICON by Steven Saylor
BONE HUNTER by Sarah Andrews
IRISH TENURE by Ralph McInerny
ZEN AND THE CITY OF ANGELS
by Elizabeth M. Cosin
DRAG STRIP by Nancy Bartholomew
MURDER ON THE LUSITANIA by Conrad Allen
THE BLACK BOOK by Ian Rankin
GUMBO LIMBO by Tom Corcoran
MURDER IN GEORGETOWN by Elliott Roosevelt
THIRTEENTH NIGHT by Alan Gordon
THE CORNBREAD KILLER by Lou Jane Temple
THE DOCTOR MAKES A DOLLHOUSE CALL
by Robin Hathaway
HUNTING THE WITCH by Ellen Hart
THE LAKE EFFECT by Les Roberts
STONE QUARRY by S.J. Rozan
BY BLOOD POSSESSED by Elena Santangelo
A PLACE OF SAFETY by Caroline Graham

ST. MARTIN'S PAPERBACKS IS ALSO PROUD TO
PRESENT THESE MYSTERY CLASSICS BY NGAIO MARSH

DEATH IN A WHITE TIE
ENTER A MURDERER
FALSE SCENT
FINAL CURTAIN

"Solid plotting, exceptional characters, and well-crafted prose."
—*Library Journal*

"With the Bill Smith and Lydia Chin mysteries, S.J. Rozan has written the most consistently compelling series of traditional detective novels published in this decade. STONE QUARRY combines the sure, controlled prose of Ross MacDonald with the fury of early Hammett. Now is the time to discover what Rozan's loyal readership has known all along."
—George Pelecanos, author of *The Big Blowdown*

"In a departure from her usual gritty urban settings, S.J. Rozan blends the elegiac beauty of upstate New York with a gripping tale of rural corruption. A solid addition to a solid series."
—Margaret Maron, author of *Home Fires*

"Rozan's seamless writing ranges from glorious to no-frills, the action is backwoods tough, and STONE QUARRY is consistently believable."
—*BookPage*

A BITTER FEAST

"Smart, crisp writing . . . The rich sights, sounds and textures of daily life in Chinatown are a sumptuous feast for jaded palates."
—Marilyn Stasio, *The New York Times Book Review*

"Superlative . . . a story that manages to satisfy all the senses."
—*Publishers Weekly* (starred review)

"Engaging, energetic Lydia is good company."
—*Philadelphia Inquirer*

"Rozan skillfully measures out the layers of double-dealing, keeping her plot just twisty enough to spin it out with consummate professionalism. If you still don't know Lydia and Bill, you'll never have a better chance to meet them."
—*Kirkus* (starred review)

"Quite a brew indeed, and one that Rozan handles with skill and verve in the most complex plot she has yet written . . . what may be the best of this uniformly excellent, well written, and entertaining series."   —*Booklist* (starred review)

NO COLDER PLACE

"A mystery gem . . . taut and beautifully written."
—*Detroit Free Press*

"Rozan is a pro at designing a good mystery."
—*San Jose Mercury News*

"The protagonists' relationship and Rozan's solid plotting ably carry this admirable series."
—*Publishers Weekly* "Best Books '97"

"The unlikely match of energetic Lydia and world-weary Bill has helped establish this couple as an engaging, quixotic pair . . . This novel firmly establishes Rozan as a major figure in contemporary mystery fiction."   —*Booklist*

"This [is] the sharpest, clearest, most purposefully focused of her four Smith/Chin mysteries."   —*Kirkus Reviews*

"A sharp, funny, and sexy detective."   —*Chicago Tribune*

"A new and absorbing voice . . . This is a series to watch for."
—*Washington Post Book World*

"Bill Smith and Lydia Chin have a chemistry between them that is as exciting and electric as any I've ever read. Combine that with S. J. Rozan's sharply drawn portrait of the dark underbelly of New York and you've got a book you won't put down."
—Steven Womack, author of *Way Past Dead*

"Rozan's intriguing tales and compelling characters make this series a continuing delight. It's truly entertainment with an edge."
—*Flint Journal*

STONE QUARRY

S. J. ROZAN

St. Martin's Paperbacks

STONE QUARRY

Copyright © 1999 by S. J. Rozan.
Excerpt from *Reflecting the Sky* copyright © 2001 by S. J. Rozan.

Front cover photograph © David Madison/Tony Stone Images.

Library of Congress Catalog Card Number: 99-35869

ISBN: 0-312-97703-4

Printed in the United States of America

St. Martin's Press hardcover edition / September 1999
St. Martin's Paperbacks edition / January 2001

St. Martin's Paperbacks are published by St. Martin's Press, 175 Fifth Avenue, New York, N.Y. 10010.

10 9 8 7 6 5 4 3 2 1

after all,
for my father

ACKNOWLEDGMENTS

my agent, Steve Axelrod
my editor, Keith Kahla
what a pair

Emily Horowitz, who first told me I was writing a novel

the experts
David Dubal, Joe Karas, Pat Picciarelli, Carl Stein
and Harvey Stoddard

the critics
Betsy Harding, Royal Huber, Barbara Martin,
Jamie Scott (and her damn owls),
and, on this one, Becca Armstrong and Steve Landau

the family
Steve Blier, Hillary Brown, Max Rudin, Jim Russell,
and Amy Schatz

the muse
Richard Wilcox

the genius
Deb Peters

and
the goils
Nancy Ennis and Helen Hester

ONE

It can be a treacherous road, State Route 30, especially rain-slick in the twilight of late winter, but I know it well. I sped along its badly banked curves faster than legal and faster than necessary. I was heading for Antonelli's; I had plenty of time. I drove that way just for the charge, pushing the road, feeling its rhythm in my fingers, its speed in the current in my spine. Water hissed under my tires and my headlights reflected off the fat raindrops that splattered the blacktop in front of me.

Years ago, 30 carried a fair amount of tourist traffic, but even then it was people on their way to somewhere else. Now that the state highway slices through the northern part of the county and the Thruway wraps around it, no one passes through Schoharie anymore unless they mean to stop, and not many have a reason to do that. The tourist brochures call this countryside picturesque. If you look closely, though, you'll see the caved-in roofs and derelict silos, the junked cars and closed roadside diners with their faded billboards. These rocky hills were never good for much except hunting and dairy farming. Farming's a hard way to make a living, getting harder; and hunters are men like me, who come and go.

The hiss of water became the crunch of gravel in the lot in front of Antonelli's. I swung in, parked at the edge. I had Mozart in the CD player, Mitsuko Uchida playing the B-flat Sonata, and I lit a cigarette, opened the window, listened as the music ended in triumph and the exhilaration of promises fulfilled.

Then I left the car and strolled over to look across the valley. I was early. City habits die hard.

Hands in my pockets, I let my eyes wander the far hills, asked myself what I was doing. Work wasn't what this place was about, for me. But on the phone, when Eve Colgate had called, I'd heard something: not her words, clipped and businesslike, but the long, slow melody under them. Raindrops tapped my jacket; a tiny stream ran through the gravel at my feet, searching for the valley.

Unexpectedly, I thought of Lydia, her voice on the phone when I'd called to tell her I was coming up here, would be away awhile. There was music in Lydia's voice, too; there always was, though I'd never told her that. She wasn't surprised or bothered that I was leaving. Over the four years we've known each other she's come to expect this, my sudden irregular disappearances and returns. In the beginning, of course, I never told her when I was going, didn't call when I got back. Then, we just worked together sometimes; if she needed someone while I was gone, there were other PIs to call. But at some point, and I couldn't say just when, I'd started calling, to let her know.

The rain was ending. Wind rolled the high black clouds aside, revealing a sky that was still almost blue. The air was full of the smell of earth and promise, everything ready, tense with waiting. Soon spring would explode through the valley and race up the hills, color and noise engulfing the sharp silence. I stood for a while, watched tiny lights wink on in the windows of distant homes. When the sky was dark I turned and went inside.

The crowd in Antonelli's was small and subdued. A golf tournament, all emerald grass and blue sky and palm trees, flickered soundlessly from the TV over the bar. A couple of guys who probably thought golf was a sport were watching it. A few other people were scattered around, at the bar, at the small round tables. None of them was the woman I had come to meet.

I slid onto a bar stool. Behind the bar, Tony Antonelli, a compact, craggy man whose muscles moved like small boulders under his flannel shirt, was ringing up someone's tab. He looked over at me and nodded.

"Figured you were up," he said, clinking ice into a squat glass. He splashed in a shot of Jim Beam and handed it to me. "Saw smoke from your place yesterday."

"Big help you are," I said. "Whole place could burn down, you'd just watch."

"Happens I drove down to make sure your car was there, wise ass. I oughta charge you for the gas."

"Put it on my tab." I drank. "How's Jimmy?" I asked casually.

Tony turned, busied himself with glasses and bottles. "Still outta jail."

I said nothing. He turned back to me. "Well, that's what you wanna know, ain't it? Make sure all your hard work ain't been wasted?"

"No," I said. "I knew that. How is he?"

"How the hell do I know? He don't live with me no more; he moved in with some girl. If I see him I'll tell him you're askin'."

I nodded and worked on my bourbon. Tony opened Rolling Rocks for two guys down the other end of the bar. He racked some glasses, filled a couple of bowls with pretzels. Then he turned, reached the bourbon bottle off the shelf. He put it on the bar in front of me.

"Sorry," he said. "It ain't you. I oughta be thankin' you, I guess. But that no-good punk pisses the hell outta me. He never shoulda came to you. He gets his ass in trouble, he oughta get it out."

"Uh-huh," I said. "How come you never gave him a break, Tony?"

Tony snorted. "I was too busy feedin' him! What the hell you see to like in that kid, Smith?"

I grinned. "Reminds me of me."

"You musta been one godless bastard."

"I was. Only I didn't have a big brother like you, Tony. I was worse."

"Yeah, well, he should'n'a came to you. And don't think you're gonna pay that candy-ass lawyer you brought here. I told you to send me his goddamn bill."

"Forget it. He owed me."

"That's between you and him. I been bailin' Jimmy's ass outta trouble for years; I got no reason to stop now. I don't like the kid, Smith, but I'm family. You ain't."

I looked at Tony, at the sharp line of his jaw, his brows bristling over his deep-set eyes. "No," I said slowly. "No, I'm not." I poured myself another drink, took the drink and the bottle to a table in the corner, and sat down to wait for Eve Colgate.

Another bourbon and a cigarette later, the door opened and a tall, gray-haired woman stepped into the smoky room. No heads turned, no conversations stopped. She looked around her, reviewing and dismissing each face until she came to mine. She stayed still for a moment, with no change of expression; then she came toward me, contained, controlled. She wore a down vest over a black sweater, old, stained jeans, muddy boots. I stood.

"Mr. Smith?" She offered her hand. Her grip was sure, her hand rough. "Thank you for coming."

"Sit down." I held a chair for her.

"Thank you." She smiled slightly. "Men don't do this much anymore—help ladies into their seats."

"I was born in Kentucky. What are you drinking?"

"Tony keeps a bottle of Gran Capitan under the bar for me." The skin of her face was lined like paper that someone had crumpled and then, in a moment of regret, tried to smooth out again. Her blunt, shoulder-length hair was a dozen shades of gray, from almost-black to almost-white. I went to get her drink.

Tony gestured across the room with his eyes as he poured Eve Colgate's brandy. "You know her?"

"Just met. Why?"

"I meant to tell you she was askin' about you, coupla days ago. Wondered about it, at the time. She don't usually talk to nobody. Comes in alone, has a shot, leaves alone. Maybe sometimes she talks cows or apples with somebody. She ain't—I don't know." He shook his head over what he didn't know. "But she's got money."

"My type, Tony." I picked up her brandy from the bar.

"Hey!" Tony said as I turned. I turned back. "You ain't workin' for her?"

"Nah. She just thinks I'm cute."

"With a puss like you got?" Tony muttered as I walked away.

Eve Colgate's mouth smiled as I put her drink on the scarred tabletop. Her eyes were doing work of their own. They were the palest eyes I'd ever seen, nearly colorless. They probed my face, my hands, swept over the room around us, followed my movements as I drank or lit a cigarette. When they met my eyes they paused, for a moment. They widened slightly, almost imperceptibly, and I thought for no reason of the way a dark room is revealed by a lightning flash, and how much darker it is, after that.

I smoked and let Eve Colgate's eyes play. I didn't meet them again. She took a breath, finally, and spoke, with the cautious manner of a carpenter using a distrusted tool.

"I'm not sure how to begin." She sipped her brandy. If I had a dollar for every client who started that way I could have had a box at Yankee Stadium, but there was a difference. They usually said it apologetically, as if they expected me to expect them to know how to begin. Eve Colgate was stating a fact that I could take or leave.

"I called you on a matter difficult for me to speak about. I don't know you, and I don't know that I want you closely involved in my—in my personal affairs. However, I don't seem to have many options, and all of them are poor. You may be the best of them."

"That's flattering."

She looked at me steadily. "Don't be silly. I can't pre-

tend to welcome the intrusion you represent. I'm too old
to play games for the sake of your pride, Mr. Smith. I may
need you, but I can't see any reason to be pleased about
it."

I couldn't either, so I let it go.

She went on, her words clipped. "However, things are
as they are. At this point, Mr. Smith, I'd like to know
something more about you. All I have up to now are other
people's opinions, and that's not enough. Is this accepta-
ble?"

"Maybe. It depends on what you want to know."

"I'll tell you what I do know. I know you bought
Tony's father's cabin ten years ago. You come up here
irregularly, sometimes for long periods. Tony says you're
moody and you drink. Other than that he speaks very
highly of you. I understand you helped get his brother out
of serious trouble recently—and went to considerable trouble to do it."

"The kid deserved a chance. He was in over his head
in something he didn't understand. I bought that cabin
twelve years ago. I sleep in the nude."

She looked at me sharply over her brandy. Her movements were small and economical. In contrast to her eyes,
her body was composed and still.

"And are you always rude to your clients?" she asked.

"More often than I'd like to be." I refilled my glass
from Tony's bottle. "I've been a private investigator for
sixteen years, twelve in my own shop. Before that I was
carpenter. I've been to college and in the Navy. I drink, I
smoke, I eat red meat. That's it."

"I doubt it," said Eve Colgate. "Have you a family, Mr.
Smith?"

I took a drink. "I had."

"But no longer?"

"I'm hard to live with."

"Was your wife also hard to live with?"

"Her second husband doesn't think so."

"And children?"

That was territory where no one went. I drank, put my cigarette out. "Look, Miss Colgate, you called me. I can use the work, but not the inquisition. I gave you references; call them if you want, ask about me."

"I have." She didn't continue.

"Well, that's all you get."

We drank in silence for a while. Eve Colgate's eyes never rested. They swept the room, probing the corners, counting the bottles on Tony's shelves. They inspected the cobwebs at the raftered ceiling. Every now and then, unpredictably, they returned to me, settling on my face, my hands, taking off again.

"Yes," she said suddenly, draining her glass. "You'll do. I'll expect you tomorrow morning. Do you know where I live?"

"You'll expect me to do what?"

"Some—things were stolen from me. They're worth a good deal of money; and yet they're not as valuable to the thief as they are to me. I want them back."

"The police are good at that sort of thing."

Her eyes flashed. "I'm not a stupid woman, Mr. Smith. If I'd wanted the police involved I would have called them."

"Why haven't you?"

She stood. So did I. "I don't want to discuss it here. If, after I tell you what I need done, you don't want to do it, I'll pay you for your time and your trip. Thank you for the drink, Mr. Smith." She walked from the room, her back straight, her steps measured.

When the door shut behind her the bar was the same as it had been before, as it had always been. Men and women who'd been stopping in at Antonelli's after work since Tony's father had run the place bought each other drinks, talked quietly about sports, the weather, their cars, and their kids. In the back, laughing, smoking, drinking beer from the bottle, was a tableful of young kids who'd been children when I first started coming here. Now that rear table was clearly theirs, Antonelli's as much their place as their parents'. Room had been made for them, and Antonelli's continued.

I swirled the bourbon around in my glass, then signaled to Marie, Tony's waitress, who was leaning on the bar chewing gum and trading wisecracks with the Rolling Rock drinkers. "Hi," she said, bouncing over to my table. "Can I get you something?" Her shaggy hair was bleached to a very pale blond, fine and soft.

"Hi." I pointed to my glass. "I need more ice, and I'm starving. What do you have?"

"Lasagna." She nibbled on a maroon fingernail that must have been an inch long. "And bean soup. And the usual stuff." She giggled.

I ordered the lasagna. Marie bounced off chomping openmouthed on her gum. I glanced up at the TV. The golf was over, the news was on. That meant there'd be NCAA basketball soon. I had a client, a bellyful of bourbon, and Tony's lasagna coming. I stretched my legs and idly watched an elderly couple a few tables over. They were eating dinner in a silence punctuated only by quiet remarks and small gestures that dovetailed so perfectly they might have been choreographed.

I'd told Lydia I was coming up here, told her I'd be away; but I hadn't said I'd be meeting a client, that I might be working.

I got up, bought a *Mountain Eagle* from the pile by the bar. Sipping my bourbon, I caught up on what had been happening since I'd last come up.

There was federal DOT money coming along and with it the state was planning to replace or rebuild three county roads. That was bad. Seven years ago they'd replaced this stretch of 30 with a faster, straighter road on the other side of the valley. Now this was strictly a local road and most of the establishments along it had died slow, lonely deaths. Antonelli's was one of the few still open.

I glanced at the other lead stories. Appleseed Baby Foods was expanding. That was good. Appleseed was the only major employer in the county. Appleseed CEO Mark Sanderson smiled from a front-page photo. I sipped my bourbon, considered the photo. In the old days, pictures of the state senator's Christmas party or the county Fourth of July bash always included a shot of Mark Sanderson with his arm around the usually bare shoulders of his stunning wife, Lena. Then four years ago she'd left him, just walked away. Consensus among the women in the county seemed to be that anyone married to Mark Sanderson would have considered that option, maybe much earlier than Lena Sanderson did, but Sanderson reported her to the county Sheriff and to the State Troopers as a missing person, made anguished televised pleas for her to come home, and waited. My professional opinion at the time was that the cops would come up empty and we'd seen the last of her, and I was right. Looking at Sanderson's round, smiling face now, it seemed to me he'd come through the whole thing pretty well.

I drank more bourbon, read on. New York State Electric and Gas had run an open meeting to get local comment on a natural gas pipeline they wanted to pull through the county. It would be heading down from Canada, where the gas was, to New York City, where it was needed. Local comment pro had to do with promised jobs. Local comment con was about tearing up fields, fencing off pastureland, polluted water, damaged crops, and the chance of major explosions. Pro won, hands down.

I lit a cigarette, turned the page. The Consolidated East girls' basketball team had won the tri-county championship in a squeaker last Friday. There was a photo with this one too, sweaty, long-legged girls grinning at the camera, arms around each other's shoulders. I imagined that picture fixed with magnets to refrigerator doors all around the county.

I was onto the Police Blotter—a lot of DWIs, one marijuana arrest—when Marie sashayed over, bringing silverware and a tall glass of ice. As she put them on my table the door swung open, letting a chill breeze push into the room.

I looked over. Three men stepped inside, chuckling as though they'd just exchanged a joke. They headed for the big table at the front. The first to sit, an angular, pasty man, cocked a finger at Marie, winking. The features on the left side of his face—ear, eye, eyebrow—were set a little higher than the ones on the right, and his nose was crooked. The other two men dropped themselves into chairs on either side of him. The big one was dark, with a thick, droopy mustache, wide shoulders, and an easy, friendly manner. The other was small and bony with bad skin and dead-brown hair.

Marie, paling, looked unsurely to Tony. Tony shook his head, lifted the gate, stepped around the bar.

"Who's that?" I asked Marie quietly.

"Frank Grice," she whispered, her eyes on Tony.

"No kidding." I knew that name: The trouble Jimmy Antonelli had been in last fall, the hole I'd dug him out of, was because he'd been dumping stolen cars for Frank Grice, cars Grice used to run dope from Miami to Albany. But Grice denied knowing the kid, and Jimmy wouldn't roll on him. Grice left the state when the sheriff picked Jimmy up and came back after my lawyer had gotten him out. I knew the name; but this was the first time I'd laid eyes on him.

I ground out my cigarette and leaned forward in my chair as Tony walked to where the three men sat.

"You ain't welcome here, Frank." He spoke low to Grice, ignoring the others. The line of his jaw was white. "Get out."

"What kind of a way is that to talk, Tony?" Frank Grice smiled widely, spread his hands innocently, palms up. "We just came by for a drink."

"Drink somewhere else."

Grice didn't answer. He took a pack of cigarettes out of his overcoat, pulled one loose. The big guy flicked a gold lighter for him. Grice looked at the flame as if it were something new and interesting. Lighting the cigarette, he looked up at Tony. Smoke streamed lazily from his mouth.

He said something softly, so softly I couldn't hear it. Tony went a deep red; I couldn't hear his answer, either. Grice stood suddenly. The other two exchanged looks, then followed suit. Grice sauntered to the door, opened it, and held it open, smiling the whole time, his cigarette dangling from his cockeyed lips. Tony half turned, searching for Marie. "Keep an eye on things," he growled. "I'll be right back." He slammed forward, past Grice, through the open door. Grice followed, his boys followed him, and the door swung shut behind them.

Before the door closed I was out of my chair, moving swiftly past the bar and through the vinyl-padded doors that swung into the kitchen. Buzzing fluorescent lights, too bright, reflected off the stainless-steel counters. The room smelled of garlic and ammonia. A skinny kid up to his elbows in greasy water stared as I slipped out the kitchen door into the winter darkness. My steps made no sound as I rounded the corner of the building, a cold wind pushing its way through my shirt. Three figures—Tony, Grice, and the big, friendly man—leaned close together in the middle of the parking lot; a fourth, the little guy, stood by the bar's front door. I worked my way in the shadows of parked cars.

I couldn't see Tony's face, but his voice came to me, tight and gravelly. "You don't get it, Frank. I want you outta here, damn fast."

"No, *you* don't get it, Tony." Grice's voice still held a smile. "If I'm thirsty, you pour me a drink. If I'm hungry, you grill me a steak. That's how it is now."

"Hell it is," Tony spat.

A nod from Grice, just a small movement of his misshapen head, and the big man slipped behind Tony like a shadow, pinned his arms as Grice smashed his fist into Tony's belly. Tony doubled over, groaning. The big man pulled him up. Grice laughed, rubbed his fist into the palm of his other hand. He stopped laughing suddenly as I slammed into him like a freight train, spreading him backwards across the rusted trunk of an old red Chevy. I back-handed him once across the mouth, just to slow him down; then I sprang back, left him there. He was Tony's.

Tony tore himself out of the big man's surprised grip and reached both hands for Grice, hauled him off the car while I grabbed the big man's shoulder, spun him around. I threw my best punch into the middle of his mustache. He wasn't any bigger than I was, and my best wasn't bad, but it didn't faze him. He staggered back; then, spreading his lips in a hungry smile, he launched himself at me. I sidestepped, drove a kick into his ribs. He stumbled; I watched. Then something crashed into me from behind, knocked me to the ground. Small, bony hands tightened around my throat, squeezing, shaking. A knee dug into my back.

Gravel scraped the side of my face as I twisted, digging with my right foot, trying to shake off the little guy as my lungs began to strain for air. I groped at his hands pressing into my windpipe. My heart pounded, raced; yellow and red explosions started behind my eyes. His breath rasped loudly in my ear. I had no breath at all. The world got smaller, darker. Closing on one finger of each choking hand I forced them back, my muscles only half obeying, beginning to tremble. I put everything into bending those two fingers; at the last minute the hands loosened and I clawed them away from my throat.

I sucked air loudly and twisted left, yanking on his right arm. He slipped from my back; I drove my right elbow hard beside me into whatever was there. It landed solidly enough to send bolts of pain ricocheting up and down my arm. From the sounds behind me, I wasn't the only one who noticed. I pulled away and got up on one knee and then the big man was back, with a fist the size of a bowling ball slamming into my chin. My head snapped back and I landed in a cold muddy puddle. I lay motionless, breathing hard.

The big man leaned over me, relaxed and smiling, for a good look. When he was near enough that I could smell the stale coffee on his breath, I shot my arms out and grabbed his jacket, pulled my knee to my chest, shoved my foot into his gut. I straightened my leg and threw him away from me, and this time when he stumbled I was right there, three fast mean punches pounding his face and another sharp kick up under his ribs. He moaned and started to sag. I clenched my hands together and swung them like a hatchet down on the place where his neck joined his shoulder. At first nothing happened; then he fell over sideways like a tree. I stepped back, panting, and looked around. The little bony guy was standing now but he was a lot smaller than I was and he wouldn't try to take me again, not from the front where I could see him coming. I grinned so he'd know I knew that.

A loud, wordless sound came from behind me. I whipped around and saw Tony sitting on Frank Grice's chest, his knees pinning Grice's arms, his square fist thumping repeatedly into Grice's already bloody face. "Tony!" I yelled hoarsely. "Hey, Tony, that's enough! Come on, man, you're going to kill him."

I pulled Tony back and off Grice, who groaned, rolled, and worked his way slowly to his feet. Tony struggled in my grip and I held him, not relaxing until he did.

"All right?" I asked, as his rocky muscles loosened under my hands. He nodded and I let him go.

Grice stood slightly stooped, breathing noisily through his mouth. He lifted a hand to his face, cupping his nose, then moved the hand away. "You'll pay for this, Tony," he hissed. "This was stupid. And you"—he turned his bloody face to me—"whoever the hell you are, stay the fuck out of my way from now on."

"Aw, Frank," I said, my voice still hoarse. "Why should Tony have all the fun?"

Something flared in Grice's eyes. I suddenly noticed how cold I was, soaked with sweat and muddy water out here in the winter night.

"Go on, Tony," Grice said, still looking at me. "You bring in all the smartass muscle you want. It won't help you, Tony." He coughed.

"I don't need no help, you son of a bitch," Tony snarled, taking two fast steps toward Grice.

From off to my right a voice like gears grinding said, "Don't do that." I spun around. Ten feet away, the little bony guy was planted, legs spread apart, holding an automatic pointed at the center of Tony's chest.

Grice and Tony saw the gun the same time I did. Everyone froze, and for a long moment no one moved in the graveled lot under the blue-black sky, scattered now with more stars than a man could count, even in a long lifetime.

My gun was pressed to my ribs under my flannel shirt, as out of reach as the stars.

Then Grice laughed, a short, guttural sound, as of something being ripped in two. "Oh, Christ, Wally. What the hell is that for? Put it away. Come on, let's go." He looked at me, then at Tony. "Next time," he said.

He turned sharply and walked to a big blue Ford, got in the front passenger door. The little guy hesitated, swore, then tucked the gun into his belt. He grabbed the big man, who looked as if he wasn't sure what day it was. Steering him to the car, he shoved him through the rear door, got behind the wheel, and sprayed gravel tearing out of the lot.

Tony and I watched the red glow of their taillights vanish down 30. "I don't like your friends," I told him.

"You got Frank pissed off at you now," he said.

I fingered my left cheek carefully. It felt hot and sore. "You owe him, Tony?"

Tony turned to me. A lead curtain fell behind his eyes. "I don't owe nobody, Smith." He wiped his hand down his sweaty face. "You shoulda stayed out of it."

"Yeah." I shrugged. "But I was hungry. Grice beats the shit out of you, I don't get my lasagna."

We turned together, headed back toward the door. The ancient, pitted tin sign that read "Antonelli's," Tony's father's sign, creaked as it swung in the wind. A smile cracked Tony's face. "Sucker," he said. "I'm outta lasagna."

* * *

Two hours later, full of food, warmer, I turned my six-year-old Acura onto the dirt road that leads from 30 down to my cabin. The single lane was rutted and slippery, ruts that fit my tires exactly because almost no one drove that road but me. I parked in the flat field next to my place and spent a long time leaning on the car, looking at the stars through the black cross-hatching of tree branches.

Inside, I turned on the lamp in the front room. The cedar-paneled walls soaked up most of the light, except where the glass frame of a photograph or drawing caught it, threw it back. When I bought the cabin it wasn't winterized, so I'd done that, insulating, finishing with cedar because it stood up well to damp and I liked the smell. I'd reroofed, too, and rebuilt the porch; this year, as soon as the weather was warm enough, I was going to replace the chimney.

I shed my jacket, threw it over the broken-in reading chair by the window. As I turned, lamplight glinted on the child's silver-framed photograph in the middle of the bookshelves. Days, weeks could go by without my looking at that picture, knowing it was there but feeling it only as a source of warmth, a hand on my shoulder. At those times I felt almost at peace; sometimes I even thought I wanted to talk about it, although I didn't know with whom and I never tried.

And then other times, like now, I'd walk by too close, too close, and slice my heart on the sharp edges of Annie's smile. Then the old pain would well up from where it lived in the hollows of my bones, and my eyes would grow hot. Ambushed by this aching, I would stare, as I did now, into this picture that never changed, and wonder why I kept it here, where it was so dangerous. Seven years ago I'd packed away the pictures I'd had in New York, and all her things. Her things were gone from here, too; this was all that I had left, all I'd kept, and I wondered why.

But I knew.

Because although the fresh prettiness of her face, the

round cheeks and soft brown eyes and the wave in her hair, had all been her mother's, that sharp, slanted smile was mine.

And because, in all her nine years, I had never seen Annie afraid.

I turned away from the picture. I poured myself some Maker's Mark, left the bottle out. I drank, then flexed my hands, palms up, palms down; they seemed all right, so I carried the bourbon to the piano bench and raised the cover off the keyboard of the old, battered Baldwin.

I ran through a series of scales, the keys cold and smooth and hard under my fingers; then, after a still minute and a few deep breaths, I started on the Mozart B Minor Adagio, trying out the phrasing that had been running around my head since morning. It didn't really work, but I played through the piece anyway, twice, and then went on to more Mozart, the Sonata in A Minor, which I'd been playing a lot longer and played better.

As I moved into it, the power and the tension in me grew until my whole body rang with them, with the exhilaration of balancing on a very narrow beam, barely controlling the lines of the music as they wove toward and away from each other, building, fading, stopping and not stopping, only my hands preventing chaos, creating just enough order for just enough time that the immense beauty of the music could exist here, now, in this dark, small place halfway down a wooded winter hillside, under a million stars.

TWO

Morning came, cold, clear, and much too early.

Groggy, I rolled across the bed out of the sunlight, tried to remember why I ached, why my cheek was stiff and sore and my jaw was tender. There must have been a fight, but I didn't remember it, and a sick, familiar feeling began in the pit of my stomach. The fights I couldn't remember were usually ones I'd started, usually over nothing, usually with men I didn't know and had no quarrel with except the quarrel that comes in a bottle of bourbon like the prize in a box of Cracker Jacks. Time had been when I would often wake sick and aching, finding nothing in my memory but shadows and regret. It had been a long time since the last time, though, and it had never happened up here. That was one of the reasons I came here, and so I worked at remembering, pushing my way through the bourbon haze and the dull thudding in my skull.

Nothing came. I groped on the table by the bed for a cigarette. I lit one, missed the ashtray with the match, rolled onto my back. I looked slowly around, to the window, the charcoal drawing on the wall, the bureau, the straight-backed chair with yesterday's clothes slung over it. Nothing. A cloud covered the sun, left the room gray and cold.

Early-morning smoke caught in my throat and I coughed, felt a pain I wasn't expecting. I touched my neck, feeling the sore, bruised places, and then memory and relief flooded in together like tide in a sand castle. It was all

there: Tony, Frank Grice, the bony hands around my neck.
The muddy puddle. The gun.

I finished the cigarette, threw off the quilt. Standing at
the window I watched the high thin clouds drifting east.
Birds searched my yard for breakfast. They moved with
the jerky speed of a silent movie, flashing from branches
to the ground.

I shrugged into a robe, went out to the front room. As
always, it was warmer there than in the rooms in the back,
the one I slept in and the other, rarely used now.

I flicked on the hot water heater in the corner of the
kitchen. I built a fire in the wood stove and put some water
on to boil. When the coffee was ground and waiting I took
a quick shower, in water I wouldn't have called hot anywhere but here.

I dressed quickly in clothes as cold as the air. I thought
about shaving, but I looked in the mirror at my cheek,
streaked and raw, and decided to skip it. Eve Colgate
would just have to live with it.

Wearing my jacket and gloves, I took my coffee outside
to the porch. Up on the ridge 30 ran, invisible, around the
rim of my land. The damp smell of decaying leaves mixed
with the dryness of woodsmoke. In the crisp and clear air
the black skeletons of trees were sharp against the sky.
The oaks up by the road I'd planted myself, the first summer I was here. They were still small; oaks are slow grow-
ers.

By the time I'd finished the thick, bitter coffee the
pounding in my head was gone. I smoked a cigarette while
the pale sun stabbed through the branches as though it
were searching for something. I grabbed a handful of bird-
seed from the can by the door, scattered it in the yard.
Then I went back inside, rinsed out my coffee cup, slipped
on my holster and my .38. I wiped the frost from the car
and headed up the road to meet Eve Colgate.

Eve Colgate's house sat on the crest of a hill along Route
10 in the north of the county. Below, the state highway

gleamed, two wide flat ribbons laid over the fields. Cars raced along it with a faint whoosh. From Eve Colgate's place you could see that, but there were better things to look at. The sky was a brilliant blue and the wind raised miniature waves on puddles by the roadside. The sun was almost warm. Eve Colgate had apple, peach, and cherry orchards, pasture for a small dairy herd, and a long, straight drive arched over by chestnut trees planted close. A stand of forsythia already showed tiny spots of green.

The house was small but solid, yellow clapboard with white shutters and a big front porch. To the right of the drive a lawn slanted up to the house. On the drive's other side, ten feet of lawn separated the chestnuts from a tangle of undergrowth and scrub trees sloping down to the forest. A hundred years ago someone had cleared the forest from that slope, probably intending to plant and harvest and prosper. But the ground was rocky and winters were hard. Some of the scrub trees were as tall as the house.

A muscular black dog came charging off the porch as I drove up. I parked behind a blue Ford pickup. In front of the house was another truck, a work-scarred red one. Eve Colgate, in a black sweater, hatless and gloveless, stood beside it talking with a thickly built man.

I got out of the car. The dog barked, planted his feet, growled deep in his throat like a dog who means business. I took a step forward. So did he. I stopped, waited.

"Leo!" Eve Colgate called. The dog looked to her, then quickly back at me, giving one wag of his tail. He didn't stop growling. "Leo!" she called again, more sharply, and he hesitated, then went to her reluctantly, glaring at me over his shoulder.

Eve Colgate stood scratching the dog's ears. I walked up the drive toward her and the heavy man. The dog bristled as I got close but he didn't move.

Eve Colgate's eyebrows rose slightly when she saw my face, bruised and unshaven. She looked from me to the man next to her; then she explained us to each other. "Bill Smith, Harvey Warner. The Warners have the next farm to mine. Mr. Smith is up from New York. He has a cabin near North Blenheim." We shook hands.

"Well, I'll call you," Warner said to her. "If day after tomorrow's good?"

"It's fine," she said. "I'll be sure to have read this by then." She gestured with a folder of papers she was holding.

"Damn thing better be all it's cracked up to be." Warner spat in the dirt. "Else I swear I'm gonna sell them damn cows, go to sharecroppin' for Sanderson like everybody else."

"You swore that last year," she smiled.

"Yeah, well, this year I'm gonna do it. Damn pipeline's gonna ruin my best pastureland anyway. Or maybe I'll just stick Sanderson with the whole damn place, retire to Florida before he figures out he's out of his mind. To hell with it. I'll call you." He swung into the red pickup, drove off down the muddy drive. The dog chased after him, yapping.

Eve Colgate watched the truck go, then looked at me, her eyes probing my face as you might test an ice field before you walked out on it.

"What did he mean, sharecropping?" I asked, to be saying something under those eyes.

She turned back to the drive, watched the dog trotting up it. "That's what they all call it. The small dairy farmers are all giving up. They're selling their herds to whomever will buy them, and their land to Appleseed. Then they contract to Appleseed, putting the pastureland into vegetables. They grow what Mark Sanderson tells them to and he pays them whatever he wants." She ran a hand through her blunt gray hair. "A lot of people are bitter about it. But they do it, because they're farmers and this is what they know, even on land that's no longer theirs." She gestured with the folder in her hand. "Harvey's grandfather settled that farm. But fifty cows aren't enough anymore. I have even fewer. We're talking about consolidating our herds and investing in new equipment."

"Will that pay?"

"I hope so. I don't know what Harvey will do if he has
to sell his cows, or his land."

"He says he'll go to Florida."

She said, "He's never been farther than Albany."

"What will you do?"

"I?" She paused. Her crystal eyes moved over the hills
and pasture, ocher and charcoal and chocolate under the
bright sun. "I have options Harvey doesn't have. Don't
misunderstand me: This farm supports itself, it's not a
hobby. But neither am I totally dependent on it. I have no
mortgage, no bank loans. I can weather bad times." She
turned away from the drive. "Shall we walk?"

I lit a cigarette, turning to shelter the match from the
wind, and we headed down the slope behind the house.
The dog sniffed at me. I showed him my hand and when
he stuck his cold nose in it I carefully scratched his ears
the way Eve Colgate had. He wagged his tail grudgingly
and bounded away.

Eve Colgate watched the dog, then looked at me ap
praisingly. "He usually won't let a stranger touch him."

"Professional courtesy," I said.

She continued to look at me for a short time, absorbing
me with her colorless eyes. Then she laughed.

"They say I'm eccentric, Mr. Smith," Eve Colgate said
as we paced over yielding earth crisscrossed by papery
yellow grasses.

"Is it true, or just convenient?" I asked her.

"It's true enough."

"Where are we going?"

"I need to show you something."

We didn't speak again, striding side by side through
last year's field. As we walked I could feel Eve Colgate's
mood change. She grew distant, tense.

Finally we came to a small outbuilding, weathered sid-
ing and corrugated steel roof in a clearing where a dirt
road curved up from the valley. We stopped at the pad-
locked door. Eve Colgate looked at me, looked down at
the mud at her feet; then, her lips drawn into a thin line,

she pulled a single key from her back pocket and thrust it into the lock, jerked it open. She pushed the wide sliding door just enough to make an opening a person could fit through and she went inside.

I followed her into a single square room, flooded with unexpected brightness from a skylight. Unexpected, too, was the fact that the interior was finished: Sheetrock walls and ceiling, white; gray deck paint on the broad-plank floor; double-glazed frosted windows, allowing light but no view out or in; and heat, electric heat from baseboards running all around the place.

The warmth and closeness of the air, after the sharp cold of the morning, was unpleasant, and it intensified the strong, heady smell of turpentine that rolled toward me as I came through the door. But that wasn't what stopped me dead two steps inside. What did that was the canvas leaning on the wall before me.

Six feet high, eight feet wide, unfinished, but already with the power of a nightmare, barely contained. Brutal, slashing lines; sullen, swollen forms whose weight seemed to threaten the canvas that held them; a darkness, a lack of clarity that made you want to shake your head, clear the film from your eyes. When you did that, when you stared long and deep enough, the thick grays and decaying browns, even the black, began to unfold, revealing the taut wires of color within them—blood red, cobalt, the green of a Kentucky sky in the minutes before a twister hits, other colors I couldn't begin to name.

I had seen paintings like this before. They were in the Museum of Modern Art, at the Whitney, at the Tate. There had been at least one in every large twentieth-century show at every major museum for the last thirty years. Landscapes, I'd heard them called, but that was only by people who needed distance, needed to name and so deflect the pain and anger that lashed out from these paintings to rip open the places inside you where you hid things you had let yourself believe were gone forever.

"Jesus Christ," I said finally, and then again, "Jesus

Christ." I looked at Eve Colgate, who was standing in front of me, a little to one side. Her back was rigid, as though she were expecting a blow, bracing herself. "You're Eva Nouvel."

She turned to face me. Two hot spots of red shone on her cheeks, but her eyes were completely calm. "Yes," she said, in a voice that matched her eyes. "And now you know something that not a half dozen other people in this world know." She pushed past me and out through the narrow opening. I turned back to the unfinished canvas for a long look, then stepped over the threshold, joining her in the crisp, bright day.

In silence we skirted a pasture where black-and-white cows nosed at a carpet of hay. Beyond the pasture was an apple orchard, where new, mature, and ancient trees ran in parallel rows up and over the hillside. We walked beneath them under branches studded with buds. The dog threaded in and out as though stitching the orchard together.

Eve Colgate, without looking at me, spoke. "You recognized my work. I didn't expect that. It may make this easier."

At the edge of the orchard a low stone wall curved sinuously along a ridge. Eve Colgate leaned on the wall, her arms hugging her chest, her back to the sun. I leaned next to her, watching the shadows of the high, cottony clouds move across the hills.

"If you know my work," she said quietly, "perhaps you know my reputation."

"Eva Nouvel is a recluse. A hermit."

"That's right." She put her hands on the wall behind her and slid onto it, cross-legged. The black dog settled into a round pile in the sun.

"I was just thirty when I left New York, Mr. Smith. I came here and bought this farm and I have lived here since, alone. I stopped painting when I came here and did not paint for some years after." She picked up a twig lying on the wall, dug it into the joint between two stones.

"That's not quite true. Within weeks of establishing myself here I did a series of six canvases. I—" She drew a deep breath. "Before I came here I had been in the hospital for—for a long time. I had been seriously injured in an automobile accident in which my husband was killed. The accident was entirely our fault, my fault. I was driving. We had been drinking heavily." She paused again, stared into the distance, past the valley, past the hills.

To my mind, sudden, unwanted, and unavoidable, came the screech of brakes, the shattering of glass, sirens and shouts. Not Eve Colgate's accident, but another one, seven years ago: the crash when Annie died. An accident I hadn't seen, hadn't even known about until days later. I'd been away then, out of town on a case, and hadn't called anyone to say I was leaving, to say where I'd be.

The sun was high by now, shining through a silence broken only by the drone of a distant plane. Eve Colgate spoke again. "The paintings I made when I first came here . . ." She stopped, restarted. "It doesn't matter. They were not successful. They couldn't have been. I stopped painting then, and did not paint again for almost five years." The twig in her hand lodged between two stones and snapped. "When I came here I brought almost nothing from my days in New York. Most of my husband's things, and mine, I disposed of. The few things I couldn't part with I brought here, packed in the steamer trunk we had taken on our honeymoon. The trunk went into a storeroom and I never looked at it again. When I realized the paintings I had made were not good, I intended to destroy them, as I do all my unsuccessful work, but I couldn't. I crated them and put them in the same storeroom." She threw the broken twig away.

"Four days ago—two days before I called you in New York—I had a burglary. I'm a prosperous woman in a poor county, Mr. Smith; it's happened before. I expect it and I survive it. But this time the storeroom was broken into. The trunk and the crate were taken, as well as some other things: tools, equipment. I don't care about any of it, not even Henri's things, which were in the trunk. I don't need to have them anymore."

She fell silent, empty clear eyes staring out over the far hills. Then she turned to me, and I saw that her eyes weren't empty. Something gleamed deep within them like gems locked in ice. "But I want those paintings back. Do you know why?"

I looked into her eyes, saw amethysts, rubies, sapphires, sparkling, infinitely distant. "I think I do."

She waited, still and silent.

I said, "Because they're not good."

She nodded, let her breath out slowly. "I want you to find those paintings, Mr. Smith. Can you do that?"

"I don't know. Have you told the police?"

She shook her head. Then she gestured over the orchard, the pasture, the hills. "Do you know what this is?"

I answered a different question. "It's beautiful."

She was quiet for a very long time. Then she spoke. "It's mud," she said. "Manure. Hay. Snow. Eight-hundred-pound cows that have to be helped to calve. Eggs that have to be collected every morning in a henhouse that stinks. Apple trees that lose their blooms in a frost, or their fruit in a hailstorm. Or produce so much fruit you can't hire help enough to pick it, at any price." She unfolded her legs, slipped off the wall to stand again on the rocky ground. The black dog leapt to his feet, tail wagging. Eve Colgate looked at me. "It's why I can paint."

We started walking again, back through the orchard, toward the house. "Eva Nouvel is famous," she said. The dog dropped a stick at her feet. She picked it up, threw it in a high, curving arc. The dog charged after it. "But Eve Colgate is a farmer. She splits wood and wrings chickens' necks. And she's the one who paints." The dog trotted back, dropped the stick. I bent down for it. He lunged but I was faster. I lifted it into the air, let him jump at it; then I sent it flying end over end through the sunlight. He raced away.

"Thirty years ago," Eve Colgate went on, "I made an

arrangement with myself. It was based on my opinion of the world as I knew it. I've had no reason to change that opinion." She didn't speak again until we came up the hill behind the house, trim and solid against the blue of the sky. "Fame is a disease, Mr. Smith. I don't want it; I won't have it. Nor will I have those paintings dissected, discussed, exposed—!"

The spots of red appeared in her cheeks again, but her voice stayed low, controlled. "I want you to find those paintings, and do whatever you have to do to get them back. Pay the market price, if you have to. I can do that." She smiled a small, bitter smile; then it faded. "But who I am is my business."

We rounded the house, stopped at the porch steps. I looked at her. Her boots were caked with mud. Her eyes were like crystal creatures caught in the net of lines around them.

"The paintings," I said, watched her eyes. "Who would recognize them as yours? An expert? A layman? Are they signed?"

"They're not signed. An expert would certainly know them. An educated layman, possibly. My work is distinctive, Mr. Smith. There are recurring images, themes that don't change."

I searched for the right way to put my next question. "If it were necessary to destroy the paintings to preserve your privacy, would that be all right?"

She didn't speak right away. Finally she said, "I don't know."

Simple and clear, that answer; and I'd made my decision. I said, "There are some things I'll need."

"What things?"

"Descriptions of whatever was in the trunk. And I'll need to bring someone else in."

She stiffened. "Why someone else? No."

"If I'd stolen your stuff, I'd forget about selling the paintings—assuming I didn't know what they were worth—and try to unload whatever looked valuable: silver, old photographs, things like that." And probably dump everything else in the county landfill, but I didn't tell her that. "But if I were smart enough to know what the paintings were worth, I'd also know I couldn't sell them up here. I'd take them to New York. I want to call someone, check that out. I could go down there myself, but I think I'm more useful up here."

She was silent for a time, her eyes roving over the sloping lawn, the drive, the tangles of forsythia. "All right," she said quietly. "I'm hiring you as a professional. If you think this is necessary, do it. But understand that total discretion is as important to me as the return of those paintings."

I couldn't help grinning. If I hadn't gotten that message already it would have been a good time to tear up my license and go fishing.

THREE

It was early for lunch at Antonelli's. Tony was alone inside except for two T-shirted guys wolfing down beers, burgers, and a mountain of fries. Tony, leaning on the bar, looked up from his newspaper as I came in.

"Jesus," he said. "You look like hell."

"And you don't. Why is that?"

He grunted. "Clean livin'." He folded the paper, put it aside. "You okay?"

"Sure," I said. "Just thirsty. Let me have a Genny Cream." He opened a bottle and put it on the bar with a glass. "Listen, Tony, I need to talk to Jimmy. Where can I find him?"

"Trouble?" His mouth tightened.

"No. Just something I need to know."

"From that punk?" He gave a humorless laugh. "If you can't drink it, drive it, or steal it, he don't know nothin' about it."

"Oh, Christ, Tony, there are some things he's good for, if you'd cut him a little slack. He cooks as well as you do. And he's better than anyone I know with a car." I was sorry the minute I said it.

Tony's face flushed. "Yeah. He can fix 'em, smash 'em, or cool 'em off if they're hot."

Oh well, I was in now. "That what Frank Grice was here about last night? Something to do with the quarry?"

"That's none of your fuckin' business!" He slammed his open hand on the bar. The T-shirts looked up from their fries. Tony shifted his eyes to them, then back to me. He dropped his voice. "You saved my ass last night. I owe you, okay? But keep out of this. I can handle Grice."

"His type doesn't handle, Tony. You give him what he wants or you shut him down."

"What the hell do you know?"

"Not much," I said. "I only know Grice by reputation. But I've met a lot of guys like him. I do it for a living."

"Then stick to the payin' customers."

I drained my glass, turned it slowly between my palms. Tony gestured at it. "You want another?" I nodded. He opened a bottle, filled my glass. I drank.

"I'm sorry, Tony," I said. "I have trouble minding my own business. And guys like Grice make my skin crawl."

"Forget it." He took the empty bottles, put them in slots in the cardboard case under the bar. "Jimmy's been workin' a coupla days a week at Obermeyer's garage over in Central Bridge. Call over there, maybe you can get him."

"Thanks." I stood. "Okay if I tie up the phone for a while?"

He shrugged. "It ain't rang in two days."

I took my beer over to the pay phone against the back wall. I thought for a minute, about Tony, Jimmy, Eve Colgate's pasture, and some paintings she hadn't seen in thirty years; about how things change and how they don't. Then I slipped in some quarters, dialed Lydia's office number in New York.

I got the bounce-line message; so she was on the phone, either actually in her office or at home on the line that rings through. Normally I would have just left a message of my own, but calling me back up here wasn't all that easy. I took a chance and dialed the other number, the one that rings at home, in the kitchen. It's not a number I call often, but it's engraved deep in my memory just the same. I tapped my fingers on the old, scarred woodwork as the phone rang and rang.

Finally a woman's voice answered in Cantonese, using words I recognized, though I didn't understand them. I gave her my dozen Cantonese words: a respectful greeting and a request. There was silence, then a snort; then the phone clattered in my ear and I could hear the voice calling to someone else.

A few moments later came another woman's voice, this time in English. "My mother says you should stop trying to impress her; your Chinese is terrible."

"What did she call me this time?"

Lydia said, "The iron-headed rat."

"What does it mean?"

" 'Iron-headed'—you know, stubborn, willful; sometimes, stupid. I guess it could mean gray-haired, too."

"You think she meant that?"

"No. In Chinese that's a *good* thing."

"Great. Why rat?"

"Don't ask."

"Someday she'll like me. Listen, are you real busy, or can you take something on?"

"She'll never even tolerate you. I'm tailing a noodle merchant whose wife thinks he's messing around with her younger sister, but it's not as engrossing as it sounds. But I thought you were up in the country."

"I am."

"You never call from there. Are you all right?" A slight quickening came into her voice.

"I took a case."

"Up there?" Now, surprise. "I thought you—"

"It's a long story," I said, even though as I said it I realized it wasn't; or at least, not the way that's usually meant. "I got a call from someone up here; that's why I came up. Can you work on it?"

"Um, sure." Her tone told me she wanted to ask more, maybe hear the long story, but she answered the question I'd asked. "What do you need?"

I told her about the burglary, what was stolen. I didn't say from whom. She whistled low. "Six Eva Nouvels? My god, they must be worth a fortune."

"Maybe two million, together," I agreed. "Could be more: They're unknown, uncatalogued."

"How unknown?"

"The client says completely. I don't know. But right now I'm not thinking anyone came looking for them. It was probably just a break-in, kids. They may even have junked the paintings by now, just kept the stuff that looked valuable to them."

"That's a cheerful thought."

"I'm going to try some other things, but if nothing turns up it may be worth a trip to the county dump. But just in case, I want you to look around down there. I don't think anyone will try to sell those paintings in New York; they'd ship them out to Europe, maybe Japan. If that's happening I want to stop them."

"What were they doing in a storeroom? Six paintings that valuable?"

"That's where the client kept them."

"Okay, funny guy. And who's the client?"

"I can't tell you."

She skipped half a beat. "You can't tell *me?*"

"Now," I said. "From here. Over the phone."

"Oh." That single word held a dubious note, as though my explanation was logical but not convincing. "Are there other things you're not telling me?"

"Yes," I said. "But when I tell them to you, you hang up on me."

"For which not a woman in America could blame me. What do I do if I find a trail? Are the police in on this?"

"No, and that's important. I don't want anyone who doesn't know these paintings exist to find out from us."

"Top-secret paintings stuck in a storeroom by a top-secret client in the middle of nowhere. And I thought it was all trees and cows and guys who shoot at Bambi up there. Silly me."

"I'll call you later," I told her. "If anything turns up, you can try the cell phone, but you might not get through up here."

"I'm surprised you even took it with you."

"You told me I had to carry one. I always do what you tell me."

"Uh-huh."

"Uh-huh. Well, anyway, if you can't get through, try this number." I gave her the number of the phone I was at. "Ask for Tony. Leave a time and a place I can call you. Hey, and Lydia?"

"Yes?"

"Tell your mother I'm a nice guy."

"I never lie to my mother. Talk to you later."

She hung up. I took out another quarter, dialed Obermeyer's garage—the number was carved into the woodwork—and asked for Jimmy. A voice muffled by food told me he hadn't come in yet. "You got a problem?"

"Lots," I answered. "If you see him, tell him Bill Smith is looking for him, okay?"

"Sure." The voice slurped a drink, went on. "If *you* see him, tell him I'm all backed up here, and where the hell is he?"

"Sure."

There were loud crunching sounds. I hung up.

The vinyl-covered phone book was chained to the shelf under the phone. I flipped it open to the Yellow Pages in the back, found Antique Shops, pages of them. Schoharie was studded with these places. Most of them were no more than someone's front room or disused garage, where chipped china and molding books shared space with broken-legged tables and chairs with torn upholstery. But a few shops were bigger or more choosy about their merchandise. It was still possible to come across the kind of finds up here that had long since vanished from areas closer to the city or more attractive to tourists. The past was one of the few things people up here had to sell.

Jimmy could have pointed me in the right direction. He'd have protested innocence, or maybe with me he wouldn't have bothered; but he'd know where to find a fence for the sort of things Eve Colgate had lost. Without him it was a crapshoot, so I fed quarters into the phone and started from A. With everyone who answered I used the same line. A teapot, I said I needed, describing vaguely a silver teapot Eve Colgate had described to me in great detail. For my wife, I said, for our anniversary. She liked that kind of thing, I didn't know anything about it, myself.

At the end of half an hour I had four promising places, all within an hour's drive of Eve Colgate's farm.

I brought my empty glass back to Tony at the bar. The T-shirts were gone; the place was empty.

"You leavin'?"

"Yeah. I'll be back tonight. Someone may call me here." I pointed a thumb at the phone.

"Okay," Tony said. "Only help me out with somethin' before you go."

"I thought I was supposed to mind my own business."

"You gonna want ice in your goddamn bourbon later, this is your business. Damn thing's busted again." Tony's antiquated ice machine had more weak points than a sermon.

"What is it, that valve? Like when I was here in the fall?"

"Yeah, and twice in the winter when you wasn't. You gotta turn it off downstairs, wait till I tell you to turn it on again. The red one. You know." I knew. "Unless you're in a hurry. It can wait till the O'Brien kid comes in, or Marie."

"No hurry."

The door to the cellar was back by the phone. Under my weight the wooden stairs creaked. The light from the head of the stairs didn't reach very far, but dusty gray daylight filtered in through the grimy windows in the back wall. The place smelled of mildew and damp concrete. I shook a spiderweb from the back of my hand.

Tony's cellar was a shadowed landscape of boxes, crates, abandoned furniture. Lying across the pipes overhead were old fishing rods, skis, a pair of snowshoes whose leather webbing was crumbling to dust. About five miles of greasy rope was heaped in a corner, next to a bureau Tony's father had moved down here before Tony was born.

Tony knew every object here, and could navigate smoothly through them in the dark. I couldn't. I waited for my eyes to adjust to the dimness, then picked my way carefully to the middle of the room, where a single light-bulb dangled from the ceiling.

I reached a hand up to it; then I stopped and froze. I wasn't the only thing moving.

Barely visible, a shadow darker than the others slid noiselessly behind a hill of boxes.

Slowly, silently, I eased the gun from under my arm. I stared through the dimness; there was nothing. Everything was still, as though it always had been. But I'd seen it. I moved to my left, to where the shadow went. My steps were silent. Maybe whoever it was wouldn't hear my heart pounding, either.

Suddenly a crash, something shattering on the concrete floor. Another flash of movement. I pressed my back against the wall, gun drawn. Before me two unblinking eyes appeared, glittering in the half-light.

The cat whose face they were in crouched on a pile of boxes, hissed, thrashed its tail. It turned, flowed through a broken windowpane and was gone.

I breathed. "Shit," I said to the vanished cat. "You could get killed doing that." I put my gun away, rubbed the back of my neck.

"Hey, Smith!" Tony yelled from above. "What the hell are you doin' down there?"

"All right!" I yelled back. I stepped over a broken bar-stool into the center of the room and yanked the chain on the dangling bulb. The sudden glare brought sharp edges and color springing out of the soft shadows. I looked around, searching for a clear path to the back of the room, but I never found it.

From the back wall near the floor another pair of eyes met mine. These didn't blink either, but they didn't glitter. They were human, and they were dull because they were dead.

FOUR

He must have been standing right up against the back wall when he was shot. Three dark rings with darker centers the size of a baby's fist stained his shirt. He'd slumped down leaving a thin smear of blood on the ancient white-wash, until he settled, sitting on the dirty floor, one arm over a case of empties as though it were a friend of his. His face was a mottled gray, like candlewax and ashes, and from his slack, open mouth a thin line of blood, now dry and cracking, had dripped down his chin to splash perfect circles onto his open, bony hand.

I knew those hands. After last night, the way they'd circled my throat, shaking and choking, after that I'd have known them anywhere.

He looked so foolish, so surprised. I wanted to close his eyes, his mouth, cover him with something. He was indecent, unready as the curtain went up on his final show, probably the only starring role a guy like him had ever had.

I knelt, felt his neck for a pulse. I knew it was stupid. I lifted the edge of his coat with a finger, looking for the gun he'd had last night. It was gone.

The sweet smell of blood was thick in the damp air. I let his coat fall and stayed where I was, prowling the floor with my eyes. I didn't know what I was looking for but I found it, a set of keys on a silver ring in the dirt by his knee. I stared at them in the dim light; then I took out a handkerchief, picked them up in it, and slipped them, wrapped, into my pocket.

I stepped back the way I'd come, careful not to disturb anything I hadn't disturbed already.

The creaking of the stairs as I went up seemed louder than before, but I could have been wrong about that.

Tony and I were sitting at the round table in the front of the room, about as far from the cellar as you could get. I was drinking bourbon; he was drinking gin. Tony had called the state troopers. Now all we had to do was wait.

A fly, early and stupid, staggered slowly around a wine stain in the red-and-white tablecloth like an old man avoiding a puddle.

I lit a cigarette, shook out the match. "Tell me about it, Tony."

Tony looked into the glass in front of him. He didn't find anything but gin. "Nothin' to tell."

"There's a stiff in your cellar says otherwise."

He raised his head sharply, glared at me. "You think I put him there?"

I shook my head. "You didn't even know he was down there or you wouldn't have sent me down. But you do know something, Tony. About what?"

Tony didn't answer. I sipped my bourbon, tried again. "What did Grice want last night?"

"Ah, shit!" He slammed his glass onto the table. "He thinks he's got somethin' on Jimmy."

"Does he?"

Tony poured himself another slug of gin. He didn't speak.

"What does he want?" I asked. "For whatever he's got?"

He shrugged, drank. "I told him to go to hell."

"Does that mean you don't know? Or you don't care?"

He started to stand, his face darkening. He started to speak, too, but stopped, clamped his mouth shut, and sat

back down heavily. He stared at his gin, then drank it as
though he were doing it a favor.

I took the handkerchief from my pocket, unwrapped it,
laid it on the table. The keys on the silver ring glinted
between us.

Tony's eyes narrowed. "Where did you get those?"

"Downstairs," I said. "They're Jimmy's, aren't they?"

Sirens wailed as cars screeched into the lot. I slipped
the keys back in my pocket. Doors slammed and the curtains at the front window pulsed red and blue.

"Tony," I said quietly, "I'm on your side."

He got up to open the door for the law.

Sheriff Garrett Brinkman, followed by a paunchy,
sleepy-eyed deputy, stepped around Tony into the room.
Their boots made hard sounds on the worn wood floor.
Brinkman wore high black boots like a motorcycle cop,
and kept them shiny enough to see your face in. He was
a long-faced, long-legged man whose hair was thinning
and hadn't been much of a color when he'd had it. His
hands were big and his eyes were small. When he was
young, he'd played right field for a Triple-A ball club. He
still held the minor-league record for spiking second base-
men.

"Brinkman." Tony scowled. "What the hell are you doing here? I didn't call you, I called the troopers."

"No, how about that?" Brinkman drawled amicably, his
eyes shifting from Tony to me, back again. "My county,
you find a dead guy, but you call the state and you don't
call me." He smiled a small, nasty smile, and waited, eyes
on Tony, for an explanation we all knew he didn't need
and wasn't going to get. Then he shrugged. "But what the
hell, Tony. We picked it up over the radio. So I thought
we'd come give the pretty boys from the state a hand, in
case they need to find their dicks or something." Brinkman
turned to me, the nasty smile widening. "And how lucky
can I get?" he said. "Look who's here."

"Hello, Brinkman," I said. "Long time."

"Not long enough, city boy." The smile pushed back

the deep creases that ran from his nose to his chin. "I hope you're messed up in this."

"Sorry." I smiled too. It was in the air. "I found him. That's all I know."

"We'll see," said Brinkman. Then, "Show me."

I pushed my chair back, got up from the table. I was about to throw back the last of my bourbon when Brinkman put his hand over my glass. "I like my witnesses sober."

"Yeah," I said. "I guess alcohol could dull the pain." I stopped smiling.

"Don't push me, city boy," Brinkman said softly.

I walked around him, opened the cellar door. Brinkman and the deputy clattered down the wooden stairs. Tony and I followed.

I'd left the light on. Sharp black shadows lay heavily beyond the circle of it. "Where?" Brinkman asked.

"In the back." I showed him how to go.

We picked our way among things once wanted, now useless and decaying. The four of us collected in a semi-circle at the back wall. The little bony guy stared at us out of sightless eyes, his arm still over the dusty bottles, his mouth still open.

"Well," said Brinkman. "This just gets better, doesn't it?" The smile twitched again at a corner of his mouth. "Know him?"

Tony took that one. "Met him once," he said tightly. "Don't know his name."

"Oh?" said Brinkman. "Well, his name's Wally Gould. Works for Frank Grice. What I hear, he does anything so dirty even Grice won't touch it. What's he doing here, Tony?"

"How the hell should I know?"

"Smith?" Brinkman said over his shoulder, without looking at me. He squatted next to the body, moved the dead man's coat aside, as I had. His boots scratched in the dirt as he stood again and turned.

"Forget it, Brinkman. I came down to shut off a leaky

valve. I found him like this, we called the troopers, got
you instead. That's it."

"I guess you didn't know him either?"

"I met him once, same as Tony."

"Uh-huh. When was that?"

Tony answered before I could. "Last night. Grice was
here with two guys—this guy, and some big gorilla. I
threw 'em out."

Brinkman raised his eyebrows, the small smile still
playing on his lips. "And they just went?"

"No. They were lookin' for trouble."

"Oh." Brinkman let the smile grow. "That what happened to your face?" he asked me.

"I was born with this face, Brinkman. Some days it just
looks worse than others."

Brinkman pushed back his hat, revealing more of his
endless forehead. "You know, a guy in your position
should show more respect for the law."

"What position am I in?"

"Hey, you're the top man on my shit list, Smith. Ahead
of Tony's little shit brother, ahead of Tony, even ahead of
Frank Grice. Right on top."

"Listen, Brinkman, I'm sorry about your little plan to
put a net over Grice, but it wouldn't have worked anyway.
Jimmy wasn't going to deal."

"He sure as hell was, until you and your New York Jew
lawyer fucked me up. Fucked me up real good. I sneeze
in this county now, my fucking county, Grice yells for his
lawyer. 'Harassment.' 'Brutality.' Where the hell you think
he learned that shit, Smith? Fucking city lawyer shit!"

"Too bad it's so easy to believe."

Brinkman's mouth twisted into an ugly shape. He made
a grab for me but the deputy, smooth and graceful the way
a fat man can be, slipped his bulk between us, his back to
me, his cushiony hands on Brinkman's arms. "Come on,
Sheriff. Everyone's upset here. I'm sure Mr. Smith didn't
mean nothing by it."

Brinkman snarled, shook the deputy off, took a step

back. "Oh, he did, Art. He sure did," he said, controlled and soft.

He turned and looked at Wally Gould, still sitting stupidly in the dirt, staring at nothing. Then he turned back. "All right. Upstairs. Art, call the pretty boys at the state, find out where the hell they are." His small eyes lit with a thought. "Smith, you packing a gun?"

"You know I am." I held my jacket open so he could see the Colt under my left arm.

"Give it to me."

I laughed. "You're not in a good enough mood for me to reach for a gun, Brinkman. You take it."

His hands clenched and he took a step toward me. Then he stopped, his eyes on mine, and the mean little smile came out of nowhere, spread like a stain across his face.

He reached for my holster, snapped the safety off, slid the gun out. It was the gun I carry when I have a choice, an old snub-nose five-shot. He looked at it wonderingly, held it out for Art to see. "Look at this shit. Christ, Smith, why don't you get yourself a piece that works?"

"It works."

"Oh?" He broke it open, sniffed at it. "Maybe so. Been cleaned lately."

"I keep it clean. I like clean things."

"How about that, Art?" He nudged the deputy. "A city boy that likes clean things."

He pocketed my gun and moved toward the stairs, pushing me aside instead of stepping around me to show he could.

Upstairs the air was better. The company was the same.

Brinkman settled on a barstool, his back to the bar, his elbows resting on it. "Where's Jimmy?" he asked Tony pleasantly.

"I ain't seen him in a coupla weeks."

"Oh, come on, Tony. Doesn't he live with you? In that big old place your grandpa built?" Brinkman jerked a thumb in the direction of Tony's house across the road from the bar.

"He moved out Christmas."

"You throw him out?"

Tony's eyes blazed. "Go to hell, Brinkman."

Brinkman smiled. "Well, I'll find him. You seen him, Smith?"

"I just came up night before last."

"Why?"

"Why what?"

"Why'd you come up?"

"I've been coming here for eighteen years, Brinkman. I never needed a reason before."

"Well, city boy," Brinkman drawled, crossing a shiny boot over his knee, "maybe you're going to need one from now on."

FIVE

The state troopers' Bureau of Criminal Investigation for the tri-county area was near Bramanville in a gray block building off the state highway. It was surrounded by a featureless field of grass and a parking lot. The grass was brown and thin now, at the chill end of winter, but spring wouldn't make much difference to it.

I was sitting where I'd been sitting for close to an hour, in a one-windowed office at the end of a narrow corridor. The walls were paneled in wood-veneer pressboard and hung with a pin-dotted county map and photos of the governor. Glass-doored bookshelves held law enforcement manuals and phonebooks. A big wooden desk with a glass top sat diagonally across a corner of the room, facing the door. I sat facing the desk.

The man whose office it was, Senior Investigator Ron MacGregor, got up from behind the desk to shut the door. MacGregor was unremarkable to look at, medium height, medium build, about as much red, thinning hair as you might expect on a man pushing fifty. A few freckles still stood out on his thin face and he had tired blue eyes.

MacGregor and I knew each other casually and accidentally. A good trout stream ran through the bottom of my land. I didn't fish it often, because from where I was it was nearly inaccessible. My land was vertical, ten acres spread down the side of a steep hill, with a few shelves like the one the cabin was on and just enough of a leveling out near 30 that a road could be coaxed out of it. Only a fanatic would bother with the long, tricky climb down to the stream over boulders and slippery leaves, especially when about five miles south the stream flowed through county land with a well-kept path to it. I wasn't that kind of fanatic, but MacGregor was, and one April afternoon a couple of years ago when roadwork muddied the water downstream, I drove in to find one of my windows forced open and some expensive-looking fishing tackle in my kitchen. A note, written in an unfamiliar hand on paper torn from a pocket notebook, was stuck on the reel. "Was fishing your stream," it read. "Sprained my ankle. Why don't you have a goddamn phone? Having enough trouble without this stuff. Eat the fish. I'll be by for the gear." It was signed "Ron MacGregor."

I looked in the fridge. There were four beautiful trout in a creel. I took one out, wrapped it in newspaper, put it back on the shelf. Then I took the creel and the rest of the gear over to Antonelli's and checked the phone book. There were two Ron MacGregors in the county; I hit it the first time. "Didn't want your fish to rot," I told him.

"You the guy in Lou Antonelli's place? Why the hell don't you have a phone? It took me an hour to crawl up your goddamn driveway."

"Get a phone, people start calling you," I explained. "You never know where it might end."

I took him his fish and his gear, and we sat drinking beer in his split-level ranch for the rest of the afternoon. Since then he'd fished my stream often. What he liked about my stream was the same thing I liked about my cabin: There was no one else around. What I liked about him was that he left his car at the top of the road and never stopped by to say hello without an invitation.

MacGregor sat back down. "You want another cup of coffee?"

"No," I said. "That one was bad enough."

I'd told my story twice, once briefly when MacGregor and his men arrived at Antonelli's, then in more detail here for the benefit of MacGregor, a uniformed trooper, and a tape machine. I'd told it patiently and completely, gave details as I remembered them, answered questions as I could. I left out only two things. I didn't say what the fight last night had been about—I didn't really know anyway—and, though I gave MacGregor the keys on the silver ring and told him where I'd found them, I didn't tell him whose I thought they were. When I was through, the trooper left, taking the tape to be transcribed.

With the door closed and the trooper gone, MacGregor frowned. He poked the eraser end of his pencil at my handkerchief, lying in the center of his desk with the keys on top. "Withholding evidence, Smith. That's a bad business."

"I'm not withholding anything. I'm giving it to you."

"Tampering, then. What if there were prints on these?"

"Then there still are. I've had them gift-wrapped, Mac. They were safer with me than they would have been with Brinkman's boys."

MacGregor sighed with that weariness that a night's sleep or a month's vacation won't cure, in a cop. "That's true. It's the only reason I'm not going to chew your ass over this—now. What else have you got? The murder weapon, maybe?"

"Nothing else."

"Why'd you pick these up?"

"I thought I recognized them. I wanted to see them in the light."

"Oh? Private citizen wants to look at the evidence, he just scoops it up and walks off with it?"

"Private investigator, Mac. It's in my blood. I'm sorry."

"And?"

I shook my head. "I'm not sure."

"What do you think?"

"I think that when I'm sure I'll tell you."

MacGregor pushed at the handkerchief some more. "You're pretty close with the Antonellis, aren't you?"

"Tony and I go back awhile. I rented his father's hunting cabin when I first started coming up here; when the old man died Tony sold it to me."

"And Jimmy?"

"He was a kid when his father died, eight or nine. He used to spend some time with me, when I was up."

MacGregor looked up from the handkerchief. "I heard you were like another father to him."

"I wasn't here enough for that, except one winter. I had troubles of my own around that time. The kid was good company. He didn't talk much."

"And when he was arrested?"

"Which time?"

"You know what I mean. Last fall."

I shrugged. "He was looking at five to fifteen. He didn't deserve it."

"Says you."

"Okay," I said.

"So you brought up a slick city lawyer and got him off."

"I thought the troopers weren't involved in that, it was a county thing. What do you care?"

"It pissed off every cop on this side of the state, Smith. We're simple folks up here; we're not used to being out-manuevered by lawyers with manicures and bow ties."

"I didn't like it either. I don't like to operate that way. But the kid didn't have a chance. Brinkman was out to get Grice and he was squeezing Jimmy hard. The whole scam was Grice's; Jimmy wasn't even in it for the money, just the fun."

"How so?"

"You know what Grice paid Jimmy to drop those cars in the quarry? A hundred bucks each. It must have been worth a lot more than that to Grice to lose them."

"So why'd Jimmy do it?"

"Because it was dangerous. You know how he did it?"

"Put the car in neutral and pushed, I'd guess."

"You'd be wrong. He drove the damn things like a bat out of hell over the edge with the door open, jumped out just before they hit the water. Twice a car rolled over on him; once he got knocked on the head. He still doesn't

know how he made it onto the rocks that time; he didn't
wake up until morning."

MacGregor shook his head. "He's crazy."

"No, he's not. Just wild. Making a lot of noise so he
won't hear the sounds in the dark. No different from a lot
of kids."

MacGregor chewed his bottom lip. He had kids, too.
Girls; but girls had their own ways of being wild.

He said, "You got any idea where I can find him?"

I said evenly, "No. Why?"

He threw down the pencil. "Oh, come on, Smith! You
got a better suspect?"

"Why would Jimmy kill Gould?"

"I've got two theories and I haven't even thought about
it yet. Maybe it was Gould who tipped off Brinkman about
the quarry, and Jimmy was pissed. Guys like Gould have
turned out to be snitches before this. Or, maybe Jimmy
was looking to move up in Grice's organization and Gould
was in the way."

"And why leave the body lying around?"

"Maybe he meant to come back for it, after he figured
out what to do with it. From the looks of that cellar, no
one goes down there from one month to the next unless
something blows."

"Things blow all the time over there. Jimmy would
know that."

"Well," he said, his eyes on the handkerchief on his
desk, "maybe he went out to his car to get something and
found he'd lost his keys, couldn't get back in." He looked
at me again. "He can hot-wire the car; maybe he's got
another set of keys to the bar at home. Maybe it's pretty
close to morning anyway, Tony'll be there soon. Maybe
he figures he'll chance it, leave the body, come back the
next night. He's big on taking chances, I hear."

I looked at him levelly. "He's not a killer, Mac."

MacGregor didn't answer, only shrugged.

"Can I leave?" I asked. "I'm starving."

MacGregor sighed and his tone changed. "In a minute.

Tell me something else. Brinkman has this bug up his ass about Grice. So why hasn't he ever picked him up?"

"What do you mean?"

"I never heard Brinkman was crooked but I never heard he was Kojak, either. All the rackets Grice runs—protection, prostitution, even drugs—some jerk or other has run in Schoharie since the Creation. Never bothered Brinkman as long as the boys were local and kept their heads down. Then along comes some minor-league bozo out of Albany to do a little muscle work and all of a sudden fighting crime is more important to Brinkman than sitting on his duff watching his pension grow."

"Jesus, Mac, I thought you and Brinkman were on the same side." He glared. I asked, "What kind of muscle work?"

MacGregor snorted. "Union-busting. For Appleseed."

"Scabbing at the baby food plant? God, that's disillusioning."

"Yeah. So Brinkman develops the same boil on his butt about Grice that he has about you—asshole from the city messing in *his* county, all that shit." I raised an eyebrow at "asshole" but that didn't stop him. "But in the four years Grice's been around, Brinkman hasn't managed to take him up even once. Why is that?"

"I don't know."

He shook his head. "You don't know. Well, maybe you know this. After your slimy lawyer sprang Jimmy Antonelli, Brinkman still had nine cars that his boys spent a week—and a hell of a lot of county money—pulling out of the quarry. If Grice was running dope up from Florida in them there must have been some other way to prove it. Why didn't he or the DA even try?"

I stood up. "What the hell do I look like, the Answer Man? Ask Brinkman. I'm going to get some lunch."

"Not even a theory?"

"Yeah, I have a theory. But you won't like it."

"Try me."

"Grice has protection, someone watching his back."

"Oh, screw that. In New York maybe. It doesn't work that way up here."

"Come off it, Mac. A jerk who'd be nobody anywhere else drifts into the county, puts all the local talent out of business, and for four years even a jack-booted sheriff with a grudge can't get near him. Did you know Grice left for Florida the night before Brinkman busted Jimmy? Left in a hurry, came back three days after Jimmy got out. It glows in the dark, Mac. Only a cop could miss it."

MacGregor turned his face to the window, stared out over the brown grass to the trees that started abruptly beyond it. After a minute he reached over, punched a button on his phone.

"Craig? You got Smith's statement yet? Well, bring it in. And bring in Tony Antonelli, too; I'm ready." He dropped the receiver in the cradle. "Sign your statement and beat it. Don't leave the county. You got a phone yet?"

"Not a chance." I didn't tell him about the cell phone. Up here in the hills, it's close to useless anyway, which I can't say I really minded. "You need me, you can leave a message at Antonelli's." I looked at his gray, tired face. "Cheer up, Mac. Fishing season starts in four weeks."

Life came into his blue eyes. "Three weeks, three days. I've been tying flies all winter."

"I don't doubt it." The door opened and Tony came in, with the uniformed trooper who'd taken my tape. The trooper handed me three typed pages; I glanced through them, signed the bottom of each.

"All right," said MacGregor. "Go on. Just don't disappear."

"When do I get my gun back?"

"When we're finished with it. Call tomorrow."

I turned to Tony. I could read tension in the set of his shoulders. His face was opaque. "See you later," I said to him. He stared at me for a moment, then nodded. I left MacGregor's office, navigated past a pair of troopers in gray uniforms sitting at gray desks. I took long, deep breaths as I headed toward my car across the gray asphalt parking lot.

The damn car was gray, too. I couldn't remember why that had seemed like a good idea at the time.

Off the highway just west of the trooper station there was a shabby Amoco station with a working pay phone. I called Obermeyer's garage, letting the phone ring long enough for a mechanic to curse, crawl out from under a car, and pick up the receiver in a grease-blackened hand; but it didn't happen. There was no answer.

I leaned against the chipped enameled steel panels of the station and watched a chunky kid in a green football jersey fill my car. I thought. Not that I had a hell of a lot to work on, but I thought.

I paid for the gas and a pack of Kents and turned back east, toward the village of Schoharie. I cut off the highway onto 1A, a county road. For a few miles 1A ran through pines and maples and birches, past some old frame houses that had needed a coat of paint for as long as I could remember, past a couple of trailers parked broadside to the road, until suddenly it opened out just before it started down into Schoharie.

Even in this season, when everything lay still and cold, not quite ready yet to take another chance, the sudden view over these hills could take your breath away. There was a promise of generosity and refuge in the soft contours, in the bowl of the hills, in the wide valley quilted with farms and fields. The river that flowed through here was choked with ice now and the hills were gray-brown where they weren't pine; and in a dark, unhealed gash in the hills you could see the old stone quarry, three played-out pits, empty now of what had made them worth ripping the hillside apart for; and farther down the hill, the smaller, working pit. Still, coming down into this valley, even in winter, could make you believe home could be more than just a word.

Schoharie's not the largest town in the county—that's

Cobleskill, where the state ag-and-tech college is—but it's
the county seat. Main Street runs half a mile, flat, straight,
and tree-shaded. In each direction, like a caterpillar's legs,
short narrow residential streets branch off it. None is more
than three blocks long, the houses thinning by the start of
the second block.

On the east side of Main in the center of town stand
the village hall and the county buildings: the executive
offices, the courthouse, the sheriff's office with the new
jail annex behind it. They're mostly brown brick, but the
courthouse, the oldest of them, is a square-shouldered
building of gray local stone, pulled from the quarry in the
busy, prosperous days.

I parked on the nearly empty street a block up from the
courthouse. I fed the parking meter—six minutes for a
penny, half an hour for a nickel—because the sheriff's
office was half a block away and Brinkman knew my car.

I crossed in the middle of the block, creating a two-car
traffic jam, and stepped onto the cracked and uneven concrete sidewalk. There was no grass verge here. Beyond
Main Street's half mile there wasn't even a sidewalk.

The Park View luncheonette was at the end of a block
of two-and three-story brick buildings with their dates set
in stone at their cornices. The luncheonette's storefront
windows were clouded, the way they always were on a
cold day. Beads of water streaked them from inside; dish
towels lined the low Formica sills, catching the conden-
sation before puddles formed and dripped onto the check-
erboard linoleum.

The chrome-legged tables at the front were empty except for two old men with plaid wool jackets and rheumy
eyes. I walked past them, sat at the counter on a stool
whose green vinyl cover was bandaged with silver tape.

At one of the rear tables a giggling group of adolescent
girls who should have been in school were drinking Cokes
and puffing on cigarettes without inhaling. At another a
young woman ate a sandwich while a baby in a high chair
rubbed his hands in his applesauce. A man and a woman

with a city look about them were spread out at the back table drinking coffee and reading the *Mountain Eagle*. There were people who said that people like them—yuppies with money to spend—would be the salvation of the county. A class above weekenders like me, they would buy the shabby farms, hire locals to repair the buildings and tend their gardens and look after their horses while they were back in the city making money. A few of the local cafes had put in cappuccino machines, and the A & P in Cobleskill was starting to stock arugula and endive, for the ones who'd come already. But the drive from New York is long, and summers are short up here in the hills. There's no cachet to a place in this county, nowhere to wine and dine your weekend guests, no one to see or be seen by. People with an eye for beauty and a need for quiet would come here, but they always had. And the moneyed crowds would continue to go elsewhere, as they always had.

Ellie Warren stepped from behind the counter to refill coffee cups and chat. She turned when she saw me sit; her thin face lit in a big gap-toothed grin.

"Well, hi there, stranger!" She came to the counter, plunked the coffeepot down, gave me a peck on the cheek. "I haven't seen you since before Thanksgiving! Where have you been?"

"I haven't been up, Ellie."

She nodded, her eyes glowing conspiratorially. "Making yourself scarce?"

"You think I needed to?"

She laughed. "Probably didn't hurt." She pushed a string of faded red hair back from her face. "Hey, hon, what happened?" Her long thin fingers touched the cheek she hadn't kissed.

I winced. "Nothing; it's okay. But I'm starving. What's good?"

She smiled wickedly. "Nothing here. Come by my place later, I'll fry you some chicken that'll make you cry."

"How about a sandwich to hold me till then?"

"If you have to."

"A BLT on toast. And coffee."

Ellie waltzed down the counter, stuck my order on a spindle at the kitchen opening. She came back, poured my coffee, leaned her elbows on the counter.

"How've you been, Ellie?" I asked through the coffee.

She spread her skinny arms, grinned again. "As you see. Not getting older, getting better."

"You couldn't get any better, Ellie. How's Chuck doing?"

Ellie's son Chuck was twenty-one, a loud, wild boy. He and Jimmy Antonelli had been inseparable troublemakers for years. Brinkman had arrested them more times than anyone could count on drunk-and-disorderlies, as public nuisances, for property damage, willful endangerment, trespassing, and once, after they'd stolen a car, for grand theft. The car turned out to belong to a cousin of Ellie's, who refused to press charges.

Until the boys were seventeen, all Brinkman could do was grit his teeth while the family court judge sent for Tony and Ellie. He'd lecture them, let them pay the boys' fines, and send them home. But finally even the judge got disgusted. As soon as they were old enough by state law to serve time as adults, he started sentencing them to weeks at a time in the jail behind the sheriff's office.

Brinkman had enjoyed that.

Ellie laughed. "He's doing great. Basic training is over and he's been at sea a couple of weeks now. I've got a picture. You want to see?"

"A picture? I thought you'd be good for a dozen, Ellie."

"He only sent me the one, so far. It's only been three months."

She reached under the counter for her purse, rummaged through it. She flipped her wallet open, smiled as she looked at the photograph, passed it to me.

Chuck Warren had Ellie's smile, with more teeth. His eyes were as challenging as ever, but his mustache was gone, and his thick blond hair was cropped close and largely hidden under a seaman's cap.

"Christ," I said. "He must have been really scared, to go and do that."

"He thought Jimmy was going to end up doing fifteen years in Greenhaven. We all did. He knew it could have been him. It made him think." She laughed again. "Sometimes, you have to hit them over the head with a frying pan to get their attention."

The bell in the kitchen rang. Ellie went down the counter, brought back my sandwich, along with cole slaw and fries I hadn't ordered. "A big guy like you needs some real food," she explained, eyes twinkling.

I salted the fries. "Ellie, I need to find Jimmy. Tony says he's been living with a girl. That mean anything to you?"

She frowned, folded her hands together under her chin. "I haven't seen him since Chucky left."

"This would be from before that. Tony says he moved out around Christmas."

The door opened, letting in cold air and two men who sat at the end of the counter. Ellie winked at me, went over and took their orders. She poured them coffee, came back, and refilled my cup. "You know, I think he did have a girl. I never met her, but Chucky told me. Oh, what was her name?" Her face furrowed into lines of concentrated thought, then melted. "Alice. Alice something."

"Alice what?"

"Come on, hon, what do you want from an old lady?"

"If I knew an old lady I'd tell you. Do you know what she looks like?"

She thought again. "You know, I do. Chucky said she was pretty; dark and sweet; but heavy-set. That sort of surprised him; I guess that's why he mentioned it. He said Jimmy'd always gone for the skinny ones, the little lost-looking ones. Alice was real different from Jimmy's other girls. She's not part of that crowd, you know, Jimmy and Chucky's crowd. I don't think Jimmy was hanging around with them either so much anymore, since he met her."

"Well, thanks, Ellie. That'll help." I reached for my check; only the sandwich was on it.

I paid her, finished my coffee as she made change from the ornate cash register. As I zipped my jacket she put her hand on my arm. "Wait," she said. "I think I did see Jimmy. I'm not sure, but I think it was him. Chucky told me Jimmy'd bought a truck—one of those stupid things with the big wheels and the light bar on the cab?"

"What about his old van, that he worked on so hard?"

"Oh, he still has that, I think. Anyhow, a truck like Chucky told me about tore through here about two weeks ago as I was coming in. Ran the stoplight, had to drive onto the curb to miss the mail truck coming from Spring Street. I think it was Jimmy's, but he wasn't driving. Some girl was."

"Alice?"

"I don't think so, not if Chucky was right. This one was small, with lots of blond hair. And laughing, as though tearing around town on two wheels was funnier than anything."

I kissed her skinny hand. She pulled it back, laughing. Then her face got serious. "Is Jimmy in trouble, hon?"

"I don't know. But Brinkman's looking for him, and the state troopers. Just to ask him some questions, for now. But I don't want Jimmy to do anything stupid if Brinkman finds him."

"Oh, lord. Sheriff Brinkman would love that, wouldn't he?"

"Yeah, he would. Keep an eye out for him, will you, Ellie? I'll see you later."

I stepped out into the afternoon. Lighting a cigarette, I looked up and down the street. A yellow dog wandered, sniffing, along the sidewalk opposite. The stoplight at Main and Spring changed. No one was at it.

It was a big county. Finding a dark, heavy-set girl named Alice, if that was all I had to go on, could take weeks.

And there was another problem. I had a client. I'd taken

Eve Colgate's money to follow a trail that was already four days old and getting colder by the minute.

I reached in my pocket, found the list of antique shops I'd made a century ago, this morning at Antonelli's. I looked at my watch. Two o'clock. If I was smart about it, I could get to the places I'd targeted and be back at Antonelli's by six-thirty or seven. If the place was open— and if I knew Tony, as soon as MacGregor was through with him and MacGregor's boys were through with his cellar, he'd be open—maybe Tony would talk to me.

If he wouldn't, maybe the Navy would let Chuck Warren talk to me.

Either way, at least I'd get a drink.

SIX

One of the antique shops on my list was in Schoharie, down Main Street from the Park View. A wooden sign in the shape of a sheep hung over the sidewalk. The proprietress, a thin, quick woman, was very nice, but as far as Eve Colgate's silver, I came up dry. I gave her the number at Antonelli's, asked her to call me if anything like what I'd described turned up, and left.

I decided to hit the farthest of the other shops first and then work my way back across the county. I U turned in the middle of Main Street, went south where Main turns into 30 and 30 turns into a four-lane highway. Down here in the valley there was nothing dramatic about this road, but it was fast. Even where it was only two lanes, it had been widened and straightened, something they did to the old roads around here when they didn't build new ones to bypass them entirely. Now 30 cut right through some of the farms that had looked so timeless and sure from the hills. Not a few farmers had retired to Florida on what the state had paid for the fields I was driving through. Asphalt was a cash crop, up here.

I turned off 30 onto a narrow road that lead up into the hills past Breakabeen. The shop I was headed for was a few miles outside town. Town was a post office, a bar, a grocery, a Mr. Softee, and a dozen houses strung out along a crossroads.

Just beyond the point where the last of the houses disappeared behind me there was a road leading up to the right—probably a driveway masquerading as a road, like mine. Faded script letters on an arrow-shaped sign told anyone who cared to know that The Antiques Barn was a half mile up.

The first hundred yards was respectable, but after that the road was badly kept, full of potholes and mud. The Acura had good suspension—the old ones did—but I wouldn't cut a diamond in it, even on the highway. I was glad to get out of the car onto ground that wasn't moving.

The Antiques Barn was a real barn, big, with flaking red paint and double square doors wide enough to drive a combine through. Those doors weren't open. Neither was the person-sized door cut into one of them, but it gave when I turned the knob. As it opened, it rang a set of sleigh bells hung on the jamb.

I stepped over the high wooden threshold into a dusky, dank room where plates and pitchers, candlesticks and jewelry, walking canes, hats, boots, and thousands of books lay in piles on wooden furniture of every description. The piles had an air of having been undisturbed since time began. Each piece, including the furniture, bore a square ivory-colored tag with a number written on it in a spidery hand.

The room went on forever, disappearing into the dusk, and it seemed I was alone in it. "Hello!" I called into the aged air. Nothing happened. Maybe in here nothing ever happened. I called "Hello!" again, louder; then went back to the door and rattled it, ringing the sleigh bells again and again.

I stopped because I thought I heard a voice. I listened, ready to go back to my sleigh bells; but I was right. Faintly, from somewhere beyond a clutch of stuffed chairs in the center of the room, came words, and with the sound came movement, a figure shuffling toward me out of the primordial twilight.

"Yes, yes!" it muttered as it inched along, placing objects from a pile in its arms onto bureaus and bookcases like a glacier depositing rocks. "My, my!" The figure came very, very slowly to stand before me. It was the figure of a man, round for the most part. His age was unguessable, as was the actual color of his hair, now a thick dust gray.

He squinted up at me over dusty glasses that seemed to have been forgotten at the end of his nose. "You must learn to curb your impatience, young man. It will get you nowhere in life."

"I've been there already," I said. "I didn't like it."

He sniffed. "Well," he said. "Well. An impatient young man like yourself hasn't come here to browse. You're looking for some particular item. Yes; you know precisely what you want. Not for yourself; a gift most likely, for someone who"—he peered at me intently—"who assuredly would rather have you at home by the fire than running all over hell-and-gone seeking out the perfect gift. But you won't hear of it, so we'll say no more about it. What was it you wanted?"

I stared at him. "Old silver," I said. "Was that just for me, or can you do it all the time?"

"Some people," he sighed. "Some people could benefit; but they won't learn."

He turned and moved off with the speed of an acorn becoming a mighty oak. I followed. Luckily we were only going around a glass-doored breakfront to an alcove where wooden shelves were piled high with platters, plates, and carving knives, teapots and baby spoons. I don't think it took us more than an hour to get there.

"Here." He made a round, inclusive gesture. "Here is old silver. But you, of course, had a particular piece in mind. What was it?"

"A teapot. I called earlier; I may have spoken to you."

"I've spoken to no one on the telephone today, young man. Perhaps my wife . . ." He turned a full circle like the light in a lighthouse. "I don't see her now, but she's in the shop somewhere."

"It doesn't matter," I said hastily. If he went wandering off to find her it might be years before I saw him again. "Is this all your silver?"

"You've looked at none of it yet, but you're unsatisfied?"

I didn't need to look at it. Everything was covered with a layer of dust so thick that the dust itself was probably on the National Register. Nothing had been put on these shelves in the last few days.

"Is this all your silver?" I asked again.

"Well," he sighed, reached up onto the shelf. "As to teapots, this one, for example, is particularly fine." He blew a cloud of dust off the graceful pot in his hands; it settled on my shoes like snow. He handed the pot to me. I took it, turned it, examined it. He was right; even tarnished as it was, it was beautiful. I handed it back.

"I do have something particular in mind." I described Eve Colgate's teapot, the chased floral pattern, the scroll handle. He pursed his lips and shook his head slowly.

"Young man, I can't help you. If you really are going to insist on a pot of that description, good luck to you; you will waste more time searching for it than the finding of it will be worth." He looked at me sadly in the dim light.

"Well, thanks anyway," I said. "You've been a great help." I started to leave before I got any older.

"Wait," he said from behind me as I rounded the breakfront and reached for the door handle. "Young man, come back and look at these. They've only just come in. There isn't a teapot, but if the one you describe is to your taste, these may be also."

I let go of the door handle, not without a pang of regret. I circumnavigated the breakfront again and found him kneeling in the dust, unwrapping newspaper from around a small silver tray. A pair of candlesticks, already unwrapped, stood on the floor beside him.

Bingo.

He smiled up at me. "You're pleased. My, my." He handed me the tray and clambered to his feet.

They were a set, the tray and the candlesticks, as extraordinary as Eve Colgate had said they were. The minutely detailed pattern of grapes and grape leaves that covered the tray was repeated on the candlesticks' shafts.

"Where did you get these?" I asked.

He frowned. "Young man." He shook his head. "If you find them beautiful, you mustn't worry about provenance. They are silver, I assure you. A pedigree does not ensure that they will give you pleasure, only that someone else will be willing, someday, to give you cash." He peered again. "And you do not strike me as a man to whom that matters very much."

"Where did you get them?"

His round eyes blinked in his round face. "Some people . . ." he quoted himself sadly. "A young lady brought them. She was given them by her grandmother and doesn't care for them. Though I must say she seemed a refined young lady; I was surprised at her taste, but—"

"When?" I interrupted.

"When? Saturday."

Three days ago. "Did you know her?"

"Not I."

"Can you describe her?"

"Oh." His face took on a faraway look. "Oh, my, she was lovely. Petite; with golden hair, not straight and pale as straw the way they wear it now, but thick and golden, like summer sunlight. Red cheeks glowing from the cold; shining eyes. Standing at the threshold of womanhood, but still with a child's eagerness and joy. Lovely."

"And you believed her?"

"Believed her? In what way?"

"These things are stolen," I told him.

"Stolen?" He looked at me as though I should be ashamed of myself. "Stolen? Oh, my, young man, you are—"

"I'm a private investigator," I said. "These things are among a group of items stolen from a client of mine last Friday." I handed him my card. He looked at it and then at me. He handed it back.

"Young man, you have been less than forthright with me."

"You do your business your way, I do mine my way."

His face took on a stern and schoolmasterly look. I went on, "Do you get much of your stock that way, total strangers bringing in pieces this valuable? Happens every day?"

"Of course not. What is there that happens every day? My stock, as you call it, comes to me from many sources. Much of it I go in search of. Some is brought here by acquaintances or strangers. Without being immodest, I may tell you that this shop is known for handling only items of the highest quality. A young lady with such valuable items to sell would naturally—" He broke off, his open mouth forming a perfect circle. "Young man! I hope you are not implying that I knowingly—"

"I don't think I am." I picked up the tray and the candlesticks. "I want these things back and I'll pay for them—assuming the price is reasonable. But I want to know everything you remember about this girl. Did she bring you anything else?"

"No, just this set." He pursed his lips. "Stolen . . . you're sure? Yes, yes, of course you are; a young man like yourself is always sure. Really, I can't tell you very much else about her. A dazzling smile, a promise of secrets. Enchanting. Many years ago, I would have been tempted to play the prince to her Rapunzel."

"Was she alone?"

"She came in here alone, though I believe someone waited in the car for her."

"What kind of car?"

"A truck, actually, I think, a blue truck, the kind that rides high on its wheels."

"And she didn't give you her name, tell you where she was from, where her grandmother lived?"

"No, no." He shook his head. "Really, young man, such a charming child—"

"Never mind. If you remember anything else, or if she comes back, give me a call at this number, okay?" I wrote

the number at Antonelli's on my card and passed it back
to him.

He looked at me as though it were I who had opened
Pandora's box and let evil loose on the world.

The price of the tray and candlestick set was very reasonable, although it was more cash than I had in my
pocket. But it didn't matter.

He took my American Express Card.

I started the car, swung it around, and headed back down
the pockmarked road. The silver was carefully wrapped
and in the trunk. I'd had on my gloves when I'd handled
the pieces, so I had fair hopes of being able to lift a good
set of prints from them, including the shop owner's.

I had less hope that anything I found would be useful.
The golden young lady's prints wouldn't be in anyone's
computer unless she had a criminal record, which seemed
unlikely.

But she might have been working with someone who
did.

I walked around that thought slowly in my mind, looking at it from all angles. The sun was thin above the over-
hanging pines and a breeze was coming up. I was driving
with the window open, as usual; I could smell the damp-
ness in the air. Maybe rain, maybe snow. The road surface
modulated from potholes to asphalt and I shifted gears,
accelerating as the road curved. I reached for the radio dial.

Suddenly I slammed on the brakes. The car rocked to
a stop about six feet from a Chevy truck parked square
across the road.

The truck was big, black, and empty. It filled the shadowed road ditch to ditch. I threw the Acura into reverse,
but not in time. Two figures leapt out from the darkness
under the trees. They had guns, one each. They came up
even with my front windows and stopped, on either side
of the car. The one on my side spoke loud and fast.

. "Turn the car off!"

I turned the car off.

"Now throw out the keys."

I tossed my keys in his direction. They rang as they hit the pavement.

"Get out. Slowly. Keep your hands where I can see them. Watch him!" he called to the other.

The second figure circled around the front of the car, his gun trained on me through the windshield. I opened the door and got out slowly, my hands open and far from my sides.

"What's up?" I asked. The face in the shadows was vaguely familiar.

"Turn around, spread your hands on the car. Search him, Ted."

I put my hands on the top of the car. Ted went over me clumsily from behind. In my jacket he found my wallet; under my arm, my empty holster. He searched my pockets but there wasn't anything he wanted. He didn't look for an ankle rig. I wasn't wearing one, but he should have looked.

"His holster's empty, Otis," Ted whined. "His gun ain't here." He backed away from me.

"Where's your gun?" Otis barked.

"State Troopers, D Unit," I said over my shoulder. "Ask for Lieutenant MacGregor." I heard my keys jingle as Ted picked them up.

"Funny," said Otis. "Look in the car, Ted."

Ted tucked his gun in his belt and searched my car, crawling into the back, running his hand under the seats, snapping the glove compartment open and closed. In the well by the gearshift he found the roll of quarters I kept there. He pocketed them with a grin, climbed out of the car.

"Nothin'," he told Otis, pointing his gun at me again.

There was a Smith & Wesson .22 strapped up behind the dash, but it would have taken a better man than Ted to find it.

"The Park View," I said suddenly. "You guys sat down the other end of the counter."

"Free country," Otis said. "Fuck the gun. Let's go. You come with me. Ted'll bring your car."

I turned slowly, stood facing him. His face was broad, doughy. The knuckles on the hand wrapped around the big automatic were hairy and thick. "Where?" I asked.

"Guy I know wants to see you." He gestured in the direction of the black truck.

"Who?"

"What do you care?" The gun was black and mean-looking. He waved it around a little.

"I guess I don't." I walked a few steps toward the truck, Otis walking behind, Ted back by my car. When I had space around me I turned again to face Otis, as slowly as before. My arms were still and loose at my sides, but my fingers and my spine were tingling.

"No," I said.

"What the hell do you mean, no? I'm supposed to bring you in, I'm goddamn gonna bring you in."

"You won't shoot me. Whoever wants me probably wouldn't like it if you brought me in dead."

"No." Otis smiled, showing thick brown teeth. "But he might not mind if you was hurt a little." We were standing no more than four feet apart. He lowered the big automatic, leveled it at my knee.

"He might not," I said. "But I would."

While I was still talking, while his eyes were on my eyes and his attention on my words, I whipped my left foot up, over, out, caught his gun hand on the inside of the wrist. His arm flew back and I dived after it, grabbed it, spun him around so he was between me and Ted. He swung at my jaw with his free hand but he was way off balance and couldn't put a lot behind it; when it landed it didn't matter much. I kicked him again, in the stomach this time, and he squealed as I twisted his arm sharply from the wrist, bent it hard in a way it was never meant to go. He grabbed wildly at me. I wrenched the gun from him and smashed it across his jaw. I pulled his twisted wrist hard up behind his back, shoved the barrel of the gun under his chin.

"Tell Ted to drop it!" I said.

Nothing happened. I yanked on the wrist in my hand.

"Goddammit, Ted!" he gasped.

Ted threw his gun down as though it were suddenly hot.

"Okay," I said. "Face down in the road, hands behind your head. Now!" I pushed Otis down. Ted scrambled to flatten himself.

I picked up Ted's gun, a smaller, older version of the Ruger 9-mm I'd taken off Otis. I went over both men for anything else of interest. I found their wallets, leafed through them. Local boys, Otis and Ted, nothing more than what they looked like. I took my wallet, my quarters, and my keys back from Ted and then stepped over to my car.

"All right," I said. "Get up."

They climbed to their feet. Otis was white, holding his wrist close to his chest. Ted just looked sullen, as though his picnic had been spoiled by rain.

"You broke my wrist, motherfucker," Otis growled.

"No," I said. "If I had, it would hurt. Let's go."

"Where to?"

"You tell me. It's your party."

He narrowed his eyes. "I don't get it. If you was coming anyhow, what was all this for?"

"Oh, a lot of reasons. One, I like to be the guy with the guns. Two, I want Grice to know I'm coming because I'm curious, not because he sent some penny-ante punks after me." Otis ground his teeth when I said that, but he didn't speak. "And three, nobody drives this car but me."

"How did you know it was Frank wanted you?"

"I didn't. But this seems like his style. Heavy-handed and amateur. Let's go."

They got into the black truck, started it up. I slid behind the wheel of my car, turned the key, and watched Ted slam the truck forward and back until it faced downhill.

I lit a cigarette, dragged on it deeply. The truck rolled

down the hill and I followed. When we came out of the pines we turned right, driving farther up into the hills away from town. The late afternoon sun was lost behind a flat lid of clouds. Geese in a V-formation sliced across the sky, heading north.

I hadn't made those guys in the Park View, hadn't spotted them tailing me. I squashed the cigarette butt against the ashtray, slammed the ashtray shut. Ted sped up, bouncing over the rough road. There was no chance of my losing him but I sped up too, hugging his tail more closely than I needed to. Maybe it would piss him off.

There was a time when I kept a bottle of bourbon in the glove compartment, but it wasn't there now, so I lit another cigarette and followed the truck into the fading afternoon.

A pale green house, dark green trim, peeling paint. Shutters slanting or missing altogether. Unpainted two-by-tens on concrete blocks stepping up to a sagging, rail-less porch. Tattered screen doors; dark, uncurtained windows, staring blind.

The Chevy turned into a swampy field to the left of the house, bounced to a stop. I pulled partway off the road, parked so a car could pass me but not park me in easily.

Not a lot of people had ever tried living up here, deep in the woods near the top of the ridge, and most of the ones who had had given up and gone away. There was nothing here, except small streams and blackberry thickets and pale snowdrops already showing through a carpet of maple leaves. By next week, wild crocuses, lavender and gold; then lilies in stands of sunrise colors on the stream banks. But you couldn't farm this land, and the streams weren't really good for fishing.

I'd driven through here a few times over the years. I'd driven just about every road in the county at one time or another. Sometimes there would be a tired woman hanging clothes out on a line, or a man with his head and arms under the hood of one of the junked cars that sprouted like

mushrooms. But mostly there were just empty frame
houses and a few desolate trailers, their aluminum doors
flapping in the wind.

The Chevy truck sat silent on the grass. I got out of my
car, crossed behind it, keeping the car and then the truck
between me and the house. Otis's gun was in my hand. I
opened the Chevy's driver-side door. "Okay, come on
out."

Ted climbed down, his eyes on the gun. He moved a
little away from me, chewing on his lip. "Anyone in the
house?" I asked. He shook his head, looked into the truck
at Otis.

"This way," I told Otis. He slid across the seat and
under the wheel, dropped to the spongy ground beside me.
"What happens now?" I asked.

His left hand still cradled his right wrist. He scowled.
"I'm supposed to call Frank when we get here."

"This his place?"

"He don't live here. But he owns it."

"Where does he live?"

"Cobleskill."

"Why come all the way out here?"

He didn't answer, just kept scowling.

"Yeah," I said. "Stupid question."

We went around the truck and up the plank steps. There
was no movement, no noise except for the sounds we
made. Otis fumbled with a key but he couldn't work the
lock left-handed; Ted had to do it, in the end.

The failing afternoon light didn't reach inside. Otis
flipped a switch and a floor lamp came on in the front
room, to our left. There was a tattered couch against the
far wall; two brown chairs, upholstery split, white stuffing
hanging out; some side tables; peeling, faded wallpaper. A
doorless doorway in the back led to a kitchen with a linoleum floor, cabinets on the wall. Straight ahead of us
was a small hallway. An uncarpeted wooden staircase ran
along the right side of the hallway, leading up into darkness.

The whole place was still and deserted and smelled of mildew and stale cooking grease. It was colder than it was outside, in the way a damp, closed place can be.

"Sit down," I said to Ted. I gestured with the gun at one of the brown chairs. "If you get up I'll shoot you. It's not a problem for me. Understand?" He nodded and sat quickly, hands gripping the soft arms of the chair. I turned to Otis. "Okay. We're here. Call Frank."

He crossed the room to a table that stood under the one lit lamp. There was a black phone there. Otis lifted the receiver with his left hand and, holding it, dialed. He put the receiver to his left ear and I put the gun to his right one, repeating in my head the number he'd dialed.

There was silence in the shadowy room, then Otis spoke. "Yeah. It's me. Gimme Frank." He waited. I gently wrapped my fingers around his swollen right wrist. He tensed and looked at me. I raised an eyebrow and nodded. "Yeah, Frank," he said back into the phone, licked his lips. "No, it's good. We're here." Pause. "Yeah." Beads of sweat stood out on his forehead. "Yeah, okay. No problem." He replaced the receiver slowly. I let go of his wrist, took the gun from his head.

"What the fuck was that for?" He drew his wrist to his chest.

"Sorry," I said. "You strike me as a guy too stupid to be sneaky when he's really scared. You did fine, Otis." I stepped back a little, included Ted in the wave of the gun. "Let's go."

Ted stood up fast. Otis said, "Go where?"

There was a door in the wall under the staircase. I backed over to it, watching the two men who stood in the yellow lamplight. I threw the bolt and the door creaked open. A gust of mud-scented air rolled into the hallway. "Downstairs," I said.

Ted and Otis filed past me. I bolted the door behind them, then went quickly out the front. There was a double-doored cellar hatch on the side of the house by the truck. It was held shut by a large bolt. I found a piece of warped

two-by-four from a rotting pile of construction lumber on
the porch and, as insurance, wedged it through the doors'
iron handles.

I went back inside, looked at my watch. Five-thirty. It
would take Grice at least half an hour to get up here from
Cobleskill. I switched on another light in the living room,
picked up the phone. I dialed the number at Antonelli's.

It rang a long time in the emptiness.

If the cops were still there they would have answered,
because all over the world that was what cops did.

If they were gone Tony should have answered. Under
the circumstances another man might have closed the bar
for the rest of the day, or the rest of the week. But as much
as the big house across the road, the bar was where Tony
lived. And unlike the house, in the bar he wasn't alone.

I pressed the cut-off button, got another dial tone, called
the state troopers.

"D Unit. Sergeant Whiteside," a woman's voice said.

"Ron MacGregor, please."

"Sorry, he's gone. Someone else help you?"

"You still have Tony Antonelli up there?"

"Hold it." The voice went away, came back. "Says here
Antonelli was just here answering questions, left hours
ago. Who're you?"

"Richard Wilcox. You guys find Jimmy Antonelli yet?"

"Who's Richard Wilcox?"

"Jimmy's lawyer. Are you holding him, or is the sheriff?"

"Far as I know, no one is," she said cautiously. "You
hear different?"

"My mistake," I said. "Thanks, Sergeant." I hung up.

Out in the kitchen an old refrigerator started to hum. I
went back there, looked around. A cast-iron pan with a
half inch of pale grease and crumbs in the bottom sat on
a splattered gas stove. Dishes and crusted silverware were
piled in the sink and a breadboard held a hunk of bread
you could have thrown through a plate-glass window. I

opened the fridge. What was in it I wouldn't have touched on a bet.

Except the three green bottles of Rolling Rock, lying on their sides on the bottom shelf. I took one out, twisted off the top, and went back to the living room. I moved one of the brown chairs so that I could see the front door from it, but someone looking in the window couldn't see me. I sat, lit a cigarette, sipped the Rolling Rock, and waited.

I was on the second bottle when I heard the faint rumble of an engine, coming closer fast. A minute later a pair of headlights swept into the front windows, stopped moving, went out. The engine stopped abruptly. Doors slammed, footsteps sounded on the loose boards of the porch.

I raised the automatic, held it steady in my right hand. The beer was in my left. The front door opened. Frank Grice stepped into the little hall, trailed by the big, friendly-faced guy with the mustache. Grice turned into the living room doorway, his mouth open as though he were about to say something.

Then he saw me. He stopped, frozen in a half-completed motion. The big guy stopped too, then started again, moved forward with a little growl. Grice put his hand up without taking his eyes off mine. The big guy stopped.

"Hi, Frank," I said. "Disgusting place you've got here."

He still didn't move. "Where are Ted and Otis?"

"Downstairs," I said. "They're not very good, Frank." I sipped the beer, waved the gun. "Sit down."

He came through the doorway, sat on the other chair, facing me. He leaned back, crossed one leg over the other. His twisted face was bruised; there were two Band-Aids over his right eye.

"You too," I said to the big guy. He looked at Grice, who nodded. He crossed to the couch and sat, leaning forward, eyes a little wide, hands rubbing his knees in opposite circles. In the light I could see that his lip was split and swollen under the mustache.

"You wanted me," I said. "I'm here. Why?"

"Last night," Grice said easily, "I didn't know who you were."

"If you had?"

"I'd have shaken your hand. Your trick-pony lawyer saved me a lot of trouble last fall, when they dropped the charges against Jimmy. I never got to thank you."

"If I saved you any trouble, Grice, it was an accident. Any trouble I can make for you," I said, finishing the beer, "will be a pleasure. What do you want from Tony?"

He shook his head, dismissing the question. "Just business." He smiled a cockeyed smile. "You're right," he said. "Otis and Ted aren't very good. They're typical of what's available around here. You ever get tired of working for Tony, I could find a place for you."

"First, I don't work for Tony. Second, I don't work for assholes like you."

"That's too bad. That was what I wanted to see you about."

I stared at him. "You sent two armed morons after me so you could offer me a job?"

He nodded. "What do you get?"

"Fifty an hour, plus expenses. Working for a guy like you, expenses could be high."

He lifted his uneven eyebrows, smiled his crooked smile. "That's all? Jesus, you're in a chickenshit business, Smith. I pay Arnold more than that." He gestured at the big guy, who smiled through his split lip. Arnold? Well, what did I know? Maybe since Schwarzenegger, Arnold was a tough name.

"What did you pay Wally Gould?"

He shook his head. "That was too bad, wasn't it? Wally was valuable. I'll miss him."

"Then why'd you kill him?"

"Me? You've got to be kidding." He looked at Arnold, who snickered. "Maybe you're not as smart as I thought. Why would I kill Wally? And if I did, why would I do it in Tony's basement?"

"Damned if I know. You were trying to shake Tony down for something last night. Maybe Wally wanted too big a piece of the action."

"Wally wasn't bright enough to want anything, except to be allowed to kill something once in a while."

"Like Tony or me, last night?"

"Sure, he would've enjoyed that. But like I say, I didn't know who you were."

"Well," I said, standing, the gun held loosely in my right hand, "you know now. Sorry I can't help you, Frank." I moved toward the door.

"Don't you at least want to hear the offer?"

"Okay," I said. "Okay, Frank. Let's hear it."

"A thousand dollars," he said. "I want to talk to Jimmy Antonelli."

I laughed. "Every cop in this county is probably looking for Jimmy by now. What makes you think I could find him first?"

Grice spread his hands, made a little self-deprecating smile. "You're a friend of his."

"Why do you want him?"

"Not your business, Smith. A grand for finding him and walking away. I'm not going to hurt him. In fact, I can help him."

"Why does he need help?"

"Murder's a harder rap to beat than disposing of stolen cars."

"There's always the chance Jimmy didn't kill Gould, just like you."

"Yeah," he grinned. "I guess there's that chance. But whether he did or not, he'll be better off if I find him than if Brinkman does."

"He'd be better off with Godzilla than with Brinkman. But I told you, I don't work for assholes."

Grice shrugged. "Think about it. The cops'll find him sooner or later. I'd like to find him first."

"Why?"

"Let's say I feel like I owe him one."

I leaned against the doorway, slipped a cigarette in my mouth. "You do owe him," I said. "But you don't know what that means or what to do about it. I'll tell you something. I was the guy he called, when Brinkman finally let him near a phone. My advice was to take the deal, sell you to Brinkman for as much as he could get. He wouldn't do it, Frank. Not because he likes you. He doesn't like you. But he wouldn't rat. Even on you."

Grice took a cigarette out of a gold case. He closed the case and tapped the cigarette slowly on it as Arnold hurried to dig a lighter out and hold it for him. Jesus.

He blew a thin trail of smoke and said, "I guess I'm a pretty lucky guy, then."

"Tell me something, Frank." I blew smoke of my own. "You're not much better than Otis or Ted. And Brinkman seems to want you a lot. So how come he hasn't been able to make anything stick to you yet?"

"Like I said: I'm lucky."

"Luck runs out, Frank. Keep away from Jimmy, and from Tony."

There was no sound of movement behind me as I opened the door and went out.

I stepped down the planks and walked to my car over the spongy earth. The night air felt sharp and clean. As I reached my car Grice stepped onto the porch. "I'll find him," Grice said. "You can make a grand on it or not, but I'll find him."

I turned to face him, saw him silhouetted in the dim light of the doorway. The silence was complete and heavy; there was no moon, no light but the glow from inside the house. Arnold appeared next to Grice. He was grinning.

I could have shot them both, two quick, surprising shots from Otis's big automatic; then to the basement, two more shots, and I could have driven away. No one would miss them, no one would wake suddenly in the night and know all over again and feel that helpless sick feeling start to grow.

Or maybe someone would. Maybe somewhere someone loved even men like this.

I started the car and pulled out hard. I drove away from that place fast, down the rutted, deserted road under a sky where faint streaks of gray light still showed in the west.

SEVEN

By the time I got to Antonelli's the clouds had thickened. The stars had given up, and the moon was a nonstarter. Patches of fog stood sentinel-like in the trees on the other side of 30, up by Tony's house.

The parking lot was as empty as the sky. The outside lights were off and the red neon Bud sign was dark, but the inside lights were on. I tried the door. Locked. I rapped a quarter on the window. The curtain moved, showed me Tony's face, jaw tight. The curtain fell back into place as I went over to the door. Tony pulled it open, locked it behind me.

The tables from the back of the room had been piled on the ones in the front and the chairs pushed between them or dropped on top. A mop stood in a steaming bucket in the middle of the empty stretch of floor. The reek of ammonia was so strong it made my eyes water.

"What the hell are you doing?" I went around the room opening windows.

"Started downstairs. Couldn't stop." Tony's words came a little thick, a little slow. "Fuckin' cops left the place a mess, just walked out when they was through."

I came back to where he was standing. "I thought you'd be open."

"Woulda been," he nodded. "Started to. But . . ." He paused, looked at me. "This happen to you before, your line of work?"

"Bodies, you mean? Once or twice."

He went over behind the bar, took the bourbon off the shelf. The gin was already standing open on the bar. Tony brought the bottles and glasses over; I pulled two chairs from the pile. We sat, bottles on the floor beside us.

"Vultures," Tony said. He gulped a large shot, poured himself another. "Phone's been ringin' since I got back here. Couldn't take it."

I looked over at the phone. The receiver was dangling from its spiraled silver cord.

"Reporters. Every goddamn paper west of Albany must have nothin' to write about." More gin. "Coupla people wantin' to know could they help. Help with what?" He gestured around the room. "An' assholes. 'Hey, Tony, what happened?' 'Hey, Tony, heard you found a stiff in the basement.' 'Hey, Tony, heard your brother killed him.' Shit!" He shrugged. "I didn't open." His knuckles whitened around his gin glass. His voice got louder. "They been comin' around anyhow, bangin' on the door. Who the fuck they think they are, these guys?"

I drank in silence and he drank too, until the silence was both blurred and sharpened and talk was easier.

"Tony," I said quietly, "did Jimmy kill that guy?"

He looked at me for a long time. The gin had cleared everything from his eyes but pain. "Looks that way," he said finally. "Don't it look that way to you?"

"How it looks and what it is might not be the same," I said. "Let MacGregor and Brinkman worry about how it looks. Tell me what's going on, Tony."

He picked up his bottle; it was empty. He got up and got a new one, walking too carefully. "I don't know," he said. He sat heavily. "Little sonuvabitch said he was gonna stay clean. Stay away from Grice. Get a fuckin' job. He was scared, Smith. You saved his ass an' he knew he was lucky." He paused, drank. I lit a cigarette, got up, found an ashtray. "He met this girl, moved in with her. Nice kid. Didn't see him much after that. Funny thing, we was gettin' along better, the coupla times he did come around."

He trailed off. His eyes roved over the silent room as though he were looking for something.

We drank. I waited a few minutes. Then, "Tell me the rest, Tony."

His face suddenly flushed. "What the hell for? Anything I say, you're gonna run to your buddy MacGregor. You gave him those fuckin' keys, Smith. What the hell'd you do that for?"

"I had to do that, Tony. You know I had to." I kept my voice even.

"Had to," he muttered, half to himself. "Motherfucker."

"Tell me the rest, Tony."

"Fuck," he said. He drained his glass. "Grice came here last night workin' that protection shit. He ain't never pulled that on me before. Maybe I ain't a big enough operation. Or maybe he figured chewin' on me would break his teeth. But last night he's tellin' me Jimmy's in deep shit, an' it's gonna cost me to keep it quiet. Cost me a piece of the action, long term. Action." He laughed softly, without humor. "I told him to shove it. You was there for the rest."

"What kind of trouble did he say Jimmy was in?"

"Didn't say. What's the fuckin' difference?"

"Maybe it's not true. Maybe he was just fishing."

"My ass." He reached for the gin bottle, closed his hand on air. He tried again more slowly, picked the bottle up. The cold night air drifted through the room, drifted out again. It didn't take the ammonia smell with it. I wouldn't have, either.

"Jimmy's girl," I said. "Know anything about her?"

"Nice kid." He poured gin very slowly into his glass.

I leaned forward. "What's her name, Tony? Where does she live?"

He gave me an unfocused gaze. "Don't know. Somewhere."

"What's her name?"

"Nice name. Old-fashioned." He frowned. "Alice. Alice Brown . . ."

"That's a song, Tony."

He stared defiantly. "'s a name, too."

"Yeah, Tony, okay. Where does she live?"

"Alice Brown, Alice Brown, prettiest little girl in town. She sells seashells. No, she don't." He rubbed a hand along the side of his nose. "No, she don't. She sells pies. Georgie Porgie, puddin' an' pie—"

I took the gin glass from his hand. "Go on, Tony. Pies?"

"Pies, asshole." He reached for the glass; I put it on the floor. He slumped back in his chair, looked at me. "Pies. Blueberry, strawberry. Chocolate cake. Cookies, even."

"Where?"

"People eat 'em. Gimme my gin."

"Where?"

He frowned, didn't answer.

"All right," I gave him his glass. "Listen, Tony. I'm going to make a couple of calls and then we're going to close this place up and go home. Okay?"

He shook his head. "Gotta clean up. Smells bad in here. Smells like blood. Shit!" His eyes were suddenly wild. "In the cellar, Smith. There's a dead guy in the cellar!"

"No, there's not." I stood, put my hand on his shoulder. "There was. He's gone. It's okay, Tony."

He stared at me, unseeing. Then he turned his eyes away. "Fuck you," he said.

"Yeah." I walked to the bathroom. I ran cold water in the cracked sink, splashed it over my face and the back of my neck. That cleared my head. I came back out; the ammonia hit me again, cleared it even more.

I picked up the mop and the bucket, hauled them to the bathroom, dumped the scummy gray water down the toilet. Half a dozen flushes later the place was almost bearable. I left the door propped open and went to the phone.

I hung up the receiver, searched my pockets for change. I checked my wallet for Eve Colgate's number. She answered on the second ring.

"It's Bill Smith," I said. "I want to ask you a couple of questions."

"Where are you?" Her voice was low and measured, the way it had been last night. "Are you at Antonelli's? Is Tony all right?"

I looked over at Tony, slouched in the chair. He wasn't drinking now, just staring into the emptiness in front of him.

"He's drunk. He's okay. You heard?"

"My foreman. He said you . . . found the body. It all sounded horrible. I'm sorry." She paused. "Not that sympathy does you much good."

"You'd be surprised," I said. "Thanks."

There was a short silence. Through the phone I could hear a Schubert piano sonata. The C Minor, written while Schubert knew he was dying. I'd never played it.

"You said you had some questions?" she prompted.

"Oh. Yeah." I cradled the phone against my shoulder so I could light a cigarette. "I found some silver today that I think is yours."

There was a very short pause, just a heartbeat. "Where? How?"

"An antique place near Breakabeen. I'll bring it over in the morning. But I wanted to ask you: Do you know a girl, probably about sixteen? Golden hair, sparkling eyes, dazzling smile?"

"Quite a description, but I don't think so. Who is she?"

"She's peddling your stuff. I was hoping you could tell me who she is."

"No," she said slowly. "But I'll think about it."

"Good," I said. "Listen, I've got to get some dinner. Tony's out of business for tonight. I'll be up in the morning." We fixed a time and I hung up, seeing in my mind the yellow farmhouse standing in the sunlight at the top of the hill.

I glanced at Tony. His empty glass had slipped from his grip and was lying on the newly scrubbed floor. He was still staring ahead of him, looking at nothing.

I fed the phone again and called Lydia. This time, Lydia answered her office number. That line rings through to her room at home, and I knew that's where she was, because I could hear her mother puttering around in the background, singing a high-pitched Chinese opera song. She obviously had no idea what a narrow escape she'd just had, not having to talk to me.

I, on the other hand, did.

After Lydia got through telling me who she was in English and again in Chinese, I said, "Hi, it's me. You have anything for me?"

"Oh," she said. "Well," as though she was thinking about it, "just information."

"What else could I want?"

"What you always want."

"Not over the phone," I said in wounded innocence.

"Since when?" I heard her rustling some papers; then she asked, "Are you all right? You sound tired."

"I am."

"Oh," she said. "That's why the lack of snappy patter."

"No, this country living must be dulling my razor sharp senses. I thought I was being pretty snappy."

"Wrong. Now listen: I haven't picked up anything about your paintings, if that's what you want to know."

"Among many other things. Where are you looking?"

"Shipping companies. Maritime and air-ship insurance. Art appraisers, auction houses." She paused. "Don't worry, I was subtle."

I hadn't said anything, but she knew me. "How?"

"Mostly I said I was looking for stolen Frank Stellas that would be being shipped as something else. People were very cooperative."

"Good old people. Anything else?"

"I went to see your friend Franco Ciardi. He remembered me and was charmed to see me."

"Isn't everyone always?"

"Of course they are, but sometimes they hide it well. Anyway, he knows nothing, but he promised he'd be interested and most discreet if I do come up with anything.

Was he offering to take them off my hands if I find them, do you think?"

"I'm sure he was. That's it?"

"Yes, but isn't no news good news? There's no sign yet that those paintings are on the market. Isn't that what you wanted?"

"Yes. How sure are you?"

"Well, I've only been on it since this morning. I may be missing something; but you can do a lot with a phone and a cab in a day."

"Okay. Any other ideas?"

"I haven't got any ideas. But I have something interesting."

"I'm sure, but you won't let me see it."

"And you said not over the phone."

"Sorry."

"Uh-huh. Anyway, listen. You know how art galleries work? On commission? Well, the normal commission is ten to fifty percent of the price of the work—the lower the sale price, the higher the commission. Artists who feel a gallery is taking too high a percentage will go with another gallery, if someplace else will take them. Okay?"

"Okay," I said. "And?"

"Eva Nouvel's work is very, very high priced. Any gallery in town would love to handle her, but she's been with her gallery—Sternhagen—since she first started to show in New York, close to forty years ago. Bill, they take seventy percent."

"Umm," I said. "How do you know that?"

"My brother Elliot? You know his wife's an art consultant. She has a friend who has a friend who used to work at Sternhagen."

The Chin network. I said, "You believe her?"

"Him. Yes."

"Lydia, I didn't ask you to check on Eva Nouvel."

She paused for a moment. "No, that's true. But I was waiting for some people to call me back and I got curious. What's the problem?"

I rubbed my eyes. "No, nothing. It's okay."

A slight chill crept into her voice. "It might be better if I knew what was really going on."

"What do you mean?"

"Oh, if I knew who the client was," she said. "If I knew why six valuable paintings were sitting around a storeroom in cow country. If I knew why you took a case up there at all. If I knew things like that, maybe I wouldn't make dumb mistakes."

"You never make dumb mistakes."

"I might if I don't know what's going on."

The windows I'd opened had made it cold in the bar. Back where I was, by the phone, the floor was empty, all the tables and chairs crowded together in the other half of the room as though something were wrong back here.

I rubbed my eyes again; that did about as much good as it had done the first time. "Jesus," I said to Lydia. "Look: You're right, and I'm sorry. But it's been a long day. Can we do this tomorrow?"

"We can do this whenever you want. You're the boss."

"That's not—"

"Apparently it is."

"Lydia—"

"Should I keep on it?" she asked, brusque and professional.

"Yes," I said. "Please."

"Talk to you later, then."

The phone clicked, and she was gone.

I walked around the silent room shutting the windows I'd opened. Then I went through the swinging doors into the kitchen, lifted Tony's jacket off the hook there, brought it to him. "Come on, buddy," I said softly, leaning down. "Time to go home." He looked at me as if he didn't know me. He rose unsteadily, pushing on the arms of his chair. I gave him his jacket. It took him some time to get into it. I didn't help, just stayed close enough to catch him if he needed that. He didn't.

I shut the lights and locked the place and we went out

into the parking lot, crunching through it to the road. The night was dark and damp and foggy. It wasn't the up-close kind of fog where you couldn't see your own hand if you held your arm out straight. It was a soft film you didn't notice if your focus was close, where everything was clear and sharp and normal, what you expected. It was only when you tried to look around, to get your bearings, that you noticed that five yards away in all directions there was absolutely nothing at all.

EIGHT

I left Tony inside his front door without a word. I waited on the porch just long enough to see him get a light on; then I headed down the steep stone steps and across the road to my car.

The fog was thickening along 30 as I drove toward my place. I kept my speed down. I was hungry, exhausted, and in spite of Tony's bourbon I could feel all my nerve ends twitching.

The car slipped in and out of silvery patches of fog. I half expected with each one to come out somewhere miles away, some bright, warm place where people had honest work to do and no one's steps echoed in an empty house. Someplace where you didn't get to be Tony's age, or mine, with nothing to show but a collection of losses.

Down at the end of my fissured road my cabin was a squat, unnatural shape hunching in the winter trees. I thought of the work I'd done on it over the years, the constant battle to keep anything man-made—no matter how small, how carefully built, how wanted—from corroding, rotting away. The processes of destruction were relentless, and had all the time in the world.

Inside, the cabin wasn't bright and it wasn't warm but it was a familiar harbor. I put on a CD, Jeffrey Kahane playing Bach three-part inventions. I built a fire. The smell of cedar and woodsmoke, the music, the shadows began to work on me. I sliced some bread, fried some eggs to go with a can of hash I found on the shelf. I drank some more bourbon and followed the music. Bach. Logic, order, clarity. I should play more Bach. The hard knots in my shoulders began to melt and my eyelids got heavy.

In the morning I had to force myself out of bed. The day was gray and I'd slept badly, prodded awake more than once by uneasy dreams I couldn't remember. I had a dull headache and though I knew it wasn't from sleeping badly, I poured a shot of bourbon into my coffee cup and downed it before the coffee was ready. It helped a little. The coffee helped some more. I showered, and this time I shaved, carefully but not carefully enough, cursing as the foam burned my cheek.

Leaning on the kitchen counter, I smoked a cigarette, worked on the day. The piano gleamed in the light of the kitchen lamp. It wasn't as good a piano as I had in New York, but it was fine, an upright with a strong, clear sound. A guy from Albany with a key to the cabin came out a few days before I came up each time and tuned it for me; and I kept the heat on low in the front room all winter, so the piano did all right. Those things cost me. But the reason I came up here and the reason I played were pretty much the same, and this setup worked for me.

I finished the last of the coffee. If I spent the day practicing, the new Mozart might begin to sound like music. Music; sleep; walking in the silent winter woods: That sounded like a good day to me.

But I thought about Eve Colgate's eyes as she told me about what she'd lost. And I thought about Tony's eyes, and about other kinds of loss. There were so many kinds.

Halfway up 30 toward Eve Colgate's there was a 7-Eleven. I bought more coffee and some other things, drank the coffee in the car with the Mozart adagio in the CD player. If I couldn't play it at least I could listen to it.

Eve Colgate's yellow house seemed to stand more somberly on the hilltop under the gray sky than it had yesterday in the sunlight, but it was still a vaguely comforting sight, like an old friend at a funeral.

I parked in the drive behind the blue pickup. As I started toward the porch the black dog raced, barking and yapping, around the side of the house. He stopped when I did, cocked his head, wagged his tail tentatively a few times; but when I started forward again he snarled and dug his feet in as he had the morning before. His breath was visible on the cold air.

Eve Colgate came around the house, wiping her hands on a stained red sweatshirt. "Leo!" she called.

"Okay, Leo," I said. "You're tough. I know." I reached into the 7-Eleven bag, brought out the doughnut I'd bought for him. "Come on." I squatted, held out a piece. He looked at it, looked at Eve Colgate.

"It's okay," she said.

He grabbed the piece of doughnut and inhaled it, wagged for more. I held out the rest. "Sit," I said. He didn't. I gave it to him anyway, dusted sugar from my gloves, scratched his ears.

"You can't buy him that easily," Eve Colgate said.

"I'm not in the market. I just want a friend." I straightened up, took the wrapped package from the back of my car. The dog escorted me up the drive, nuzzled Eve Colgate's hand when he reached her.

"Good boy." She scratched him absently. Her eyes swept over my face as though registering small changes since she'd last seen me. Then she looked at the package I was holding. "Come inside," she said.

I followed her through a vestibule where a yellow slicker hung on a peg into a single room running the width of the house. On the right was a kitchen, not new but ample and serviceable. On the left an antique dining table and chairs, carefully refinished, stood under the front window. There was a woodstove like mine on the hearth, its flue running up the fireplace chimney. A couch, an easy chair, a side table, a cedar chest on the bare, polished floor. A few framed watercolors—none of them Eva Nouvels—

hung on the walls and on the mantel there was a china pitcher and bowl painted in the bright yellows and purples of spring.

I shrugged off my jacket, looked around for a place to put it. Eve took it from me, pausing as her eyes caught the worn shoulder holster with the .22 from the car slipped into it.

"Do you always wear that?"

"Yes." A long time ago I'd stopped answering that question with anything more elaborate.

She turned, hung my jacket in the vestibule. She pulled off her sweatshirt and hung it there, too. Under it she wore a thick white turtleneck tucked into flannel-lined jeans.

The air was warm, and pungent with cinnamon. There was music, too, strings. Schubert, maybe.

"Do you want coffee?" Eve asked. "I've been baking."

"Sounds great. Smells great."

She handed me a plate of sticky looking sweet rolls. "How do you take your coffee?"

"Black." I bootlegged a piece of roll for Leo, who was walking between my legs, head twisted to sniff at the plate.

I put the plate and the wrapped silver on the cedar chest, sat on the couch. Eve brought over coffee in two white mugs. She made good coffee; better than mine, much better than the 7-Eleven's. The rolls were warm and sweet and crunchy with walnuts.

She kicked off her shoes, sat cross-legged on the other end of the couch, her back against the armrest. "How's Tony?"

"I haven't seen him today." I could have guessed how he was, but she could guess, too.

"The police are looking for his brother, aren't they?"

"That's what I hear."

She poured cream into her coffee from a round jug. "Tony used to work for me, before his father got sick. Spring, summer, and fall, as a laborer. I was sorry to lose him when he took over the restaurant." She cupped her hands around her coffee. "I don't have anything to offer him, except sympathy and money. He won't want my sympathy. He won't want my money either, but he might need it." She sipped at her coffee, was quiet a moment. "I'll say this to Tony later, but I'll tell you now. If there's anything he needs—lawyers, whatever it is—I can take care of it."

"Why tell me?"

"So somebody with a more level head than Tony will know what options he has."

"You're right," I said. "He won't want it."

"Trouble can be expensive. Especially . . ." she paused. "Do you think Jimmy could have killed that man? I hardly know Jimmy. When he was young Tony brought him by occasionally."

"Could have?" I said. "He could have. I don't know anyone who couldn't, for a strong enough reason."

She fixed me with her pale, disturbing eyes. "Do you really believe that?"

"It's true. Reasons vary, but everybody's got one he thinks is good enough. If you're lucky you never get the chance to find out what yours is."

She explored my face briefly, then looked away, as though she hadn't found something she had hoped, but not expected, to find.

The flashing, contrapuntal figures of the music filled the air around us. I put down my coffee, picked up the wrapped package. I laid it on the couch between us, unwound the paper, watched her face as she watched my hands.

At first she didn't react. Then her face drained of color and her hand went slowly to her mouth. She stared at the candlesticks and tray resting on the crumpled paper as though she needed to count every vein in every leaf engraved on them.

She reached out a hand. I stopped it with mine. "Don't touch them. There may be prints."

She looked surprised, as though she'd forgotten I was there. She drew back her hand, shook her head slowly. "They were a wedding gift from Henri's mother," she half whispered. She looked away, hugged her chest. Her face was still pale but her voice was stronger as she said, "I deal with my memories in the way I can. I kept these, but I haven't looked at them in thirty years."

I drank my coffee, gave her time.

"I'm sorry," I said. "You had to identify them. I didn't realize it would be hard."

"No," she said, shaking her head again. "It's all right. What do we do now?"

"Two things. We try to lift prints from these, and we try to find the blond girl who fenced them."

"What if she's not from around here?"

"I have a feeling she is. She could have gotten more for things like these in New York, or even Albany or Boston; if she's not local, why fence them here?" I put my mug down. "You know, both finding the girl and identifying the prints would be a lot easier if you'd report this to the police."

She flushed angrily. "And when they found her and my paintings, the whole world would know who I am."

"If this girl or anyone else has any idea what the paintings are, the whole world will know soon anyway," I pointed out.

"Maybe she hasn't. Or maybe it won't occur to her that I made them, just because I had them." She stood abruptly, paced the room, her hands in her back pockets. The dog, curled in the chair, lifted his head and followed her movements. She stared out the window for a time; then she turned again to face me. "It's important," she said. "Maybe it's not rational. But I'm past apologizing for it. It's why I hired you in the first place. If you can't do it the way I want it done, I don't need you."

The music had stopped, leaving nothing in the air but the fragrance of cinnamon and coffee and the weight of Eve Colgate's anger.

"I'm working for you," I said. "We'll do it however you want. But I've got to give you the choices the way I see them."

She nodded, said nothing.

I rewrapped the silver. "I'll send these to New York. There's a lab I use on Long Island that can pull the prints." I stood. "Can I use your phone?"

Lydia's machine answered my call. Well, that was okay; the machine liked me better than Lydia's mother did. Right now, maybe better than Lydia did. I told her to expect a package on an afternoon Greyhound out of Cobleskill, and that I'd call again and tell her when it was due. Then I called Antonelli's.

Tony's voice sounded hoarse and tired.

"How're you doing?" I asked him.

"Sick as hell. You?"

"I feel great. Maybe you should switch to bourbon."

He grunted. "Can't afford it."

"I'll come over and buy you a bottle. You open?"

"What's the difference? Wasn't open last night. Didn't stop you."

"True. You heard from Jimmy?"

Silence. Then, "No. Brinkman called an hour ago, asked me the same thing. He ain't called me, he ain't gonna call me. Why the hell should he?"

"He's in trouble. You're his brother."

"Hell with that. I'm through with that."

"Tony—"

"Don't preach to me, Smith. I got no time for it."

This time it was I who was silent. "I'll be over later," I finally said.

"Yeah," Tony said. "Whatever. Listen, you got a call. If you're gonna keep givin' out this number, you better tell people it ain't my job to know where you are when you ain't here. An' tell 'em it don't help to try an' impress me with who the hell they are, 'cause I don't give a damn who the hell they are."

"You tell them," I said. "You sound like you enjoy it. Who called? MacGregor?"

"That trooper? Nah. One of your big-time pals. Lifestyles of the rich an' famous."

"What are you talking about?"

"Mark Sanderson."

I frowned into the phone. "Mark Sanderson? Appleseed Baby Foods? I don't know him."

"Well, now's your chance. He left a number. Want it?"

I found a scrap of paper in my wallet. "Yeah, go ahead." He read it off to me. "Did he say what he wanted?"

"To me? I'm just the hired help."

"Okay, Tony, thanks. Listen, there's something else. Two things. Last night you were telling me about Jimmy's girl. Do you remember? Alice. You said something about pies. What did you mean?"

"Oh, Christ, Smith, what do you care?"

"Look, Tony, I know what you think, that Jimmy killed that guy. I think you're wrong. And even if he did, he can't hide forever. In the end it'll make things worse. I want to talk to him. Maybe I can help."

"Maybe he ain't around. Maybe he already beat it, Mexico or someplace. Maybe you helped enough."

"Maybe."

Neither of us said anything. I heard footsteps from the floor above, looked around to find I was alone.

Tony gave a tired sigh. "Alice Brown. I don't know where she lives. Not around here."

"What about the pies?"

"When they started comin' around, she started bringin' me pies, or cakes. Couple at a time. Fancy stuff. She said she made them. I served them here. They were good." He paused. "She's a sweet kid, Smith. Only met her three or four times, but I liked her. Don't know how she got tied up with Jimmy."

"And you wouldn't know where to find her?"

"No."

"Do MacGregor and Brinkman know about her?"

"I didn't tell 'em."

"Good. Here's the other thing. I'm looking for a girl, long blond hair, small, pretty. She may be a friend of Jimmy's. Does she sound familiar?"

"No, but I ain't met his friends, except the ones he gets arrested with. What's she got to do with it?"

"Nothing. A friend of mine asked me to find her. It's something completely different."

"Eve Colgate. I knew you was workin' for her."

"Not your problem, Tony."

"Shit. *You* tellin' *me* to mind my own business?"

"I get your point. I'll be over later, okay? If you do hear from Jimmy, try to talk him out of anything stupid."

"Spent half my fuckin' life tryin' to talk him outta stupid things. I'm no good at it."

"Try again. He might listen this time."

We hung up. Eve Colgate was still upstairs, giving me privacy while I used her house as a public phone booth.

I looked at the number Tony had given me for Mark Sanderson, started to dial it, but stopped. I called the state troopers instead.

"D Unit. Sergeant Whiteside." It was the same officer I'd spoken to yesterday.

"Ron MacGregor, please."

"Hold on."

Thirty seconds of electronic silence; then, "MacGregor."

"It's Bill Smith. You get any sleep lately?"

"You kidding?"

"Well, I'm glad to know country cops work as hard as city cops. Can I have my gun back?"

"Yeah. Come get it."

"What killed Wally Gould?"

"He was shot."

"Oh, come on, Mac. Is it a secret?"

"What interest you got in this investigation, Smith?"

"I'm a friend of Tony's and Jimmy's. As long as Jimmy's a suspect, I'm interested."

"That's it?"

"Why, he's not?"

"Yeah, he is. You know where to find him?"

"No."

"Would you tell me if you did?"

I thought about it. "I'd tell you I knew. I'm not sure I'd tell you where he was."

"Wait, let me get this straight. You want information from me on an ongoing police investigation, but you're not sure you'd turn over my chief suspect if you had him?"

"I'm not sure I wouldn't. What killed Wally Gould?"

He paused. "Three close-range shots from a nine-millimeter."

"When?"

"About four A.M."

"You found it?"

"The gun? Not yet."

"Well, I have two you can look at."

"Two what?"

"Nine-millimeters."

MacGregor exploded. "Goddammit, Smith! If you've been holding out on me again I'll lock you up!"

"I didn't hold out on you about the keys and I'm not now. I took a pair of Ruger nine-millimeters off two of Grice's monkeys yesterday." I told MacGregor the rest of the story, my conversation with Grice, the green house, Otis and Ted. He didn't ask what I'd been doing on the potholed road by Breakabeen and I didn't tell him.

I also didn't tell him that Otis and Ted had picked me up at the Park View while I was talking to Ellie Warren. I wasn't paid to give him ideas.

"So Grice doesn't know where Jimmy is," he said thoughtfully when I was through. "And he's willing to pay a lot to find out."

"Maybe not," I said. "I imagine it's one of those fees I'd have a hard time collecting."

"You could be right. You want us to pick them up?"

"Who, Otis and Ted? Don't bother. Everybody'd deny it and I'm sure everybody's got a nifty alibi."

"Yeah, probably. We had Grice down here this morning on the Gould killing."

"Let me guess. At the time Gould was shot, Grice was

drinking tea with his congressman and the Bishop of Buffalo."

MacGregor answered that with a grunt. "What do you think he wants Jimmy for?"

"Grice? I think the same as you, Mac. Grice knows something about Gould's death and he's looking for a fall guy."

"Is that what I think? What else do I think?"

I left that alone. "I'll be by this afternoon to pick up my gun."

"If you have evidence to turn over, you'd damn well better make it this morning. Now."

"An hour."

"Half an hour. If not, in thirty-one minutes I'll have every unit in the county looking for you."

"I'll be there."

Now it was time to call Mark Sanderson.

"I'm sorry." Mark Sanderson's secretary's voice was so carefully modulated and inflected that I regretted not being a radio producer calling to offer her her big break. "Mr. Sanderson is unavailable. Perhaps I can help you?"

"I don't think I'm the one who needs help, but I could be wrong. Mr. Sanderson called me; I'm returning his call."

"Oh, I see. In that case, please hold the line a moment."

I did, passing that moment and some others listening to watery Muzak through the phone. I heard footsteps again from upstairs, the sound of doors opening and closing.

"Mr. Smith?" the modulated voice returned. "Mr. Sanderson will be right with you."

A few more bars of Muzak, and then a man's voice, deep but not booming, calm but with an edge somewhere behind it. "Mark Sanderson."

That left me to introduce myself, which was silly, since we both knew he knew who I was. But it was his court, his rules. "Bill Smith, Mr. Sanderson. I understand you've been trying to get in touch with me."

"Smith. Yes. I expected you to call before this; I left that message some time ago. I want you to come by here right away."

This was a man who didn't waste words. In fact he didn't use quite enough of them for my taste.

"Mr. Sanderson, we don't know each other."

"We will. I intend to engage your services."

No one said I had to make it easy for him. "As what?"

That threw him off his stride. There was silence; then, in the voice you'd use to explain to a gardener the difference between roses and ragweed, he said, "I understand you're a detective. I have a job for you."

"I don't come up here to work, Mr. Sanderson. I can give you the name of a good investigator out of Albany, if you'd like."

"No," he said, struggling to hide his impatience, and losing. "It's you I want. You in particular. How soon can you get here?"

From the newspaper photograph I remembered him as a broad-shouldered man with a receding hairline that emphasized the roundness of his face. I imagined that round face frowning now behind a heavy oak desk in a corner office with a picture-window view.

I asked, "Can you give me more of an idea what we're talking about talking about?"

"Not over the phone. We're wasting time, Smith. Where are you? At the bar where I left the message?"

"No. And how did you know to reach me there?"

"I was told you had no phone, but that the bar would take a message. I was also told there was a good chance you'd be there, whatever time I called," he added nastily. "I'll expect you in half an hour."

"I have to be over by Bramanville in half an hour." I looked at my watch, thought some unsatisfying thoughts. "I'll get over to you as soon after that as I can."

"Look, Smith—"

"No, you look, Sanderson. You want me. In particular. I don't want your job, but you're not listening when I say no, and I'm just curious enough to come over and hear you out before I say it again. If that's not good enough, call someone else."

Through what sounded like clenched teeth he said, "All right. I don't suppose it will make that much difference, in the end." He hung up without saying good-bye.

NINE

Schoharie was a detour off the route between Bramanville and Cobleskill, but I thought it was a detour worth making. I'd dropped the Rugers with MacGregor, picked up my Colt, exchanged some small talk about civilians interfering in police work. I'd tried out the golden blond girl on him.

"Sounds like half the kids at Consolidated East. You got a picture?"

I shook my head. "She doesn't ring a bell, part of Jimmy Antonelli's crowd?"

"Not with me."

An idea came to me. "You think your girls might know her?"

"I doubt it. My girls go to school in Albany. Adirondack Prep."

"I didn't know that."

"Yeah." MacGregor sighed. "This is a dead-end place, Smith. Kids got no future here. The boys join the service and the girls get pregnant." He picked up a pencil, bounced it on the desk. "How long you been coming up here?"

"Eighteen years."

He nodded. "Those days, you could make a good living around here. Farming; or the young guys from town, they worked at the quarry. Now the quarry's down to one pit. And that one's almost played out now, did you know that?"

I hadn't. I shook my head.

"Yeah. Next year, maybe year after. Then that'll be

gone, too. My father-in-law had a dairy farm. My brother-in-law, too. My father-in-law's place you could see from that window." He pointed across his office but he didn't look where he was pointing. "They're both working for other guys now. Broke their butts all their lives, what've they got? What've their kids got?" He looked up from the desk. "Where my girls go to school, all the kids go on to college. It's expected. My girls can speak French, play the piano, paint. Their friends are congressmen's daughters." Tilting his chair back, he stretched, smiled tiredly. "Aaah, what do you care? You got no kids. You don't have to worry about this crap. You're a lucky guy."

I didn't answer.

MacGregor raised his eyebrows. "What do you want this girl for, anyhow?"

Now was as good as any other time. "I'm working a case."

"Goddammit!" The front legs of his chair hit the floor and his smile collapsed like a house of cards. "Why the hell didn't you tell me that yesterday? What case?"

"Private problem for a private client."

"Who just happens to be looking for a friend of Jimmy Antonelli's when everyone else in the goddamn county is looking for Jimmy? What's the case, Smith?"

"I can't tell you. But it's not police business and it's not connected to Gould's death. And the girl might not be a friend of Jimmy's," I added. "I'm just guessing."

MacGregor sat motionless, looked at me. "God, I'm tempted."

I knew what he was tempted to do. "What for?"

He threw down his pencil, stood, yanked open the office door. "Being stupid and ugly in public. Raising the blood pressure of a Senior Investigator. Get the hell out. I'll be watching you."

That had been about it, there, so I'd started for the Greyhound depot in Cobleskill. The Appleseed plant was west of town; I could make my appearance at Sanderson's office after I got the silver squared away.

When I got on the highway, though, I had a better idea.
I went east to 1A over the ridge, down into the softly
quilted valley and through to Schoharie, same as yesterday.
Main Street seemed exhausted under the leaden sky and
leafless trees, as though it had stretched out for a rest and
hadn't yet found the strength to get up and move on.

The smell of coffee and bacon grease inside the Park
View was warm and familiar. The windows were still
steamy, and the two old men in hunting jackets were at
the same table in the front. Or maybe it was two other old
men. I slid onto a stool and waited for Ellie to finish bringing them sandwiches.

Ellie came back to the counter, spotted me. Her faded
brows knit together above her sharp nose; she squeezed
my hand. "Hon," she said without preamble, "why didn't
you tell me yesterday that what you were looking for
Jimmy for had to do with a killing?"

I wasn't sure of the answer to that. "I didn't want to
worry you, Ellie. How did you find out?"

"Sheriff Brinkman was here. He's going to call Chucky
in North Carolina."

"I thought you said Chuck was at sea."

"Well, sure. And I suppose Sheriff Brinkman will find
that out, sooner or later."

She grinned and I grinned back. "They have telephones
on ships now, Ellie."

"Hon, I called him myself last week, for his birthday.
You wouldn't believe the red tape before they let you call
a ship at sea." She poured me a cup of coffee.

"Thanks." I tasted it. Not as good as Eve Colgate's, or
mine; but still better than the 7-Eleven's. I was getting to
be an expert. "Did Brinkman ask you anything about Alice, or the blond girl you told me about?"

"No. I don't think he knows about either of them. And
Chucky won't tell him."

"I know he won't. Listen, Ellie, try this: Tony says Alice's last name is Brown, and that she bakes. It sounds to
me as though she may do it for a living. If you were or-

dering desserts for the diner, where would you get them from?"

"What, this place? Ralph would kill you if he heard that." She pointed to a sign over the glass-shelved pie cabinet behind her: All Baking Done On Premises.

"Okay," I said. "But what if?"

She compressed her lips in thought. "I don't know. You want to talk to Ralph? He's here."

Ralph Helfgott owned and cooked at the Park View. He was a large soft man with the look of a hard man gone to seed. The blue tattoos on his forearms were blurred and his white hair was unkempt and wispy. He followed Ellie out from the kitchen, wiping his hands on the apron that surrounded him.

"How're you doing?" he asked, shaking my hand. "Haven't seen you around in a while."

"Haven't been up. Finally got so I couldn't stay away from Ellie another day, so I came back."

He put a thick arm around her. "That's my girl you're talking about."

She pulled away grinning, slapped his arm lightly. "Knock it off, Ralph. Bill wants to ask you something important."

Ralph leaned over the counter, spoke confidentially to me. "She don't know yet how crazy she is about me. But I got time, I can wait." He slipped his hand below the counter, pinched Ellie's rear. She let out a squeak, slapped him again. He straightened up and looked at me out of choir-boy eyes. "What can I do for you?"

I told him what I wanted to know, but not why. He massaged his chins. "Desserts? Baked goods, you mean?"

"Fancy ones, I hear. And good."

"Well, there's really no place around that's any good. There's Glauber's, and there's Hilltop, over in Cobleskill. But they're both pretty lousy. That's why I do my own. There's nothing worse than serving a customer a soggy pie, you know," he said earnestly. "Except wait a minute. There is a new place. I got a brochure or something. Wait, let me think." He rubbed the stubble on his chins again with a hand like a rubber bath toy. "Yeah. Some girl called me. About six, eight months ago, I don't know. A new bakery, commercial, but small. I told her no thanks, but she asked if she could send me a brochure anyway. Of course, I don't know if they're any good."

"Did she send the brochure?" I asked. "Do you have it?"

"Of course he does," Ellie said. "He has every piece of paper anybody ever gave him. Go find it, Ralph."

"You want it?" he asked me; I nodded.

He gave Ellie a friendly leer and went off down the counter to the back. Ellie patted my hand and, taking the pencil from behind her ear, went to see to a family with three kids who'd taken over one of the rear tables. I watch the over-sized Slush Puppie cup slowly rotating on top of the milk shake machine.

Ralph came back first. "Got it," he said, spreading a flyer on the Formica in front of me. "This what you want?"

It was a price list, typeset on heavy stock. Cakes, pies, cookies, other sorts of pastry. At the top of the page was a line drawing of a cozy snowed-in house with smoke coming from the chimney, circled by the words Winterhill Kitchens.

"I hope so," I said.

"Well, you can have it. I still think I'm going to keep baking my own."

Ellie came back to the counter. "Find it?"

"Yeah. Kiss me?" Ralph closed his eyes and puckered his lips.

"Oh, in your dreams! Bill, hon, will this help?"

"I hope so," I said again. "Let me call and see."

I used the pay phone by the front door to call the number on the brochure.

The young woman's voice that answered the phone was fresh and direct, the kind of voice that goes with a clear complexion and great skill at outdoor sports. I asked for Alice Brown. The fresh voice said that Alice Brown was at the market, and that she'd be back at three-thirty. Would I like to leave a message? I would, and did, leaving my name, identifying myself as a friend of Jimmy Antonelli's, saying I'd call again. We thanked each other and hung up.

I went back to the counter, dropped some coins on it for the coffee. I squeezed Ellie's scrawny hand. "I think we found her. I'll see you later. If you think of anything, call me at Antonelli's."

"Found who?" Ralph asked. "What's going on?"

"None of your business, Ralphie," Ellie answered. "How's Tony?" she asked me. "Should I call him?"

I shrugged. "You know him. The more trouble he has, the less help he wants. He's got Jimmy convicted already."

Ellie shook her head. Ralph patted her shoulder, and she didn't pull away.

I walked back to my car, unlocked it, sat with the flyer spread on the steering wheel. The bakery had an address in Jefferson, in the south end of the county, far from here but not far from my place. I could be there in forty minutes if I stood up Mark Sanderson. I could camp out there, wait for Alice Brown to come back. And hope she knew where Jimmy was. And hope she'd tell me.

And hope Brinkman didn't get there first.

I fished a cigarette from my pocket, put a match to it, started the car. I pulled out onto the empty street and headed for the bus station in Cobleskill. I didn't know many of Jimmy Antonelli's friends, but even law-abiding citizens didn't have much use for Brinkman. He probably wasn't getting a lot of cooperation from people who'd be in a position to help him. And MacGregor hadn't asked me about Alice Brown when I was up there this morning, so he might not know about her either.

It seemed to me I might be a few hours ahead of the law on this. If that was true, I had the luxury of enough time to find out what was on Mark Sanderson's mind.

The bus station in Cobleskill was in what passed for down-town, a shabby area of two-story industrial buildings and three-story frame houses on both sides of the railroad tracks. There were no trains through here anymore, and most of the industrial buildings were only half used, as warehouses now. I parked in front of a peeling brown house with a gate hanging on one hinge and bedsheets for window curtains.

I looked around as I took the package from my trunk under the heavy sky. A car rolled down the cracked street, turned the corner. It hadn't been following me. I was making sure of that now, as routinely as I did in the city. A kid on a thick-tired bike bounced along the opposite sidewalk, and a couple of college-age girls came out of the bus station, wearing backpacks. Otherwise the street was deserted. Whatever happened in Cobleskill these days didn't happen here. It happened in the office parks and Pizza Huts and Friendlys and multiplex cinemas that lined the state highway as it ran into and out of town.

I put my package on the next bus out to New ·York, a one o'clock local due at the Port Authority at eight forty-five. Very local. I didn't insure it. The fewer people who knew it was worth something, the more likely it was to get where it was going. Cobleskill had a Federal Express office and I'd considered that, but this was still faster, and Lydia wouldn't have to sit around waiting for delivery.

I called her again, got her machine again, sketched in what was going on. I left the time of the bus and the number of the receipt. I told her to messenger the package in the morning to Shelley at the lab, tell her it was for me, tell her to rush it. I started to tell Lydia something else, but I wasn't sure what it was, so I stopped and hung up.

Tomorrow I'd have to figure out how to get MacGregor to run the prints for me, if they found any. I had cop friends who would've run them in New York, but that wouldn't show up anything strictly local, as for instance if someone had been arrested by a county sheriff. Maybe MacGregor could be bent; maybe I could bribe him with a new pair of waders.

*   *   *

Appleseed Baby Foods was west of town, at the end of a three-mile spur off the highway built just for them. The white concrete panel building spread in various directions from the center of a sprawling parking lot. A low office annex connected to the processing plant through a glass-enclosed entranceway.

I gave the guard at the desk my name, which he passed along over the phone to someone else. He listened, nodded, and hung up; then he told me to sign in, pointed at a pair of double glass doors, said "Upstairs."

I went up open-riser oak steps with an oak rail and a skylight at the top. Ferns hung in the light well in white plastic baskets. At the top was a hall lined with oak doors. The pair at the end were labeled President. I went through them into a large outer office with a beige carpet, and framed pictures of carrots, zucchini, and tomatoes on the walls.

A young woman with a heart-shaped face smiled behind a white desk in the middle of the room. Her glossy blond hair was an organized cap cut neatly at chin length. She wore a blue wool dress, and her nails were an understated length and an understated color.

"Did anyone ever tell you you have a beautiful voice?" I asked before she spoke.

She blushed but kept her composure. The effect was becoming. "Mr. Smith? Mr. Sanderson has been expecting you. Please have a seat; I'll just tell him you're here."

She picked up the phone on her desk, spoke into it, smiled at me again. Smiling was something she did well, probably from practice. I sat on a beige fabric-covered chair, the kind that puts you too low to the ground. I admired the vegetables. Five minutes; ten. For a man who'd been anxious to see me, in particular, Mark Sanderson didn't seem very excited now that I was here.

I took out a cigarette, rolled it around in my fingers a little, lit it. After the first drag the phone on the desk buzzed. The secretary answered it, hung up, smiled again.

"Mr. Sanderson will see you now. Go right in." She nodded toward a door in the wall behind her.

Funny how often that cigarette thing worked.

Mark Sanderson's office was a corner office, as I'd imagined, with a view out over the plant, the parking lot, and the soft hills wrapping the valley. Sanderson's desk, though, was facing the door I came through. He'd have to turn his back on his work to get the benefit of that view.

"Smith." Sanderson rose, came out from behind the desk as I came in. He extended a well-kept hand in a solid handshake. A smile came and went on his round baby face, leaving no trace. His steel-colored eyes studied me. Then, with the casual tyranny of a man so used to being obeyed that he rarely gave orders, he said, "Sit down."

I sat.

Sanderson perched on the edge of the desk, one foot still on the floor, one hand folded over the other. I watched the action behind his hard eyes. "Look," he said, "I think we may have gotten off to a bad start earlier. If it was my fault, I apologize. I can be abrupt, I know." The smile blinked on and off again.

"I can be pretty rough myself," I said. "Let's forget it. What was it you wanted to see me about?"

"Frankly, I need your help." He walked back around the desk, sat in a leather swivel chair. I was left trying to read his face against the glare from the uncurtained windows. "I need to find a boy named Jimmy Antonelli. I've been told you can help me."

The cigarette I'd started in the outer office hadn't been much fun. I took out another, lit it, looked around for a place to throw the match. There was an ashtray on a credenza against the wall. Sanderson didn't move, so I got up, walked around him, picked it up. I repositioned my chair before I sat back down.

I pulled on the cigarette, breathed out some smoke. "Why do you want him?"

"It's a personal problem."

"Jimmy's got some of those, too. Why do you want him?"

"Well." He smiled again. This one was longer-lasting than the others, but it vanished as completely. "Well, I really don't want him. But my daughter seems to have run off with him."

"Alice?" I asked.

He looked at me blankly. "My daughter. Ginny. Who's Alice?"

"Never mind. What makes you think your daughter's with Jimmy?"

"They've been seeing each other. Two nights ago Ginny didn't come home. I haven't seen her since."

"Did you call the police?"

"Naturally." He frowned impatiently. "And they came to the same conclusion I had already come to."

"If you've talked to the police you know they're looking for Jimmy, too. So why call me?"

"You're a friend of his."

"That doesn't mean I can find him."

"Have you tried?"

"I'm not a cop."

"Doesn't that mean you're likely to do better than they have?"

I said, "Do you have a picture of your daughter, Mr. Sanderson?"

He started to say something, but stopped. He picked up a photograph from his desk, stood and handed it to me. It was a studio portrait, maybe a yearbook picture, of a small, beautiful girl with thick golden hair billowing around a delicately boned face. A hint of a smile, high red cheeks, and something in her deep blue eyes that sent a chill up my spine. Sanderson watched me. "She's fifteen," he said, unexpectedly softly.

I looked up quickly. His face had lost none of its arrogance and his mouth was still hard, but his eyes held a sudden tenderness, a familiar desperation that cut through me like a knife.

He stood abruptly, turned to the window, hands in his pockets. "I didn't want Ginny growing up around here, with the kind of punks that hang out in McDonald's and drag race down the highway. I sent her to boarding school. But like any kid, she probably thinks the grass is greener where she's not allowed to go, and she's naive enough to fall for an SOB like Antonelli if he came on to her."

"Do you know Jimmy?"

He turned back to me. "By reputation."

"How did they meet, if she's in boarding school?"

He regarded me silently. I thought he wasn't going to answer; but he said, "She was sent home—suspended—a month ago."

"For what?"

"Her roommate, a first-year girl, was selling drugs. When they caught the little bitch, she claimed Ginny was involved, too."

"It wasn't true?"

"Of course it wasn't." There was ice in his words and his eyes. "Ginny didn't like that girl from the first day. She was loud and crude, Ginny said. I wish she'd told me that then. I'd have had that girl moved in two seconds flat."

I put my cigarette out. "So Ginny was home, with nothing to do, and she met Jimmy at the soda shop?"

His eyes hardened. "I don't have any idea how they met. And believe me, if I'd known they were seeing each other, I'd have forbidden it."

"How did you find out?"

"I was told yesterday morning, by a friend."

"Why didn't your friend tell you sooner?"

"How the hell do I know?" he burst out, then clamped his jaw shut immediately, the jutting tendons in his neck proof that he was working to contain anger he hadn't wanted to show.

I leaned forward, put the photograph back on his desk. "I don't know where she is, Mr. Sanderson."

"I know where she is." His voice was tight. "She's with

Jimmy Antonelli. All I need is for you to tell me where he is."

I didn't say anything. His hard eyes looked me over. He said, shaping his mouth as though the words tasted bad, "Of course, I expect to pay for this information. Whatever a man like you would expect to be paid."

The sun broke suddenly through the dark clouds behind him, streaking the sky with slanted rays. "Mr. Sanderson," I said, "I don't know where Jimmy is. I don't know that your daughter's with him. I don't know that I could find him if I wanted to. But you're right about one thing: I'm a friend of his. I won't obstruct a police investigation, but that doesn't mean I have to be point man on this."

"Goddammit!" he exploded. "Goddammit, Smith, we're talking about my daughter!"

"I'm sorry," I said, toughening myself against the pain in his eyes.

For a moment he didn't speak. Then suddenly his eyes became hard again, and he smiled that firefly smile. "You have a cabin near North Blenheim, don't you? Off Thirty? I hear you come up here a lot. It's a long way from New York. You must like it here."

"Your friend tell you that, too?"

"Actually, I know a good deal about you. I like to know a lot about the people who work for me." He sat, leaned back in his chair, smiled a smile that lasted. It reminded me of his daughter's eyes. "Route Thirty." His manner was musing. "You know, we used to use that road a lot, to truck to our eastern markets, but it's winding and narrow. In my father's day it was fine, but competition's stiffer now. My father founded this company," he interrupted himself. "Did you know that?"

"No," I said.

"Fifty years ago. When I took over, I modernized a lot of things. I updated factory operations and office procedures. But transportation was the big problem. The demand was there, and we had the product, but we couldn't get to market fast enough. I almost moved the whole plant to Georgia. But you know what happened?"

"No."

"The county built me a new road. They were set to upgrade 30, until they saw that a new road on the other side of the valley made more sense. I helped them see that. And they got the state to put in a new highway spur for me, right out here. They want to keep me here, Smith."

I said nothing. He went on, "Now, that new road is good, but cuts too far east to do us any good if we want to get to 17. Binghamton, Elmira, central Pennsylvania— those are big markets for us."

He looked out over the parking lot, where a truck painted with vegetables and smiling babies was pulling into a loading dock. "So I've been thinking about 30. You know, there's a place about two miles from North Blenheim where you could take 30, drop it down the valley, then pull it through around the other side of the mountain. Then you could widen it as it runs south. That would still leave a narrow stretch before North Blenheim, but it's pretty straight there, so that wouldn't be a problem." He turned back, steepled his hands over his chest. "That's a pretty good idea, don't you think?"

He didn't expect an answer and he didn't get one. "I think I'll suggest it to the County Economic Development people. I think I'll suggest that while they study the idea of improving 30 like this, they start condemning the land they'd need to do it. That won't be costly, because none of that land is worth anything. Most of the people who live around there"—he paused, locked his hard eyes on mine—"most of them would be glad to take a few dollars from the state and clear out. Some won't like it, of course. But luckily, they won't have a choice." He spread his hands, palms up. "And if the state decides not to build the road, they can always sell the land again. That would be years from now, of course. These things always take a lot of time."

I watched him across the desk, the two of us sitting

motionless in the carpeted room while on the other side of the window cars and trucks crawled around the parking lot and dark clouds scudded across the sky.

"You're blowing smoke," I finally said. "You can't do it."

"Oh, you're wrong." His voice was rueful, self-deprecating. "There are a lot of things I can't do. I can't play cards and I can't sing a note. And I can't seem to find Jimmy Antonelli. But get land condemned in this county? That I can do, Smith. That I can do."

He shuffled some papers on his desk. "Well, I imagine you're a busy man, so I won't keep you any longer. I'll expect to hear from you soon." He rose, stuck out his hand.

I stood. I looked at the outstretched hand, at the baby face, at the beautiful girl in the silver picture frame. I turned, walked to the door, left it open behind me, and went out.

The secretary with the beautiful voice began to smile as I came through the door, but the smile faltered and died when she saw my face.

TEN

I pulled the car hard out of the Appleseed lot and onto the spur road. My jaw didn't start to unclench until I hit the state highway, which Sanderson didn't own.

I fished in my jacket pocket for a cigarette and found that was all I had: one. I shoved it in my mouth, crushed the pack, flung it against the passenger-side door. It bounced. I smoked the cigarette right down to the filter, ground it in the ashtray as I hit the turnoff that would take me to 10 and south through the county to Jefferson.

An Appleseed truck, painted with enormous peaches and cherries, rumbled past me going the other way.

Cherries flowered early in the spring, up here; the three on my land, halfway up the slope between the cabin and 30, were always the first color on the hillside. For years I'd made it a point to be up here when they blossomed, if I could.

I checked to make sure I wasn't being followed. I checked to make sure I didn't have any more cigarettes. I checked to make sure I hadn't missed 10, because the way I felt, I could have zipped right by it and been halfway to Buffalo before I caught on.

In Jefferson I had to stop and ask directions. The ones I got, from a toothless guy in a John Deere cap, were complete to the point of idiocy. My fingers tightened slowly on the wheel as he leaned in my window and ticked off every curve and corner between the center of town, where we were blocking the intersection, and Winterhill Road.

It turned out the drawing on the flyer wasn't half bad; I might have recognized the little house even without the wooden Winterhill Kitchen sign that stood on the lawn. The house was freshly painted, blue with a darker blue trim and deep red accents. There were carved bits of gingerbread at the eaves and lace curtains in the windows. The porch light was lit, a warm yellow glow in the chilly afternoon.

I parked in a gravel lot by the side of the house. There were three other cars there. None of them was Jimmy's Dodge Ram van and there was no blue truck.

A sign on the front door said Open—Come In in the same calligraphy as the logo on the flyer and the hanging sign. A bell tinkled as I opened the door and stepped inside. The air was scented with spices and the warm, sweet smells of vanilla, yeast, butter, chocolate.

To my right was a staircase, small but with an elegant curve to the bottom steps. Straight ahead was a closed door, and on the left a wall of french doors, which stood open. I went through into a lace-curtained room that held four tables, an antique garden bench, and a display case.

Inside the display case were latticework pies, deep purple filling showing through woven crust; a tall, darkly glossy chocolate cake, and a smaller white one with crushed pistachios sprinkled over it and one slice missing; a tray of cupcakes glazed in pastel colors; and a basket of star-shaped cookies with tiny gold and silver balls in their white frosting. Pots of coffee and hot water steamed on burners behind the counter, a cappuccino machine gleamed, and a rush basket held foil-wrapped envelopes of fancy teas.

It occurred to me that I was hungry.

A slight young woman with fawn-colored hair and round glasses came through a door behind the counter. I caught a glimpse of bright lights, white tiles, and pies cooling on tall racks. She wore jeans and a smudged white apron. She asked shyly, "May I help you?"

"I'm looking for Alice Brown," I told her, handed her my card.

She read it, nodded, disappeared through the door, and was back in moments to say, "Alice is on the phone, but she'll be right out when she's through. Would you like to sit down while you're waiting?"

I pointed to a plate of thick slices of cranberry bread. "What I'd like," I said, "is to have one of those and a cup of coffee while I'm sitting down."

Smiling, she poured coffee into a dark blue mug, slid the cranberry slice onto a blue china plate. I paid her, took a seat at a table by the window.

The shy young woman disappeared behind the door again.

The coffee was good: fresh and strong with a faint bitter taste of chicory. I put it somewhere up around Eve Colgate's. The bread was rich and crumbly, the cranberries moist, tart, and plentiful.

Outside, the view was over a treeless field curving gently up away from the house. The sky was silvery at the horizon, with heavy iron clouds above.

I'd finished the bread and was halfway through the coffee when the kitchen door opened again and a different young woman came through. She was in her early twenties, I judged, and heavy, as Ellie had said; but she moved with graceful ease, self-assured and quiet. Her white kitchen jacket contrasted with her rich, shoulder-length chestnut hair. Her eyes were large and dark, and there was a scattering of freckles on her high cheeks.

I stood. "Alice Brown?"

"Yes, I'm Alice Brown," she said, looking at me not with hostility but with a clear reserve. Maybe it was just her way; or maybe she had some idea why I was there.

"My name is Bill Smith," I said. "Please, sit down." I held the chair for her and she sat, her back straight, her shoulders relaxed. She folded her hands loosely on the table, gave me a direct gaze.

"I'm a friend of Jimmy Antonelli's," I said as I sat again. "It's important that I speak to him, and I think you know where he is."

"Jimmy," she said. She dropped her eyes to the table-top. "No, I don't know where he is."

"I'm a friend of his," I repeated. "He's in trouble. Maybe he deserves it, maybe not. Either way, maybe I can help."

"I know who you are," she said evenly. "But I can't help you."

"Tony thought you might."

"Oh " She smiled a little. "I like Tony. I wish he and Jimmy had gotten along better." She stood abruptly, went behind the counter, made a business of making herself a cup of sweet-smelling herbal tea. "Do you want more coffee?" she asked.

"Please. It's terrific coffee."

She brought the pot over, poured, returned the pot to the heat, sat again. She sipped her tea. I waited to see what it was all about.

"Jimmy talked about you a lot," she said, cupping her tea in both hands. "He said you were the only other person who ever took him seriously. He said you didn't make him feel like a punk."

"Besides me. I was the other person?"

"—— only other person?"

"Besides me. I was the other one."

I didn't say anything. She went on, "I suppose Tony told you Jimmy was living here with me for a while."

"This is your house?"

She nodded. "I grew up here. I live alone here now; my father died a year ago." Her face said she still wasn't used to it.

"I'm sorry."

She smiled softly. "Thank you."

I drank my coffee. "The bakery is yours, then?"

"Laura's and Joanie's and mine. That was Joanie you met when you came in."

"And Jimmy?"

She was quiet for a moment, looking out the window. Then she went on. "I got to know Jimmy in the fall. We needed a delivery van and none of us knows about cars. I take my Plymouth to the garage where Jimmy works. I could tell he knew what he was doing, so I asked him to help us find a used van and put it in shape. That's how we got to know each other, driving around looking at vans. At first he did his tough-guy act, but I wasn't interested. Finally we started to just talk. We talked a lot. He wasn't used to that, he said. He said nobody had ever cared what he had to say, except you."

"He never gave anybody much of a chance."

"That's what I told him."

Outside the window the wind ruffled the grasses. I said, "And he moved in with you?"

"Just before Christmas. I knew his reputation, but I didn't care. I knew Jimmy, I thought. And you know what?"

"What?"

"I was right. It wasn't a mistake and I'm not sorry."

"But something must have gone wrong."

She nodded. "He wasn't ready. He just wasn't ready. He started seeing someone else. It didn't last long, a couple of weeks. It was over by the time I found out. He felt terrible about it, he said. It w~~as just~~ ~~one~~thing ~~that hap~~pened, it didn't mean anything. But ~~I~~ ~~with~~ ~~I~~ ~~didn't~~ even want to start playing that game. I told him to leave."

"When was that?"

She swirled the floating leaves around in the bottom of her teacup, watched their patterns as they settled. "That he moved out? Maybe a week ago."

"Who was the someone else?"

She pushed her teacup away. "Maybe I'm talking too much."

"You haven't said anything that could hurt Jimmy," I

said. She didn't answer. "Please," I said. "It's important."

"Her name is Ginny Sanderson."

"Mark Sanderson's daughter?"

"Do you know her?" she asked, eyebrows raised.

"No. But her father is looking for her. She hasn't been home for a couple of days."

Her answer surprised me: "Would you go home, if he were your father?"

I asked, "Do you think she's with Jimmy?"

"No."

"Why not?"

"He . . ." she hesitated. "He said she'd dropped him for somebody else."

"Do you know who?"

She shook her head.

"And you don't think she and Jimmy could have gotten back together?"

"No," again.

"Alice," I said, "I've got to find him. I'm not the only person looking for him. A man's been killed. The police are calling it a homicide and they think Jimmy's involved."

"I know." Her fair, clear skin flushed a deep red. "I mean, I know about the killing, and I know it happened at Tony's bar. It was on the news. The man who was killed — Jimmy had talked about him. He talked about all those people. I told him he didn't have to explain things to me, but he said he wanted me to know." She looked at me seriously. "He said that was over. He said he wants something different now." She added quietly, "I hope he finds it."

She peered through the window to the pale horizon, but I didn't think she was watching the clouds. Her dark eyes turned back to me. "I don't think Jimmy killed that man."

"Why do you say that, if you haven't seen him?"

She didn't answer right away. Finally she said, "You don't think he did either." It wasn't a question.

I said, "I want to talk to him."

She gave a small shrug, spread her hands helplessly.

"If he does get in touch with you, will you tell him I'm here and I want to help?"

She nodded.

"My cell phone number is on the card. Or you can always reach me at Antonelli's. Jimmy knows that." I stood. She stood too, and hesitated; then she offered me her hand. We shook; her skin was soft and smooth. She smiled a quiet smile which didn't so much light up her face as allow it to glow softly, from within.

I went back down the porch steps and out to my car. The wind had come up and the clouds had thickened. I drove out of the lot and down the driveway, turning left onto Winterhill Road, the way I had come. The land up here on the ridge was gently rolling. I looked for a spot to pull off and I found a good one, behind a little slope about two hundred yards from the house. The road curved here; someone concentrating on driving, especially at dusk, might pass a parked car and never even notice.

I pushed the seat back, stretched my legs. I turned the CD player on, slipped in the disc of Uchida playing my Mozart Adagio. I could never hope to play with the control she had, the enormous technical mastery that made the piano respond to her precise intention every time, but I could learn from it. My fingers started to feel the music, to move the way your foot will move to where the brake pedal should be when someone else is driving the car. The Baldwin in the cabin, recently tuned, had sounded good these last two nights in the cedar-scented darkness. Now, in the still car, the tips of my fingers, looking for the smoothness and hard edges of ivory and ebony, found only denim and leather and the coldness of the air.

Color drained from the fields and the sky as the day grew old around me. I turned the car on twice, to get a little heat, trying to thaw that deep bone chill that can come from sitting in the cold, not moving. I kept reaching for a cigarette, remembering I had none, cursing first silently, then out loud.

Three cars passed me during the time I sat there, two from the east, one from the west. With each I turned off the tape, listened with the window open for the sound of brakes or slamming doors. In the wide, treeless emptiness the wind, blowing east, would have brought me those sounds, but there was nothing, so I stayed where I was and I waited.

It was longer than I thought, almost two hours, the day close to darkness, when the yellow Horizon I'd been waiting for whisked by. It had been the only Plymouth in the Winterhill lot. I started the car, pulled out without haste. I wanted plenty of room between us on roads as deserted as these.

She drove down into Jefferson and beyond it, picking up 2 heading east. There was a Stewart's a few miles along and she stopped there. I pulled into the lot, engine idling while I watched her shop under the harsh convenience-store light.

She was wearing a blue parka, her glossy chestnut hair half hidden under a blue knit hat. She filled a basket and it didn't take long. Cold cuts, milk, coffee, a six-pack of Bud. After a moment's hesitation, a second six-pack. Something from the sandwich counter in the back, micro-waved before it was wrapped and handed to her. At the checkout she bought the *Mountain Eagle* and the Albany paper, and added a carton of Salems.

Maybe she'd pick me up a pack of Kents, if I asked.

She loaded the paper bag into her trunk, rolled out of the parking lot. She turned north on 30 as far as Middle-burgh, then suddenly left it and started threading her way over back roads. I kept my distance. She wasn't acting as though it had occurred to her she might be tailed; she hadn't even scanned the Stewart's lot. But she wasn't stu-pid and I didn't want to scare her off.

She knew the roads well, choosing the better-paved shortcuts, working her way north. I kept her in sight close enough so I wouldn't lose her when she made a turn, but no closer. A couple of times I killed my lights, not for long, just long enough so that she'd think the headlights in her mirror belonged to three or four different cars, if she thought about it at all.

About half an hour after we'd left 30, twisting and turning along dark roads where the trees crowded close, she turned onto a well-kept county road and I suddenly caught on. She drove west about two hundred yards. I didn't follow her, just watched as she turned left into a space in the trees that was a road only if you thought it was. I didn't need to follow her now; I knew where she was going.

After the Plymouth's taillights disappeared I parked on the shoulder across from the mouth of the hardscrabble road she'd turned up. I locked up the car, started to pick my way. I had the flashlight from the car and I needed it. The sky was a thick steel gray, no moon, no stars. Branches pressed against its underside. The darkness around me started at the edge of the flashlight beam and was complete.

There were no night sounds, no birds; just my footsteps scraping softly, as softly as I could manage, up the stony road.

The road wasn't long; I knew it wasn't. I switched off the flashlight as I came near the top. The path leveled out and the trees stopped abruptly, staying behind. In the darkness there were darker shadows, but mostly there was a sudden feeling of openness, an empty plain where, if I stood long enough, I would begin to be able to see what I knew was there.

Close in, there would be piles of boulders and slag standing on the dead earth; farther off, a pit, an enormous hole maybe five hundred yards across and half that deep, sudden and sharp-sided and filled with inky water. Beyond the pit, a wall of rock, thin trees scratching for a living. On top of the wall was a road that ran straight along the top of the mountain. The only way to get here from that road was to scramble down the rocks.

About a third of the way around the pit there was a bigger road than the one I'd come up, and there were three other pits like this one, vast canyons separated from each other by ridges which in places narrowed to ten feet. When this pit was active the gravel trucks had used that other road, kicking up dust, rumbling through the daytime hours with loads of stone crushed and ground to order in a towering collection of connected timber structures that clung to the side of the hill. Fist size, egg size, pea size, dust: There was nowhere in this part of the state that gravel from this quarry hadn't been used to build roads, line drainage ditches, mix into concrete.

This pit was abandoned now, and so were two of the others, but the fourth—the one MacGregor had said was close to played-out, too—was for now still working, lower down on the hill. Each of the exhausted pits was as huge and desolate as this one, and each, as it was abandoned and the dewatering pumps removed, filled with water from the interrupted springs that bled down the face of the rock. The local kids used these pits to swim in in the summer, diving from the rocks into the cold, bottomless pools. It had been one of those kids who, early last August, on the last warm night of the year, had discovered something strange here: a late-model Nissan Sentra come to rest on a ledge a few feet below the surface.

To my right two cars were parked: the yellow Plymouth, and a familiar Dodge Ram van. The van's rear windows were hung with Mylar shades from which a stag on a huge boulder stared, impassive, over a winter scene as desolate as this.

Just beyond the cars a dilapidated shack with a tin roof leaned into the night. Light shone through its grimy windows, reflecting weakly off the cars' chrome trim.

My footsteps were silent walking up to the shack. It seemed likely that Jimmy was armed, and though he wouldn't shoot me if he knew it was me, he was liable to be jumpy as hell.

I stopped about ten feet from the door, stood facing it. Anyone looking out through the glass could have seen me clearly then, a tall, solid shape on the barren plain. Inside my gloves, my palms were sweating.

"Jimmy!" My voice echoed off the rock wall, repeating, fading, dying. The light in the shack went out; nothing else happened. "Jimmy!" I called again. "It's Bill Smith. I'm alone. Let me in."

Nothing, again.

Then Jimmy's voice, loud, tough, and blustery. "Mr. S.! Talk to me! You alone?"

"I said I was. Let me in."

I waited. The door creaked open; the doorway gaped emptily. I walked forward, stepped through into the darkness. The door slammed shut and the blinding beam of a powerful flashlight hit me full in the face.

I jerked, raised my hand to block the glare. The beam switched off and the small flame of a match lit a kerosene lamp. Wavering shadows were thrown against the bare walls, shadows of two figures standing, some distance apart, before me.

"Jesus," I said, trying to clear my eyes.

"Had to make sure." Jimmy's voice, nonchalant.

"You know a lot of guys my size, sound like me?"

"You never know."

We faced each other across the small, dusty room. In the flickering light Jimmy looked drawn and tired, his stubble-covered face smudged with dirt; but the grin, the cocky set of his shoulders under the plaid-lined parka were the same as always, the same as they'd been on the kid I'd taught to hit a baseball and to drive a nail straight and to split a log without chopping his own foot off.

And to shoot. I'd taught him that, too.

Loosely by his side Jimmy held an old Winchester .30-30, maybe the one Tony had given him when he was twelve. The shack smelled of stale beer, kerosene, and disuse. Shadows danced on the walls, moved over our faces. It struck me then how much Jimmy looked like Tony: the same short, powerful build, the same square jaw and dark, unyielding eyes. But where Tony looked as if he'd been put together by a rockslide, Jimmy had been carved more carefully. His nose was straighter than Tony's, his eyes set less deep; but the take-it-or-leave-it in them was Tony's, too.

To Jimmy's right, next to the wall, Alice Brown stood with her arms wrapped around her. She had taken off her hat, but not her parka; the potbellied woodstove in the corner wasn't giving off enough heat for that. She was watching me with guarded eyes.

"I'm sorry," I said to her. "I didn't believe you."

"You had no reason to," she answered calmly.

"I wanted to. But I couldn't afford it."

"I had to make sure Jimmy wanted to see you," she said.

I turned back to Jimmy. "Did you?"

"Hell, yes!" Jimmy leaned the rifle against the wall, reached into the Stewart's bag on a rickety table by the stove. He pulled out a six-pack, freed a can from its plastic collar, tossed it to me. He held out another, said "Allie?" in an unsure voice. Alice shook her head.

I dropped onto an upended wooden box, popped the top of the beer. Jimmy leaned against the table. There was one spindly chair in the room and he gestured Alice to it with his beer and a tentative smile.

"No," she said, with no smile at all.

So the chair stayed empty as I sat and Jimmy leaned and Alice stood. On the table next to the Stewart's bag was a half-eaten meatball hero, melted cheese and tomato sauce congealing on aluminum foil. "You mind if I finish this?" Jimmy asked me. "I'm starving."

"Go ahead," I said. He scooped up the sandwich, bit into it. Tomato sauce dripped on the floor, kicked up tiny craters in the dust. I asked, "When was the last time you ate?"

"Yesterday," he said, his mouth full of bread and meat-balls. "Lunch."

I put my beer can on the floor, went to the table, took the carton of Salems from the bag. I shook out a pack, found a book of matches in the bottom of the bag. I lit a Salem as I sat down again.

Jimmy watched me. "You hate those," he said.

"Damn right," I answered.

I smoked and Jimmy ate. I asked, "Where were you yesterday?"

"Here," he said, wiped his mouth on a wadded-up paper napkin. "Been here for a few days."

"How many?"

He looked uncomfortable. "About a week," he answered. "Since Allie threw me out."

Over by the wall, Alice dropped her arms, turned around to stare out the window at the impenetrable darkness.

"Allie—" Jimmy said.

She shook her head, didn't turn around.

Jimmy looked at me, helplessly. "I come up here sometimes. To think. You know. Nobody comes here, except in summer. When Allie . . ." His eyes shifted to her; she didn't move. "Where was I gonna go? I didn't want to crash with nobody. No way I was going back to Tony's. So I came here. I mean, just for a while. Just, you know, to get it together."

I said nothing, tasted the cool taste of menthol, wished for a Kent. Jimmy went on, "I was on my way to work yesterday, in the van. Had the police scanner on just to listen to the cop talk. Heard about Wally. Heard Brinkman was looking for me. Well, no shit, Sherlock!" He grinned, but the grin seemed strained.

"What did you do?"

"Turned the hell around and came back here. What'd you think?"

"Did you talk to anybody?"

"What do you mean, talk?"

"You have a CB in the van, don't you?"

"Oh, yeah, and I said, 'Breaker, breaker, this is Jimmy Antonelli, tell Brinkman I'm up at the quarry.' What're you, fucking nuts?"

"How did Alice know you were here?"

"He called me," Alice said, without turning around. Her voice was strong, but waiting to crack, like spring ice. "In the middle of the night, from someplace closed. He asked me to come after dark, and bring him some things."

I looked around the shack, at the leaning walls, at the cardboard jammed over the missing windowpane, at the sleeping bag spread on the floor, at the dirt and the darkness in the corners.

"How long you figure to be here?" I asked. "A couple of months? A few years, maybe, until everyone forgets?"

"Years? What the hell are you talking about?" Above the grin Jimmy's eyes were confused. "A few days, that's all. Just till the heat lets up a little."

"Then what?"

"Then I'll take off. Time I left this dead-end place anyhow." He crumpled his empty beer can one-handed, flipped it into the Stewart's bag, popped the top on another.

"And go where?"

"What's the difference?" He slurped beer off the top of the can. "New York, Chicago. Hell, L.A.! I hear it's nice out there. You been there?" I didn't answer. "Anywhere. I got a million choices, man. I'm gonna disappear. Change my name. You know." He laughed. "I'm gonna grow a big fuckin' mustache, be a real dago wop, like my grandaddy! Hey, whadda-you a-think?" He looked from Alice's back, which didn't move, to me. His grin was desperate for company.

I dropped my cigarette butt in my empty beer can, listened to the hiss it made. "All right," I said, looking up at Jimmy. "Now listen to me, and hear every goddamn word." The grin wavered a little. "You don't know shit about life on the run. You'll never get out of the county. If you do you won't last six months. You'll be spotted in Asshole, Texas, by some pork-faced sheriff who sits around reading wanted posters because he's got nothing else to do. And you're a cowboy, aren't you, Jimmy? You'll pull out that Winchester when they come for you in the hole you're hiding in, which'll be just like this one except instead of cold and filthy it'll be hot and filthy and the water'll taste bad. And they'll blow your head off. And that'll be it, Jimmy. That'll be all of it."

He stared at me for a long moment; then he pushed sharply away from the table. He turned away, ran a hand over his hair, turned back. He stood looking at me, his empty hands opening and closing.

"What the fuck you want me to do, man?" For the first time the fear stood out in his eyes. "Brinkman's after my ass, you know he is. He's gonna hang this on me if he can. What am I supposed to do, just let him?"

Alice turned from the window then. Her lip trembled as she looked from him to me and back again.

"Did you kill Wally Gould?" I asked him.

Color drained from his face. He sank down slowly onto the chair.

"You think so, Mr. S.?" he asked quietly. "That what you think?"

I lit two cigarettes, passed one to him. He took it, hunching forward in the chair. He rubbed his eyes with the heels of his hands.

"Listen," I said, in a voice gentler than the one I'd been using. "Listen, Jimmy. That's not my only question. I've got a lot of questions, and you're going to have to answer them all. Jimmy?" I waited; he looked up at me. "You'll have all of me, either way. Either way, Jimmy. But I want to hear it from you."

He took in smoke, exhaled. He stood, walked around aimlessly, sat down again.

"Wally. That stupid little fuck," he said in a half-whisper. "He was real into making trouble for me. With Frank, with Brinkman, with anyone he could think of. And now check it out: He's fucking *wasted,* and he can't stop!" He laughed shortly, looked up at the ceiling, back at me. "Ain't that a kick in the ass?" He did what I'd done, pushed his cigarette into his beer can, watched it disappear.

He lifted his eyes to mine. "I didn't kill him, Mr. S."

By the window, Alice's hand moved slowly to her mouth, and she started to cry.

Jimmy jumped from the chair, moved to Alice's side. He folded an arm around her shoulders, spoke her name softly, but she pulled away. She wiped her eyes, leaving her face streaked with grime.

"I want to go home," she said, voice quavering. She pulled together her mittens, hat, car keys. "You don't need me now. I can go."

"Baby—" Jimmy reached out a hand; she shrugged it off.

"Alice, wait," I said.

"Why?" she asked unhappily. "Jimmy has you now. You'll know what to do. I just want to go home."

"It's not him I'm thinking about. It's you."

She pulled on her mittens, stood thin-lipped, waiting.

"Remember I said I wasn't the only person looking for Jimmy? One of the other people is Frank Grice. He offered me a thousand dollars."

Jimmy's eyebrows shot up. "What the hell for?"

"You."

They were both silent, digesting that.

I went on, "If I found you, Alice, Grice can too. He's not a nice man."

She threw Jimmy a confused look, then back to me. "I don't understand. What do you want me to do?"

"I don't want you out there in that house by yourself. Is there someone you can stay with?"

"That's ridiculous!" she snapped. "It's my home. I've always lived there. I'm not afraid of those people."

"That's a mistake," I said. "I am."

That stopped her. "Well . . ." She frowned. "Laura and her husband live in Schoharie."

"Good," I said. "Go there tonight. And I don't want you alone during the day. You know Grice by sight?"

She nodded.

"You even think you see his shadow, call the state

troopers." I described Arnold to her, and Otis and Ted. "And if anyone does ask you anything, do you think you can lie better than you did to me?"

She flushed crimson, and for the first time she smiled. "I think so."

"Good," I said again. "You haven't seen Jimmy since he started cheating on you and you threw him out." Jimmy started to protest; I ignored him. "You don't know where he is, and you hope he rots in hell. Right? Tell them to go ask his new girlfriend. And tell them if they find him not to bother to tell you about it because you really couldn't care. Can you do that?"

"Yes." Her voice was clear again.

We looked at each other, the three of us, in the cold, dingy room. The kerosene lamp sputtered.

"If you need me," I said, "you have the number; or try Antonelli's."

Alice opened the door, shut it silently, and was gone.

Jimmy watched at the window as the yellow Plymouth backed into position, headed down the stony road.

He sat down, nodded toward the door, gave me a shamefaced smile. "I messed that up, huh?"

"Big time," I said. "Was it worth it?"

He shook his head.

I lit another Salem, tried to taste the tobacco through the mouth-numbing menthol. "Okay," I said. "Let's get to work."

He grinned his old grin. "You're the boss. What do we do now?"

"I ask, you answer. Who killed Wally Gould?"

"Oh, man, I *told* you, I wasn't there!"

"No, you didn't. You only said you didn't kill him."

"Well, I wasn't. Happier?"

"Lose the attitude, Jimmy. This isn't a game."

His grin spread, and he reached for a cigarette. "Sure it is, Mr. S. It's a big fucking game, and you're my ace in the hole. You're gonna pull it out for me, just like before."

I pushed to my feet so fast the box I'd been sitting on

fell over, clattered on the floor. I took two steps across the room, grabbed Jimmy's parka, slammed him up against the wall. His cigarette dropped and his fists clenched but all he did was stare at me through eyes suddenly grown huge.

"What the fuck—!"

"Shut up, you stupid bastard!" I felt the blood rush hot to my face. "Now listen to me! There's no game. A man's dead: The game's over. I don't know if I can pull it out for you, but I know this: There's only one way now. My way! You got that, Jimmy?"

He didn't answer, didn't move.

Our eyes locked in silence. In his eyes I saw the kid who, years ago, had skated out onto a frozen pond on a dare, triumphantly clowning at first, then hearing the ice crack.

I didn't know what he saw in mine.

I spoke slowly, controlling my voice. "You're going to give me everything you know."

I released him ungently, took a step back, drew in a long breath. My Salem had scorched the table where I'd left it. I set the box on end again, sat down.

Jimmy still hadn't moved.

"You never knocked me around before," he said, angry and accusing but with a note of wonder. "My dad did, and Tony, but you never did."

"Maybe I never thought it would do any good before."

He pushed off from the wall, yanked his parka back on straight. He turned the chair around, straddled the seat, arms crossed along the back. I took another drag of the Salem, dropped it and crushed it.

"My way?" I asked.

Jimmy nodded.

I began: "Who killed Wally Gould?"

"I don't know. I wasn't there."

"You don't have any ideas?"

He shrugged.

"Why was he killed at the bar?"

"I don't know, unless to make me look bad."

"Who'd want to do that?"

He smiled a little. "Mostly, Wally."

"All right, try this. Frank Grice tried to soften Tony up the other night. Why?"

Surprise stiffened his body. "Frank? Tony? What happened? Is Tony okay?"

I told him about the fight, Gould, and the gun. "Grice told Tony he had something on you, and it would cost him to keep it quiet. What does he have?"

"Oh, shit, Mr. S.! What the hell could he have? I've been clean, man, *months* now. You know, working. Allie could tell you . . ." He gestured toward the door, left his sentence unfinished.

"She did tell me." I opened another beer; my mouth was as dry as the rock dust that coated everything in the shack. "She also told me that a couple of weeks ago you started fooling around with Ginny Sanderson."

"Yeah" was all he gave me, and that reluctantly.

"Where'd you meet her?"

"At the Creekside."

"Grice's place?"

"Uh-huh."

"I thought you told Alice you were through with those people."

"I just stopped by for a beer, man. Just a beer, with the guys. They were all starting to say stuff. You know, about how I wasn't hanging out no more . . ."

"Yeah, Jimmy. Okay. Where's Ginny now?"

"Where's Ginny? How the hell do I know? Who cares?"

"She dropped you for another guy. Who?"

He pulled out a cigarette, tapped it on the pack. "I don't know."

"She didn't tell you who it was?"

"Uh-uh. She only said he was tougher than me. That's what she likes, tough. She thinks she's tough, too." He lit the cigarette, licked his thumb and forefinger, squeezed out the match. It made a sizzling sound. A smudge of smoke rose, broke up, and vanished. "She told me to get lost. She said . . ." He trailed off.

"What?"

He glared, but he answered. "She said she was tired of little boys."

"Jimmy," I said, "she hasn't been home for two days. Her father's worried."

He laughed. "Worried? That jerk? He's lucky she didn't split a long time ago."

"Why should she have?"

"He's on her case all the time. Won't leave her alone. He's the king of *don't,* like she was a kid or something. Don't do that, don't go there, don't hang out, don't be late. He's a tightass with money, too. She hates him."

"She told you that?"

"Uh-huh."

A gust of wind shook the window in its frame. A storm was coming up. There were scratching sounds as pebbly dust was flung against the shack.

"You know Eve Colgate, Jimmy?" I asked. "She lives along Ten outside of Central Bridge."

"Sure. Tony used to work for her, long time ago. Sometimes he took me over there with him. She used to give me, like, cookies and stuff. I mean, I was a kid." He flushed self-consciously.

"Last Friday she was robbed," I said. "She lost some pretty valuable stuff, but it's not stuff just anybody could unload. I want to know who did that job, Jimmy. Was it you?"

His face was the face of a kid who'd been smacked even though, for the first time in his life, he'd been nowhere near the cookie jar.

"Oh, man!" he said. "No, it fucking wasn't! What do I got to do for you, man, draw you a picture? I'm clean! Ask Allie. Ask Tony. Ask fucking *Frank!*"

"Okay, Jimmy," I said, "Okay. It wasn't you. Who was it? Frank?"

"No way. Even if it was his idea, it wouldn't've been

him. He keeps his hands clean. Only he'll find where to fence your shit for you later, for the right price. What the hell's the difference, anyway? I got a murder rap hanging over my ass and you're asking about a robbery I never even heard of! What do you want from me?" He stood abruptly. "You keep asking me all this shit I can't answer. What do you want?"

"I'm trying," I said evenly, "to dig your ass out of a hole so deep it hasn't got a bottom. Your keys to the bar were found next to Gould's body."

His face went white, stranding his eyes, big and dark and frightened. "What?" he almost whispered.

"Your keys to the bar, on a ring with some other keys. Door keys, car keys. Where's your truck?"

"My what?" He looked blank; then the color rose in his face again.

"Oh, come on, Jimmy. Ellie Warren says you bought a four-by-four. It's not up here. Where is it?"

"I don't know," he said.

"You don't know? What the hell does that mean, you don't know?"

"I don't fucking know! One of the guys must have borrowed it. They do sometimes, you know, like when I'm working and shit."

"How long is it that you don't know?"

He paced the small room. "Couple of days, maybe. How the hell'd my keys get in the bar?"

"You tell me."

"Oh, man! I wasn't there. I wasn't! I didn't know nothing about it, until I heard it over the goddamn scanner." He stopped pacing, turned to me hopefully. "They were left there on purpose. Like Wally was killed there: to make me look bad."

"Planted? Maybe. Who had the truck?"

"Oh, shit, Mr. S.! I don't know! One of the guys took it, Andy or Rich, somebody. I leave the keys in it sometimes when I'm at work. Bad habit, huh?" He tried to grin.

"Same keys? The ones on the silver ring?"

"Yeah. I guess so."

I pushed to my feet, stood facing him. "This is a load of crap. You don't just lose track of a new four-by-four. I don't know how that truck figures into Gould's murder, but your keys say it does. I want to know who had it. Was it Frank?"

"Frank? I wouldn't lend Frank a nickel, forget about my truck!"

"But you did lend it to someone. Andy and Rich didn't just come and take it, did they?"

"No, man, I told you."

"You told me bullshit."

"Hey! Hey, you don't like it, go to hell!" he exploded. "No one asked you to come up here, man! You don't owe me nothing. I don't need you. I was doing great before you came!"

"Were you?" I asked quietly.

He turned away with a curse, pounded a fist on the wall. Wood groaned, glass shivered. He stared out the window at the bleak plain. The shaky flame of the kerosene lamp was mirrored in the glass.

I put a hand on his shoulder. He didn't turn around but he didn't shrug me off, either.

"Okay," I said. "I'm leaving. I'll do what I can. I'll be back when I can. Jimmy?" I waited for an answer. I got a grunt. It was enough. "If they find you, give up. Let them take you. Don't shoot it out, Jimmy. You'll lose. I don't want that."

He didn't answer again. I zipped my jacket, stepped out the door into the moonless, starless night.

ELEVEN

There were more cars than usual in the lot at Antonelli's. I parked up by the road, watched the tin sign swing in the wind, blowing stronger now, out of the north. As I left the car two guys I'd seen around over the years came out the bar's front door, talking, smoking. One poked the other's ribs, said something low as I passed. I felt their eyes on me as I crossed the gravel, pulled the door open.

Inside was crowded, for Antonelli's, for a Wednesday in late winter. There were new faces and faces only half familiar. The winter regulars were sitting at tables along the walls as if they'd been stranded there by a flood.

Marie passed, looking harried, carrying plates of burgers and a bowl of chili. I winked at her and she smiled ruefully.

There was an empty stool at the end of the bar and I put myself on it. Tony spotted me, nodded. I waited for him to finish mixing two 7&7s that Marie came back and snatched up off the bar. She called, "Scotch rocks, two Buds, and a Fog Cutter."

Tony stared. "An' a *what?*"

Marie lifted her shoulders helplessly.

Tony looked at me. "Grenadine, mixed fruit juice, one-fifty-one rum," I said.

"Figures you'd know." Tony reached the Buds up onto the bar. "Can I charge 'em five bucks for it?"

"Charge them whatever you want. Most people you'd have to pay to drink it. What's going on here?"

"Vultures," he shrugged. "Same as yesterday." He dropped ice into a glass, poured Jim Beam over it. The ice cracked under the bourbon.

"You got the ice machine fixed," I said as he handed the glass to me.

"Did it myself."

I drank. "I need to talk to you."

He started to answer, then looked at me. After a moment he turned, pushed open the door to the kitchen. "Ray!" he called to the short-order cook. "Take over here a minute."

He swung the gate up, stepped out to the customers' side of the bar. I took another swig of bourbon, left it sitting on its cardboard coaster, waiting for me. Tony and I walked out together into the parking lot.

We stopped at the same time, as if we'd reached some prearranged place, and turned to face each other. Tony hooked his thumbs into his belt and stood waiting.

"I've seen Jimmy," I said. "I just left him."

Tony spat in the dirt. "Where is he?"

"He says he didn't kill anyone."

"Where the hell is he?"

"He's up at the quarry."

"Alone?"

"Yes. He's scared and he's armed."

"But he didn't do it, huh?"

"He says not."

"An' you believe him."

We looked at each other in the red neon glow. "Yes."

Tony shook his head. "He say who did?"

"He says he doesn't know."

"An' you believe that, too?"

"I'm not sure."

"He's so goddamn innocent, why's he hidin' out?"

"Come on, Tony. Last time he was in jail Brinkman beat the shit out of him. And guys have gone to prison before this on less than Brinkman and MacGregor have on Jimmy right now."

A car swept down 30, the beams from its headlights brushing the trees, illuminating nothing.

"Shit," Tony said. He kicked at a patch of gravel. "You gonna tell that trooper buddy of yours?"

"No."

He rubbed at the back of his neck. "What do I do?" he asked, but I didn't think he was really asking me.

"Maybe nothing, for now," I said. "I wanted you to know he was all right. But maybe you don't do anything."

"Yeah," he said. "Yeah, maybe." He spun around, stalked back into the bar.

I watched him go, gave him a minute. Then I went too, back inside, picked up my drink from the bar, carried it to the phone in the back.

A pretty young girl with a lot of blue eyeshadow was on the phone, talking animatedly with the receiver pressed to one ear and her index finger in the other. I waited, drinking bourbon.

Finally she was through. She hung up and sashayed across the room to a table where a skinny boy with a skinny mustache was waiting. I picked up the receiver, to which the scent of her perfume still clung. It was nice perfume. I fed the phone, dialed Eve Colgate. When she answered there was Schubert in the background again.

"I just wanted to make sure you were home," I told her. "There's something I want to talk to you about. Can I come over?"

"Yes. When?"

"Soon. After I get something to eat."

"Where are you?"

"At Tony's, but I'm not staying. Too many people here for me."

I could hear the small smile in her voice. "I know how that feels." A hesitant pause; then, "Why don't you come here?"

As she spoke the jukebox started up, filling the room with Charlie Daniels. "Sorry?" I said.

'For dinner. Come here. I have beef stew. There's plenty."

"Well, I—" I stopped myself. "Thanks. I'd like that."

When I left, the bar's door swung closed behind me, as though, if allowed to drift out, the light and the music, the talk, the taste of bourbon and gin would dissipate like woodsmoke in the vast darkness, and Antonelli's would be as empty and desolate as the night.

I crunched up through the gravel of Tony's lot toward the road, hearing nothing but my own footsteps and the hissing of the wind, seeing nothing but the shadowy forms of trees moving restlessly. In those trees, patient and alert, owls waited.

My car, up by the road, was a mound of flat, featureless black in the surrounding murk. No moon or stars threw careless light to be reflected off it; no cars rushed past it to emphasize by their motion its own stillness. Dark, and still, and silent, full of things I could only sense, not see: The night up here was always like that, and in that sense, comforting.

But here, now, in this night, something moved. Beyond my car, a red glow, the tip of a cigarette drifting lazily through the air.

Such a small thing, an everyday thing.

My skin sizzled. All my senses were instantly alert and bare. I reached, but there was nothing else, no sound, scent, nothing more I could see from that place.

But the night had changed completely.

I eased the zipper of my jacket down, slid my .38 out as the red glow vanished. If this was someone just finishing off a last smoke out in the night before driving home, he'd get in his car now and pull out. It didn't happen. Or if he'd just wanted a few moments of peace before heading down to Antonelli's, his footsteps would start soon, and he'd pass me, nodding a greeting, going on.

That didn't happen either. The smoker, quiet as the night, didn't move. Up by my car, he waited for me.

I didn't slow my steps. I could be walking into a setup, but it wasn't likely. If he'd wanted me dead without fuss he could have picked me off as I stood framed in Tony's doorway. This was someone who wanted to talk, just us two.

Still, I slipped the safety off the gun as I covered the last few yards.

He was on the far side of my car, a dark form between it and another I could now see parked beyond it. On this side of my car, nothing, no one else visible. A few more steps. Then I swung the gun up sharply, the car still between us, and snapped, "All right, don't move!"

The stillness changed; I could feel the smoker's body go stiff, maybe with surprise, maybe obedience. But not that, because although there was no movement, a girl's soft voice breathed, "Wow! Are you going to shoot me?"

I was at my car now, facing her across it. At this distance we could see each other, though shadowed and indistinct. She was small, her face pale, her clothes dark; I was large, and I was armed. For a moment nothing moved. The entire night was waiting for us. Then slowly she lifted her hands. She wore gloves without fingertips, the gloves you need if you're hammering nails or selling apples by the side of the road; and I could just make out her mocking smile as she wiggled her fingers like a child saying bye-bye, showing me they were empty.

I held the gun steady. She hesitated, then shrugged. Reaching up, she pulled her knit cap off, shook out her thick, golden hair.

"Fuck this hat. I fucking hate hats." The words were spoken with a careful casualness, the way you'd try out a phrase when you found yourself among native speakers of a language you'd been studying. "But it worked." Her voice held a self-satisfied tone. "You didn't see me until you got close."

A dark turtleneck sweater, much too big for her, engulfed her tiny frame in soft folds. Her tight jeans were tucked into high leather boots; even with the heel on the boot, she was barely five feet tall. Without looking, she tossed the unwanted cap onto the hood of her car.

"The cigarette was a big mistake," I told her.

"Well, shit, I've been freezing my ass off out here for a fucking hour! Guys keep coming in and out of that stupid bar. How was I supposed to know this time it was you?"

"Doesn't matter. If you don't keep your focus, you lose."

"Oh, is that detective stuff?" she asked archly. "Well, if you have to stand around in the cold all the time waiting for some asshole you don't even know to show up, it's a pretty shitty job." She started to move around the car toward me.

"Stay where you are."

"Oh, give me a fucking break," she snapped, but she stopped.

Gun still on her, I walked around, peered into the car that wasn't mine. It was as empty as the night around us.

"You're afraid I brought somebody?" Close enough now to read each other's faces, I could see amused contempt in her smile. "Is that what real detectives do?"

"It sometimes helps." I holstered the gun; I felt stupid, alone out there in the huge night, holding a gun on a tiny fifteen-year-old girl. "Did you know I was looking for you? Is that why you're here?"

She frowned up at me. Although there were no stars, no moon, the gold of her hair seemed to shine. "Looking for me? How do you know who I am?"

"Detective stuff," I told her. "You're Ginny Sanderson, and your father's worried about you."

"Oh, him." Impatience and disappointment equally filled her words. "You work for him?" The idea didn't seem at all to surprise her. She slouched against my car and scowled.

"He wanted me to," I said, "but I'm not."

She glanced up at that, and I saw her eyes glow, like the sparkling of the stars and the snow and the air itself on the coldest of winter nights.

"You crossed my dad? You won't last long up here. What did he want you to do?"

"Find you. Where's Jimmy Antonelli's truck?"

With a laugh she pushed herself up to sit on the hood of my car. As she moved she brushed close to me, and I caught the scent of her perfume, a heady, complicated fragrance, rich and old-fashioned, not what I might have expected of such a young girl.

"I get it," she said, swinging her legs against the wheel well. "That's a dumb detective trick, right? You say something out of nowhere to confuse me?"

"Do you have it?"

She pointed to the Trans-Am parked between my car and the road. "That's my car. I'm not supposed to drive at night until I'm sixteen, but it's mine."

"That's not an answer."

"Sure it is. Besides, you should like that car. My dad gave it to me. But he won't give you one. He's not that nice to his employees."

"I told you I don't work for him."

"Maybe you think you don't. Everyone around here does, whether they know it or not."

I pulled a cigarette out of my jacket. She held out her hand automatically, unthinkingly. I gave her that one, took out another for myself. She waited for a light; I did that, too.

The match was a brief flare in the darkness, reflected in her hair, her eyes. I shook it out, threw it away. "A man was killed Monday night by someone with the keys to that truck."

"Yeah. Wally." She pulled deeply on the cigarette. "Dumb little shit."

"You knew him?"

"Oh, sure. I know all those guys." She tossed her head, elaborately uninterested. "What kind of stupid cigarettes are these?" She looked at the Kent I'd given her, threw it away. She reached under the baggy sweater, brought out a filterless Camel, waited without speaking for another light.

The still-burning cigarette she'd abandoned lay among gravel and dry leaves. I crushed it with the toe of my boot, then lit for her the one she was holding.

"Shit!" she snapped, brushing ash from my own cigarette off her sweater, where it had fallen. "Watch it! This is my mom's."

"Your mom's?" I said, then stopped myself. Her family's troubles weren't my business.

"Yeah, you know all about it, right?" she said scornfully. "Everybody around here knows all about it. So she walked out on my dad, so what? Who wouldn't? Fucking jerk-off. Anyway, when she comes back, she's gonna want her stuff." She hugged the soft black sweater around her, looked away as she smoked.

I watched her in the empty night. She brushed again at the spot where ash had fallen. I said, "I'm sorry."

"Oh, don't be an asshole!" she hissed. She might have been about to say something else, but the bar's door opened, spilling light, music, and four laughing people out into the night. They stood briefly in the lot, ending the evening together, the men's voices loud, the women's harder to hear. Car doors opened and closed, engines growled, and two sets of headlights swept past us onto 30.

Ginny Sanderson jumped lightly off my car, moved beyond it to where the headlights didn't reach. "Nobody better see me here," she said.

"Why not?"

She looked at me with a nasty smile. "Because if my dad knows you found me and didn't bring me home you'll be in really deep shit. He'll probably fuck you up anyway if you don't find me, but this would really piss him off. He said that, right? That he'd fuck you up?"

I didn't answer, but whatever she saw in my face made her nod. "That's him," she said. "He never just asks you to do something. Like it never occurs to him you might want to anyway, or you don't but if he paid you or something you would. He always has to tell you how bad he's going to fuck you up. That's why my mom ran away. You know," she said, fast, as though to prevent me from speaking, "you're some dumb detective. You never even asked me what I'm doing here."

"You want something," I said.

"Well, duh! If you're so smart, what do I want?"

"I don't know. But I want something too: I want Jimmy's truck, and I want the things that were stolen from Eve Colgate's storeroom."

Her eyes widened quickly; then she laughed. "You used that one already, saying something to confuse me. Are you supposed to be a good detective?"

"Probably not. But I get the feeling you're not such a good kid, either."

She snorted. "Different meanings of 'good,' Mr. Bigshot. Don't do that shit with me. I'm in Honors English."

"Not anymore this semester, from what I hear."

"That was bullshit!" She glanced at me sharply.

"That's what your father told me, too. Not his innocent little princess."

"He's an asshole," she couldn't help saying. "But anyway, now I can go somewhere else next year. Maybe Europe or something. I hated that dump anyway."

"If I tell Sheriff Brinkman you've been fencing stolen property, you might not be going anywhere."

"Who, Robocop?" She was scornful, unimpressed with my threat. "You think my dad would let him anywhere near me? Besides"—she leaned back against my car, blew a stream of smoke into the sky—"I don't know what the fuck you're talking about."

"I don't believe you."

She eyed me thoughtfully. With a well-bred, ladylike smile, she inquired, "Who fucking cares? Anyway, forget that crazy lady and her shit. I thought you wanted to know who killed Wally."

I dropped my cigarette to the ground, crushed it. "Do you know?"

She shrugged. "Everyone says it was Jimmy."

"Was it?"

"How the hell am I supposed to know? But Jimmy's in deep shit, huh? Do you know where he is?"

"That's what you were looking for me for? You want to know where Jimmy is?"

"Hey, you figured it out! You *are* a great detective!"

"Why do you want him?"

Her voice became coy. "I can help him." She waved her cigarette casually in the darkness. "You're not the only one who knows smart lawyers and shit like that. I can help Jimmy more than you can. Only I bet you don't even know where he is."

"Why would you want to help him? You walked out on him."

"He told you that?" she asked slyly.

"Everyone knows," I countered.

She shrugged again, temporarily out of dumb detective tricks. "So what? I can still want to help him."

"Then tell me who has the truck."

"Okay," she said teasingly, "if you tell me where he is."

"Did you use the truck when you robbed Eve Colgate?"

As I spoke, a car cut around the curve of 30, swept us with headlights as it pulled into the lot. Ginny Sanderson stepped into the shadows again. When Antonelli's door had shut behind the driver and the night was ours again, she threw her cigarette away, still burning, like the one before it. "Oh, fuck this shit," she said. "I'm getting the fuck out of here. This is a drag."

She brushed past me to her car, pulled open the door, slid behind the wheel. As the engine roared to life and the loud bass thump of the stereo began to pound, she lowered the black-glass window.

"If you want to know where the fucking truck is, just tell anyone at the Creekside you want to see me."

She reversed hard, close to me, then tore onto the road.

Her red taillights whipped around the curve much too fast, and were gone.

The drive to Eve Colgate's wasn't long. The bare branches of the trees were being tossed violently now, and dead leaves scraped across the road in front of me. I drove carefully, my mind on other things.

Leo came charging to the doorbell, barking loudly. I heard Eve reassuring him as she shot the bolt and drew the door open.

She smiled, stood aside to let me pass. I walked through out of the cold wind into the warm, neat room, where the odor of damp earth was replaced by a rich confusion of herbs, garlic, tomatoes, meat. Steam fogged the windows. The table was set with woven mats, wineglasses, white china. There was music, not Schubert anymore, but Chopin, a nocturne I used to play. Hearing it now, I couldn't remember why I'd stopped.

Leo followed me, wagging, looking up; I reached down to pet him and he sniffed my hand expectantly. "Oh," I said. "Sorry, old buddy. Nothing for you."

"It's just as well," Eve said. "You were spoiling him." She took my jacket, hung it in the vestibule next to the yellow slicker. I shrugged off my shoulder holster, slipped it over another hook.

Her eyebrows raised slightly. "You don't have to," she said.

"It makes you uncomfortable."

She moved around me into the kitchen. "I just wonder how it must feel to live with what it means."

"You get used to what protects you."

"Yes," she said. "Yes, I suppose that's true."

She lifted the cover from an enameled steel pot on the stove. A cloud of steam rolled up as she added wine from an open bottle.

"Sit down," she said. "It'll be another few minutes."

I stood on the polished floor by the ivory wool couch like a tractor at Tiffany's. "Let me clean up first."

"There's a bathroom under the stairs."

I went and used it, scrubbing rock dust from my hands, my arms, my face. I examined the face critically in the mirror as I dried off on a thick, soft towel. Dark eyes, too deep and too tired; the etched lines that smokers get, on the forehead, around the eyes and mouth; crooked nose and a lumpy jaw. Dark hair, rapidly graying. And the new addition, a collection of scratches and bruises in the ugly colors of healing on the left cheek. Clean, the face was better, but it would never be good.

Back in the living room, I chose the chair, whose dark upholstery gave it a fighting chance to handle the dirt I hadn't been able to brush from my clothes.

"Do you want wine?" Eve asked. "I haven't got anything else except brandy. But this is good."

She brought over the glasses from the table, handed me one, poured a garnet-colored wine into it and into the other. I tasted it. It was liquid silk and it had no argument with Tony's bourbon.

Eve settled on the end of the couch nearest the chair. Her clear eyes swept over me, face, hands, dirt, everything. She said, "Shall we talk business before dinner?"

I put my wineglass down. "The blond girl," I said. "When I called you before, it was because I thought I knew who she was. Now I'm sure, I've seen her. It could be a problem for you."

She said nothing, watched my face.

"Her name is Ginny Sanderson. She's Mark Sanderson's daughter."

"He's a powerful man," she said after a moment. "Is that what you mean?"

"Only part of it. I also think she's mixed up in this murder, the guy in Tony's basement. If she is, your robbery may be, too."

She sipped her wine while Chopin's ambiguous tones flowed around us.

"Why do you think that?" she asked quietly.

I told her about Ginny, and about Wally Gould and

Frank Grice and who Frank Grice was. I told her about
the blue truck waiting outside the antique shop for Ginny
Sanderson, and about the keys that I'd found on the concrete floor by Wally Gould's body.

"The keys were to that same truck? How do you know
that?"

"I don't, not for sure. But Jimmy Antonelli owns a blue
four-by-four. It's been missing for a couple of days. The
keys I found were his."

"Oh," she said softly. "Poor Tony. Does he know that?"

"That the keys are Jimmy's? Yes. But I haven't told
him about Ginny Sanderson and the truck."

Eve's lined face seemed paler than before. Leo nuzzled
her hand and she scratched him absently, sipping wine,
thinking her own thoughts. She said, "You say you spoke
to her . . . ?"

I nodded. "She claims she doesn't know anything about
your robbery. I'm pretty sure she's lying, though I guess
it's possible she's just fencing things and doesn't know
where they came from. But, Eve, if she's got the truck, it
could connect her to both crimes. If that's true I don't
know how long I can keep your robbery a private problem."

She searched my face. "There's something you're not
telling me."

I thought about Jimmy, alone up at the quarry, and nodded again. "But it wouldn't help."

She surveyed her own living room minutely, intensely.
It was something she must have done a million times.

"Is there something you want me to do?" she asked me
finally.

"No. Give me more time. I'll try, Eve. I know how
important it is; that's why I didn't push Ginny when I saw
her tonight. I wanted to talk to you first. If there's any way
I can keep it from coming out, I will. But I wanted you
to know."

Eve was silent. Dragged by the wind, branches scraped

across her roof. The approaching storm weighed on the air.

"All right," she said, standing. "If things have to change, will you tell me first?"

"I promise."

She looked at me for a few moments. Then she walked over to the stove. Leo jumped to back around the couch stood, too.

"or not," she said, "there's still beef stew. Why don't you pour more wine?" She put the enameled pot on the table. "And you can change the music, or turn it off, if you want. I should have said that before."

The nocturnes had given way to Chopin mazurkas. "No," I said. "It's fine. I haven't heard these pieces in a long time."

"You know this music?"

"Yes."

She smiled. "I'm intrigued. I suppose I always thought of the detective business as rather sordid."

"It is. But I'm not sure it's any dirtier than cows and chickens."

She brought a round, crusty loaf out of the oven, set it on the table next to a dish of butter flecked with herbs. "Cows are much more decent than people," she said.

"Well, maybe. But not chickens. My grandmother kept chickens in our backyard in Louisville. I know all their secrets."

"Is that where you grew up? Louisville?"

"We left there when I was nine, but yes, until then."

"Where did you go then?"

"Thailand," I said. "South Korea, West Germany, the Philippines, Holland. My father was an army quartermaster. We lived in a lot of exotic places; when I was fifteen we moved to Brooklyn."

She nodded. "Exotic."

The last thing she did before sitting was to feed two more logs into the iron stove on the hearth.

"Well, it's not fancy," she said. "But you won't be hungry."

It wasn't fancy, but it was great. The stew was thick with beef, and the beef was tender. Chunks of carrots, potatoes, onions, and stewed tomatoes glistened in a garlicky broth. The bread was dense and slightly sour, butter sweet.

Eve Colgate and I drank more wine, and we talked, the in the silences we listened to Chopin and to the wind.

I admired her house, the spare completeness of it.

"I've been here thirty years. Things get completed, over time."

"Not always."

She poured wine for me, some for herself. "Where do you live, when you're in the city?"

"Downtown. Laight Street."

"What's it like?"

"The neighborhood? Changing."

"Your place, I meant."

"A friend of mine owns the building, and the bar downstairs. Years ago I helped him fix up the bar and the two upstairs floors. He has storerooms and an office on the second floor and I live on the third."

"You have no neighbors?"

"It's better that way."

"Why do you come here?" she asked me.

I sipped my wine. "Even fewer neighbors."

That was true, and in some ways the real reason; and in some ways, about as evasive an answer as I'd ever given to any question. Eve looked at me. She smiled, and in her smile it seemed to me she understood both the truth and the evasion.

I buttered a last piece of bread. "Why did you choose this place, Eve? When you left New York, why come here?"

She didn't answer right away. "Henri and I had come here for three summers, renting a cabin, the way you did

"Well, it's not fancy," she said. "But you won't be hungry."

It wasn't fancy, but it was great. The stew was thick with beef, and the beef was tender. Chunks of carrots, potatoes, onions, and stewed tomatoes glistened in a garlicky broth. The bread was dense and slightly sour, the butter sweet.

Eve Colgate and I drank more wine, and we talked, and in the silences we listened to Chopin and to the wind.

I admired her house, the spare completeness of it.

"I've been here thirty years. Things get completed, over time."

"Not always."

She poured wine for me, some for herself. "Where do you live, when you're in the city?"

"Downtown. Laight Street."

"What's it like?"

"The neighborhood? Changing."

"Your place, I meant."

"A friend of mine owns the building, and the bar downstairs. Years ago I helped him fix up the bar and the two upstairs floors. He has storerooms and an office on the second floor and I live on the third."

"You have no neighbors?"

"It's better that way."

"Why do you come here?" she asked me.

I sipped my wine. "Even fewer neighbors."

That was true, and in some ways the real reason; and in some ways, about as evasive an answer as I'd ever given to any question. Eve looked at me. She smiled, and in her smile it seemed to me she understood both the truth and the evasion.

I buttered a last piece of bread. "Why did you choose this place, Eve? When you left New York, why come here?"

She didn't answer right away. "Henri and I had come here for three summers, renting a cabin, the way you did across her roof. The approaching storm weighed on the air.

"All right," she said, standing. "If things have to change, will you tell me first?"

"I promise."

She looked at me for a few moments. Then she walked back around the couch, over to the stove. Leo jumped to his feet, followed her. I stood, too.

"Trouble or not," she said, "there's still beef stew. Why don't you pour more wine?" She put the enameled pot on the table. "And you can change the music, or turn it off, if you want. I should have said that before."

The nocturnes had given way to Chopin mazurkas. "No," I said. "It's fine. I haven't heard these pieces in a long time."

"You know this music?"

"Yes."

She smiled. "I'm intrigued. I suppose I always thought of the detective business as rather sordid."

"It is. But I'm not sure it's any dirtier than cows and chickens."

She brought a round, crusty loaf out of the oven, set it on the table next to a dish of butter flecked with herbs. "Cows are much more decent than people," she said.

"Well, maybe. But not chickens. My grandmother kept chickens in our backyard in Louisville. I know all their secrets."

"Is that where you grew up? Louisville?"

"We left there when I was nine, but yes, until then."

"Where did you go then?"

"Thailand," I said. "South Korea, West Germany, the Philippines, Holland. My father was an army quartermaster. We lived in a lot of exotic places; when I was fifteen we moved to Brooklyn."

She nodded. "Exotic."

The last thing she did before sitting was to feed two more logs into the iron stove on the hearth.

Tony's father's. I suppose I wanted to be where I'd been happy. With him."

She rose, went to the kitchen, put water on for coffee. I started to clear the dishes. "I'll wash," I said.

"No," she said. "There's almost nothing. I'll do it later."

"It's my only domestic talent. Let me exercise it."

"I doubt that that's true. I think you're capable of being quite domestic, in your way."

"In my way," I agreed. I did the dishes.

We drank coffee, ate pears and some Gorgonzola cheese that looked older than I was. We talked some more. Then the Chopin was over, and the coffee was gone, and I had work to do.

I called Lydia before I left. It must have been both my night and not my night: She answered the phone herself.

"Where's your mom?" I asked her.

"Playing mah-jongg at Mrs. Lee's. Don't try to make up by being solicitous about my mother."

"Still mad?"

"Why wouldn't I be? Has something changed? Are you about to tell me what's going on?"

I looked over at Eve putting dishes in cabinets. "Not here," I said. "Not now."

"Uh-huh. Well, good-bye. I have to go to the Port Authority to collect your package. I assume I still work for you?"

"God," I said. "Yeah, uh-huh, sure. And there's something else I want you to do."

"You're lucky I don't have another case right now. But I'm raising my rates."

"I'll pay anything." I had a feeling that was truer than I knew. "You know Appleseed Baby Foods?"

"Baby food's not exactly my specialty. Is that the one with the babies and fruits all over the label?"

"Yes. It's owned by a guy named Mark Sanderson. He lives up here; I'm not sure where. The Appleseed plant is up here, too," I added, realizing she probably didn't know that. "I want dirt. Get a skip tracer, someone with a computer who can chase paper for us."

"Us?"

I let that one drop. "Get Velez, he's good."

"Are *we* looking for anything specific?" she asked.

"No, and there may not be anything at all. It's just a hunch. But whatever there is, I want it. Tell Velez sooner is better than later. You have anything new on the other thing?"

"The paintings? I would have told you if I had," she said. "You're sure they were stolen? You're sure they exist?"

The woodstove clanged as Eve opened it, fed another log into the fire. "Yes," I told Lydia.

"Well, I'll keep looking. But if they do, I think they're on ice."

"I think you're right. I'll call you in the morning."

"Lucky me."

We both hung up. Eve brought my jacket and shoulder rig in from the hook where I'd left them. "What are you going to do now?" she asked.

"I'm going to talk to Ginny Sanderson again."

"At her father's?"

"No, she's not there. He told me this afternoon she hadn't been home for a few days. But Grice lives in Cobleskill. I'm going there."

She caught my eyes with hers. "If these people are what you say, if they're involved in murder . . . Be careful, Bill. My paintings aren't that important."

"To you they are."

"Not that important."

We walked together across the porch, down the steps. "Thanks for dinner," I said.

She smiled. "I don't have guests very often. I'm glad you came."

Leo bounded down the steps and sniffed circles in the driveway. The cold wind tossed the tops of the trees around as yellow light spilled from the windows of the house. I took her hand, squeezed it lightly; then, feeling suddenly unsure, I let it go. I turned up my collar against the wind, walked down the driveway toward my car.

TWELVE

I headed along 10 in the direction of Cobleskill, but I didn't get that far.

After the driveway there was a wide curve around the wooded slope where Eve's land came up to meet the road. The other side of the road was flat farmland, and my eyes traveled restlessly over the fields and down the slope, for no reason I could name. In the deep emptiness of the wind-swept night there was nothing to see.

But there was: off to my right, way down the slope, lights. Headlights, double, one set white, one piercing yellow, spaced widely, the way they would be on a truck. And near them, a paler glow, light through a window.

I stopped the car. This was Eve's land. Her studio stood at the end of a road, a road from the valley. I wasn't sure that clearing was what I was looking at now, but as I watched the headlights swing around and start to move off, it suddenly seemed like something I wanted to know more about.

I didn't know where the road came out down in the valley and it would have taken me twenty minutes to get there anyway. The truck would have to do without me. But the paler light still shone, and there might be something in that. I pulled off, parked, started down the slope on foot.

The darkness and winter brush made it slow going. Wind swept through the trees, swirled leaves, shook branches. It carried on it the scent of rain. There was no moon to help me; my footing was uncertain. I could have used the flashlight, but there might be someone still down there, and getting myself noticed wasn't the point.

From the bottom of the slope across thirty feet of clearing I saw my hunch was right: The building with the lit windows was Eve's studio. The glow was gentle and even, the light diffused through the frosted glass. The door was open a few inches, throwing a rod of light across the clearing toward where I'd stopped at the edge of the woods.

I began to inch around the clearing, keeping behind the trees, to where I could approach the building from the rear. There was only the one door, but I could work my way back to it against the wall of the building, which seemed a better idea than strolling across thirty feet of empty space.

It might have been, too; or it might have worked out the same in either case. I never had time to think about that. The only thought I had, as a shadowed figure rose suddenly at the edge of my vision, pain exploded in the back of my head, and the world turned red for an instant and then softly black, was that my woodsmanship wasn't what it ought to be.

I was dreaming of a dark beach, late night, winter. Billowing sheets of rain, gray-green water folded into sludgy, pounding waves. I shivered on the wet sand; icy spray broke over me.

In the shelter of a dune was a house with golden windows. Music came softly from it. Schubert, I thought, but I wasn't sure. It would be warm inside; someone kind would be there. I tried to head toward it, but my feet wouldn't move.

I turned my back on the house, walked slowly down the beach into the cold, thick water, looking for something I knew I wouldn't find.

There was water everywhere, cold water, rushing past me, sweeping over me. I opened my eyes, saw nothing. I was lying face down in water, tasting it in the mud in my open mouth. But this wasn't the ocean, and the dream was over.

I tried to look around. A pounding in my head made it harder. There was darkness, there were trees. There was rain, lashing through the trees and darkness, racing over the ground where I was.

I was soaked through. The skin on my thighs was numb where I lay in the cold water. My scalp was tight with the cold and I felt my back trying to pull away from the heavy weight of my sodden jacket. I started to shiver.

I pushed my shoulders off the ground, to get up, but hot nausea rose in me and I collapsed back onto the leaves and twigs and icy water. I lay there, listening to my breath rasping in and out, as the dizzying pain in the back of my head faded.

I tried, very slowly, to get up again. I became aware of noise: wind shrieking through the trees, branches creaking and cracking against each other, the percussion of rain pounding the ground around me. The duller, desolate sound of the drops as they hit my jacket. My own voice, wordless and hoarse.

I made myself stand.

Water ran down my neck, oozed inside my sleeves. I shook uncontrollably. My body tried to fold in on itself, to escape the icy, burning bitterness. The wind changed directions, blasted me from the front; my eyes began to tear, but they hadn't been clear anyway.

I didn't know where I was. I didn't know where to go. I didn't know anything at all, except the agony of the cold and the dazedness I couldn't clear. Finally I took a clumsy step, then another, because movement was better than standing still and anywhere was better than here.

After a time that was not long, or maybe a thousand years, I had to rest. I leaned against a tree, tried to catch my breath. All the world was in motion. The wind screamed and the rain drummed and I was shaking and unsure. I looked up, around.

Above me, up a slope through the trees: light. Yellow

light. I blinked, passed a hand over my eyes. The light was still there. Lights, maybe; or maybe that was me. But something was there and I headed for it, crashing through what I could, going around what I had to, always my eyes fixed on the light.

It was uphill and I climbed. I pushed my feet into the mud, strained against tree roots and branches. My legs were sluggish, slow to respond, as though they were only half listening.

There was a searing flash and a bone-splitting thunder crack. Negative became positive and then black again and what I'd reached for wasn't there. I slipped and fell. The pain in my head wouldn't quit, and needles of rain swept across my face as I lay listening to rushing water and the pounding of my heart.

I wanted to stop trying then, to stay where I was, to wait for the cold and the pain and the noise to end.

But there was light; I could see it. Where the light was maybe it was warm and maybe it was quiet.

Better than quiet: Maybe there was music.

With a groan I rolled to my feet. Slowly, as though with glue in my veins, some steps forward; then some more.

The trees ended.

I held onto the last one, looking. The space before me was dark and full of rain, but nothing else. Nothing to hold onto; but nothing, anymore, between me and the light.

It was harder, without the trees and brush. Each step had to be sure. The ground still sloped uphill and the wind was hard. But the light was closer now, I could tell that. It was golden and square and must come from windows, from someplace warm, a house, someone's home. It had to.

And then it was gone. I blinked, stared, tried to bore through the darkness with my eyes. Maybe I was wrong about the trees. Maybe something was standing between me and the light, something I could go around.

I took some more steps; my knees became rubbery.

There were no trees. There was nothing there, nothing hiding the light. It was gone.

Like a puppet whose string had been cut, I sank slowly to the ground. The water rushed past me, splattered over me, pushed by a screaming wind. As I was swallowed by darkness and cold, I was sorry that I hadn't reached the glowing house, because I'd wanted to hear the music.

THIRTEEN

Silence. Warmth. A pale, gray light. Softness against my skin when I moved; but pain then, too.

Later, the gray light again, and less pain, pain that had shrunk, settled behind my left ear and in my left shoulder. There was softness everywhere, around me and under me, and warmth, and quiet.

In the gray light things came slowly into focus, soft-edged and gentle. A table; a cedar chest; a woodstove set into a fireplace between two uncurtained windows. Through the windows, rolling clouds and the blowing tops of trees.

I was lying on my right side. Heavy wool blankets wrapped me closely. A pillow was under my head, with a smooth, cool cover. I tried to stretch my stiff legs and found I couldn't: there was something in the way.

In a minute, I thought, I'd look and see what.

My mouth was cottony. My bare skin was sticky and tight with dried sweat. I could smell coffee, and the dry sting of woodsmoke in the still air.

I pushed back the blankets some, tried my legs again. They still wouldn't stretch, so I pushed back the blankets some more and tried something else: sitting up.

It was easy, if you didn't count the stiffness and the dizziness. The stiffness stayed with me, but the dizziness passed.

I looked around from my new perspective. I saw my boots, on spread newspapers by the woodstove. I was sitting on an ivory-colored couch not as long as I was tall. I knew this couch; I knew this place. Eve Colgate's house, her living room.

On the easy chair was a pile of clothes, my jeans, my shirt, my underwear, all folded and stacked as if they'd just come back from the laundry. On the cedar chest, in a big wooden bowl, some other things: my wallet, keys, cigarettes, junk from my pockets. My gun, the holster coiled beside it.

The story behind this, I told myself, has got to be good. I couldn't wait to hear it.

I stood, creaking like a rusty hinge. I made my way to the pile of clothes on the chair, pulled on my shorts. Minimally decent, I kept going, to the small bathroom under the stairs.

I took a piss it felt like I'd been waiting a week to take. Then I turned on the water in the sink. The rush of it, loud in the silence, made me vaguely uneasy. I filled the bathroom tumbler, drained it three times. The water was sharp and sweet.

The face in the mirror looked worse than it had last time I'd seen it: pale, stubble-covered, and old.

I soaked a hand towel in hot water, used it to wash everywhere I could reach. I took a look at my shoulder. A messy-looking bruise was coming up inboard of the shoulder blade, more or less in line with the aching place behind my ear.

Something, or someone, had hit me pretty hard.

I wandered back out to the living room, pulled on my jeans. They were as stiff as I was. I maneuvered my undershirt on with as little use of my left shoulder as I could manage, which was not little enough.

Then I had done enough hard work for a while. I reached into the wooden bowl for the unopened pack of Kents that lay there, then went to the woodstove for a kitchen match.

I dropped back down onto the couch, rested my elbows on my knees. I drew smoke in, streamed it out, probed the blank space in my memory for a way in. The cigarette was almost gone when I heard the front door open.

I grabbed my gun from the bowl, held it out of sight. I didn't stand; I was steadier seated. The door closed; there were sounds in the vestibule. The inner door opened and Leo trotted through.

When he saw me he scrabbled over to the couch, wagging everything from his neck back. He put his front paws on my knee and stuck his face up near mine, licked my chin. I scratched his ears with my left hand, which was holding the cigarette. I figured that was better than my right one, where the gun was.

"Leo!" Eve said, coming through the inner door. "Get down!"

He did, sitting in front of me, lifting a paw excitedly, scratching at my knee.

I put the gun down as Eve walked around the cedar chest, came to stand in front of me.

"How do you feel?" she asked.

"Tired." A half dozen other words came to mind, but that one got there first.

She nodded. "You had a bad night. You ran a fever. I don't think you really slept until almost dawn."

"What happened?" I asked her.

She frowned. "I was waiting for you to wake up so you could tell me that."

I made no answer.

Eve moved around the couch to the kitchen. "Do you think you could handle a cup of coffee?"

"God, yes."

She brought me one, and one for herself. The coffee was rich and fragrant and hot. I gulped at it.

She moved what was left of the laundry pile onto the cedar chest, settled herself in the chair.

"I found you," she said. "About an hour after you left here last night, just down the hill." She gestured toward the slope outside the windows, where the scrub trees began about ten yards from the house.

"Found me," I repeated stupidly. I wasn't sure I was following her.

"Well, Leo did. Something strange happened. Something . . . frightening."

"Tell me."

She sipped at her coffee. "I got a phone call, maybe forty-five minutes after you left. A man's voice, I think, but whispering, so I really don't know. 'Your friend Smith,' it said. 'He's down the hill from your place. It's a bad night to be out.' "

I sipped my coffee, tried to understand this. She went on, "He hung up. I didn't know what he meant, down the hill, but I took Leo and went out. Leo found you, lying just where the trees start, only half-conscious." She stopped, studied me. "You don't remember? You were soaking wet; you were freezing."

I shook my head. "No. How did I get here?"

"Back to the house? You walked." She smiled her small smile. "You didn't want to. You kept telling me to leave you alone. I began to get desperate. It's a way of conserving heat, that refusal to move, but it really would have killed you. Alcohol's not the best thing for someone whose body temperature's dropped as low as yours had, but it feels good, and you needed motivation. I came back for the brandy." Her smile faded. "You don't remember any of this?"

I shook my head. Leo, who had climbed onto the pile of blankets beside me, rearranged himself with a happy sigh.

"Actually," Eve said, "I think Leo saved your life."

I raised my eyebrows, looked at the dog.

"Besides finding you, I mean. When I ran back here for the brandy, I covered you with my slicker and told him to get under it and stay with you until I came back. I think his being there kept you just warm enough to stay conscious. Then I gave you brandy and told you you'd die if you didn't get up and come with me." She smiled again. "And you told me to go to hell.

"But you got up. It took a couple of tries. I was afraid that you couldn't. It was obvious you were hurt. I was trying to think what to do if you really couldn't walk, but you did get up, and you leaned on me and we came here."

She made that last part sound easy.

When she'd come through the door her cheeks had been glowing from the wind, but as we'd talked the color had faded, and I saw now that her eyes were dark-ringed and her skin was patchy and dull.

"You haven't slept," I said.

She shrugged, finished her coffee. Over her shoulder, framed in the squares of the window, leafless branches danced in a gusting wind.

"Thanks," I said. It was dust when it should have been diamonds, but when I said it she lifted her eyes to mine and smiled.

She stood, got the coffeepot from the stove, refilled our mugs. Small, everyday blessings. I drank.

"Why were you there?" she asked. "Why did you come back? Who called me?"

I passed my hand over my eyes. Something was in the back of my brain, but it was darkness and noise. "I don't know." .

I drank more coffee. "I remember leaving after dinner, driving away. No, wait—" The coffee was nudging something forward, like an indulgent aunt with a shy child whose turn it was to recite. "Light. I wanted to reach the light." That seemed right, but I didn't know what it meant.

"Where?"

I pulled out another cigarette, dropped the pack back in the bowl. I lit another match. With the flare came a sudden burst of memory. "Your studio. In your studio. There were lights down there as I came around the curve, so I parked the car and went down to look."

"Lights in my studio? Last night? What—who was there?"

I reached, but there was nothing. "I don't know. I came close, but I don't think I got there." A dark figure, a shadow in the shadows. "Someone was waiting. He hit me from behind. I didn't see him."

"Someone was waiting for you? Someone wanted to kill you?" Her voice might have cracked, but if it did she got it back under control fast.

"No. They couldn't have known I'd come, couldn't have even known I'd see the light. And I would've been easy to kill, once I was down. I was even carrying a gun, if he didn't want to use his own."

"But you could have died. But they didn't want you to, or they wouldn't have called here. I don't understand. Why do that to you, and then call me?"

I thought about that. "Something was going on that someone didn't want me to know about, or screw up. But there's been one death already; maybe they thought another would call down more heat than they were ready to take. I suppose they could have ditched my body where it wouldn't be found"—Eve cradled her coffee as though her hands were suddenly cold—"but I'm too high-profile right now to just disappear. Brinkman would love nothing better than for me to just turn around and go back to the city, but he knows I won't, so if I disappeared he and Mac-Gregor would know something was up. No, as long as they make sure I don't know what the hell's going on, I must be less trouble alive than dead. So they got me out of the way, got their business done, and called you."

"Got their business done. In my studio." Eve's mouth was drawn into a thin line.

I picked up the gun again and did what I hadn't done before: broke it open, emptied it, tested the action. It worked. It always worked, rain, snow, sleet, or gloom of night. The mail used to be like that, too.

I reloaded the gun, put it down, went and got my socks and boots. The boots were tight and not quite dry, the laces squeaking a little through the eyeletted holes.

"What are you going to do?" Eve asked me.

"I'm going to have a look around, see if I can figure out what it is I'm not supposed to know."

"Are you sure you're all right?"

"I'm fine." I buttoned my shirt. I slipped my holster on, moved the strap around on my left shoulder searching for a comfortable, or at least bearable, way to wear it. There wasn't one. I took it off.

Leo had jumped off the couch as soon as I stood; now he was sitting by the door, brushing the floor with his tail. Suddenly his back bristled. He spun to face the door, started to bark.

"Someone's coming," Eve said.

She opened the inner door, stepped through the vestibule, Leo barking furiously beside her. I followed her out onto the porch, in time to see the sheriff's car roll to a stop in the driveway in front of the house.

Brinkman unfolded his long, booted legs from the car's passenger-side door. The heavy deputy got out the other side. Eve told Leo to stay on the porch with us and he did, growling deep in his throat.

Brinkman's face was unreadable as he stood at the bottom of the porch steps looking up. "Well," he finally said. "You sure do turn up in the strangest places, city boy."

"Is there a problem, Sheriff?" Eve asked.

"Well, ma'am, maybe not," Brinkman drawled. "I just came by to ask what you know about a car parked a half mile west of here, along Ten. An Acura." He looked at me. "Six, seven years old. Gray." Back to her: "Before I get it towed."

"Oh, Christ, Brinkman," I said wearily. "You know it's mine." Even on the protected porch the wind was cold. I suppressed a shiver.

He nodded unhurriedly. "What's it doing there?"

"I had trouble."

"When?"

"Last night."

"In the storm?"

"Before that."

"So you came here and bothered the lady?"

"Thank you for your concern, Sheriff," Eve said. "But Mr. Smith is a friend of mine."

"Well, that's fine. I worry about you, is all, Miss Colgate. All alone out here like you are."

Eve smiled. "I've managed over the years, thank you."

"Yes, ma'am, you have. Though you might want to be a little careful how you choose your friends."

"I am," Eve said. "Very careful."

Brinkman smiled pleasantly, nodded. "Your power and phone back on yet?"

"Yes," she answered. "Since about nine."

"Good. Then Smith can get a tow truck for that car. Save the county money." His grin turned nasty. "Why don't you call Obermeyer's? I hear they got a kid there real good with Jap cars."

"I hear he hasn't been in much lately," I said.

"That so? You suppose he's on vacation?"

I shrugged. "Florida's popular this time of year."

"Yeah, but it's no fun alone. You know a girl name of Alice Brown?"

"I met her yesterday."

"You were looking for Jimmy Antonelli, she says."

"That's true."

"You find him?"

"She said she didn't know where he was."

"She told me that, too. You believe her?"

"Most women don't lie to me until they know me better."

"I got the pretty boys from the state to put a tail on her."

"Good luck."

"She's too high class for that punk, anyhow."

"I liked her, too."

"But what I hear," he said, lifting his hat, scratching his high, domed forehead, "what I hear, he had a new sweetie anyway. Mark Sanderson's little girl. Sweet, blond, and fifteen. And guess what?"

"Tell me."

"Her daddy hasn't seen her for days." He settled his hat. "God, I hope you're right about Florida, Smith. Lot of state lines between here and there." He shook his head, chuckling to himself. "Hey, he's not at your place, is he, Smith?"

"No."

"Well, you're right. We looked."

"You searched my place?"

He made an innocent face. "We had a warrant. Nice place, too. Nice piano. Course, alls I can play is 'Chopsticks,' none of that culture stuff you city folks go in for. But it sounded pretty good. Didn't it, Art?" Behind his sunglasses the deputy nodded.

The thought of Brinkman's long, mean fingers banging on my piano brought hot blood to my face. "Brinkman—" I started, stopped as Eve's hand closed on my arm.

Brinkman smiled, walked back around the cruiser, pulled the door open. "Get that car taken care of, Smith," he said. "That's a bad stretch, and I don't want no more trouble on that damn road."

"No more than what?"

He leaned on the top of the car. "You folks had better things to do last night than listen to the radio, huh?

"Well, seems someone else had a problem, too. Someone in a blue Chevy truck. Ran off the road down there in the valley, flipped into the gorge. We're pulling it out now. Made a helluva mess." He grinned a grin that showed me all his teeth.

My heart jolted. "Who?" I asked. He didn't answer. "Goddammit, Brinkman, who was in the truck?"

"What the hell you getting so excited about? Who're you expecting was in the truck?"

I started to move down the steps toward him, but Eve held my arm.

"Sheriff, who was it?" she asked.

"Well, ma'am," Brinkman drawled, "well, that's the strange thing." He adjusted his hat again. "Doesn't seem to have been anyone in it."

"What the hell is this, Brinkman?"

"You tell me, city boy. Why would someone send a new Chevy four-by-four into the ravine, just to stand there and watch it fall?"

"How do you know no one was in it?"

"Shape that truck was in, if anyone'd been in it we'd be scraping 'em off the insides now."

"Maybe the driver was thrown."

"Well, now, we thought of that, too. Checked the area, but damned if we didn't come up empty." He started to get into the car, paused as if struck by a sudden thought. "Now, no one being in that truck doesn't mean it wasn't interesting."

"In what way?" I asked. My hands were clenching and unclenching themselves.

"Two ways. One, seems to be a little blood smeared on the seat. Not a lot, just a little. And the other, there's this nine-millimeter automatic we pulled from the cab." He grinned a final grin, said, "See you around, Smith. Miss Colgate, you take care of yourself."

He and the deputy climbed back in the car. They U-turned in the driveway, drifted slowly under the bare chestnuts back to the road.

"Why does he dislike you so?" Eve asked as we headed down the hill behind the house, Leo charging back and forth beside us.

"Last fall," I said, "when he picked up Jimmy, what he really wanted to do was get his hands on Frank Grice."

"The man you told me about?"

"Yes. He wants Grice badly. But he can't make anything stick to him. Grice is always a step ahead. It drives Brinkman crazy."

"Well, he is the sheriff, and this man Grice is a criminal."

"It's beyond that. This is Brinkman's county. Grice isn't just a crook, he's an outsider. Like I am."

Pushed by a strong wind, the heavy clouds were rushing west, but the sky they left behind remained dull and gray.

I turned up my collar. Eve, beside me, wore only her sweatshirt over a sweater, and didn't seem to mind the cold. Or maybe it really wasn't that cold at all.

I went on. "Grice had people running drugs from Florida to Albany for an Albany boss, then ditching the courier cars here. That was Jimmy's job, getting rid of the cars. Everybody knew it, but no one could prove it, and Jimmy wouldn't talk. He was offered a deal but he wouldn't take it. He was prepared to go to prison." I shook my head.

"Honor among thieves?" Eve suggested.

"He's a brave, stupid kid. He thinks he's tough, but he'd've been eaten alive. But we were lucky. Brinkman wanted Grice so badly he beat the shit out of Jimmy—" I caught myself. "I'm sorry," I said.

"About what? Your language? Don't patronize me. Besides"—she smiled—"you should have heard yourself last night."

"I can imagine. Anyhow, I got Jimmy a slick city lawyer and we parlayed Brinkman's mistakes into a dismissed case. Brinkman lost Jimmy and he lost Grice and he looked like a fool."

"And he blames you?"

"He's right."

We were walking the way we had walked two days before, through fields now oozing muddy water under every step. Twigs, leaves, and branches forced down by the storm lay on the earth among sprawling puddles. This way to the clearing was longer than the way straight down the slope—the way I'd fought my way up last night—but it was also easier and faster.

"You got quite angry when the sheriff talked about your piano," Eve said, her eyes on me. It occurred to me that she might want to keep talking to keep her mind off where we were going.

"That he played it," I said.

She nodded, but said, "Or that he knows now that you play it?" I didn't answer. "We talked a good deal about

music last night, but you never told me you were a pian-
ist."

My response to that was silence; hers, to my silence,
was an ironic smile. "I suppose, coming from me, that's
an odd complaint."

I smiled at that. "I don't play for other people, ever.
Very few people understand about that. Mostly I don't care
whether they do or not."

"I understand," she said.

"I know," I answered.

We went on in silence for a time, the only sound the
soft grasping noises made by the mud as our feet passed
over it.

"Brinkman asked about the power," I said. "Did the
power go off last night?"

"Yes," she answered. "Not long before I found you. I
saw the lights go off in the house just when Leo ran back
to me, barking."

I'd seen the lights go off in the house, too. I wondered
what it would cost me to get the 7-Eleven to deliver a
doughnut a day to Leo for the rest of his life.

In the clearing the studio looked sturdy and deserted. I kept
my hand on the gun in my pocket just the same.

"Stay here with Leo," I told Eve. "Let me look around."
They stood on the edge of the clearing while I prowled
the road that came up from the valley, but the rain had left
nothing I could read.

I did the same in the clearing, looking for whatever I
could find, but I couldn't find anything. Eve joined me as
I neared the studio door. Things looked in order, but when
she put her hand on the padlock, it twisted open. It had
been cut through.

A tingle went up my spine. I motioned Eve behind me,
took out my gun. I lifted the lock off the door, slid the
door aside, moving with it. Nothing happened: no shots,
no booming voices. I stepped through the doorway in a
quick crouch, swung first left, then right.

No one was there, but they had been.

I stood, pocketed the gun, stretched my arm across the doorway to bar Eve from stepping over the sill.

"My God," I heard her say tonelessly behind me.

The floor of the studio was a storm of color. Paint swept across the wide boards, red and green and purple and blue, mud where they clotted together. Ropes of pigment squirted from stomped tubes across smears and swirls. White gesso puddled around broken quart jars, colors bleeding into it. Thick lumps of black were smeared over stains of crimson and magenta; a yellow pool near the window mocked the gray day. Cans and brushes and palette knives lay in the glistening mess like the branches the wind had brought down last night.

Just inside the door a broom lay in an eddy of paint. It had been used to push and pull and smear the colors on the floor; its paint-covered bristles were broken, sticking out in all directions.

There were no footprints in the paint. The broom had obliterated them.

"My God," Eve said again. Her fingers dug into my arm and she started to move past me.

I grabbed her wrist. "Wait," I said. "Look first."

Her face was flushed. Her eyes flared as she said, "At what? Why?"

"At everything." I searched the floor, starting from where we stood, my eyes sweeping slowly back and forth. "The painting." I pointed across the studio to the half-finished canvas I'd seen Tuesday morning. "Is it all right?"

She stared across the room. "Yes," she said, and I felt her relax slightly. I let go of her wrist.

"What else?" I asked. "What else is wrong?"

"How can I tell?" she exploded, her voice rough-edged. "How can I see through this? What do you want me to tell you? Get out of my way!"

"Eve," I said, and took her hand.

She stood trembling for a moment in the doorway, her eyes moist; then she wiped them with the back of her hand.

Her fingers closed on mine and she was still.

"I'm not sure," she said huskily, after a few moments. "Except for the floor, and the paints and brushes from over there, everything looks all right. The big painting is all right. I can't tell about the ones in the rack from here, but they don't look as though they've been touched. Is that what you want to know?"

"Yes," I said. "It looks that way to me, too." The smells of oil paint and mud mingled in the open doorway. The windows weren't broken; they'd come and gone through the single door. In the city, in the middle of this much deliberate ruin, I'd have expected taunting words, filthy phrases scrawled on the walls, but that hadn't happened either. There was only the sea of paint, submerging the floor. "Let me check around out here once more; then we'll go in."

"Bill," she said suddenly. "Last night you had paint on your neck and chin. Not a lot. I thought it was mud, but it wouldn't come off with water. Is that from when they hit you?"

"It could be."

I circled the building, examining the ground for anything that wasn't mud or leaves or broken branches, but they were all I found.

We went into the studio, Eve and I. Eve told Leo to stay outside and he did, whining. He lay down with his paws on the threshold, followed our movements with his head.

Inside, Eve stopped, stood, as though unsure of what to do. I searched in corners and under furniture for something that would help.

There was nothing.

It took us an hour to clean up.

"There's no reason for you to have to stay," Eve said. "But I can't leave it like this."

I stayed. Eve picked through the paint with an archaeologist's concentration, evaluating each brush and palette

knife according to criteria I didn't understand. Some she
dropped into the garbage bag I was filling; others she left
covered with turpentine in a shallow tray.

We scraped the floor and scrubbed it with turpentine-
soaked rags until a streaky purplish film was all that was
left of the mess. Then we opened the windows to let the
turpentine fumes out, and we left too.

"I'll paint it," Eve said, as we walked back up the hill
to the house. It was close to midday, but the skimmed-
milk sun was having trouble fighting its way through the
clouds. "In a couple of days, when it's really dry, I'll get
deck paint and paint it." She'd been like a taut wire since
we'd entered the studio and we hadn't spoken. But as she
talked about the next step her mouth relaxed and the deep
creases on her forehead smoothed out, the way it happens,
unconsciously, when you step from a dark, unfamiliar
space into one that's lit. "A new lock; maybe even a security system. And I suppose I'll have to go into the city,
to get more paints and things. That's all right. I would
have had to go soon in any case."

"Why?"

"I've completed a painting; in fact it's been done for
weeks. I made the mistake of telling my dealer it's done.
He's too much of a gentleman, and an old friend, to bother
me about it, but I know he's anxious to see it."

"Sternhagen?"

"Ulrich, yes."

"He's a friend of yours?"

"Probably my oldest. He was my dealer thirty-five years
ago; we were friends in art school, before I had anything
to sell. He's the only person in New York who knows
where to find me—where to find Eva Nouvel, I mean."
She paused to look at me. "How did you know who my
dealer was?"

"You're famous."

"Do you know who Robert Rauschenberg's dealer is?"

"No."

She waited. I said, "The investigator I called in New

York thought your gallery would be an obvious place to check, to see if anyone had tried to sell your paintings there. She told me."

"Had they?"

"No."

"It would be a pretty stupid thing to do."

"Not necessarily. It's not that easy to unload stolen art. They might take a chance that your gallery would be interested in splitting the profits on six new paintings without having to cut you in."

"Ulrich would never do that."

"Are you sure?"

"Of course I'm sure! He's a marvelous man and a good friend. If he hadn't been willing to cooperate with me in this—eccentricity—for thirty years, I could not have managed to live the way I have. The way I've wanted."

At the side of the house I dumped the garbage bag in a buried can. We walked around front. On the porch, as she unlocked the door, Eve turned to me. "Ulrich has been good to me in more ways than you can know. I don't think I like the idea of someone bothering him, possibly worrying him on my account."

If she didn't like that idea she'd hate some of the others I was having.

"Eve," I said as I followed her into the living room, "Lydia did some checking in New York, some things I hadn't asked her to do, but I'm glad she did. One of those things was a background check on Sternhagen and his gallery."

She spun to face me, her eyes flashing. "She did *what?* How dare you!"

"She told me he takes an unusually large share of the profits from your work."

Color choked her cheeks. "My arrangements with Ulrich are not your business! I hired you to protect my privacy, not to pry into my life!"

"Lydia's instincts are good," I said. "Maybe it has nothing to do with anything else, but it's unorthodox and she thought I should know. And if you can tell me, I'd like to know why."

"Who the hell do you think you are?" She was taut and trembling, the color gone from her face. The night she'd spent keeping me alive and the morning she'd had and the last six days were suddenly crashing over her like a tidal wave. She was fighting it with anger and the anger was aimed at me, and maybe I deserved it. Nothing good had happened since I'd started working for her.

I watched her struggling for control. I might have gone to her, held her, given her the illusion of safety that someone else's arms can give; but control is different from safety, though they sometimes feel the same. I turned, went quietly out the door, past Leo, who wagged his tail uncertainly as he looked from Eve to me.

I sat on the porch steps, lit a cigarette. I weighed my options, Eve's options, Tony's and Jimmy's options. On the broad sweeping lawn bare tendrils of forsythia were moving lightly in the wind. When the right time came they would flower, flaring like solid sunlight around houses all over these hills. Forsythia lived easily among us, nestling against buildings and fences. It didn't need much care, but it didn't do well alone.

The cigarette was almost gone when I heard the door open behind me. Eve crossed the porch, came and stood near me, arms wrapping her chest as though now she were cold.

"I'm sorry," she began.

"No." I cut her off. "You haven't got anything to apologize for. I'd expect you to be upset and I don't blame you for being upset with me. I haven't done you a hell of a lot of good."

She sat on the step above mine, stared into the distance. "I'm frightened." They didn't sound like words she was used to. "What's happening, Bill? Is it—am I a target for somebody?"

Admitting she was scared gave me an opening I

wouldn't get again, for one of those ideas I knew she'd hate. "Eve, there's something I want you to do. Hear me out before you decide."

Her crystal eyes were uneasy. "What is it?"

"I don't want you to be alone for a while. I want to bring someone up to stay with you."

She looked at me blankly for a moment; then, unexpectedly, she laughed. "You have to be crazy," she said. "I'm the person with two *names*, for God's sake. I'm an eccentric recluse. I'm a hermit. I'm the person who'll do anything to protect her privacy, even hire a private detective!" She laughed again.

"No," I said. "Eva Nouvel is all those things. Eve Colgate is a farmer. She's the least sentimental person I've ever met. She makes decisions and doesn't look back. And she's scared."

The laugh had subsided into a smile; now the smile faded. She looked away. "I don't want this," she said.

"I know you don't."

We watched the forsythia sway with the wind. She said, "You don't think it's vandalism. You don't think it's coincidence."

"No, and you don't either."

"No." She tried a small smile. "But I was hoping you did."

"If there hadn't been a murder," I said, "if Mark Sanderson's daughter hadn't been fencing your things from a truck that rolled over the ravine last night, if everybody I met weren't so anxious to get his hands on Jimmy Antonelli, then I'd say sure. I'd say someone stole the paintings, then got curious about where they came from. They came back to have a look. Maybe they were drunk or stoned and found they could make a hell of a mess and were just getting into it when I came around." I lit another cigarette, cupping it against the wind. "And maybe that's what happened. Maybe the only thing that's tying all these things together in my head is my inability to mind my own business." I turned, faced her. "I don't think so, but of course

I wouldn't. Make your own decision; but I can tell you it will affect what I do from now on."

"How do you mean?"

"If you don't let me get you some protection, I'll spend a lot more time and energy keeping an eye on you, and concentrating on the people I think might be a threat to you. That might not be the same thing as solving your case, or figuring out what the hell is going on around here."

"What if I don't want an eye kept on me?"

"Fire me."

That one dropped to the ground between us.

"Maybe the police will figure out what's going on," she said.

"Maybe they will. But they'll only figure out what they need to know to solve the crime they know about."

"You would feel more free to act," she said slowly, "if I had a baby-sitter?"

"Bodyguard."

"I can't even bring myself to say that. It's so ridiculous."

I didn't answer that. She thought silent thoughts and I smoked and the forsythia danced.

"Who?" she asked me finally.

"Lydia."

"That same detective? The one who snooped into Ulrich's accounts? Living in my house?"

"She's good," I said. "She's done this kind of thing before. She can stay by your side and keep out of your way at the same time. You'll like her."

"I don't think so."

"Eve, remember, when she checked out Sternhagen, she didn't know who my client was. She still doesn't."

"You didn't tell her?"

"No. I told her the client had lost six uncatalogued Eva Nouvels. That's all she had to go on. She was trying everything she could think of, and your gallery was a smart idea."

She stood, hands in her back pockets, and paced. Stopping, she said, "How long?"

"I don't know. I hope not long. I can't tell, Eve."

She paced some more, but not much. "All right," she finally said. "All right. Because I *am* scared. And because you didn't tell her who your client was."

"Good. Let's call her now."

She hesitated. "I've lived alone for thirty years. Now you want me to have someone with me twenty-four hours a day. I won't be good at it."

"Lydia will."

We went back inside. Eve lit the fire in the stove, put on water for coffee. I dialed Lydia's number. I said a prayer, keeping in mind the danger of answered prayers, and when the phone was picked up I got what I'd prayed for: It wasn't the machine and it wasn't her mother.

"Oh," Lydia said coolly, once she knew it was me. "Hello. I wasn't expecting you to call until later. I got Velez, but he's only just started. Should I call him and call you back? In case he has something already?"

"No, that's not why I called."

"Why did you?"

"There's trouble up here, and I need help. Can you come?"

The ice in her voice thawed a little, probably in spite of herself. "What do you mean, trouble?" she asked cautiously. "Are you all right?"

"I'm fine, but things are getting rough. I need someone to stay with the client."

"A baby-sitter?"

"Bodyguard."

Her voice almost smiled. "The client's right there with you, huh?"

"Yes."

She hesitated. "When would I start? Right away?"

"Yes."

She was silent. An image focused itself in my mind, Lydia in her back-room Chinatown office, cloudy light drifting in the pebbled glass window. Maybe she was look-ing at one of the pictures on her wall as she thought; maybe the one I'd given her for Christmas, a shadowy, somber photograph of a city street at night, the buildings dark, the people gone.

"I know you're pissed off," I said. "We can talk about it when you get here. I need you, Lydia."

More silence; then, briskly, "I'll have to organize my mother, and I'll have to rent a car. I could leave by two. For how long?"

"I don't know."

"How do I get there?"

I gave her directions.

"How long will it take me?"

"About four hours, the way you drive."

"How about the way you drive?"

"Two and a half."

"I'll see you at four-thirty."

"Lydia—"

"This isn't just a ploy to get me up there where it's rustic and isolated and romantic?"

The unexpectedness of that question stopped me, made me laugh. "If I thought that would work I'd have tried it long ago."

"You've tried everything else."

"Nice of you to notice."

"See you later."

"Lydia?"

"Umm?"

"It's been rough. It could get rougher."

"Promises, promises," she said in her sweetest tone, and hung up.

Eve brought the mugs to the counter by the phone, filled them.

"Do you want something to eat?"

"No, thanks. I'm not hungry."

"You haven't eaten since dinner last night."

"I'll get something later." I drank my coffee slowly, savoring it.

"She wasn't frightened?" Eve asked. "When you told her it was dangerous?"

"No," I said. "She liked it."

We leaned on opposite sides of the kitchen counter, finishing the coffee. She looked at me over her mug, said nothing, hid her thoughts.

I took my rig from where I'd dropped it on the cedar chest, slung it over my shoulder. I was loading up my pockets with what she'd taken out of them when the phone rang.

"Hello?" she said into the receiver; then, "Yes, in fact, he is. Are you all right?"

I stopped what I was doing, listened.

"All right," she said, half smiling. "I should have known better than to ask. Hold on." She held the receiver out to me. "It's Tony. He's looking for you."

I grabbed it. "Tony? Something wrong?"

"How the hell do I know?" Tony's voice growled out of the phone. "I'm just the messenger boy. You okay?"

"Yeah. Shouldn't I be?"

"You sound lousy."

"Thanks. What's up?"

"Your buddy Sanderson called here lookin' for you. He got kinda steamed when I said you wasn't here drinkin' at ten in the mornin'."

"He has no sense of humor. Did he say what he wanted?"

"No. Place was empty anyhow, so I closed up an' went over to your place, but you wasn't there, either. So I figured I'd check around. Nothin' else to do. Hope I didn't interrupt nothin'."

"You didn't. Thanks, Tony. Anything else new?"

"Not a goddamn thing."

"How're you holding up?"

"Great," he grunted. "Just goddamn great."

"Tony," I said, "You don't know where Frank Grice lives in Cobleskill, do you?"

"How the hell would I know that?"

"Didn't think so. Listen, I'll see you tonight, okay?"

"Yeah, whatever. What do I tell Sanderson if he calls again?"

"Tell him I'll call him when I have something to say."

"You gonna tell me what that means?"

"No."

"Ah, to hell with it, an' you too. An' Sanderson."

"And the horse he rode in on. See you later."

"Yeah," he said, and hung up.

"What was that about?" Eve asked.

"I'm not sure." I stuffed my cigarettes into my shirt pocket, my wallet into my jacket.

"Where are you going?" she asked.

"I have some things to do. You'll be okay for a while; I don't expect anyone will come back so soon."

"I won't be here long, in any case. Harvey's coming to pick me up in half an hour."

I must have looked blank.

"We're going to Albany to look at farm equipment."

"Oh, milking machines. I remember. You'll be with him all afternoon?"

"Yes."

"That's even better." I zipped my jacket. "Meet us at Antonelli's tonight."

"Us?"

"Lydia and me."

"Oh," she said. "Yes, all right." She looked into her coffee; then her crystal eyes met mine with an unexpected swiftness. "Bill?" she said in an unsteady voice. "Who could be doing this to me? Why?"

"I don't know." They were very empty words, but they were what I had. "Maybe," I said, "maybe they're not doing it to you. Maybe you're just in the way. But I don't want you to get hurt."

"The way you did last night, when you were in the way."

"I'm paid for it."

"It's not what I'm paying you for."

"Well, now I'm going to go do what you're paying me for."

I went down the driveway, walking slowly, not stiff anymore but bone-tired. The arched limbs of the chestnuts took me as far as the road, and after that it was spruce and maple and oak, white birch and thin, leggy stands of wild roses, waiting. They lined both sides of 10 as far as the bend, a half mile west, where I'd left my car.

FOURTEEN

There was nothing wrong with the car, but I'd never said there was. I pulled onto the road and drove, not fast, not slowly, maybe a little beyond what the road was used to but not beyond what it could easily handle.

I'd lied to Eve. I was starving. But there were some calls I wanted to make and I didn't want to make them from her place, or from Antonelli's. Some things were starting to come together for me, but others weren't, yet, and if there were going to be any surprises I didn't want anyone to be surprised but me.

I had the cell phone with me, but the static, the fading in and out, the disruptions caused by these hills were more than I could face right now. The 7-Eleven down 30 had a pay phone, and it also had food, if you weren't picky. I got turkey and tomato, and a pint of Newman's Own Lemonade to go with it, though I had doubts about that stuff. I'd never seen Paul Newman drinking it.

I sat in my car and ate, Uchida's Mozart in the disc player again. I hadn't touched the piano in two days now and I could feel the rust in my fingers.

The sandwich was finished before Mozart was, but I waited. Then I took the roll of quarters from the well, ripped it open, flipped the first one. It was tails. I flipped it again. Heads. That was better. I pocketed the quarters and headed for the phone.

The first number I tried was the one Otis had dialed from the green house, and the second was the number of the green house itself, and they both just rang. Either Grice wasn't home or he was too busy to answer the phone. Well, that's what I got for flipping coins. I dialed the state troopers, asked for MacGregor.

"What the hell do you want?" he greeted me.

"Warmth and fellow feeling. I must have the wrong number."

"By a mile."

"Where do I find Frank Grice?"

"You don't find Frank Grice. If I want Frank Grice, I find Frank Grice. Do I want him?"

"I have no idea. Did you test those guns?"

"Yeah."

"And?"

"Smith, I told you, stay the hell out of my case."

I eased a cigarette from my shirt pocket. "No, you didn't. You told me not to withhold evidence and not to get in your way."

His voice was impatient. "How do they do this in the big city? They write you a Dear John letter? This is a police investigation and you're included out."

"Actually, it's not. What I want Grice for is something different." So far, I added silently.

"Yeah? What?"

"Tell me about the guns."

"The guns were a washout. Your turn."

My turn. "Mark Sanderson asked me to find his daughter. I think Frank Grice knows where she is." Close enough, I thought, and all true.

Silence. I had an image of MacGregor rubbing tired eyes. Then, "I hear she's with Jimmy Antonelli."

"You listen to the wrong little birds."

"That so? What tree do you recommend?"

"The Creekside Tavern."

"Some swell dive."

"Grice owns it. Ginny's been hanging out there lately."

"How do you know this?"

"Jimmy's friends could tell you."

"They haven't yet. Of course that crowd wouldn't tell me it was raining if I was standing there getting soaked."

"So where do I find him?"

"Forget it, Smith. Do yourself a favor. Go home, light a fire, have a drink. Let me play policeman."

"Mac—"

"Or do yourself an even bigger favor. Go back to the city."

"Brinkman hinted he'd rather I didn't do that."

"I'll tell him he changed his mind."

"Mac, what the hell's going on?" I moved the phone to my right ear, rolled my left shoulder to ease the ache.

"Nothing's going on, except I've got a rent-a-cop on the phone too dumb to know good advice when he hears it."

"I want to find Ginny Sanderson."

"I'll deal with it."

"How? When? The kid's been missing for three days."

"Depends how you define missing."

"She hasn't been home. Her father doesn't know where she is and he's worried. He's a shit, but he's her father and he's worried. How's that?"

"You know that kid, Smith? You know her father?"

"A little," I offered, ambiguously.

"Well, the kid takes after her mother and her father still hasn't caught on."

"Caught on to what?"

"Christ, where've you been? Lena Sanderson ran around, almost from the day they were married. Everyone knew it but Sanderson. He was the only one surprised when she left him."

"And Ginny's like her mother?"

"We've hauled her in three times since she was thirteen."

"For what?"

"Knowing the wrong people. And this is a kid doesn't live in the county, Smith. She's away at school making trouble there most of the time."

"Not now."

"No, not now."

"What happens when you arrest her?"

"We don't. We learned. We call Sanderson and he comes and gets her and reams us out for holding his angel in a nasty place like this. Never mind she's been batting her blue eyes and practically climbing into the uniforms' laps."

"So how come you didn't tell me about her when I described the girl I was looking for?"

"Ginny? That's who that girl was—Ginny Sanderson?"

"Sounds like her."

"Smith—"

"Mac," I interrupted, "did Brinkman tell you he found a nine-millimeter pistol in a Chevy truck that rolled into the gorge last night?"

"Yeah. Yeah, he told me. How the hell do you know?"

"He told me, too. Have you tested it yet?"

"No, I haven't tested it yet. And when I test it, you'll be the last to know."

"Whose was the truck?"

A hesitation; then, in a tired voice, "Jimmy Antonelli's."

I drew a last drag on my cigarette, dropped it, ground it out. "I guess I knew that."

"I guess you did. What else do you know?"

"Not a goddamn thing. Where do I find Frank Grice?"

"Christ, Smith! What the hell's the matter with you? I see you anywhere near Frank Grice, I'll pull you in and stuff you in a hole. Is that clear enough, or you want me to say it some other way?"

"No," I said. "No, I get it."

"Smith," MacGregor said, "this Ginny Sanderson thing isn't the case you came up here to work, is it? You said you came up Sunday night. That kid's only been gone since Monday."

"It's part of it."

"Smith, you'd better—"

I stopped him before he painted us both into a corner. "I told you, Mac, it's not a police matter. I'll call you later, see about that gun. 'Bye."

I hung up, leaned against the scratched glass wall of the phone booth. I spun another quarter in the air, thought about what MacGregor had said.

I'd given him Ginny Sanderson at the Creekside Tavern for free. Underage drinking could close the Creekside down, and the threat of closing down might buy Mac-Gregor something that might help break the Gould case. That, in turn, should have bought me something, but it hadn't.

Cops had a lot of ways of telling you things they wanted you to know.

MacGregor wanted me to know something was going on. Maybe he was getting pressure from above on the Gould murder; maybe it was something else. But what he wanted me to know was that I couldn't count on his help. If I got myself into trouble, even with him, I'd have to get myself out.

I stuck the quarter in the phone and called Mark Sanderson.

"Where the hell have you been?" he demanded, after I'd gotten past the receptionists and the secretary with the beautiful voice.

"Mr. Sanderson, has your daughter ever mentioned a man named Frank Grice?"

He stopped cold, as though he'd lost his place in the script. "No," he finally said. "She doesn't know him. How would she know him?"

"But you do?"

"I've heard of him. Some of the people I do business with have had trouble with him."

"Bullshit," I said. "Grice first came here because you brought him here. What happened, Sanderson, he get out of hand?"

His voice exploded out of the phone. "Goddammit, who the hell do you think you are? The sheriff tells me he found

Jimmy Antonelli's truck this morning, in the ravine. If anything happened to Ginny—"

"There was no one in the truck when it went off the road, Mr. Sanderson."

"So where the hell are they?"

"Wherever Jimmy is, your daughter's not with him."

The phone hissed his words the way a pot lid hisses steam. "Damn it, Smith, you're trying to protect that kid, and it's obvious and stupid. I'm getting impatient."

"I can't help that."

"Yes, you can. You can tell me where he is, and where my daughter is, or I promise you you'll be one sorry bastard."

I hung up without telling him I'd been a sorry bastard most of my life.

I had lots of quarters. I called Alice Brown to tell her the troopers would be watching over her.

"Me? You're—oh," she said. "Oh, I understand."

"I thought you would. Have you been okay?"

"Yes. But the sheriff was here, and right after him one of those men you told me about. The one with the cast on his wrist."

"Otis. They wanted to know where Jimmy was?"

"Yes. I told them both the same thing—about Jimmy cheating on me and how I threw him out. And I said if anyone found him they shouldn't bother to tell me because I couldn't care less."

"Good. When was this?"

"This morning, about eleven. I called you at Antonelli's but no one answered."

"Did they believe you?"

"I don't know."

"Will you be okay there?"

"I'm all right. What should I do?"

"Keep on doing what you're doing. As far as you're concerned it's a normal day, because you don't know where Jimmy is anyway. I'll check back with you."

I was about to hang up when she asked a sudden question: "Will it be all right?" Her voice through the phone was shaky and brave.

For a moment I couldn't answer. Then I said, "I want it to be. Alice, I'll do what I can."

"I know," said Alice. "Thank you."

I depressed the silver cradle, kept the receiver to my ear. I dropped in another quarter, tried the green house again, and the number Otis had dialed from it, but they both rang into emptiness.

I crossed the parking lot back into the 7-Eleven, bought another pack of Kents, a lemon, and a box of teabags. As a last-minute thought I grabbed a bottle of aspirin. Back in the car I washed three pills down with the last of the lemonade, turned the car and the music on, and headed down the road.

FIFTEEN

A loud buzzing cut like a chainsaw through my dream. Bare winter trees, dark sky, cold. A stream, two ways to cross it: one a bridge, ugly and new; the other shadowy, undefined. People in the shadows, people I thought I knew but couldn't see. Movement in the darkness. And then the buzzing, and I was awake, disoriented in the twilit room.

I groped for the clock, hit the button. The buzzing stopped. I lifted the clock and focused on it: four o'clock. Christ, what a stupid time to get up. No, but it was afternoon, not morning; and Lydia was coming. Right, at four-thirty. Get out of bed, Smith, take a shower, make yourself bearable.

Groggy and stiff, I stumbled to the bathroom. I'd been asleep for an hour, since I'd gotten back from the Creekside Tavern. I stood under the hot water, tried to make the steam clear my brain.

The Creekside. Shabby mustard-colored shingles, brown vinyl trim, windows full of lit beer signs, most for brands the Creekside didn't sell anymore. Inside, wood-grain Formica dimness and a stale smell. No sign of the drug dealing that went on from the bar or the bookmaking business in the back room, but it was early in the day.

Two guys my age were curled over beers at the bar; two younger guys and a girl with a fountain of hair springing from the top of her head were playing pool. They all looked up, measured me, an intruder in their territory, and just how tough was I, if it came to where that mattered? I sat on a barstool near the door, not near the other guys, the etiquette of the stranger.

"Haven't seen you here before," the bartender said, put my Bud on the bar. He was blond and big, shirtsleeves pushed up past his elbows.

"No," I said. "I'm from North Blenheim. I don't get over this way much."

That placed me for them, told them where I'd been before I walked into their lives.

"What brings you over here now?" he asked.

I drank some beer. "Frank Grice."

He made a show of looking around the near-deserted room. "He's not here."

"Been in lately?"

"I don't remember."

"Buy yourself a drink. It might help your memory." I dropped a twenty on the bar.

"Why, thanks, friend." He scooped up the bill, rang it into the register. He poured a shot of Dewar's, downed it, smiled, and shook his head. "I don't think that helped."

"Think harder," I suggested.

One of the pool players straightened up from the felt, strolled around the pool table, cue loose in his right hand. I drank more beer, put the glass down on the bar as he came to stand beside me.

"Something I can do for you?" I asked, not looking at him.

"You look familiar. You look like a cop." A nasal voice, belligerent and edgy.

"I never liked my face much, either," I said.

"What do you want Frank for?"

"He's got something I want."

"What?"

I looked him over. Smallish; fish-belly pale; eyes a little out of focus. Close up, he was younger than I'd thought, too young to be drinking in the Creekside in the early afternoon.

"Tell you what, Junior," I said. "You tell me where Frank is, and I'll tell him my secret, and afterwards, if you're good, he'll tell you."

"Sonuvabitch," he growled. He hefted the pool cue, moved closer.

I slipped off the barstool toward him, took a quick step in, too close for him to swing the cue. I socked him in the stomach, fast but not all that hard; but his eyes had told me he'd drunk enough that I didn't need to hit him hard. He made a small noise, doubled over, was quietly sick.

"Hey!" came from his friend on the other side of the pool table. He headed for me.

"Mike!" said the bartender sharply. "Hold it!"

The second pool player halted, his hands rolled into fists. He glanced from the bartender to me, back again.

"You're not going to break up my place," the bartender said. "You," he turned to me, "get the hell out."

Standing, I realized that the beer was hitting me harder than it usually did. The room wasn't as still or solid as I liked rooms to be. Getting out didn't seem like a bad idea.

I dropped my card on the bar. "Tell Frank I know about Ginny Sanderson, and the truck," I said to them all. "Tell him he'll have to deal with me. I'll be at Antonelli's tonight. Tell him that."

And I left the Creekside, my clothes still carrying that stale, sour smell as I drove, slowly and carefully, back to my cabin, to sleep.

The hot water faded to warm, lukewarm, cold. After a few minutes of cold I gave it up. I dried, dressed, built a fire in the stove, put the kettle on. Four twenty-five. I sat at the piano, worked at slow, even scales until I heard a car crunch down the driveway. Four-forty. I closed the piano, opened the front door in time to see a Ford Escort roll to a stop next to my Acura.

I crossed to the car as Lydia got out. I hesitated, then kissed her cheek, caught the scent of freesia in her hair.

"Don't squeeze," she said. "Where's your bathroom?"

I pointed to the cabin door. "Just inside, on the left. I'll bring your things."

She scuttled up the porch steps, disappeared inside.

I reached into the car, brought out a zippered, snapped, strapped, and buckled carry-on of soft black leather. I followed her inside, dropped the bag on the couch. The bathroom door opened and she came out, combing her hair back from her face with her fingers.

"Didn't you stop?" I grinned.

"I wouldn't have made it by four-thirty if I'd stopped."

"I always stop," I told her. "Twice."

She made a rude noise.

"That's just what your mother always says to me."

"I'm not surprised. What happened to your face?"

"I'll tell you all about it. Do you want some tea? It's only Lipton's, in a bag," I apologized. "It was all I could get."

"When in Rome," she sighed. I took that as a yes.

Lydia shook off her leather jacket, unclipped her holster from her belt. The lamplight was gold on her smooth skin; it caught highlights in her hair, which was black and asymmetrical, like her clothes. While I made her tea, and coffee for myself, she wandered around the room, investigating my drawings, photographs, books. She stopped at the small silver-framed photo. She picked it up in both hands, looked at it silently, then looked over at me; but I was busy with cups, spoons, and teabags, and I let her look pass.

"It's just the way I thought it would be up here," she finally said, coming over to the counter, collecting her tea.

"I didn't know you ever thought about it."

"Don't play dumb." She settled onto the couch, drew her legs up. The cushions molded themselves to her as if they'd been expecting her, as if they were already used to her being here.

"I'm not," I said. "Playing, anyway. I'll tell you the whole story."

"That's only part of it."

"Part of what?"

"What I'm mad about."

"I thought the problem was I wouldn't tell you who the client was, why the paintings were here."

"The other part is there's a client at all."

"I don't get you."

A log shifted on the fire. I could see sparks through the stove grate; then everything was still again.

"I thought you came up here," Lydia said, "to get away from work."

"I always have, before this."

"But this time, someone from here called you in New York to hire you."

"That's right."

"When you left you didn't tell me that."

I sipped my coffee. "I wasn't sure I was going to take it."

"So? When you did take it, you called me to work on it. To work for you."

"With."

"No, for. If it was with, you'd have told me from the beginning. Even if you weren't sure."

"I've turned down cases before," I said. "Without telling you."

"And taken them. And I didn't care. But I thought things were supposed to be different now."

"Am I supposed to consult you on every decision I make?"

"God, I knew you'd say that! No, and you're not supposed to play dumb again, either." She pulled her legs in closer, wrapped both hands around her mug. "This is a big deal, you working up here. You can't pretend it isn't."

"I'm not pretending anything."

She nodded, but I had the feeling it wasn't because she agreed with me. "I think you did it for the same reason you didn't tell me about it or tell me who the client is."

"What reason is that?"

Her eyes confronted mine. Her look was hard under the soft lamplight, but there was more than anger in it.

"Caring about you," she said, "is a big problem for me."

I reached onto the side table for a cigarette. "I'm not sure what that means, and I don't know how to answer it."

"Before," she said, "when we just worked together, just sometimes, that was easy. Now, if we're supposed to be partners and . . . and maybe whatever, then I can't do it unless you really mean it too."

"You think this has to do with that?"

"I know it does. You're used to working alone. You took a case up here and didn't tell me about it because you're not so sure being partners is a good idea. Maybe it's not: but if it isn't, then I can tell you right now that all that other stuff you've been saying you wanted all these years is a worse one."

I put my coffee mug down on the side table without looking at it. I didn't have to look; years of sitting in this chair, reading, smoking, listening to music, had given me the measure of that table, of this room and everything in it.

"I don't know," I told Lydia. "If that's what I did I didn't mean to do it."

"You didn't mean to, or you meant to but you just didn't know you did?"

Briefly, I met her eyes, then looked beyond them to the shadows gathering on the porch I'd built, the dusk starting its business of disputing the daylight's confident disposition of the facts of time, depth, distance.

"I don't know," I said again.

"Well," she said, "you'd better figure it out. Because I'm not going down this road if this is what's there. I can still help it. So think about it."

We sat in silence for a while, no sound but the crackle of logs in the stove, the hiss of a match as I lit another cigarette when the first was gone. I was beginning to think bourbon would have been a better idea than coffee when Lydia spoke again.

"Okay." She surprised me with a grin. "Anyway, you have this case and I'm here. So tell me about it."

I told her. I went through everything that had happened since Monday, everything I thought had happened before. I told her what I was sure of and what I wasn't, what I was worried might be coming next. We talked the way we always talked, going back, forward, back again. I gave her everything, even things I didn't understand.

She sipped her tea, listened, asked a few careful questions. When I had said all I had to say she was quiet; then she asked, "These people are very important to you, aren't they?"

"Tony and Jimmy . . ." I began. Then I didn't know anything else to say besides "Yes."

"And Eve Colgate, too."

"Eve, too."

"And this place." Her eyes moved over the room, stared into the woods, dark now beyond the windowpanes, then came back to me. "Bill, can he really do that? Have your land condemned?"

I looked into the murky depths of my coffee, answered, "I'm sure he can."

"Is it worth it?"

I looked up, met her eyes. "Jimmy didn't kill Wally Gould."

"If you did what Sanderson wants," she said, "Jimmy would get arrested, but your land would be safe, and if he's innocent—"

"It wouldn't matter. Between Brinkman and Grice, Jimmy'd be sent up for life, if he lived long enough."

"So it's worth it?"

"It's got to be."

In the silence I could hear the wind moving in the trees around the cabin, the whispering, the rustling and creaking as familiar to me as my own breathing, my own bones.

Lydia stood, crossed the room. She sat on the arm of my chair, kissed my bruised cheek very gently. Freesia and citrus mingled in the cool air.

"Okay," she said. "Just making sure." Her face grew serious. "I just hope you're not—missing something," she said. "Because of how you want things to come out."

"That's one of the reasons I asked you to come. I wanted someone I could trust, someone who's detached."

"Well," she said doubtfully, "detached hasn't ever been my best thing."

"You'll be fine. And besides being detached," I said, "you have that beautiful, anonymous, rented car. I have plans for that."

"My car," she said, standing. She clipped her gun to her belt. "I drive."

"Always. Besides," I added casually, "it's probably not a stick shift. I bet it wouldn't be any fun anyway."

"Forget it. I drive."

So she drove, up my driveway and on to 30, north under the bare winter trees spread against the dark sky.

Our first stop was the 7-Eleven, where we picked up cigarettes, beer, and a chicken parmesan hero. The clerk stared at Lydia as though she were a black-petalled orchid that had sprung up in the daisy patch. Back in the car, Lydia grinned, said, "Not many Asians up here, huh?"

"Especially in black leather."

"You think I'm too downtown?"

"I think you're adorable."

"Seriously, Bill. Will it be a problem? That I can't blend?"

I shook my head. "Outsiders don't blend here, no matter what they look like. I've been coming here for eighteen years; once I lived here through the fall and winter into the spring. I'm still a weekender. Brinkman calls me 'city boy.'"

"When did you do that?"

"What?"

"Live here."

I lit a cigarette, found the ashtray in the unfamiliar dash. "Seven years ago."

Lydia said, "Mmm." I didn't say anything.

She rolled down her window. The wind blew her silky

hair across her forehead. She combed it back with her fingers.

When the first cigarette was gone I pulled out another.

"If it makes you that crazy," Lydia said, "you can drive."

"Do all Chinese read minds?" I pushed the cigarette back in the pack.

"Only me and my mother."

"I love your driving. Hear that, Mrs. Chin? I love your daughter's driving. Turn here."

We had reached the steep hardscrabble road. We bounced up it, emerged from the trees onto the flat, rock-strewn plain.

"We're here," I said.

Tonight there was a moon. The ridge was clearly visible, towering on the other side of the great pit, in whose glassy surface stars glittered.

"God," Lydia said, staring. "Where are we, Mars?"

"It's an abandoned quarry pit. The one I told you about, where Jimmy dropped the cars."

A truck went by on the ridge road, its headlights passing behind trees a hundred yards above where we sat.

"That's weird," she said.

"There's a road up there, but you can't get here from it, except on foot. Stay in the car a minute."

I got out, moved away from the car. The shack was dark and silent. "Jimmy!" I shouted. "It's Bill. I have a friend with me. I need to talk to you."

A short silence. Then from behind me, some distance away, Jimmy's voice, hoarse and loud: "Who's with you?"

I turned. There was a great mound of jagged rock, with smaller mounds piled at its feet like the ritual remnants of some brutal civilization. Nothing moved. I called, "No one you know. Another PI." I motioned Lydia out of the car. She stepped out cautiously, her jacket unzipped but her hands empty.

Scraping sounds came from the mound. The moon covered everything with a silver light that had no dimension.

The scraping stopped, and Jimmy, rifle in one hand, jumped from a rock that jutted sharply from the mound's face.

"Man, where've you been?" he demanded. His face was haggard, sleepless. His jumpy eyes flashed from Lydia to me. "Where's your car?"

"My car's too obvious. I wanted to come up here in something Brinkman wasn't looking for."

He eyed Lydia again.

"This is Lydia Chin," I told him. "We work together sometimes, in the city. She's okay."

"Thanks," said Lydia dryly.

We followed Jimmy into the shack. He lit the wobbly kerosene lamp. His clothes stank of sweat and smoke; there was a pile of cigarette butts on the table.

Jimmy shifted uneasily.

"You scared the shit out of me."

"For Christ's sake, Jimmy, what's wrong?" I put the 7-Eleven bag on the table.

"Someone was here."

A chill went through me. "Who?"

"I don't know, man! Last night, in the rain. Someone came up the truck road. A car. I saw his lights."

"Did he see you?"

"I don't know. He could've. I had the lamp lit, you know, just . . ." He shrugged. "I killed it when I saw his lights, but he could've seen it."

"And you didn't see him?"

"No, man. It was raining, it was dark."

"Did he drive close to the shack?"

"Uh-uh. Just to the top of the truck road. He was here maybe five minutes, then he split."

"Did he get out of the car?"

"I don't know! I couldn't see him!"

"Okay, Jimmy, okay. Here, we brought you some dinner. And some beer. You look like you could use it." I reached into the bag, put a six-pack on the table. Jimmy yanked a can off the plastic; I did the same. He looked unsurely at Lydia. "You want one?"

"No, thanks," she said. She had stationed herself by the window, listening to us, keeping an eye on the empty landscape.

Jimmy sat on the rickety chair. I perched on the edge of the table. He unwrapped the sandwich, bit into the end as I asked him, "What did you do?"

"When?" he asked, muffled by chicken and cheese.

"Last night."

He swallowed. "What did I do? I didn't do anything!" He took a long pull on his beer. "I thought about it, man. I thought, soon as he's gone, I'm history! I figured with the rain and all, I could make the Thruway and be in Canada by morning."

"Why didn't you?"

He stared at me. "Because you said not to! Because you said stay put!"

"Good."

"But then you didn't come last night, and you didn't come today . . ." He looked at me out of eyes that seemed as tired as mine. "Jesus, Mr. S. What's gonna happen?"

"What's going to happen is that you're going to tell me the truth."

"Oh, man—"

"Don't start that shit, Jimmy!" I slammed my beer down on the table. "Here's what happened last night: Someone cracked me on the head, left me lying in the woods in the rain. That I'm not dead is pretty much an accident. And someone tore up a shed belonging to a friend of mine. I want to know why. And someone drove your truck off the road into the ravine."

He paled. "What the hell are you talking about?"

"It's what I said the other night: This is no goddamn game, not anymore."

"Game," he muttered. He shook his head. "Are—are you okay?"

"No. My head is killing me, my shoulder's sore, I'm

stiff, I'm tired, and I'm generally pissed off. So now tell me, Jimmy, it's Ginny who had the truck, isn't it?"

He shook a Salem from the pack in his parka. "Yeah." He lit it, looked at me in silence, as though he didn't want the answer to the question he was about to ask.

"There was no one in it," I told him.

He let out a breath, nodded. "Jesus," he said.

"Since when has she had it?" I asked.

"Last week. Thursday, I think."

"You think?"

"Some time Wednesday night, Thursday morning."

"Right after she told you she didn't want to see you anymore? What the hell did you give her your truck for, if she was kissing you off?"

He dragged on the cigarette, blew smoke into the cold room. "I didn't. She has her own keys. I gave her a set. Well, loaned them to her. The ones on the silver ring." He looked up at me. "She loves that truck, man. She loves to drive it. She's so little, it's so big. She gets a real charge out of that truck. When it was missing, I knew that's who took it."

"So she took it, and she's had it a week, and you didn't do anything about it?"

"What the hell was I supposed to do, report it stolen? She's fifteen, man. And her father, he thinks she's a fucking saint. He'd kill her if she was in trouble with the law."

"That's why she hangs around with guys like you?"

He shrugged. "Just because he thinks she's a saint, that don't make her one. Maybe if he got to know her a little better she wouldn't run around looking for trouble to get into." He hesitated. "Mr. S.? What about my truck?"

"From what Brinkman says, it was totaled."

"Shit." He shook his head slowly, gave a short laugh. "Ain't that a kick in the ass?"

"Jimmy," I said, "there was blood in the cab. And a nine-millimeter automatic."

"A gun? In my truck?"

"And I'd bet the rent it's the one that killed Wally Gould."

"Oh, Jesus."

"Yeah. Whose is it?"

"Please, man. Please. You gotta believe me. I don't know whose it is. It's not mine."

"Do you have one? A handgun, any kind?"

He shook his head. "Just the rifle. It's all I ever owned. Ever." He glanced at the Winchester standing against the wall. "Tony gave it to me. A long time ago."

"I know, Jimmy."

"I'd've told you," he said. "About Ginny. I almost did. But when you said about my keys being at the bar . . ."

"Jimmy," I said, "I know you're trying to protect her, but you're not doing her a favor. I saw her last night."

"Ginny?"

I nodded.

"So what're you asking me about the goddamn truck for? You knew she had it."

"No. She was in her car. I didn't find her, she came and found me, at the bar. She wouldn't tell me about the truck. Unless," I said, "I told her where to find you."

"Find me?" He had the look of a man trying to make sense of the half-remembered incidents in a dream. "Ginny wanted to find me? What the hell for?"

I drank some beer; it just made the cold room colder. "Any ideas?"

He shrugged wearily. "Frank. You said Frank was looking for me. She's always trying to impress fucking Frank, he's always telling her go away and leave him alone. Maybe she thought if she found me, that would work."

I looked around the room, the wavering lamp flame, Lydia in black leather at the dusty window. "Jimmy," I said, "remember I told you Eve Colgate was robbed?"

He nodded.

I said, "Someone made a real mess in a shed on her farm last night. I was on my way to see what was going on when I was hit."

"I don't get it. Who hit you?"

I gave him the short version. When I was through he didn't move, didn't speak. Finally he said, through tight lips, "Jesus, man. You could've been killed."

"Yeah. By whom, Jimmy?"

He rubbed his grimy face. "Honest to God, Mr. S., I don't know," he said. "But if I find out, I'll kill him. I swear I will."

I laughed, shook my head.

Jimmy looked at me in surprise. He smiled weakly. Lydia, looking over, smiled too.

"Jimmy, listen, what about the burglary?"

He gave me a blank look. "What about it?"

"Could Ginny have done that?"

He shrugged. "I guess she could have. She's always trying to prove she's tough. Bad, you know. Like she smokes Camels, without filters. She could've done it to show, like, that she could."

"To show whom?"

"The guys. You know, everyone."

"Frank?"

"Yeah, she does a lot of shit like that. But it never works. Frank don't want nothing to do with her."

"Why not? She's too young?"

"Frank don't give a shit about that. He's just, like, he just don't want her around." He stood, paced the gritty room. "Jesus, Mr. S., I feel like I don't know a fucking thing. Except I know I'm sick of this place. I'm sick of these clothes, and that goddamn stove, and hearing the goddamn wind all day. Tell me what to do." There was nothing guarded in his eyes now, nothing hidden. All there was was weariness and fear. "Whatever you say, I'll do it. You think I should turn myself in?"

I thought about it. "No. Someone's trying to set you up for Gould's murder. My choice is Frank. That's pretty straightforward, but there's something else going on and I don't want Brinkman to get his hands on you until I know what the hell it is."

He lifted his shoulders in a helpless gesture.

"Where does Frank live in Cobleskill?" I asked.

"Those condos over the bridge. You know, the ones with the pool. The first building, on the third floor. His name's not on the bell."

"What name is?"

An embarrassed look. "Capone."

"Capone?"

"Uh-huh."

"Too bad," I said. "A sense of humor almost makes a guy human. I'd hate to think that about Frank."

Jimmy added his cigarette butt to the pile on the table. "But he's got this other place he uses sometimes, in Franklinton."

"A grungy green house at the top of Endhill Road?"

Jimmy's eyes widened. "Uh-huh. How do you know that?"

"I know all sorts of things," I said. "And if I knew why Wally Gould was killed at the bar, I could die a happy man."

"Christ, Mr. S., I've been thinking about that for two days. That basement—Jesus! Why would anyone go there? There's nothing to steal. Tony hasn't got anything."

I said, "Maybe they went there because that's where they had a key to."

"A key—you mean, mine? That they would've got from Ginny? Yeah, but still . . ."

I finished my beer, set the can down. "Yeah," I said. "But still." I zipped my jacket, pulled my gloves on. "Okay, Jimmy. Give me another day. But if I come up with nothing, then I think you should turn yourself in. Not to Brinkman, to the troopers. I have a friend there. And Jimmy? What I said the other night, about if they find you?"

"Yeah, I know. Don't shoot nobody." He tried to grin.

"Right," I said.

He stood in the doorway watching us leave. An unsteady shaft of light from the kerosene lamp pointed over the dust and rubble.

"Mr. S.?" he called after us. I turned. "How's Allie?"

"She's fine," I said. "She's worried about you."

"Tell her . . . I don't know. Tell her I was asking."

In the car, picking our way down the rocky road, I said to Lydia, "I know he's hard to take."

"I liked him," she said.

"You're kidding."

"No. He reminds me of you."

"Oh, thanks."

"You said this wasn't a game anymore. Did he ever really think it was?"

"He said he did. But no. He didn't."

She steered onto the blacktop. "Where to, boss?"

I let the "boss" go. "Back to my place for my car, then to Antonelli's. You're going to meet our client, and if I'm lucky, Frank Grice will come to me."

"Ancient Chinese wisdom," Lydia said. " 'That kind of luck you don't need.' "

SIXTEEN

Eve Colgate was at the bar talking quietly with Tony when Lydia and I walked into Antonelli's. The whole place was quiet, almost back to normal. *Sic transit gloria.* Tony poured me a drink, put together a club soda with lemon for Lydia. Eve and Lydia, appraising each other, headed for a back table. As I picked my bourbon off the bar to follow them Tony said, "Smith, I gotta talk to you."

I glanced at Lydia and Eve, found myself thinking how balanced they were, one quick and dark and small, the other tall, pale, still. "In a few minutes?"

"Okay." Tony went back to wiping glasses, his face unreadable.

Eve's clear eyes regarded me steadily as I sat. "How were the milking machines?" I asked her.

"They might do," she said. "Harvey thinks it will work."

"I'm glad." I sipped some bourbon, reminded myself about the beer at the Creekside, put the bourbon down. "Eve, I've told Lydia everything that's happened, and everything else she needs to know. She understands what's important to you, and she'll try as hard as I'm trying to keep your private life private."

Eve turned her eyes to Lydia, said nothing.

"I also understand," Lydia said, "that you don't want me here. I don't blame you. I'll try to make it as easy as I can." She met Eve's eyes with her own polished obsidian ones.

"I find it difficult," Eve said slowly, "to understand how you"—she indicated both of us—"can do what you do."

"You mean dig out things people buried on purpose, and want to keep buried?" Lydia asked.

"That's exactly right."

"Well," Lydia said, "but someone's doing that to you, right? Or you're afraid they will. Having us on your side just evens the odds."

"Are you always sure you're on the right side?"

"No," Lydia said simply. "Sometimes I make mistakes."

Eve looked at me. "And you?"

"All the time," I said. "Morning, noon, and night. That's why I need Lydia. She's right at least sometimes. Can you two excuse me a minute? I have to talk to Tony."

As I stood, I caught a look passing between Lydia and Eve that seemed to augur well for their getting along, though I had the feeling it didn't do much for me.

I walked to the bar, leaned on it while Tony finished mixing someone's scotch and soda. "What's up?" I asked.

"C'mon outside," he said, wiping his hands on a towel, not looking at me.

We left the warmth of the bar for the damp night chill. This was Tony's call, so I followed him, stopped when he did, waited.

He had trouble starting. We hadn't gone far from the door, and he stood with his back to the building, hands in his pockets, neon glowing over one square shoulder, the pitted tin sign in the air behind him. "I gotta tell you," he said. "I gotta tell you what happened. What I did."

"Okay," I said.

"Last night—" he began, then suddenly stopped as his eyes flicked from mine to something behind me. Fear flashed across his face. I tried to turn, to see what it was, but Tony slammed into me like a wrecking ball. I crashed onto the gravel. Maybe I heard tires squeal, maybe I heard shouts; the only thing I was sure I heard was the whine of bullets cutting the cold air.

I twisted over, yanked my gun from my pocket, emptied

it at the taillights tearing out of the lot. I couldn't tell if I hit anything, but I didn't stop them.

Now there were shouts, running feet, shadows. I turned, saw light from the open door cutting a sharp rectangle on the ground. Tony lay just beyond it, two spreading pools of red merging on his chest.

I ripped off my jacket, tore my shirt off and wadded it up. I leaned hard against the places where Tony's blood welled. A forest of legs surrounded me, too many, too close; and then Lydia's voice: "All right, people! Move back, give them room. Come on, move!" The legs receded. Tony moaned, opened his eyes.

"All right, old buddy," I said, pressing on his chest. My heart was thudding against my own. "Don't move. Don't talk. It'll be all right." In the cold air the blood seeping under my hands was sticky and hot. I called, "Lydia!"

"Right here," she said.

"Get me something to use for a bandage. Call the nearest rescue squad."

"They're in Schoharie," said a calm voice beside me. Eve crouched on the gravel, took Tony's hand. He focused his gaze, with difficulty, on her face.

"Shit!" I said. "It'll take them fifteen minutes to get up here."

"What the hell happened?" A face bent over me; a voice echoed other voices on the edges of my attention.

"Back off!" I spat. The face retreated and the voices became background noise again.

Lydia reappeared clutching a roll of gauze and a pile of clean towels. "They're calling the ambulance," she told me, kneeling.

Tony's eyes closed. His breath scraped through lips tight with pain.

"No time," I said. "I'll take him. Lean here. Hard."

I reached for a folded towel, but Eve took it from me, said calmly, "I'll do this. Get the car."

She began peeling my shirt back from Tony's bloody

chest, laying clean cloth, directing Lydia's help with short, quiet words.

I grabbed my jacket off the ground, searched it for my keys as I sprinted across the lot. I backed the car down the lot, pulled as close as I could to the place where Eve and Lydia knelt.

Eve was knotting the ends of the gauze. The dressing on the wounds was neat and tight, better than it would have been if I'd done it. I picked a big guy out of the wide-eyed crowd; he helped me lift Tony, manuever him into the back seat, strap him in as well as we could.

As I climbed out of the car, Eve slipped in. She perched on the seat where Tony lay. Someone pushed through the crowd, passed Eve a blanket. It was Marie, white under the deep shadows of her makeup.

I looked around for Lydia; she was at my side. "Call the state troopers," I told her. "Tell them I'm taking 30 to 145, 145 to 1, to the highway to Cobleskill. Tell them to pick me up wherever they can." She repeated the route back to me. "Good," I said. "When they get here, tell them what happened, but nothing else. Stay here until I call you from the hospital."

"Good luck," she said. There was blood on her cheek, Tony's blood.

As I started the car, I called back to Eve, on the seat beside Tony. "You sure?" I asked.

"Yes."

I wound up the engine, let the clutch up fast. The front tires spat gravel. The car started to slither across the parking lot. I cursed, stopped, closed my eyes. I breathed deeply, forced my shoulders to relax, my fingers to loosen on the wheel, focused the electric current sizzling on my skin into a thin beam I could draw on, in my gut. I started the car again, accelerated quickly and quietly out onto 30.

Thirty was easy. I knew every inch of it, the bends, the dips, the places where dirt would have washed onto the road from last night's rain. I knew the turns where I could let the steering go light, where there was room to catch it on the far side. It helped that it was dark. I drove the whole road, dipping my headlights at each curve to check for the swell of oncoming light that would warn me I wasn't alone. The rhythm of the road was bad but my rhythm was good, and I snaked through at seventy, faster in short bursts.

When we hit 145 it got harder. More people lived along it, and I knew it less well. There were hidden driveways, there were potholes I wasn't prepared for. I was deep into turns before I knew they were there. Trees grew thickly, close to the road. I had to come down to sixty, which was still too fast for the road, but not fast enough to keep the adrenaline of anger and frustration from pushing through to my fingertips. My hands began to sweat. The steering wheel, sticky with Tony's blood, now became a slimy, slithery thing on which my grip was not sure. I pressed my fingers into the ridges at the back of the wheel to keep my hands from slipping. I wished for my gloves, but I didn't know where they were. At Antonelli's, on a back table, by a half-finished drink, a half-started conversation.

Ahead, from the right, lights swung onto the road. A hulking truck body followed, filled my vision, my world. I didn't slow because I couldn't have stopped. I flicked the wheel left, flew out past him, and eased right. I felt the left front wheel search for the road, then claw its way back onto it. The rear wheel hung in the soft shoulder another second, then followed. We dug up dirt as we thudded back onto the asphalt. Then we were running smoothly, except for the staccato hammering of my heart. Sounds came from behind me, soft words, but I didn't pay attention. I'd lost my focus, thinking about gloves; we were lucky to have made it through that, and you don't get two of those.

My world became a moving, headlight-lit band and the shadows on either side of it. The texture of the road, the car's banked angle, the sound of the engine as we headed into a curve were all I cared about. My breathing became

as regular as a metronome. My heart slowed again, and I
had no purpose and there was nothing I wanted but to push
this car down this road and onto Route 1 as fast as it was
willing to go.

And we made it. There were other cars, other headlights, migrant leaves and branches huddled across the
road, but we made it through all that, and burst out onto
1 like a sleeper screaming himself awake from a dream.

One was a good, four-lane road. It was one of the ones
the county had widened and straightened, and it gave me
room and a clear view. I pushed up to eighty.

As I hit 1 the insistent flash of circling red and white
lights appeared in my mirror. A siren howled. I held my
speed steady. The lights moved up close behind me. Then
he pulled beside me, in front of me, opened a distance
between us, kept it even. I flashed my lights, inched up
behind him to show I could match his speed. He accelerated.

A mile and a half of that, running straight and fast, the
siren clearing the way for us as we lay each well-banked
curve smoothly onto the one before. Sometimes we sped
by a car cowering in the right lane; most of the time the
road was empty, ours.

The state highway was even better, six lanes, and we
took the six miles, on and off, in four minutes. The hospital
was only two miles away now, a long, long two miles
through residential streets whose posted speed was thirty.
The cop ahead of me, with his screaming siren and flashing
light, kept us near sixty. I felt as though I'd come down
to pleasure-drive speed, Sunday afternoon meandering. I
wanted to pass the cop, to drive the way Tony needed me
to drive; I wanted to arrive.

A car skidded to a stop as we ran a light; his screeching
brakes faded fast into the night behind me. The cop ahead
of me signaled and swung right, taking a turn I didn't
know. I followed; we zigzagged through night-sleepy
streets whose quiet we ripped apart. The cop darted right
again, and we were in the hospital lot.

The medics were waiting as I swung under the canopied emergency entrance. They spoke little to each other, nothing to Eve or me, as they lifted Tony from the back of my car onto a gurney, sped him out of sight through glass doors that opened without help.

I watched them vanish, medics like parentheses bent at the ends of Tony's wordless sentence. Suddenly I had no words either, and no ability to move. I stood in the cold, drained and empty, staring at the door because I was facing that way.

A voice said, "Go inside." I turned, uncomprehending. Eve stood close, her hand warm on my bare arm. "You've got nothing on. I'll park the car. Go inside."

I spread my hands, looked down at myself. I wore a sweat-drenched, blood-streaked undershirt. There was blood on my pants, my hands, my arms. Even the blue snake curling his way up to my left shoulder was smeared with Tony's blood.

Eve took the car keys from my hand. I did what she said, went inside, to a room where a nurse sat behind a cheerful yellow counter beside yellow double doors you couldn't see through. It was warmer inside, but I didn't feel warmer. The smell was cold and the shiny vinyl floors were cold and the deserted silence was very cold.

The nurse asked me some questions about Tony and I filled in some forms. There were a lot of things I didn't know. Eve came in with my jacket. I put it on. She went around a corner, came back with a steaming paper cup, handed it to me. The hand I took it with must have been shaking; hot coffee slopped over my fingers, dripped onto the floor. Eve took the cup back, waited, handed it to me again. I held it in both hands. The coffee was bitter, with oily green droplets floating on the surface, but as I sipped it I finally began to warm.

Eve said, "Do you feel better?"

"I'm all right." My voice sounded loud in the stillness.

"You probably saved his life, driving like that."

I reached a cigarette from my pocket, lit it without an-

swering her, because we both knew that Tony might not
live, even so.

The nurse behind the counter glanced up at the sound
of the match. She rested a long look on me, on the cigarette, on Eve. Then she went deliberately back to her pa-
perwork as though nothing was amiss. I wondered whether
some people were born understanding the true nature of
kindness, or if it was something you had to learn.

A state trooper came through the glass doors, knife-
sharp creases in his pants smoothing at the knees as he sat.

"You the guy I was following?" I asked him.

"Uh-huh. Donnelly." He had crinkly blue eyes and a
wide smile. He stuck out his hand.

I reached for it, then saw my hand, dirt, blood, and
coffee in equal parts darkening my skin. I withdrew it,
said, "Thanks."

"What happened?" he wanted to know.

I finished the coffee. "Drive-by."

"Yeah?" he said. "Like the movies?"

"Yeah."

"You know who it was?"

"No."

"You know why?"

"No."

"Anybody else hurt?"

"No."

"Well," he said, "none of my business. I'm just supposed to keep an eye on you until someone who knows
something gets here."

"On me?"

"Sure." He was a little surprised. "You're a witness.
From what I hear, you're *the* witness. You're gonna be a
popular fella around here."

Somehow, I doubted that.

I stubbed out the cigarette, found the men's room, lath-
ered liquid soap on my arms, my face, my neck. I took off
the undershirt, threw it away, washed again. There weren't

"He's in surgery. They haven't told me anything yet."

"You think he saw who it was?"

"He could have."

"I'll send someone over, to be there when he wakes up."

"You've got someone here now."

"Who? Donnelly?"

"Yeah."

"He should've been Highway Patrol. He drives great, but he doesn't think so good."

"Does the Highway Patrol know you feel that way?"

"Yeah, and so does Donnelly. Smith, listen—"

An electronic voice interrupted him, asked me for more money. I fished around past the gun in my pocket for quarters, shoved them in the slot. I said, "I'm listening."

"Whatever it is you've been sitting on, I want it. Don't give me client confidentiality, don't give me it's not police business. I've got one dead body and I might—I almost had another. I cover three counties here, Smith. This is more homicides than I had all last year. So your time's up. Give."

"I can't, MacGregor."

"You can, and you will. If you don't, I'll send somebody over there to pick you up. You won't like my jail, Smith. It's not nice and comfy like the ones you've got in the big city."

A nurse squeaked down the hall on crepe-soled shoes.

"Oh, Christ," I said. "Yeah, okay, Mac. But tomorrow, okay? I want to stay here until—until I know something. And I'm beat. I'll come in the morning."

He was silent a moment. "You going to spend the night there?"

"Yes."

He sighed. "Am I going to be sorry if I don't make you come in now?"

"No. Nothing else is going to happen tonight. All the bad guys have gone home to bed."

"You'd better be right."

"I'm right. Listen, it's been fun, but I didn't call to chat with you. What are the chances of my speaking to Lydia Chin?"

"The little Chinese dish in the leather jacket?"

"You'd better hope she didn't hear that."

"Who is she?"

"She's a friend of mine, for Christ's sake. She came up to spend a couple of days."

"You sure know how to show a girl a good time."

"Can I speak to her?"

"Yeah, sure. Oh, and look—Brinkman's on his way to the hospital, to talk to you."

"Jesus, Mac, did you have to do that?"

"I didn't want him screwing up my crime scene. Tell him what happened, tell him you're coming in to see me in the morning, tell him to leave you alone."

"Sure, Mom. Can I tell him my big brother'll beat him up if he doesn't?"

"Tell him any damn thing you want." MacGregor's voice became distant as he called Lydia's name.

I waited, not long. "Bill? How's Tony?" Lydia's voice was both soft and urgent, like spring rain.

"I don't know. He's still in surgery. MacGregor give you a hard time?"

She said noncommittally, "He's a cop." With a smile in her voice, she added, "And he's listening."

"Talk dirty."

"You wish. What should I do? They took my statement; I can go."

"Come to the hospital. I want you to take Eve home, stay with her."

"What are you going to do?"

"I'm going to stay here." I wasn't sure why. Tony wasn't likely to wake until morning, if then; and I was desperately tired. But it seemed, somehow, as though it would help.

I went back to the little waiting area. Eve and Donnelly were sitting companionably, silently. I asked the nurse behind the yellow counter whether she could tell me anything about Tony yet. She smiled a gentle, practiced smile, said she was sure Doctor would let us know as soon as he could.

I sat down next to Eve. Donnelly and I looked each other over; then I leaned back, stretched my legs, closed my eyes. Eve rested her hand on mine. It was rough, warm, and sure. I twined my fingers with hers, and slept.

SEVENTEEN

I didn't sleep long. The sound of boot heels clomped through the confused images in my mind. I felt Eve squeeze my hand just before a deep voice drawled, "Well, look at Sleeping Beauty."

I opened my eyes but I didn't sit up. The fluorescent hospital lights seemed harsher, brighter than before. I squinted against them.

"Every time I see you, city boy," Brinkman said, dropping into the chair next to Donnelly, "you look worse. Why d'you think that is?"

"In the eye of the beholder, Brinkman." Now I sat up, took my hand from Eve's. I lit my last cigarette, drew on it hungrily. The nurse looked up again, her face more disapproving this time. I crumpled the empty pack, showed it to her. She smiled and bent over her papers again.

Brinkman half turned, spoke to the man next to him. "You Donnelly?"

"Yessir," Donnelly said cheerfully.

"He say anything I should know about?"

Donnelly scrunched up his face, thought about what I'd said. "I don't think so, Sheriff."

"Okay," said Brinkman. "You can go." He turned back to me. "You shoot Antonelli, Smith?"

I felt color fill my face like a flood tide. I could have leapt out of that chair and broken his neck.

Eve said quietly, "Sheriff."

I stepped on her word as I said, "Brinkman, you're an idiot."

"You were alone out there. No one saw what happened but you."

"Other people saw the car."

"A car driving out of a parking lot. In a hurry to get to the next drink."

Wordlessly, I let my eyes meet his. Then I pulled my gun out of my pocket, held it out to him.

He smiled delightedly. "Why, how'd you know? Just what I wanted."

"Tony's a friend of mine, Brinkman," I said quietly.

"Wouldn't be the first time a man crossed up a friend." He sniffed at my gun. "Could even be you had a good reason."

"The gun's been fired," I said. "At the car."

"At the car." He nodded. "Now tell me the whole story."

I told him. It was a short story. Donnelly, dismissed, didn't move, but sat gaping at the excitement he'd missed.

"And, of course," Brinkman said when I'd finished, "you have no idea who might be shooting at Antonelli, or at you. Do you, city boy?"

I told him what I'd told MacGregor. His response surprised me. "Frank Grice," he said. "You and me, that's something we think the same on."

"Then what's this shit about me shooting Tony?"

"Well, that was mostly to get a rise out of you," he grinned. "See, the way I look at it, anybody'd rather shoot you than him."

"Brinkman," I said carefully, "it's been a long, long day. If you're through, I'd appreciate it if you'd go to hell."

But he wasn't quite through. First he took a statement from Eve. Her calm, low voice was like a warm place to watch a storm from. Then he wanted to hear about the car, so I told him about the car. Then he asked me where Jimmy Antonelli was.

"You think Jimmy shot Tony?" I asked.

"It would make me happy."

"Making you happy isn't high on my list, Brinkman, or Jimmy's either."

"Maybe he's dead," he said thoughtfully. "Maybe that's why I can't find him."

"Well," I said, "maybe if he's dead, he'll come looking for you."

That made Donnelly laugh. It made Brinkman narrow his beady eyes and scowl. "When I find him," he said, "and he tells me you knew where he was all along, that'll make my day."

"Glad to help," I said.

Then he gave me the usual warnings about not leaving the area, about making myself available. Then he left, about a year after he'd come, with my .38 in his hand and Donnelly trailing behind him.

The waiting area was very, very quiet without cops. I stood. "You want coffee?" I asked Eve.

"Yes, I suppose I do."

I got coffee and peanut butter crackers from the vending machines. "Dinner," I said. She smiled and we ate crackers and drank coffee and said nothing.

I spent the night in Tony's hospital room. It had been close to an hour before Lydia had arrived, and another half hour after that until the surgeon, discreetly triumphant in a red-streaked green gown, had pushed through the doors to tell us Tony had lived through surgery and had a good chance of staying alive.

Eve had been willing to go home then. While she was in the ladies' room, Lydia asked me, "What do you want me to do?"

"What you came here for: Keep an eye on Eve."

"This doesn't change things?"

"I don't know what this does. I feel as though I've been working blindfolded for days. Every time I think I'm close, something happens I don't understand."

"Think about it," Lydia said slowly, "as though you didn't know these people. As though you really were an outsider."

"What do you mean?"

"Well, I'm not sure. It's just—I can't lose the feeling there's something you're not seeing. I wish I could see it, Bill. I wish I could help."

I gave her a tired grin. "Just standing there, you help."

"God, you're impossible. If you didn't look so pathetic I'd slug you."

"That's why I practice looking like this. Actually I feel great."

Eve came back, asked me to call her in the morning. I promised I would. I watched through the glass doors as they crossed the parking lot together, saw Eve incline her head to catch Lydia's words, saw Lydia's smile flash as she unlocked her car.

After they'd driven away I sat back down, thought about what Lydia had said. My mind chased ideas around like a greyhound after a whole pack of mechanical rabbits, until I finally gave up and got up to talk to the nurse.

Tony didn't wake that night. Because it was a country hospital, the nurses found a cot for me—"From Pediatrics," they confided—and pillows and blankets and even a toothbrush in a cellophane wrapper. Because it was a hospital, I didn't sleep well anyway. Nurses came and went all night, checking Tony's tubes and bandages, his temperature and his breathing. I woke each time, and then lay awake, breathing the bitter, antiseptic air, watching the moon, tired but dutiful, move across the sky. It finally gave up and set, discouraged.

A long time after the moon had set, the sky began to show streaks of red and iron blue, like a slow-to-develop bruise. Sometime after that I heard the jingle of glass and metal that tells you the doctors are making rounds, accompanied by nurses with trays of syringes and pills and other things patients need. By then the sky was a sullen gray, as bright as it probably meant to get. I got up, washed and dressed, zipped my jacket over my bare chest because I didn't want anyone's sympathy.

I stood watching Tony, who with the aid of a complex network of machines and tubes and drugs was able to successfully complete each breath he started. His face was pallid, yellow-tinged, his eyelids dark and sunken. He already looked like a man who'd been sick a long time, a man who'd be a long time getting well.

The attending physician, a younger, colder man than the surgeon, asked me to wait outside while he did his work. When he came out he was noticeably friendlier. He told me Tony was doing well. I recognized that thaw, that softening of the armor in which he wrapped himself in case he had to deliver bad news. Relax, I wanted to tell him. You get used to it. Eventually the armor turns to stone around you. Then it doesn't soften anymore; but then you're never caught without it, either.

I didn't go back into Tony's room when the doctor was gone. Tony was not likely to wake until later. The cop MacGregor had sent was sitting patiently in the hall—had, it turned out, been sitting there most of the night, while I was tossing on the cot. Let him wait to hear from Tony. I had to move. I had to do something, while the ideas slugged it out in my head until a winner was declared.

The hospital cafeteria wasn't open yet, so I drove to Friendly's, just before the state highway entrance—E-Z-Off, E-Z-On. I had fried eggs because I knew they couldn't make fried eggs from powder, and I had bacon and potatoes and toast and coffee and orange juice and more coffee, but before any of that I called Eve Colgate.

She answered on the second ring.

"It's Bill," I said.

"Are you all right?" Eve asked. "I just called the hospital. They've upgraded Tony's condition to 'stable.' They said you'd gone."

"He's doing all right, but the doctor says it'll be a slow recovery."

"Did he wake up? Did you speak to him?"

"No."

"So he doesn't know you were there."

"It doesn't matter."

"If you're not staying with him, maybe I'll come down. He should have a friend there when he wakes."

"He'll tell you he'd rather be left alone."

"When he tells me that, I'll leave," she said easily. "Bill, how are you?"

"I'm okay. How are you two doing?"

"We're fine. We're having breakfast." A note of amusement crept into Eve's voice. "We just got back from doing the morning chores."

"What's funny?"

"Lydia did quite well," Eve said gravely.

"Oh, God," I said.

"She wants to talk to you."

A pause, and then Lydia. "Bill? Do you know how big cows are?"

I chuckled.

"Don't laugh!" she demanded. "The closest I ever was to a live chicken before is the Grand Street kosher market. Did you know chickens get annoyed when you take the eggs away?"

"Only if your hands are cold."

"Oh, you're so smart. Did you ever milk a cow?"

"Did you?" I asked, impressed.

"Well, sort of. Eve showed me. I wasn't real good at it. I mean, they do it all by machines anyway. We just got enough for breakfast." She stopped for breath, then asked, "How's Tony?"

I repeated what I'd told Eve.

"It sounds as though he'll be all right," she said. "I'm so glad."

"Yeah," I said. "Me, too."

"What are you going to do now?"

"I'm going over to Frank Grice's place, on the other side of Cobleskill. If I can't find him I'm going to try that other dump."

"Be careful."

"I'm always careful."

"Uh-huh. I'd feel better if I were with you."

"I'd feel better if you were with me, too. But I want you to stay with Eve. And think of all you're learning. This will be good, for when we buy our little rose-covered cottage. You can milk the cows and collect the eggs and bake cherry pies while I split firewood and shoot things for food for the winter."

"If this were my phone I'd hang up on you."

"If this were your phone your mother would already have hung up on me. I'll call again later. 'Bye."

I drank the coffee and worked my way through all that food. I wondered if the gun in Jimmy's truck actually was the one that killed Wally Gould. I wondered why Wally Gould was killed. I wondered if Lydia's hands had been cold. I wondered who had shot Tony, and whom they'd meant to shoot, and why.

A half mile from Friendly's there was a Valu-Center, a supermarket as big as a New York City block. They sold everything there: food, lawn furniture, hardware, clothing. I bought a T-shirt, a sweater, and a carton of Kents, and I bought gloves. Back in the car I pulled the clothes on, lit a Kent, and headed across Cobleskill, to the place Jimmy had said Grice lived. I went past once elegant frame houses, a couple of public buildings built out of gray stone from the quarries, and a municipal park that looked tired and old in the dull morning light. As I crossed the bridge over the state highway I caught a glimpse of the Appleseed plant, enormous painted trucks coming and going, pale smoke pouring into the sky from a stainless-steel chimney. On a day like this even the stainless steel didn't shine.

The complex of three-story buildings Grice lived in was the only one like it in Cobleskill, maybe in the county. Luxury Condos, a sign announced. Balconies, Euro-style kitchens, 1½ baths. Pool. The buildings were tan-colored stucco. The pool was empty, except for a small congealed lump of winter leaves. The paint on the sign was peeling.

The first building, Jimmy'd said, on the third floor. I found the bell labeled Capone. I pushed it; nothing happened. I started, methodically, to push all the second-floor bells. I was halfway through them when the intercom barked, "Who's there?" I put my mouth very close to the speaker, growled something loud and unintelligible. The question came again and I growled again. I was buzzed in.

I found the first-floor garbage room and waited there, gave my benefactor a chance to give up and stick his head back in his door. After a few minutes I slipped out, continued along the corridor to the fire stair and up to the third floor.

Grice's apartment wasn't hard to find and it wasn't hard to break into. That was disappointing. What I really wanted was to talk to Grice; this little excursion was just an irresistible side trip. I wasn't looking for anything in particular, and it seemed likely that a man who made it so simple to get into his place wouldn't have left anything to find.

That turned out to be true. The apartment didn't have quite the ambience of the green house near Franklinton, but there was nothing about it to make me want to spend my retirement there. A thick gold carpet lay prostrate under a large brown leather sofa and matching La-Z-Boy recliner. In a smoked-glass wall unit there was an enormous projection TV and VCR. There were three used highball glasses on the glass coffee table, and a full ashtray. I examined the butts. Marlboro Lights, mostly; but among them, two Camels. Without filters.

In the bedroom the bed was unmade, but it would be hard to say how many people had slept in it, or when. There were dirty dishes in the Euro-style kitchen sink.

The whole place had an air of grease and uncaring that made me want to open a window, open all the windows. I resisted because I didn't want any movement up here to be seen from outside.

Wearing my new gloves, I worked fast. I opened everything that was closed, pawed through drawers, rifled through piles. I found both cocaine and marijuana in a kitchen cabinet, but in small amounts, like what a host might keep on hand for guests. There was change and a pile of bills in a bowl by the bed, and in the same bowl a pair of jeweled and tinkling earrings, which I pocketed, but no large amounts of cash. No phone bills, which I would've been interested in. No credit card receipts, no datebook.

No lists, no ledgers, no maps to the pirate gold.

Okay, the hell with it. What had I expected, a signed confession? "I killed Wally Gould and I've been trying to frame Jimmy Antonelli for it. I did it because he was an ugly little creep and he got on my nerves. I'm writing this because the guilt is too much to bear. Yours truly, Frank Grice."

I was wasting time.

I left. Down the way I'd come, out the rear door this time, around the side of the building. Out of habit, I surveyed the parking lot before heading across it to my car. It was almost empty, and I didn't see any bad guys.

The only thing I saw that I wasn't expecting was Lydia.

EIGHTEEN

She was sitting in her rented car, parked next to mine in
the condo lot. As I stepped from the shadow of the building she flashed me a smile, opened the door, got out. The
smile turned down the voltage on the jolt that had gone
through me when I saw she was alone, but I still covered
the lot in fast strides and I still called, "What's wrong?
Where's Eve?"

"No, she's all right," Lydia answered as I reached her.
"She's at the hospital, with Tony. There's a cop there and
everything. She won't leave until I come back. It's just
that I called Velez right after we talked to you, and he
gave me something Eve and I thought you should have
right away."

Velez. I'd forgotten about Velez; but that had been a
grudge match anyway, what I'd hired him for.

"Eve and you thought, huh?" I said to Lydia.

"Uh-huh. I told Eve where Grice lived and she told me
how to get here after I dropped her at the hospital. I was
afraid I'd miss you, but I found your car. I figured I'd give
you time to toss the place if that's what you were doing.
If you'd been much longer I'd have come up to see if you
were okay."

"I appreciate that, I really do. As it turns out, it was
what I was doing. No one's home, and I didn't find a thing.
Well, almost not a thing." I lit a cigarette, leaned next to
her on the car.

"What did you find?"

"You first. What's Velez's big news?"

"He says to tell you first it's not dirt," she said. "He hasn't found anything illegal, which is what he thinks you wanted."

"That was what I wanted, but I'm flexible."

"Good. Now, you know for a couple of years Appleseed's been buying farms all over the county?"

I nodded.

"Well, one thing is, Velez says they've been consistently paying more than the land is appraised at."

"How much more?" I interrupted.

"Not a fortune. Ten or fifteen percent."

"Hmm. Not enough to ring any alarms, but enough to make a seller grab it before Appleseed comes to its senses."

"I guess," she said. "The other thing is, it's not really Appleseed."

"Oh?" I said. "Do tell."

"Velez says he needs more time to work on it, but it looks as though it's Appleseed's money that's making the purchases, but the title to the land is actually put in the name of a thing called Appleseed Holdings, not Appleseed Baby Foods. It's a whole different company, a partnership with two partners."

"And the partners are . . . ?"

"That's the good part," Lydia said. "Mark Sanderson owns forty percent. The other sixty is in the name of Frank Grice."

Lydia looked at me for a moment, then laughed. "Boy," she said, "that's an expression I don't see on you very often. I'll have to tell Velez."

"Son of a bitch," I said. I dropped the cigarette, crushed it underfoot. "Are you real busy right now?"

"I could probably make some time. What did you have in mind?"

"How about we go see Mark Sanderson?"

"Sounds lovely."

We left her car in the condo lot, rode to Appleseed in

mine. In the car, Lydia went on. "Velez says to tell you Sanderson's wife disappeared about four years ago."

"I knew that. Did Velez find her?"

"No, and he looked. Her credit cards haven't been used since the day she left. Her social security number hasn't either. There were no unusual withdrawals from their joint bank accounts in the couple of months before she left. Since then all the activity has been Sanderson's." She added, "She supposedly ran away with some guy, but Velez couldn't find anyone."

I nodded. "MacGregor said she had a reputation. He said everyone but Sanderson knew it." We passed the state college campus, turned onto the spur road to the Appleseed plant. "Were her credit cards canceled?"

"Lena Sanderson's? They weren't renewed when they expired, but they weren't canceled. She could have gone on using them for a couple of months."

"Except that would have made her easier to find."

"She must have really wanted to stay lost."

"You don't know Sanderson. It's a natural reaction."

Mark Sanderson didn't keep us waiting long this time. We didn't even have time to sit and enjoy the vegetables. As soon as the secretary's beautiful voice announced us, the door to Sanderson's office flew wide and Sanderson filled the opening.

"Where is she?" he demanded.

"Ask your partner," I said, pushing past him into the corner office, where the windows offered two different views of the same sullen sky. Lydia followed me, looked Sanderson over. He shot her one glance and then ignored her.

"What the hell are you talking about?" he barked. "Where's Ginny? That Antonelli punk, his brother was shot last night. What the hell is going on? Where's my daughter?"

"Why didn't you tell me you were still doing business with Frank Grice?"

He stopped dead, his eyes fixed on me as though I'd suddenly mutated into a form of life he'd never seen before. He looked at Lydia again. "Who the hell is this?"

"Lydia Chin," I said. "Lydia, this is Mark Sanderson." Lydia put out her hand. Sanderson didn't move. Lydia shrugged. "Lydia and I are business associates," I told him. "Like you and Grice."

"Smith," he pushed through his teeth, "it's none of your fucking business, but if you mean Appleseed Holdings, that's a completely legitimate operation."

"Yeah," I said. "Seems to be, so far. What I really want to know is why you didn't tell me about it."

"Because it was none of your fucking business!" he said again. "It has nothing to do with my daughter, who is the only reason I let a man like you into my office at all!"

"How about a man like Grice?"

Sanderson forced the muscles in his jaw to relax. He walked around behind his desk, sat down. "Appleseed Holdings is a profit-making venture. Sometimes business decisions get you involved with people you'd otherwise rather not be involved with."

"Profit-making for whom? The money that goes into it is Appleseed's. Yours. But Grice owns a bigger share than you do."

Sanderson smiled a hard, cold smile. "For us both."

"But not yet?"

"No," his smile widened, then flicked off. "Not yet."

"Uh-huh. That's what I thought."

Lydia lifted her eyebrows, waited to be enlightened.

"The gas pipeline," I said to her, but with my eyes on Sanderson. "I'll bet I could map the properties he's bought. North to south down the county, mostly in the valley. When NYSEG starts buying up land for the pipeline, they'll have to come to him. What if it doesn't happen, Sanderson?"

Sanderson practically laughed at me. "It'll happen. You forget," he said, "I have friends who tell me things."

"But I thought they condemned land for things like

that," Lydia said. "So you couldn't speculate that way."

Sanderson looked at her as he might at a retarded child with whom he was forced to deal. "They do. But they have to pay a fair market price. And this is very, very productive land. We lease it to Appleseed Baby Foods at very good terms. Appleseed—Appleseed Baby Foods—is making huge profits on the crops we grow on this land."

"Because you pay chickenshit to the people who grow them, the people who used to own that land," I said.

He shook his head. "Doesn't matter why. Profit is profit."

"And what about Grice?"

"What about him?"

"I could understand if there were strong-arm work involved. But I haven't heard that. People are falling all over themselves to sell their farms to you. So how come you're willing to invest in Grice's future?"

"Smith, let me tell you again: This is none of your business. My daughter's safety should be concerning you. It should be keeping you up nights. Because if anything's happened to Ginny—" He stopped as the earrings from my pocket skidded, jingling, across his desk. He looked up. "What's this?"

"Hers?"

Sanderson glanced at them. "No. They're too flashy for her."

"Christ, Sanderson, you're a case." I picked up the photograph from his desk, passed it to Lydia, who, as usual, was leaning by the window. She studied it, handed it back to me. I offered it to Sanderson. The spun gold of Ginny's hair and the tilt of her head combined to hide all but the tip of one earring, but the amethyst bauble was unmistakable.

He paled, picked up one earring between finger and thumb. He said, "Where did you get them?"

"You really didn't recognize them? That picture's right under your nose every day, Sanderson."

He scowled.

"Sanderson," I said, "there's a lot you don't know, and a lot I don't know. Let's fill each other in." I sat, put a match to a cigarette. Then I had to get up and retrieve the ashtray, as I had two days before. "Your daughter," I told him, "met Jimmy Antonelli in a bar sometime last month." At the word *bar* his eyes flashed and he started to say something, but I went on. "It was Grice who told you they were seeing each other, wasn't it? You're a pawn, Sanderson. Grice couldn't talk me into finding Jimmy for him, so he thought maybe you could. By the way, did he tell you he owns the bar where they met?"

He didn't answer, but the look in his iron eyes told me I wouldn't have liked anything he'd said anyway.

I went on: "Ginny dropped Jimmy about a week ago. She told him she'd met someone else. Someone tougher than he was, she said. There are probably a lot of men in this county tougher than Jimmy, but I found those earrings in Frank Grice's apartment."

Suddenly a pencil broke in Sanderson's grip. He looked at the yellow splinters, then at me. "This is crap!"

"There's more. Last Friday someone broke into a house near Central Bridge and stole some valuable things. Your daughter has been fencing those things."

"What the hell are you trying—"

"There's at least one witness who can identify her, and if I have to I'll find more. But here's where what you want and what I want may come together. The stuff from that burglary that's already been sold we'll forget about. But there was a crate with some paintings in it. Six of them. They haven't surfaced yet. The police don't know about this. If I get the paintings back, they never will."

Sanderson was livid, his jaw clamped shut in his round face until he found enough control to speak. "You stupid bastard," he hissed. "You think you're smart enough to set Ginny up and blackmail me? You don't know what league you're playing in, Smith. Where did you get these? Where is my daughter?" He crushed the earrings in his shaking hand.

"Ask Grice," I said. "Get my paintings back. And who knows? Maybe you can talk your daughter into coming home."

"You bastard," he repeated. His eyes shone with a molten rage.

"Sanderson," I said softly, tapped my finger on Ginny's picture, "you threw it away."

"Get out of here!" Sanderson screamed, apoplectic. Lydia looked at me. I nodded. She straightened up, walked unhurriedly before me out Sanderson's office door.

"That was exciting," Lydia said as we left the plant. "But you didn't tell him you'd seen her."

"It wouldn't have helped. Actually, I think it would have made things worse. That I was so close, but I didn't bring her home."

Lydia nodded. "There's something peculiar."

"All of this is peculiar. What do you have in mind?"

"Well, Jimmy said Grice didn't want anything to do with Ginny. Why wouldn't he? And if Jimmy was right, what made Grice change his mind?"

"Maybe he didn't. There are lots of guys tougher than Jimmy."

"But the earrings—?"

"I'm not sure. But this should loosen things up."

"You think Sanderson will go straight to Grice?"

"Wouldn't you?"

"I don't know. I've never been anyone's father." She looked up at me quickly, said, "God, Bill, I'm sorry."

I didn't look at her, shook my head. "You don't have to tiptoe."

"I'm sorry," she said again.

Now I met her gaze. Usually, Lydia's eyes are a hard, pure black, like polished ebony or basalt; but sometimes, unpredictably, they soften to an infinite liquid depth. They were that way now, and I thought of the quarry, Jimmy's shack next to the wide black water deep with secrets, like Lydia's eyes.

I said nothing, and she understood.

We'd reached the car I'd put it close to the building, in a "Reserved" space in the Executive Parking area around the back. I unlocked her side, went around to mine; but I didn't get a chance to get in.

A big blue Ford was parked nose to nose with my Acura. Three of its four doors sprang open together, three figures jumped out, and in three hands guns glinted, even in the dullness of the day.

Lydia, halfway into the car, froze. I did the same. "Tell her to get out!" Otis snarled. "And to keep her hands where I can see 'em!"

"She speaks English," I said evenly. Lydia stepped out of the car, her hands raised. "Lydia," I said, "this is Otis and Arnold and Ted. They're creeps." To Arnold I said, "You guys must be running out of cars. You used that one already." It was the one they'd been in Monday night at Antonelli's, Grice and Arnold and Wally Gould, and I should have spotted it the minute we walked into this lot.

"Shut up!" Otis ordered. Ted came over and frisked me. "This time he ain't even got a holster, Otis," he complained. "Do the girl," Otis said in disgust. Ted crossed to Lydia's side of the car. Otis jerked his head at Arnold, who came and went over me again, more expertly and roughly than Ted had. Arnold stepped away, shook his head. Ted, meanwhile, pocketed Lydia's .38. He didn't bother to search my car, so he didn't even come close to the .22 I'd strapped back under the dash between the visit to Grice's place, where I'd thought I might need it, and here, where I hadn't.

"Who's the gook?" Otis demanded. Lydia's cheeks flared hotly but she said nothing.

"She's a friend of mine."

"Your friends all carry guns?"

"Yours do."

"Yeah? And where's your goddamn rod this time?"

"This time the sheriff has it. Can you really shoot lefty?"

"Fuckin-A right I can! You wanna see, just keep flappin' your yap!"

Lydia spoke. "Who writes his dialogue?" she asked me.

"Mike Tyson. So what now, fellas? You shoot us here in the parking lot in the middle of the day and drive away?"

"You see anyone around who'd care if we did?" Otis snickered. The secluded area was empty except for us. "But I'm not supposed to shoot you till after Frank talks to you."

I shook my head. "I don't get Frank. I've been looking for him since yesterday. I even dropped by his place this morning. How come every time he wants me he thinks he has to send armed assholes to pick me up? And which of you assholes shot Tony Antonelli?"

Arnold growled, started toward me, but Otis said, "Uh-uh. Not here. Get in the car." He waved his gun around. Ted echoed gleefully, "Get in the car."

Lydia and I got in the car, in the places where they told us, Lydia in the middle of the back seat, me next to her. Arnold climbed in behind Ted, who was driving, Otis having been put on the Disabled List.

Otis waved his gun at me. "Turn around." I shifted in the seat. Arnold pulled out a set of handcuffs, leaned across Lydia. Ratchets clicked as steel closed tight around my wrists.

Otis put the gun about two inches from the end of Lydia's nose. "Now, we got no cuffs for you, cutie pie," he said. "But we also got no use for you. So if you or smartass here do anything dumb, even once, I'm gonna blow your pretty face off, and no one's gonna care. Got it?"

Lydia said, "I've got it." Her voice was clear and steady.

Ted threw the Ford into gear and we started down the road.

*   *   *

It took us half an hour to climb to the green house through hills heavy with the weight of the sky. Maple trees shimmered with the shiny red-brown of buds waiting to open. A pair of hawks wheeled low against the clouds. In the heaviness of the day even the snowdrops seemed dulled, subdued.

From the corner of my eye I watched Lydia concentrate on the road, the turns and the miles we covered. Otis smoked. Every cell in my body begged for a cigarette, but I didn't give Otis the satisfaction of turning me down.

I knew where we were going; I had no need to do what Lydia was doing. I stared out the window, saw other things. I saw Eve Colgate's eyes, tiny jewels glowing in them; I saw blood from her heart spread across six paintings, blood which was still, after all this time, too fresh for the world to see. I saw Tony's blood, and Tony's face, backlit in red neon, trying to find a way to tell me something he needed me to know. I saw Jimmy as I'd seen him last night, filthy, exhausted, scared, but his eyes full of the same mixture of bravado and belief that had been there, years ago, when he'd followed me onto a wobbly rope bridge across a swollen creek because I'd said it was safe. And I saw a little girl with those same eyes.

And I heard voices, words: Lydia's; MacGregor's; Brinkman's, at the hospital.

And suddenly I knew.

A late-model Buick Regal was parked between Otis's black truck and a dark green Aries in the spongy place next to the house when we got there. The Aries had a triple-A sticker above the left taillight and cracks spiderwebbing out from a small hole in the rear window.

The air as we crossed to the decrepit porch was sharp, bringing on it the scents of pine and water; but that was only outside. I saw Lydia's nose wrinkle with distaste as we walked through the door.

Grice stood in the living room opening. "Well," he said. "It's about time. Nice of you to come, Smith."

"I've been looking for you. You didn't need this."

"Yeah, I heard you wanted to see me. I didn't like the way you put it."

"How'd I put it?"

He shrugged, smirked at Lydia. "Who's this?"

"A friend of mine."

"She got a name?"

"Lydia Chin," said Lydia, looking steadily at Grice.

"Cute," Grice said. He reached to touch her cheek. She slammed his hand aside. Her eyes blazed. "Grice!" I said sharply. My arms tugged uselessly against the cuffs. "You want to deal, leave her alone."

Grice stopped, open mouthed, eyes on Lydia. Then he laughed. "Well," he said, "maybe later." He looked at me. "Deal? I don't think so." Smiling, he asked Otis, "Where'd you find them?"

"We was lucky," Otis said. "When we was crossing the bridge, Ted spotted that fancy car of his going into the Appleseed lot. We sat and waited till they come out."

Grice whipped to face me. "You talked to Sanderson?"

"Yes."

He started to say something else, but recovered himself. Turning to Otis and Ted, he said casually, "Thanks, boys. Make yourselves scarce for a while. I'll let you know." Ted gave a mock military salute, headed to the kitchen. He lifted a six-pack of Miller from the fridge, clomped behind Otis up the stairs.

Grice waited until we heard the canned laughter of daytime TV drifting down after them. Then he looked at me, asked softly, "Did you tell him?"

"No. I didn't know. I didn't catch on until about ten minutes ago, on the way here."

He looked at me strangely. "Bullshit. You told Mike you knew, at the Creekside. You told everyone. Why do you think Arnold tried to take you out last night?"

At the Creekside. What had I said? I thought back, seeing the hostile faces, smelling the dull air, hearing my words.

"That wasn't my idea, by the way," Grice went on. "I was busy last night." He winked at Lydia. "So Arnold had to decide what to do about you, and Arnold gets a little carried away sometimes."

Arnold, who'd settled on one of the shabby brown chairs, smiled sheepishly.

"I figured that's why no one's found her yet," Grice went on. "Because you and that painter lady, or whatever she is, were going to try to shake me down." He grinned.

"No," I said. "That's not why. Eve doesn't know anything about it. And I didn't have it at the Creekside, Grice. I knew Ginny was with you. I knew she had the paintings and the truck. That was all I knew."

"You're kidding." His crooked mouth pursed. "Christ, you disappoint me, Smith." He shook his head in mock sorrow, spoke to Arnold. "See? I told you we could afford to back off. Plus, of course," he added, to me, "you're not worth as much to me dead, yet."

"You set Jimmy up for it, didn't you?" I said. "Like with Wally Gould? That was your frame, even though you didn't kill him, right?"

Grice laughed out loud. "Maybe you're not so dumb. That was good, wasn't it? Quick thinking in a crisis, I mean."

"Any idiot would have thought of it. What was she doing, just showing off?"

"Uh-huh." He took a cigarette case from his pocket, opened it. Arnold jumped up, did the number with his lighter. "Give one to Smith," Grice told him. "He looks like he needs it."

I did need it. Arnold lit a cigarette, held it about six inches from me, grinning. Finally he stuck it in my mouth. I drew deep on it with the resentful gratitude of any addict who's waited too long for a fix.

Grice perched on the arm of Arnold's chair. "Sit down," he offered.

"I'll stand."

"Ma'am?" courteously, to Lydia.

"Go to hell," Lydia said.

Grice winked at her again. He went on: "Ginny thought I'd be impressed by the paintings. They were worth a cool million, she said. She talked like that. 'A cool million.' Shit." He shook his head, laughing. "She wanted me to fence them for her." He mimicked a prim young voice. " 'We're gonna be rich, Frank. You and me!' "

"But you couldn't fence them, so they weren't worth anything."

"Sure I can. There's nothing can't be fenced. But that kind of shit takes time. I mean, *years*. She didn't want to wait."

"And you didn't want her trying it on her own."

"She was a fucking idiot. She couldn't keep her god-damn head down pushing nickel bags at Pussy Prep."

"And you couldn't afford for her to get caught. That would've screwed up your deal with Sanderson, if she'd dragged you in and he found out you'd been messing with his baby."

"Maybe it would've, maybe not," Grice shrugged. "But why take the chance? That pipeline thing is worth two, three million, all legal. 'Go back to Daddy, baby whore,' I told her. 'You're not ready for the big time.' 'Oh, no?' she says. She smiles that smile she had, kind of scary, you know? She walks up to Wally, presses her tits against him like she's been doing for days. He gets all hot. He was so dumb, Wally." Grice took a drag on his cigarette. Arnold nodded solemnly. "He never noticed when she pulled his gun outta his pants. Three fucking shots she put in that jerk. Then she said, 'Is that big time enough?' You know, she never stopped smiling."

Grice pressed his cigarette down into the ashtray. He smiled, folded one hand over the other in a gesture of finality.

My cigarette wasn't finished yet. I watched him through the smoke that drifted up past my eye. "And after you had Jimmy set up for that one, you figured you'd make it two," I said.

"Well, what the hell was I gonna do, send her home? She was bragging to everyone and his brother-in-law about the burglary, like she was the only broad ever stole anything. She would've called the *newspapers* to say she'd *killed* somebody."

"And that would have gotten you involved."

"You bet your ass. Besides, I was thinking about the paintings. I didn't want her to fuck that up for me."

"For you?"

"That's right. For me." He smiled the smile of a python thinking about a mouse. "We went back to my place. Christ, that's what she wanted. We spent the whole next day in the sack. Just me and those tits and that pink ass. She was a great lay, Smith. You ever have her?"

I couldn't do anything but shake my head.

"Well, you should've. You missed something. She told me she talked to you, that night."

I spat my cigarette butt onto the floor, squashed it under my foot. "She was looking for Jimmy."

"She told me. She thought I'd be impressed if she found him for me. I would've, too. But you wouldn't tell her shit."

"After that," I said, trying to keep my voice calm, even, "that night, you took her to Eve's studio?"

"Hell, she took me! She still thought I just didn't believe her. She thought showing me where the goddamn paintings came from would change my mind. 'She's real famous, Frank.' " Mimicking, again. " 'I learned all about her in school.' Christ, a million-dollar education, that broad was still dumber than shit."

"She was fifteen, Grice."

"And she'd've been sixteen one of these days, if she'd kept out of my way. I tried to get rid of her. I told Mike and those guys, Jimmy too, not to let her hang around, but she was balling 'em all, what were they gonna do?"

Grice stood, faced me close, slipped his hands in his pockets. "So tell me, Smith. Why hasn't the shit hit the fan yet?"

I ignored the question. "What was the setup?"

He stared, then shrugged. "I found Jimmy's gloves in the truck, left one of 'em next to her in the shed. Didn't you notice?" he asked sarcastically.

"That was all?"

"What did I need? Everyone knew he'd been screwing her. I had the truck, I had the gun. I had Brinkman chasing all over the county hunting Jimmy for doing Wally. The glove was plenty."

"The blood in the truck was hers? And the gun you killed her with—Gould's gun?"

"You know so fucking much, how come the whole county isn't screaming about it? You expect me to believe you weren't counting on a little shakedown?"

"Blackmail's your game, Grice. It isn't mine."

He was starting to speak when the telephone shrilled loudly. Grice may have jumped; I know I did. Lydia was still as stone. Grice backed over to the phone, picked it up. "Yeah?" Silence. His twisted face twisted some more. He tried to speak a few times, finally yelled, "Hold it! Dammit, hold on! No. No! Look, I'll call you back." He dropped the receiver back between its prongs, said to Arnold, "Take them upstairs." He stood by the phone, watching, as Arnold pressed his gun against my spine and showed us the way upstairs.

On the next floor were three disheveled bedrooms and one closed door. Arnold, with a lift of his eyebrows, rousted Otis and Ted from a decaying couch and a *Gilligan's Island* rerun. He passed Ted something from his pocket, nodded toward the closed door, and thumped back down to join Grice.

"Doesn't he ever talk?" Lydia asked into the cold air as we were shepherded up the steep steps beyond the door.

"He talks to Frank," Otis said. "He don't like to talk to no one else."

The stair stopped in a small, slant-ceilinged room. It

held two chairs and a table, a sink full of ancient dishes, and a sense of chill neglect.

"Now what?" I asked Otis.

"Now you stay here until Frank wants you somewheres else." He turned to go.

"I don't trust him, Otis," Ted whined.

"It's too damn cold to stay up here with 'em."

"Maybe we should cuff him to something. The radiator," Ted suggested.

"Yeah," Otis agreed. "Good idea." He took the gun Ted had been pointing and he pointed it while Ted came around behind me and opened the cuffs.

I was ready. As soon as the first steel claw released I twisted, dropped, hooked Ted's legs from under him. I saw a blur of black as Lydia dove for Otis's gun.

Ted thudded to the floor, me on top of him. I slammed my elbow into his face, and then I did it again. He softened under me. I rolled off, was pushing to my feet when I heard an explosion, the shattering of glass.

Lydia had Otis bent back against the sink. She had one hand around the gun, which had just gone off, and the other on his throat. Dimly aware of pounding footsteps, I grabbed at Otis's fingers, pried the gun loose. Lydia drove a hard punch into Otis's exposed gut, seized him by the shoulder, threw him across the room. I swung the gun to face the door opening at the bottom of the stairs. Then another explosion, roaring, blinding, knocked me down, endlessly down.

NINETEEN

My name, spoken faintly in the darkness. I tried to answer, and to move; I couldn't do either. The soft voice spoke my name again, more urgently this time. It came from far away, the other end of a long, dark tunnel. It was hot in the tunnel, stifling; or maybe it was deathly cold. I wasn't sure, and it didn't seem to matter anyway.

I heard my name again, and this time with the sound came the blessed cool of a damp cloth pressed to my temple. A pale shape formed in front of me, gradually resolving, sharpening into a face, Lydia's face. She was sitting on the floor next to me, wringing out a dish towel in a bowl of water. The water was pink with blood.

I was sitting too, my hands behind me, sharp ridges pressing uncomfortably into my back. I tried to shift position, bring my hands around, but it wasn't possible.

"Don't try to move," Lydia said. "You're handcuffed. To the radiator." She dabbed at my face with the wet towel, then laid it against the side of my head again.

I leaned my head back, resting it between two cold metallic ridges. "What the hell happened?" I managed.

"Arnold shot you. Just a graze. There's a lot of blood, but I don't think it's bad."

She didn't think it was bad. "Are you okay?" My voice sounded like someone else's.

"Uh-huh."

I tried to look at her; my eyes wouldn't focus. I couldn't tell whether what she said was true.

"Where are they?"

"Downstairs. Grice isn't here. They're waiting for him to get back before they decide what to do with us."

Chances were good they'd already decided, but I didn't say that to Lydia. "Is there anything to drink?"

"Not the way you mean it. There's water."

"Water's good."

She brought me some and it was better than good. I drained the chipped glass twice. Doing that exhausted me, and I leaned my head back again, closed my eyes. "How come you're not chained to something?" I asked her bitterly.

"They're out of cuffs. They tied me, but only with a rope."

"Only with a rope." I opened my eyes again, saw through the throbbing and the haze a snaky length of hemp lying limply on the floor. "You're amazing. Can you pick a lock?"

"You taught me. But I don't have my picks."

"In my wallet, in my jacket, left side."

She searched my jacket, both sides. "Your wallet's gone."

"Shit. What about the cell phone?"

"You really think they're dumb enough to leave you a cell phone?"

"I thought maybe they were too dumb to recognize one."

"Six months ago you wouldn't have recognized one," she pointed out.

"Oh, Christ, all right. Just remember, I told you the thing was useless. Do I still have cigarettes?"

She fished one out, lit it for me, and then, while I smoked, Lydia prowled the room, collecting things that could be used to pick a lock. She sat on the floor, worked on the handcuffs with the bent tine of a fork, with the prong from my belt buckle, with the straightened end of a wire hanger she'd found hanging from an empty curtain rod. Finally she sat back on her heels, spread her hands emptily. "I'm sorry, Bill. It's not working."

"You must have had a lousy teacher."

Sounds came from somewhere in the house below, the loud slamming of a door, voices. We both froze, eyes on the stairs. Lydia's hand tightened on my arm.

When no footsteps came up the stairs and the voices stopped we breathed again.

"What's outside?" I asked. "Something you could climb on? Could you make it out a window?"

Lydia looked around without getting up. "Maybe I could. But I'm not going to leave you here like this."

"Lydia, please, don't be a hero, just go call a cop."

"It'll take me an hour to find a phone."

I started to shake my head, realized that was a mistake. I leaned back again, but I didn't close my eyes. "There's a Hess station a quarter mile north, where this road hits the paved one." We'd come from the south. She wouldn't know I was lying.

She hesitated. Then she said, "They'll kill you."

"Christ, Lydia!" I put as much into it as I had, which wasn't much. "You think you can stop them, if you stay? If you're here when Grice gets back they'll kill us both." It crossed my mind that I didn't know why they hadn't done that already. "I don't want to die here, but if I do, I want someone to pay. Please, Lydia."

"If it were the other way around, you wouldn't leave me."

"Bullshit! I'd leave your Chinese ass in the dust so fast it wouldn't know what hit it."

She laid her hand very gently on my cheek. "Can you look at me and say that?"

I turned my head to her, looked into her eyes, which had become liquid, bottomless. I didn't say anything.

After a moment she kissed me, her lips soft and warm, resting as lightly on mine as her hand on my cheek. Then she stood. She walked around the room, looked out each window in turn. She paused at one in the wall to my right, one I couldn't see. I heard her open it, felt the cold wind push in. A soft slithering sound, a quiet thud, and then nothing. Nothing for a long time. I started to breathe again.

And then the crack of a rifle shot. Another. Voices, yelling; words I couldn't make out. Adrenaline surged through me, rammed my spine straight, scraped my nerves. I strained to hear, through the hissing wind, through the pounding in my ears, but the voices had stopped and there was nothing else. I found I was yanking, stupidly, repeatedly, at the cuffs that pinned me where I was, in this dim attic room, alone and useless.

I didn't have much time to be alone; I didn't have much time to wonder. Feet thudded, the door crashed open, Arnold and Otis and Frank Grice exploded up the stairs and into the room. They stopped when they saw me. I could feel them relax.

"Well," Grice grinned. "So it looks like your girlfriend skipped out without you."

I couldn't see their faces well; they were standing too close, towering too high. The radiator wouldn't let me tilt my head back. Hoarsely, I said, "If you hurt her, Grice, I'll kill you."

"Yeah," he snickered. "Sure." He squatted, brought his face level with mine. "Would it bother you if I told you she was dead?"

I couldn't answer; I was frozen in ice. Then Grice laughed, clapped me on the shoulder as though we were drinking buddies sharing a good joke. "Well, she's not. She's not even scratched. She was lucky," he said. "Just like me. Get him up, boys. You're lucky too, Smith. Come on, we'll go for a ride."

Arnold knelt behind me, unlocked the cuffs. He and Otis hauled me to my feet. Otis propped me up while Arnold pulled my hands behind me again, slid the handcuffs shut around my swollen wrists.

I needed the support. The room was swaying; my knees were like water. I shut my eyes to fight the dizziness, but it got worse. Grice's voice came from a long way off: "Sit him down." I felt myself dropped onto a chair. I'd have slipped off if someone hadn't been holding me there. The world rolled sickeningly around me.

Then something hard was pressed against my mouth. Fire burned my tongue, my throat. I swallowed, coughed. Time out. Then there was more, and I swallowed again, and when I opened my eyes the room was almost still.

"All right?" asked Grice. "Because the boys don't want to carry you."

"More." A croaking half whisper seemed to be the only voice I had.

Arnold held the bottle for me, and I gulped as much as I could get. Whiskey trickled down my chin, splashed wet patches onto my shirt. When Grice said, "Enough," Arnold took it away, stood it on the table.

I let my eyes shut, made them open again. I wasn't ready for Grice's face; I focused on the bottle. Canadian Club. I gave a short, harsh laugh. "I had you figured for the Four Roses type, Frank."

"He's ready," said Grice. "Get him up."

This time as they pulled me to my feet the room lurched but it didn't flip over. The stairs were difficult, but Arnold's iron grip kept me upright all the way down to the living room, where Lydia sat, pale but, as far as I could see, whole. Her hands were tied behind her. Opposite her, on the other shabby chair, Ted held a deer rifle casually on his lap.

"You okay?" I asked, in a voice as strong as I could make it.

She nodded. Then she shrugged, smiled with a corner of her mouth, said, "Sorry."

I gave her back the same smile. Then I turned to Grice. "I want to deal."

"Smith, what the hell you think you have to deal with?"

"I must have something. I'm not dead yet."

"Oh." Grice grinned. "And you think that's because you have something I want? Well, you don't. You're just going to help me out a little. Now," he crossed to Lydia's chair, laid his hand on her head, "*this* is something I want. But it's not yours anymore."

Lydia jerked her head from under Grice's hand. He laughed. I ignored what he was doing, and the way it made me feel. I spoke evenly. "So why aren't I dead?"

"Because you're lucky. You see, when I had the boys bring you up here, I was still looking for Jimmy. Just to help Brinkman out, you know. I'm that kind of guy. Arnold was going to persuade you to tell us where he was. You wouldn't've enjoyed that, but Arnold would." He smiled at Arnold, who smiled back. "But then I had to go all the way to fucking Cobleskill to calm Sanderson down, because you got his balls in an uproar. And driving back, I'm thinking about you, I'm thinking about Jimmy, I'm thinking about last fall. And bang! It comes to me. That's where he's got to be. He's up at the quarry."

He waited for an answer. I didn't give him one. "Well?" he said.

I met his eyes. "I don't know."

Grice looked at me for a minute, then laughed again. "Okay," he said. "But let's go look. If he's not there, Arnold can ask you nicely where he is. If he is there, you can be my insurance. I don't think he'll shoot me if he has to shoot through you."

"I still want to deal."

"With *what?*"

I took a breath. "I have the paintings."

Grice smiled a big, slow, crooked smile. "No," he said. "Yes."

"And I thought you were a straight-arrow type."

I shrugged. "They're worth a lot of money."

"So you stole them."

"I just moved them. Nobody else seemed to have any idea they were there. I didn't know how they got there but I knew what they were."

Lydia was watching me closely, her eyes narrowed. "So where are they?"

"That's the deal."

Grice flipped open his gold cigarette case. Arnold snapped his lighter. Grice sucked at the end of the cigarette, said around it, "Okay. You tell us where they are, we'll let you go."

I laughed. "Bullshit. I'm dead, Frank. You think I don't know that? The deal is this: You let Lydia go. Then I tell you where the paintings are."

"If you're dead," he said, streaming smoke at me, "how come she's not?"

"Because she's not as dangerous as I am. What the hell does she know? She heard you confess to one murder and to being an accessory to another, but you've got Jimmy framed for both. By the time she gets to tell anyone her story, Jimmy and I'll be dead and you and the boys here"—I spat the word "boys"; I couldn't help it—"will have an airtight alibi, probably provided by Sanderson in return for whatever it is you've got on him."

Grice smoked, a contemplative look on his uneven face. I wasn't sure he'd bought it, so I went on. "In fact, if she's smart—and she is—she won't say anything to anybody. Why bother? Isn't that right, sweetheart?" I looked at Lydia, my face blank, everything I'd ever wanted to say to her in my eyes.

Lydia's obsidian eyes widened slightly. She said, "That's right. I like to stay out of trouble."

"Okay," Grice decided. "We go find Jimmy. Then we go get the paintings. Then she goes home."

Even through the protective layer of Canadian Club the throbbing in my head was making it hard to think and my legs were getting rubbery again. I had to end this. If I passed out here Grice would just pile us all in the car and forget about making any deals.

"She comes with us," I said. "She gets out where I say, so I can see. Then I tell you. Nothing else, Grice. Nothing else."

Grice finished his cigarette. He nodded slowly. "Sure. Why not?"

Thank God, I thought, as the six of us crossed the swampy lawn to the blue Ford. Thank God. Now just keep it together, Smith, one more play and you can sit out the rest of the game.

Because I knew what Grice was thinking: Let her go. Find out where the paintings are. And then deal with her later.

He could do that. I knew he could. Lydia wouldn't be able to prove what she'd heard today, and she wouldn't be safe from him, ever.

But I had one more play. And if Grice was stupid enough, and Lydia was smart enough, we just might pull it off.

TWENTY

The rhythm of the car was soporific with my eyes closed, sickening with them open, but I needed, desperately, to stay awake. One chance; one place.

An argument started in the front seat and I concentrated on it.

"It ain't on the goddamn map, Frank," Ted was complaining. "I never been there."

Papers rustled loudly, Grice unfolding a highway map, not nearly detailed enough to show them the way to the quarry from the green house near Franklinton.

"Here," Grice said, with his finger on a place on the map. "This is where the truck road starts. Get us here. I can find it from there."

Ted peered over. The car drifted; he yanked at the wheel, swung us back from the shoulder. "Okay, Frank," he said. "Sure."

Arnold had brought the bottle. I asked for a drink. Arnold looked to Grice, in the front seat next to Otis. Grice shrugged, Arnold held the bottle for me, and against its better judgment my blood started to move again.

I wondered if Ted had been promoted to Wally Gould's old job, and how Otis felt about that. We drove north, hit the paved road a mile away at a featureless intersection. Lydia threw me a look, muttered, "Hess station, huh?"

Grice turned around. "What?"

"Private joke," I answered.

We kept moving. I kept trying to stay awake. Not much

longer, I promised myself, feeling a trickle of blood slide down along my jawline from the throbbing place near my eye. For Lydia. For Jimmy. And not much longer.

I almost missed it. There was only one good way to the quarry from where we'd been; that was the basket all my eggs were in. But when we got to where I'd been waiting to get to, I was almost gone. The road climbed, ran straight, fell. I pushed myself back to consciousness, said, "Here."

"Here what?" Grice asked.

"Lydia gets out here."

Grice gestured to Ted. The car slowed, stopped. "Why here?"

"Because it's deserted. Because it'll take her an hour to find anyone, if she's looking. So she can't stop you doing whatever it is you're planning to do. So you'll let her go." Buy it, I begged him silently. Buy it. It's all I've got.

Grice nodded. Arnold reached across Lydia, opened her door. He untied her hands as Grice said, "Get out."

Lydia hesitated, looked at me. I met her eyes. "Walk back the way we came," I told her. "Don't turn around. And Lydia?" I added, "it's okay. Remember, it's just a game."

A light flashed in the depths of Lydia's eyes, or maybe I just needed to think I saw it there. She turned, slid swiftly from the car, and stalked rapidly away. She didn't look back.

I leaned back against the seat, shut my eyes. That was it. My part was almost over.

The car started to move again. "That was touching," Grice said.

"Screw you," I murmured.

"Where are the paintings?"

"Screw you."

Arnold grabbed my jacket, jerked me close to him. He smacked me with his open palm once, and again. Howling pain shot through my skull, blinding my left eye.

"No," I said weakly. "Wait." I didn't want to be hurt

any more, and I was lying anyway. Arnold pushed me back against the seat. I lay there breathing unevenly, not speaking, as long as I dared. Make them look at you, Smith. Make them think about you, focus on you.

I felt Arnold's hand tighten on my collar again. "No," I whispered. I didn't even try to open my eyes. "Cobleskill. Self-storage rooms near the college."

"Where's the key?" Grice demanded.

Key. I hadn't thought about a key. "No key. Combination. Room number's one-twenty-four. Combination's eleven, twenty-five, fifty-one." I swallowed, said, "Give me a drink."

"Screw you." Grice laughed, Otis laughing with him. Arnold was probably grinning, but I didn't look to see.

I was cold. A drink would have helped, or a cigarette. Or a soft voice, or music. Schubert, maybe. I began to hear the soft opening chords of the B-flat Sonata, the one I didn't play. They faded, along with everything else, as the darkness thickened around me.

I woke when the car stopped moving. Outside, a silver sky pressed down like a weight on thick slate-colored clouds. Ted had brought us by the truck road to the flat, exhausted plain. I stared across the pit to the shadowed ridge rising against the sky. We had come along the road up there, the ridge road; from Franklinton it made sense. But the drive from there to the truck road was long, roundabout. You couldn't see the quarry pits from the ridge road, even in winter. If you didn't know the area well, if you didn't know where you were, you might not be able to tell anything about that road when you were on it, except that it was deserted, far from anywhere.

That was the reason I'd given Grice for letting Lydia go there.

"Is that where he's been staying?" Grice's words tore the silence. He pointed toward the shack.

"I don't know." My voice sounded like sandpaper on a board.

"Drive closer," Grice told Ted. He drew his gun from his coat; so did Otis. Arnold's was already out, aimed casually at my belly.

We rolled slowly over the stones scattering the plain. Ted angled the car toward the shack. My heart, beating fast, jarred, then stopped as Jimmy's van came into view.

Lydia hadn't made it. She hadn't understood, or maybe she hadn't been able to handle the climb down. Whatever; it didn't matter; she hadn't made it.

The car stopped again. Arnold leaned across me, as he had across Lydia, and opened my door. He nudged the barrel of his gun against my temple, against the place where the blood was drying. "Out," said Grice. I swung my legs through the door, stood with an effort. From behind, Arnold grabbed my arm. We moved clear of the car. Grice got out, kept behind me. "Jimmy!" he shouted into the empty sky. The word echoed, faded; there was nothing else. "Jimmy! I just want to talk to you, kid. Come on out for a minute." There was no movement, no wind in the trees. "Jimmy! I got your friend here, kid, and he doesn't look good. You don't talk to me, Jimmy, he could get to look worse."

More silence. The clouds could have been painted; the surface of the water was polished marble. Grice tapped Arnold's arm, and we walked forward again, toward the shack.

Then, crashing through the stillness, a gunshot exploded, magnified by silence, multiplied by echoes. It seemed to come from everywhere around us, but as Arnold's grip suddenly slackened I spun around, ran with everything I had left toward the rock pile at the mouth of the other road.

What I had left wasn't enough. As shots came from behind me and another from ahead I tripped, stumbled, fell, and knew I couldn't get up; but strong hands seized me, yanked me forward, around the fortress of rock.

The world was reeling. Shots screamed through the air. I was hauled up, over stones and loose pebbles, until fi nally I was dropped, battered and breathing dust, my shoulders and arms burning with pain wherever I had feeling at all.

From somewhere above, Lydia said, "Is he okay?"

Jimmy's voice: "I guess." I was helped to sit, my back against a rock. At first my eyes showed me nothing but shape and movement. Then things started to make sense again. I squinted, made out Lydia's black-wrapped form kneeling between two boulders. She squeezed a shot out of Jimmy's Winchester, pulled back, and reloaded fast as a bullet chipped the stone at her shoulder.

"What the hell are you two idiots doing here?" I coughed on stone dust.

"Christ, he's crabby," Jimmy said to Lydia.

"He gets like that when he doesn't feel well," Lydia answered. She took aim, shot again. I heard glass shatter.

"I got my goddamn ass busted trying to save yours," I told them. "You were supposed to be gone by the time we got here."

"They weren't going to keep hauling you around if Jimmy was gone," Lydia pointed out. "They'd've killed you and dumped you here."

"So now they'll kill us all. I don't suppose it occurred to you two superheroes to go for help?"

"Not to me. Jimmy?"

"Uh-uh." He shook his head. Then he grinned at me. "I mean, not after we put it out on the CB."

The CB. Oh, beautiful consumer audio technology. "You called for help?"

Jimmy grinned again. "Man, I was so scared, I told the guy who picked it up to call the sheriff. Brinkman, man. Me—I called the fucking sheriff!"

But it wasn't Brinkman whose car came rocketing up the truck road, scaring a cloud of dust into the air.

Since the first storm of shots, Grice and his boys hadn't moved out from behind the Ford. They had reasons not to. Lydia was a deadly accurate shot. Otis and Ted were cowards. And Arnold was out of the picture, stretched still as stone where Lydia's first bullet had dropped him.

But we couldn't go anywhere either, and we had only one gun. Sooner or later, if we had to keep sniping to keep them pinned, our box of shells would be empty. They would know that moment, and that moment would be theirs.

We had no escape; we needed a rescue.

So fifteen minutes later, when we heard the whine of a heavy engine, the screech of brakes echoing off the stone walls, they were good sounds. "The fucking marines!" Jimmy cheered.

But Lydia, peering around a boulder, said, "It's not a cop."

She was wrong, but she was right.

"Civilian," she said. "One man." She whipped her head back as a bullet spewed stone chips into the air. She took aim, fired back, pulled her head in again. "He's out of the car. I can't see him now. He must be behind the other car with Grice." She reloaded, inched her head out. "Nothing." A pause. "But maybe he is a cop. There's a red light on the dash, the portable kind."

"What does he look like?"

"I couldn't really see. Thin face, reddish hair."

A cold shock hit me. I heard a wordless sound of surprise and sorrow; I realized it had come from me.

This was the piece I hadn't had.

"Smith!" MacGregor's voice burst, loud and distorted, from the electronic bullhorn all state cop cars carry, even unmarked ones. "Don't shoot. I'm coming up there."

Lydia turned to me. I said, "Let him come."

I heard MacGregor scramble up the rocks, watched as he appeared, crouching, in the narrow cleft we occupied. His face darkened when he saw me, the cuffs, the blood.

"What happened?" His voice was tight, cold.

"Your friends."

"They're no friends of mine."

"Crap, MacGregor." A shiver overtook me. "You're

Grice's hip-pocket cop. You're why he's always a step ahead."

MacGregor exploded. "I warned you, you son of a bitch!" His voice was driven, full of fury. I squinted to look at him. "I begged you, stay out of this fucking case! I told you to go the hell back to New York!"

"That's true," I agreed quietly. "You tried. And I smelled something wrong with the way you did it. But I didn't add it up. I guess I didn't want to know."

"Oh, Christ, Smith, don't get holy on me! Small shit, that's all it is. I pass on what I hear. I bury a file or take a guy off something before he gets too close. So what? I don't have the manpower to go after every crook around. Someone's going to get away with something. What's the difference if it's Grice?"

"Uh-huh," I said. "And the kids shooting up in the Creekside? And guys who're barely squeezing out a living, then splitting their chickenshit take-home with Grice so they don't get their legs broken? That's okay with you, Mac?"

"Oh, come off it! If it weren't Grice it would be some-body else!" His face was purple with anger, but in his eyes there was something like pleading.

"And Ginny Sanderson?" I said softly. "That's okay with you?"

MacGregor looked quickly from Jimmy to me. "What about her?"

"She's dead. Grice shot her. I think you'll find her if you drag the quarry." I looked at Jimmy. He was white as marble.

"She was a *kid*," Jimmy whispered. "She was a *kid*."

"Yeah," I said. "A kid. That's what it was about, right, Mac? Kids?"

It took MacGregor a long time to answer. "Tuition," he said, not to anyone, not looking at anyone. "Books, clothes. Travel. Piano lessons, painting lessons. There had to be something for them besides this. I had to find them a way out." He faced me suddenly, the pleading back in his eyes. His voice wavered. "I had to, Smith. I'm their father; I had to."

I had trouble speaking, too. "Ginny Sanderson had a father, Mac."

"I didn't know about her. I didn't know."

No one spoke. We watched each other, motionless, silent. Statues, all of us, cold and separate, powerless, and alone.

Lydia, finally, broke the silence. A quick, worried glance at me; then to MacGregor, "What do they want?"

MacGregor gave her a blank, lost look. "What?"

"They let you come up here. They're holding their fire. Why?"

He swallowed. "Jimmy. They'll let you two leave with me. They want to talk to Jimmy."

"Do it." Jimmy's words came fast, but they caught in his throat.

"Talk, bullshit." I didn't look at Jimmy, spoke to MacGregor. "They'll kill him. Then they'll call Brinkman. Here he is, the guy who killed Wally, the guy who killed Ginny. Sorry he's dead, but it'll save the cost of a trial. Any problems, call MacGregor." I paused, said, "Then they'll come for Lydia and me later."

He met my eyes, nodded slowly. "I know that. It was all I could think of, to get Grice to let me come up here. It'll buy time."

"What do you mean?"

"I'm not the only cop who picked up the CB call. Brinkman's on his way, but he wasn't close."

I looked closely at him. "You could have stayed away, then," I said. "You could have kept out of it, and maybe you'd have stayed smelling clean."

"Yeah," he said. "But they said it was Jimmy, and he was asking for help. I had a feeling what was happening. And I'm a cop, Smith. Whatever you think."

An engine roared to life below us.

"Hey!" Lydia yelled. "They're moving!"

"What the hell—!" MacGregor stuck his head up next

to hers, dropped down again as a shot sliced the air. With a cop's instinct he reached for his gun, pawed an empty holster. He cursed, looked at me, shrugged. "Grice has it," he said. "That was the deal."

Grice's voice blared from the speaker on MacGregor's car. "You've got thirty seconds, folks. Come down, everyone can leave but Jimmy. How about it?"

"Do it, for Chrissake!" Jimmy said again.

Lydia and I exchanged a look that MacGregor caught, and MacGregor understood it. For the first time, he grinned. "Fuck you!" he yelled over the rock, and his words echoed in the dusty air.

"What's happening?" I asked Lydia. I struggled to sit up straighter, as though it would help me think.

"They're moving the Ford around this way. I can't get a shot."

But they could. As the Ford's engine shut off, a barrage of gunfire from our right almost hid the sounds of someone scrabbling up the rock. Lydia whipped around, fired where she couldn't see. Sudden silence; then a shot from behind her, the side MacGregor had climbed. She answered that, too, and then the Winchester was empty and Ted's sneering face appeared behind a Luger where the first shots had come from.

He swung the barrel of the gun to Jimmy, who was frozen, pressed against the rock; but before Ted could fire, MacGregor tackled him. They fell, struggled, tumbled down the rocks out of sight. Then a shot. Then nothing.

Lydia had reloaded. Suddenly we were fired on from both sides. Lydia shot again, twice, looked at me with frightened eyes. There was nothing I could give her. She shook herself, reloaded again, and as she did, a siren screamed and tires crunched and car doors slammed and a voice I had never been glad to hear before hollered, "Give it up, Grice! I got two more cars on the way!"

Shots screamed from our right, and two or three from ahead, near the shack. Lydia crept forward to the cleft she'd been shooting from before, craned her neck. She yelled, "Sheriff, on your left!" She stood to get an angle, fired down the face of the rock.

Then, at the whine of another shot, she jerked, lost her footing, fell hard against the rock. She didn't get up, didn't move.

"Oh, Jesus, no," I heard myself plead. I was dimly aware of Jimmy grabbing the rifle, more shots, then silence, sudden and total. I saw nothing but Lydia's face. "Lydia, please," I whispered. "Please."

The silence ended, broken by shouting voices, slamming car doors, a confusion of smaller sounds. Through it all, Lydia's pale, still face.

"Antonelli, you bastard!" I heard Brinkman yell. "I'm coming up there. You gonna shoot me?"

"No," Jimmy answered, but it came out as a whisper, so he had to say it again: "No!"

"Stand up—where I can see you!"

Jimmy did, leaning the rifle against a rock, showing the cops below his hands were empty. Grunts and curses as Brinkman hauled himself up the rock pile. He appeared from behind a boulder like Godzilla coming to crush a city.

"Well," he drawled, with the mean little smile. "Don't you two look like shit."

Lydia groaned, moved her hand a little in the dirt.

"Help her!" I looked from Brinkman to Jimmy. "Jesus, help her!"

"Yeah," said Brinkman. He dropped to one knee, bent over Lydia. "Calm down, city boy. Nothing wrong with her. Just a bump on the head. I got the Rescue Squad coming."

"Sheriff," a voice called from below, "two of these guys are alive."

"Yeah?" Brinkman yelled back. "Which two?"

"The one with the cast. And Ron MacGregor."

Lydia groaned, stirred. "Don't move, little girl. You'll be fine," Brinkman told her.

Lydia's eyelids fluttered, opened. "Little girl," she murmured. "I'll kill you."

"It'd be a waste," Brinkman said. "You saved my life. Now just don't you move." He took off his jacket, covered her with it. He swiveled to face me, said, "You know, city boy, you look a hell of a lot worse than she does. Who has the key?"

I had no idea what he meant.

"The cuffs. The key to the cuffs."

I tried to remember. "Arnold."

"Arnold Shea? The big guy?"

"Yes."

Brinkman narrowed his eyes at Jimmy, smiled a little smile. "He's stretched out there by your van, Jimmy, deader'n hell. Go get the key off him. For your buddy here."

Jimmy swallowed hard, turned, climbed down off the mound of rock.

"You didn't have to do that, Brinkman." I coughed, closed my eyes.

"I like to see that kid sweat," he said. "Now how about you telling me what went on here?"

"Later," I said, my voice sounding distant, even to me.

TWENTY-ONE

MacGregor died in the ambulance on the way to the hospital.

After Brinkman had unlocked my handcuffs, he'd told Jimmy to get me down to the cruiser, where it was warm. He moved Lydia there also, laying her on the back seat while I slumped in the front, and we were there like that until the ambulance came; but before that, after I had worked my way down the rocky mound with Jimmy's hand tight on my numb arm, I had crouched by Mac-Gregor, motionless in the dust.

Brinkman's fat deputy had covered MacGregor with a blanket from the cruiser. There was blood on the blanket. MacGregor's face was ash gray and his breathing was shallow, ragged.

I spoke his name. His eyes opened. "Smith." The corners of his mouth moved weakly. "I guess no trout this spring, huh?"

"Summer," I said. "They'll be bigger by then, anyhow."

"Yeah." His face contorted with pain. He said, hoarsely, "I wouldn't have done it, you know." He gestured toward Jimmy with his eyes. "If you'd left it alone, I'd have found a way to let him off. I knew it was a frame. I wouldn't've let it happen."

I had no way to tell if that was true, but MacGregor's gray eyes were locked onto mine, and I said, "I know, Mac. I know."

His eyes closed. I saw him struggling to keep them open, not to lose yet.

"Take it easy," I said. "They've got an ambulance coming."

I tried to find something else to say, but there was nothing. Jimmy tugged gently on my arm, and I stood, my eyes stinging in the cold gray light.

The "later" I had promised Brinkman happened in the outpatient department of the hospital in Cobleskill. Lydia was in a room upstairs. Brinkman had been right: She had a concussion, not serious. Prognosis excellent. I'd waited until they could tell me that before I let them take me down the hall and put four stitches next to my left eye. I lay now on a bed in a curtained-off stall in Outpatient because, although they'd made a room ready for me upstairs too, I had refused to be admitted. The doctor who'd sewn me up, a round man named Mazzeo, popped in every ten minutes to tell me a man in my condition couldn't leave the hospital.

"You can't drive," he pointed out, a pudgy finger smoothing his thick mustache. "You probably can't even see straight. You have a headache to beat the band, am I right? And your hands won't be much good for hours."

I flexed my swollen fingers. The numbness was receding slowly, leaving the billion pinpricks of returning circulation behind. My wrists were bruised, red and purple under the icepacks that wrapped them.

"No," I said. "I'm leaving." I didn't try for anything else. I knew that I couldn't argue with him, but I also knew I wasn't staying. Everything here was sharp and bright, and outside the curtain I could hear voices and footsteps and the sounds of endless activity. There was no peace here, no darkness, no silence. No music. I couldn't stay.

Immediately after the third or fourth of Dr. Mazzeo's disapproving visits the curtains parted again and Brinkman stood smiling and very tall next to the bed. "Shit," he said, took his hat off. "I brought in four corpses today, Smith, and they all looked better than you do."

"Go to hell."

"Christ! For a man whose life I saved, you're an ornery son of a bitch."

"Yeah," I said. "I always was." I paused, went on, "But I owe you for that, Brinkman. And for Lydia and Jimmy."

"So pay up, city boy. What the hell's going on around here, and how come I shouldn't lock you up, you and Jimmy and that china doll of yours?" He dropped his hat on the bed, pulled a stool close.

I turned my pounding head carefully, groped with thick fingers for the button that would raise the bed. Brinkman vertical and me horizontal was bad odds to start with.

I tilted the bed as upright as it would go, and then I asked Brinkman to find me some water. By the time he got back I'd found a way to tell it, very close to the truth.

"Ginny Sanderson," I said, after a drink.

"Snotty little bitch," he drawled. "What about her?"

That jolted me, but then I realized he didn't know.

"She's dead, Brinkman. Grice killed her."

Nothing moved but his eyes. They narrowed into slits. "The hell you say."

I drank more water, spoke slowly. "She wanted to be part of Grice's in-crowd. But Grice wasn't having any. She thought it was her, so she tried harder. She took up with Jimmy; she robbed a house."

"Robbed what house?" Brinkman interrupted.

"Eve Colgate's."

"Miss Colgate didn't report that."

"No," I said. "She called me instead."

"Why?"

I shrugged. "Some people aren't crazy about cops."

"Smith—"

"Oh, Christ, Brinkman, will you shut up and let me finish? Let me get through this, then you can arrest me or shoot me or whatever the fuck you want."

His face darkened, and I wondered briefly whether it

was beyond him to beat up a man lying in a hospital bed. Maybe I'd get to find out.

Meanwhile, I went on. "I traced the burglary to Ginny pretty easily. She denied it, but sooner or later she'd have come across. But there was a wrinkle: Some of the stuff she'd stolen was really valuable. She thought Grice would be impressed with that, so she showed him. He wasn't."

Brinkman asked through gritted teeth, "Why not?"

"Well, he was, but it was hard stuff to fence. And Grice had a sweetheart deal going with her father. He didn't want to blow that by getting caught fooling around with her."

"Grice? You're telling me Frank Grice was making deals with Mark Sanderson?"

"Uh-huh. Based on blackmail, I think."

"Blackmail over what?"

"The murder of Lena Sanderson."

"The *what?* Jesus, city boy, what the fuck are you talking about?"

"When Lena disappeared," I said, "Sanderson called the cops, it's true; but it would've looked too odd if he hadn't. But he didn't hire anyone to look privately, after you guys turned up nothing. Okay, so maybe he figured good riddance. But he also didn't cancel her credit cards. He didn't close bank accounts she had access to. He never filed for a legal separation. He didn't make any effort to protect himself from her. All I can figure is he knew he didn't have to."

"You're saying—"

"I think Sanderson killed her. Either that, or he hired Grice to do it; but my money's on him. In anger; probably by accident. She played around one too many times; the whole county was full of it, from what I hear, but it took him forever to catch on.

"Then I'll bet he lost his nerve. He called Grice. They knew each other: Grice did muscle work for Sanderson. So Sanderson calls. I've got this body in my living room, get rid of it. No problem, Grice gets rid of it. And suddenly Grice is a big shot. He's running the county. Sanderson buys him a cop, Sanderson buys him information, and he and Sanderson go into business together."

Brinkman's eyes were hard, his mouth tight with anger. I thought he was going to tell me to shove my theories, but when he spoke, it was to ask, "What business?"

"Appleseed Holdings." I told him about that.

Brinkman sat silent for a while when I was through, then stood abruptly. "City boy," he said, "the Sandersons fought under George Washington. When that war was over they came up here and settled this county. My county, Smith. Now you want me to believe Mark Sanderson murdered his wife and bends over for Frank Grice?" He shook his head. "I don't know, city boy. I don't know."

"I don't give a shit what you believe, Brinkman. I'm telling you what happened. A real cop would check it out."

"A—" His hand curled into a fist, but he said, "Ginny. You're so fucking smart, what about Ginny?"

I told him about Ginny, Wally Gould, Frank Grice. He asked what it was Ginny had stolen that was so valuable, and I told him the only lie I had for him. "I don't know."

After a long silence, he asked, "Where are they?"

It took me a moment; then I caught on. "The bodies? I'll bet you'll find them if you drag the quarry."

Brinkman looked at me long and hard, his small eyes like a cold, close weight, stones on my chest. "All right," he said at last. "I'll check it out. Otis Huttner's still alive; I'll see what he has to say. And I'll drag the quarry. And you'd better be right, Smith. You'd better be right, or you're fucked."

He turned and strode out, the curtain closing behind him.

I was right, I knew I was. The part about Lena Sanderson was theory, but it fit too well to be wrong. I thought about Mark Sanderson, what it would be like for him when Brinkman faced him with the two bodies in the quarry, the one he knew about and the one he didn't.

I was grateful for the emptiness of the room after Brinkman was gone. I'd worked hard to give him what he'd needed to know, but to hold back the one part I'd told no one. I hadn't been sure I could do it. In the end I had, but the exhaustion I felt now, alone in the curtained alcove, was in my nerves, my muscles, and bones, a tiredness so deep I was, finally, unable to move.

I lay back, my eyes closed, prepared to surrender whenever Dr. Mazzeo bustled back in. I slept for a while; then I heard the metallic slide of the curtain rings. I opened my eyes to see Eve Colgate pulling the curtain shut.

I reached out my hand. She took it, smiling slightly. "Well," she said, "you don't look as bad as Al Mazzeo said you did."

"I don't feel as bad as he says I do."

"How do you feel?"

"Battered." A thought hit me. "Jesus, you've been here all day, haven't you?"

She nodded. "I was stranded. Lydia was supposed to call me. I waited until afternoon. When I hadn't heard from her, I called the state troopers. Was it they who found you?"

"Sort of," I said. That must have been why MacGregor had reached the quarry so fast after Jimmy's call came over the CB. He'd been on his way to Franklinton, to the green house. He'd known right where to head for when Eve told him Lydia and I had gone off radar.

"How's Tony?" I asked Eve.

"Improving. He was awake for a while. He asked for you. He's anxious to talk to you. But he doesn't know who shot him."

"Arnold Shea," I said. "He's dead."

"Bill, what's going on? What happened to Lydia? The sheriff's men won't tell me anything."

"Lydia'll be okay. A concussion, not serious. And it's all over, Eve."

"What do you mean, over? What happened? What's happening?"

"You're safe. You always were; you weren't the target.

I'll tell you about it. And I think I know where your paintings are."

She was speechless for a moment, her clear eyes widening. "Do you?" she asked. "Do you?"

"I think so. If I'm right, I'll get them in the morning."

"Where? Who has them?"

"I don't want to tell you, in case I'm wrong." I wasn't wrong, but the whole story was something I hoped she would never know. "But Eve, I need a favor."

"What do you need?"

"A ride. The doctor wants me to stay here. I want to leave. But he says I can't drive yet and I know that's right."

She hesitated. "Are you sure that's a good idea?"

"Yes."

Another hesitation, then an ironic smile. "All right. But what am I supposed to use for a car?"

"Oh," I said. "A car." I thought. "Mine's at the Appleseed plant. Lydia's is at Grice's condo."

"Yours is closer. I'll call a cab."

"Is the cab company still open?"

"They're open until eight. It's only four-thirty."

"Four-thirty? Jesus."

I'd thought midnight, at least.

When Eve was gone I got gingerly out of bed. I dressed, moving very carefully. At first I was light-headed, clutching the door frame for support until a wave of dizziness passed, but I was feeling more solid by the time I got to the admissions desk to check out. After I did that I asked for Lydia's room number, bought myself a cup of coffee, and rode the elevator to the second floor.

In Lydia's room the lights were out, leaving the room to settle softly into the purple dusk. I stood silently by the bed, sipped my coffee, watched the bedclothes rise and fall with the gentle rhythm of Lydia's breathing. The white bandage around her head made her features look delicate, her face small and vulnerable. She'd hate to know I was even thinking that.

When my coffee was almost gone Lydia's eyelids fluttered, opened, closed again.

"Bill?" Her voice was faint.

"I'm here."

"Are you all right?"

"I'm fine."

"Thank God," she breathed. "Now go to hell."

"Lydia—"

"Passwords, for God's sake." I leaned to hear her better. " 'It's only a game.' I almost broke my neck climbing down that cliff. You smell like a brewery."

"Distillery."

"Go to hell," she whispered again.

"I'm sorry," I said.

"No, you're not. You're standing there thinking how very clever you are, how you managed to save everybody after all."

Not everybody, I thought. In the twilight I saw MacGregor's ashen face.

I stood silent, not knowing what to say. She was silent too, and for a while I thought she was asleep. Then, her eyes still closed, she slipped her hand from beneath the blanket, found mine. I closed my tingling fingers around her small, soft ones.

"Bill?"

"It's okay. You'll be okay."

The sky outside the window faded slowly to black. I stood holding Lydia's hand until the soft rhythm of her breathing told me she was asleep again, and for a long time after that.

When I left Lydia I took the elevator again, this time to the third floor, to Tony's room. In here the lights were on, but Tony was asleep, his face pale and, even in sleep, reflecting pain.

Suddenly deeply weary, I pulled a chair next to the bed,

leaned forward in it. I spoke Tony's name once, twice. His lips moved, without sound; then his eyelids rose slowly. He looked blankly around. "Tony," I said again. With an effort, his eyes found mine.

"Smith." His whisper was almost inaudible.

"Don't talk," I said. "Just listen. I came to tell you it's over. Jimmy didn't kill anyone, Tony. Ginny Sanderson— the little blond girl—Ginny Sanderson killed Wally Gould and Frank Grice killed Ginny Sanderson. Tony, do you understand what I'm saying?"

He moved his head minutely, a nod. "Blood," he whispered. Pain shadowed his face. "All over everything."

"Uh-huh. But Jimmy wasn't involved in any of it. Any of it, Tony. He ran because he was scared. He didn't have the keys and he didn't have the truck. Do you understand?"

"The truck," he whispered. "I was followin' the truck."

"I know, Tony. Don't talk, don't tell me. All right? What Frank told you about Jimmy—he told you about Eve's burglary, right? That night at the bar? He said Jimmy did that, that he could prove it, he could get Jimmy sent away for a long time? It wasn't true.

"Jimmy told you he was going straight. That was true. He's clean, Tony. He had nothing to do with the burglary, he had nothing to do with the murders. Tony, don't talk," I said again, as he tried to speak. His mouth closed; he watched me.

"Grice is dead. Jimmy messed things up a little trying to protect Ginny Sanderson, but it probably would've come out the same anyway. He saved my life, Tony, just like you did.

"Those bullets you took, they were meant for me. From one of Grice's boys." I stood. "That's what I came to say, Tony."

"Smith—"

"No," I said. "I don't want to hear it. Rest. You need to rest, Tony. You'll be all right, but it'll take time." We looked at each other in silence for a few moments. Then I said, "I'll see you, Tony," and I left.

* * *

Eve Colgate was waiting in the lobby when I got downstairs, but so was Brinkman.

"I got to talk to you, city boy."

"Jesus, Brinkman, can it wait until tomorrow? I'm a wreck."

"No. Now."

Eve put her hand on my arm. "I'll wait outside. I'm tired of this place." She turned to Brinkman. "I'd appreciate it if you kept it short, Sheriff." She walked out the smoky glass doors.

Brinkman watched her go. " 'I'd appreciate it . . .' Shit."

"What the hell do you want, Brinkman?" I sat, exhausted.

"I've been talking to Otis Huttner. He's going to live. He's not even hurt bad."

"Great. Can I go now?"

"He says everything you said is true, except he claims he didn't know a goddamn thing about Lena until after it was over."

"Uh-huh, sure. And?"

"And he says the cop Sanderson bought Grice was Ron MacGregor."

I rubbed my eyes. Flashes of red and yellow played behind my lids.

"Why the hell didn't you tell me that, Smith?"

I thought of saying I didn't know, but I had nothing left for that kind of show. And there was something more important, so I said that instead. "Brinkman, does it have to come out?"

"What the hell are you talking about? I'd've had Grice years ago, except for that bastard! I don't—"

"Brinkman, look. Grice is dead. MacGregor's dead. Any organization Grice built you'll be able to take apart pretty easily now, and it probably doesn't amount to much anyhow.

"But I don't think you're going to get much else out of

this. You might get Sanderson for the murder of his wife, but you'll have to drain the quarry pit to find her, and I don't think you'll have enough to go to court on, even if you do that.

"So pretty much it's over. You'll give press interviews and get reelected. The DA and NYSEG and the Feds, and whoever else wants to, will start investigations into Appleseed Holdings. Sanderson's pet politicians will suddenly lose his phone number. He'll be nobody in this county anymore, but he won't go to jail.

"And Ron MacGregor will get buried, but as a hero, Brinkman. That's what his family thinks. That's what everybody thinks. What the hell good is it going to do anybody, if the truth comes out?"

Brinkman's small eyes fixed on me for a long time. "You're just so goddamn smart, aren't you, city boy? You can just tell what's good for everybody, and how everything oughta work."

"No," I said, standing. "If I were smart, I could make things come out the way they should, instead of being left behind to clean up the mess."

I turned away from him, followed Eve Colgate out the gray glass doors.

In the car I told Eve the story from the beginning. I told her more than I'd told Brinkman, because the paintings were hers; but the part I'd kept from him I kept from her also.

I found myself telling her about MacGregor, though, which was something else I had decided not to talk about. But I needed to talk about it.

"I didn't catch on." I said. "At first he just told me to keep out of his way. He was a cop; that's standard. And he started asking me why I thought Brinkman, with such a grudge on, hadn't been able to get at Grice. I wondered why he was asking me. But he was fishing, looking to see if I'd figured out Grice had protection. And I had, but I wasn't smart enough to see where it was coming from.

"Then suddenly he was ordering me off the case, out of the county, pissed off, as though I'd done something. I guess that was when he found out Grice really was involved and trying to set Jimmy up. He was afraid I'd get too close. He wanted to protect me. And I didn't get it."

"He was a friend of yours," she said. "You trusted him, and he couldn't afford to trust you. What would you have done, if you'd known?"

"I don't know. Honest to God, I don't know."

We rode in silence for a time, back over the route we'd taken last night with Tony. The night seemed very quiet, very dark.

"That little girl," Eve said at last. "Do you think she really did that?"

"Shot Gould? Yes. If Grice had done it he'd've been proud. He wouldn't have manufactured a story, at least not for me. Yes, I think that was true."

There was more silence, more narrow, curving road, the smell of damp earth and woodsmoke in the air.

"Eve?"

"Yes?"

"I want to know something. You told me it was none of my business once, but I'm asking again. What's behind your arrangement with your gallery?"

She didn't answer for some time. Finally she said, "You have to have all the pieces, don't you? That's what drives you."

"That's part of it," I said. "Part of it."

She shifted, turned onto 30. Her driving was smooth and sure, even in my unfamiliar car.

"I told you," she said, "how my husband died. In a car accident. I was driving; we had both been drinking. I didn't tell you why." A pause; then, "Henri had just told me he'd made another woman pregnant."

She didn't look at me. I said, "Someone up here?"

"Yes. He'd been seeing her for over a year. I didn't understand it then, and I don't now. I thought we had . . . I thought . . . my God, how I loved him!" Her voice quavered. "And so I killed him. I don't think I meant to. I don't think so. But I don't think I'll ever know.

"Henri's daughter was born not long after I got out of the hospital. Her mother, Henri's . . . Henri's mistress . . . she wasn't a tramp. She ran a plant nursery. She was older than I, as Henri was. Smart, kind, and strong.

"She never knew who I was. I used to go to the nursery regularly. My cherry trees are from it. I watched the child grow."

The night had grown foggy as 30 climbed into the hills. I shivered slightly in the clammy air.

"I tried, through Ulrich, to give her money for the child. She knew it was from Henri's widow; she turned it down. But when the child was ready for school, she found she had a dilemma.

"We had gotten to be friends, of a sort. I don't know if you'll understand that . . ." For the first time, she glanced at me.

I said, "Yes. Yes, I do." In the darkness I couldn't see her eyes.

She nodded, went on. "She wanted the child to be educated well. She told me she had promised the child's father that. She told me—she said she had loved him very much." Eve drew a breath. "But the public schools here were not good. The only nearby private school was Adirondack Preparatory, which at that time was just a finishing school. There was no other place to send her daughter close to home, and she couldn't bear to send her away.

"And at last I had found something I could do. I made arrangments with Ulrich. On my behalf, he met with the trustees at Adirondack Preparatory. In the beginning I endowed chairs. I sponsored scholarships. I donated a new building, for the visual and performing arts.

"Eventually, as happens, my money attracted more money. Other people began sending their daughters there, and giving generously.

"By the time Henri's daughter was ready to enter the fifth grade, Adirondack had changed a great deal. She was sent there on a scholarship; she did quite well. She went on to college, and to medical school. She lives in New York now. I look her up when I go in, an old friend of her mother's.

"I've continued to support the school, and the answer to your question is that that's where my money goes. I'm not alone anymore in this, so now I concentrate my efforts in two areas: I sponsor a number of scholarships, and I underwrite Adirondack's programs in the visual arts."

The road curved, straightened again at a place where, in daylight, the view stretched fifty miles. Now there was only blackness, and distant lights.

"Do you see," she asked, "why I was unhappy with Lydia's prying into this? I knew it was unrelated to the burglary. And I had kept it secret for so long."

"Yes," I said. "I do see. And thank you for telling me. I know it was hard."

She surprised me with a wry smile. "Telling you wasn't as hard as I thought it would be."

I hesitated, said, "Eve? Who chooses the scholarship recipients?"

She threw me another glance, said, "There's a panel. They have certain criteria. Occasionally I recommend someone. I don't abuse my position and my candidates are never turned down. Why?"

"MacGregor's girls go to Adirondack," I said. "His arrangment with Grice was paying their tuition. That's what it was all about, his girls."

Eve said, "And you want me to make sure they can continue? You want to do that for him, even now?"

"Especially now. It's what he sold his soul for."

We spoke very little after that, as we covered the dark miles. I lit a cigarette and stared out the window and thought about Eve educating two generations of girls, other people's daughters, helping them to see so much, and so clearly, that in the end a nurserywoman's daughter becomes a doctor, and a wild fifteen-year-old can identify, with certainty, unsigned canvases no one has ever seen before.

TWENTY-TWO

Eve unlocked my cabin door, came in long enough to turn the light on in the front room. Her eyes fell on the piano, which gleamed softly. "I am sorry," she said, "that you won't let me hear you play." She smiled her small smile, studied me. "I imagine you're quite good."

"No. I'm not."

She smiled again, didn't answer.

Her eyes swept over the room, came back to me. "Are you sure you'll be all right?"

"Yes," I said. "Now that I'm here."

"Then I'll leave you here. Do you want me to come in the morning with your car?"

"No. I'll find my way over tomorrow. Thank you, Eve."

She took my hand, held it a moment. Then she turned and left.

I worked my way out of my jacket, found a glass and the bourbon bottle. I needed music, and I knew what I wanted: ensemble playing. Music made when people know each other, can anticipate and understand each other. I put on Beethoven, the Archduke Trio. I stretched out on the couch, sipped at the bourbon, felt the music flow around me. The soloistic, separate parts of the trio wove, danced, glided forward and back, created together what none of them was, alone.

It was an illusion, but it was beautiful.

I slept until one the next afternoon. Sometime after the music was over and the bourbon was gone I'd made my way into bed, and after that I was aware of nothing except the strange, sad images of my dreams.

When I awoke I was aching and stiff. My head hurt, but not as badly as the day before, not as badly as I'd expected. I stumbled to the outer room, clicked on the hot water, built a fire, put the kettle on. The day was gray again, silent, but with an expectation in the air.

I put bourbon in the coffee and made the coffee strong. After it was gone I showered, tried to soothe my aching shoulders under the rhythm of the pounding heat. I shaved, inspected in the mirror the shiner ringing my left eye, blood under the skin from the bullet that might have killed me. I was a mess. You could read the week's accumulation of trouble on my face.

Still, I didn't have to wait long on 30 before a pickup, heading south, stopped for me. Antonelli's was north of my place, and Eve Colgate's house north of that, but before I did what I needed to do today I had to eat.

"Thanks," I said as I climbed into the truck. "I wasn't sure anybody would stop for someone who looks like this."

The driver, a big, unshaven man, laughed a big, friendly laugh. "You kiddin'? Safest guy in the world to be with is a guy who's finished makin' trouble for someone else."

We shared a smoke and some idle talk about the nearness of spring. He let me off at the Eagle's Nest, a small, shiny diner that still had most of its original aerodynamic chrome.

At the counter I ordered steak and eggs, homefries, toast, and coffee. I took the first mug of coffee to the phone, called the hospital. I asked them how Tony was and they told me he was better, out of danger now. Then I asked for Lydia's room.

The phone rang five times and I was about to give up when a groggy voice answered in slurred Chinese.

"English," I said. "It's me."

"Oh, goody, it's you," she said. "Where are you?"

"At a diner, having breakfast. How do you feel?"

"Sleepy, and I have a huge headache. Is this what it's like when you have a hangover?"

"No, a hangover's worse because you know it's your own fault, too. Listen, I'll be up to see you later. I just wanted to know how you were."

"I can't wait. Bill, is Jimmy all right?"

"He wasn't hurt. I haven't seen him since yesterday, but he's okay. Go back to sleep."

"Wait. You don't really have Eve's paintings, do you?"

"No. That was for Grice. It was all I could think of. But now I know where they are. I'm going to get them after I eat."

"You do? Where are they?"

"I'll tell you about it when I come up," I said, and I knew I would. The part I hadn't told anyone, I would tell Lydia. "Hey, Lydia?"

"Umm?"

"You want me to call your mother, tell her what happened?"

She sighed, but just before the sigh I thought I heard a stifled giggle. "You," she said, "are an idiot."

"Yeah," I said, "I know. I'll see you later."

I hung up, went back to the counter, where my breakfast was waiting. I ate, filled with immense gratitude toward chickens and cows, offering a prayer of thanks for grease and salt. The homefries especially were almost unbearably good, burned in the pan, flecked with onions and peppers.

Finally finished, I lit a cigarette and worked the room, found somebody who was headed north on 30. He turned out to be a weekender, like me, and as we sped past my driveway and the empty parking lot at Antonelli's we talked about the city and, again, the approach of spring.

He dropped me on 30; I caught another ride into Central Bridge, walked the mile and a half to Eve's house. It felt good to walk, even in the dullness of a late winter day that made the promise of spring seem like just another damn lie you'd let yourself be suckered, again, into believing.

I was halfway up the drive when Leo came charging around from the back, barking, growling, yipping, and wagging all at once. I gave him the jelly doughnut I'd brought from the Eagle's Nest, scratched his ears, looked up to see Eve standing on the porch.

"Hi," she smiled. "How are you?"

"Much better, thanks."

"Come in. There's coffee and cake."

I shook my head. "Later, Eve. I want to finish this."

She gave me the keys to her truck and I headed back south. I pulled into the gravel lot at Antonelli's, slowed to a stop close to the door. I let myself in with the keys I had taken from Tony's hospital room.

I was steeled for an eerie silence, a sense of something ended, lost. But inside, the tables were set and a strong smell of garlic and oregano came from the kitchen. The jukebox was playing Charlie Daniels. As the door slammed behind me a voice yelled from the kitchen, "Marie?"

"No," I called back. "Bill."

The kitchen door swung open and Jimmy came through wiping his hands on a towel. "Hey, Mr. S.!" he grinned. "You okay? I called the hospital. They said you went home. What're you doing here?"

"I came to pick something up. What are *you* doing here?"

"Oh," he shrugged. "Well, you know. Tony's gonna be in the hospital a long time. That kind of stuff costs a lot. The hospital, they said Miss Colgate was taking care of everything, but that ain't right. You know? I mean, he's my brother. Hey, you want a drink?" He started to move behind the bar.

"No," I said. "No, thanks. Does Tony know you're doing this?"

"Nah. He don't want to talk to me."

"Did you go up to the hospital?"

"Uh-uh. He'd just tell me to get lost. That's what he always told me. You know."

I knew. I gestured around the bar. "You think you can manage here?"

"Sure. No problem. I called Marie and Ray. And Allie's coming in later, to help."

"Alice? Hey, Jimmy, that's great."

"Yeah, well, she says just to help. For Tony. The rest of it, she says we'll have to figure it out."

We stood looking at each other, suddenly awkward. Then Jimmy said, "So—what'd you come to get?"

"Jimmy," I asked, "how much did Lydia tell you yesterday?"

He grinned, a little color seeping into his face. "I was scared, man. Real scared. She just sorta kept talking, you know, until you guys showed up."

"What did she say?"

"Well, about what happened." He told me what Lydia had told him. It was the same story I'd given Brinkman: the truth, except for details of what it was Ginny had stolen from Eve Colgate.

And except, of course, for the part Lydia didn't know.

"Well," I said when he was through, "here's what comes next." I pulled a chair out from the nearest table, sank into it. I got a cigarette going before I went on. "That stuff Ginny stole that turned out to be so valuable? It was also big. Too big for her to take home and hide, and she didn't trust Wally with it."

"Wally?"

"Wake up, Jimmy. He's who she left you for. He was a lot closer to Frank than you were, and that's what she wanted."

"*Wally?*" He shook his head in disbelief. "Fuckin' Wally?"

"Yeah," I said. "Anyhow, she needed someplace safe to store this stuff for a while."

Light dawned in his eyes. "Here?"

"She had your keys. She must have known about Tony's basement. She probably figured no one would ever notice."

Jimmy flushed. "I told her. About downstairs. I was, like, goofing on Tony one day."

"So she hid it there. And she showed it to Frank Monday night. She'd already told him about it, and he was already figuring the angles. At the very least, he could frame you for the burglary and shake down Tony. That's what the fight was about.

"But when Ginny and Wally took him down here and showed him what they had, he acted cool. He wasn't impressed. Ginny was just a stupid kid, an amateur, he said. He told her to go home, back to daddy."

"She must've hated that, being treated like a kid. Like she wasn't tough."

"She did hate it. She hated it so much she showed how tough she really was by killing Wally, on the spot."

"Yeah," Jimmy muttered. "Yeah, that's what Lydia said. Jesus."

I didn't say anything. After a moment Jimmy asked, "Mr. S.? Why did Frank kill her?"

"She was in his way. She had just gotten to be too much trouble."

Jimmy rubbed his hand along his forehead.

Neither of us spoke for a long time. The jukebox moved from Charlie Daniels to Crystal Gayle. Finally Jimmy said, "Where is this—this stuff?"

"In the basement. Come help me with it."

We went down the creaking stairs. The basement still had the same dank smell, the same decades of dust covering things that once mattered to someone. The disturbances made by the finding of Wally Gould were already aging, rounding, fading.

Jimmy found his way to the middle of the room with an unconscious familiarity. He pulled the chain hanging from the bare bulb and in the light I searched the room from where I stood.

I found it immediately, a plywood crate about six by six, partially hidden behind other boxes. It was carefully made, fastened with screws at the corners, and it was practically dust free.

Jimmy and I carried it up, maneuvering carefully through the basement door, past the tables and barstools, out into the lot. I let down the back gate of Eve's truck and we hefted the crate onto the metal bed. My sore shoulders ached, my arms trembled a little as I closed the gate again.

Jimmy had been silent since we'd entered the basement. Now he turned to me, asked, "What's in it?"

"Eve asked me not to tell anyone, Jimmy. I'm sorry."

"No, it's okay. I sort of—I don't want to know, you know?"

I started around to the cab. As I put my hand on the door handle Jimmy said, "Mr. S., I don't get it." He frowned, rubbed his hand over the back of his neck, Tony's gesture.

"Don't get what?" I asked, but as I said it, I knew.

"Frank was framing me for killing Wally, right? And Ginny too? That's what Lydia said."

"That's right."

"But you told that trooper Ginny's body was in the quarry. Why would he, like, ditch her body, if he was setting me up? Is that who came up that night in the rain? To drop her there?" We looked at each other in the dull afternoon light. "Mr. S., that wasn't Frank, was it?"

I looked around me, the gravel lot, the tin sign swinging against the graying sky. The air had gotten colder since I left the cabin; there was a bite to the wind.

And suddenly I thought, tell him. Maybe something can be salvaged out of what happened here, if he knows. And so I told Jimmy what I had kept from everybody else. "No," I said. "That wasn't Frank. That was Tony."

It took him a minute to answer, and when he did his voice was shaky. "What the hell are you talking about?"

"Tony'd heard what Frank had to say about you. When I found Gould's body, Tony came down to the basement. He knows every inch of it, every broken piece of trash there. He must've spotted the crate right away, knew it didn't belong. Then your keys, the whole frame. He bought it all.

"Wednesday night he went looking for you. Marie would probably tell us, if we asked. Maybe he closed up early, maybe he just left her in charge. He was on his way to the quarry, I think. I'd told him you were there; I wanted him to know you were safe.

"But he saw your truck, on the road. He followed it. He didn't know it was Frank and Ginny; how would he know that? He thought it was you.

"He followed them to Eve Colgate's shed. He stayed back, to see what was going on. He's lucky he did that; Frank would have killed him. But what he saw was two people going into the shed, one coming out. Remember how dark it was that night, Jimmy, right before it rained.

"The truck drove away, but Tony stayed. Frank must've driven right by Tony's car, never saw him. I checked that road up from the valley. You could pull off and hide in the dark, lots of places.

"Tony went to the shed. The lock had been cut through; it was easy to get in.

"And he found Ginny, in a pool of blood on the floor. Your glove beside her. Your truck driving away.

"He bought this frame, too. Just like the other one."

"He thought I did that?" Jimmy spoke slowly. "Ginny, like that? He thought I did that?"

I waited before I went on.

"He took her body to his car. Her body, and the glove. He tried to clean up the blood, but there was too much. So he did something else: He covered it up. With paint, which Eve—which she stores there. With anything else he could find. That mess in the shed? It was only the floor. The windows weren't broken, the walls weren't scrawled on. Only the floor.

"But just as he started—probably even before he moved the body—I came along. He heard me coming; he couldn't let anyone see. Couldn't let anyone know what you'd done. So he waited, and he hit me, knocked me out."

"No, man," Jimmy said. "Uh-uh. If that was Tony, even if he thought it was me, he'd've told you. You, man. You saved my butt that other time, he knew that."

"I also gave your keys to MacGregor. Tony and I had fought about that. He didn't trust me to protect you, Jimmy. Not when it came to hiding a murder, a fifteen-year-old kid."

Jimmy started to speak, but I stopped him.

"Just before he left he came back to check on me. To make sure I was alive. There was paint on my chin, on my neck, when Eve found me."

"No!" Jimmy burst out. "This is crazy! Tony don't even like me! Why the hell would he do this, he thought I did something like that? Hide her body and shit? And you, man, he wouldn't hurt you. You're his best buddy, man."

"Someone called Eve Colgate that night to tell her I was in trouble. And Tony called her place in the morning," I said quietly. "Looking for me, to tell me nothing: I'd gotten a phone call, someone wanted me. He said he'd closed up, gone to my place to find me; when I wasn't there he started calling places I might be. Eighteen years I've been getting phone calls at the bar, Jimmy. When I come in Tony hands me scraps of paper. Did you ever know him to go looking for me before?"

Jimmy shook his head, back and forth, back and forth. "No, man. You're crazy. You coulda died out there. Tony wouldn't do that shit to you."

"I'd've been all right, if it hadn't rained. Tony called Eve; then he went up to the quarry, to dump Ginny's body. He may have seen your light; anyway he knew you were there, but probably the last thing in the world he wanted was to talk to you.

"And then what could he do? He couldn't come back and find me. What would he have said? All he could do was wait, and wonder if I was all right. And think about you, and what he thought you'd done. It must have been a hell of a night."

Jimmy stood motionless. His right arm started a gesture, abandoned it, fell back by his side. "I . . ." he said, sounding choked; he didn't finish.

I turned, climbed into the cab of Eve Colgate's pickup. I put the key in the ignition. As the engine roared to life I leaned out the window, said, "He's in room three-oh-nine, the new wing. Go see him."

I backed the truck around, rolled slowly out of Antonelli's lot. I drove with great care; I was very tired.

TWENTY-THREE

The wind was picking up as I turned the truck up Eve's chestnut-bordered drive. Hard dark clouds pushed through the sky from the north.

I pulled in front of the house, silenced the engine. The front door opened and Leo bounded onto the porch, left Eve framed in the doorway. She waited until I jumped from the cab, then came forward slowly, walked down the steps and around the back of the truck. She looked at the crate. With her eyes still on it, she asked me, "Are they all right?"

"I didn't open it."

Together we pulled the crate from the truck bed, carried it inside the house, Leo wriggling through the vestibule along with us. The house had a soft, sweet smell, vanilla and brown sugar.

We laid the crate on the dining table. I waited while Eve brought a screwdriver. She unscrewed the cover, dropped each screw in the wooden bowl on the cedar chest before going on to the next one. When she was finished she used the screwdriver to pry the cover loose. We each took an edge then, lifted the cover, leaned it on the wall.

The canvases were stacked facedown. Eve touched the top one, pulled her hand back as though it were hot to the touch. She stared a moment longer; then, suddenly, she hefted the painting out of the crate, stood it on the floor against the chair without looking directly at it. She repeated the action, her mouth set in a hard, determined line, like a diver forcing herself over and over into icy water to search for something lost.

Then all six paintings were out, spread around the room, and Eve was standing as still as I was, in the center of the storm.

Like other powerful storms, this one was violent, frightening, and heartbreakingly beautiful.

Thin razor-sharp wires of color were stretched across canvas, pulled so taut they broke apart; or, released, they bunched together in choking knots. These were colors other painters never found, colors you recognized instantly from the dreams you could never remember.

But unlike the Eva Nouvels I'd seen before, these paintings were not dark. The colors twisted, tangled, pierced each other, bled; but the field they were on was luminous, and the color wires glowed against it like lightning against the sun.

I was without words, looking from canvas to canvas as the storm raged around me. From the canvases I looked to Eve. She stood silent, her arms wrapped tightly around her chest. Her crystal eyes swept each painting, moved to the next. Then she covered her mouth with one hand and began silently to cry.

I took two quick steps, gathered her into my arms. Her shoulders felt sharp and thin, made of glass. She pressed hard against me. I held her more tightly. At first she wept noiselessly; then came great wracking sobs that shook her again and again. I rocked her, smoothed her hair, whispered useless, meaningless words as the storm pounded and battered her.

Finally, like other storms, it ended. I held her as long as she wanted, after the sobbing stopped, until she softened, pulled away. She turned without looking at me, stepped out of the circle of canvases, walked to the bathroom under the stairs. The door closed and the water ran for a long, long time.

I felt a pressure against my leg. I looked down to see Leo sitting, looking up. He whined, lifted a paw anxiously.

I crouched, scratched his ears. "It's okay, boy," I told him. "It's okay."

When Eve came out her eyes were pink-rimmed, her lined face pale. She hesitated outside the circle I still stood within, then stepped to my side. "Will you help me?" she asked.

We repacked the crate, each canvas facedown, and we tightened the cover. We carried the crate together out the back door, around into the storeroom, which had a new, heavy padlock and hasp. My eyebrows lifted at our destination; Eve saw that and shrugged. She gave me a small, tired smile. "It's where they go," she said.

We went back inside. Eve poured coffee, asked me to put some music on. "If you'd like," she added. I found Haydn, string quartets. Eve sliced a pound cake, brought me a piece. It was warm, rich, with a brown sugar glaze. She sipped her coffee, and the music calmed the air.

After a while I said, "They're beautiful, you know."

She shook her head.

"You'll probably never see it," I said. "But they are."

There was more music, more peace. She asked, "Bill, where were they?"

I looked into my coffee, watched the deep blackness release steam, which wandered out of the mug, lost itself in the open air. "They were at Tony's, in the basement," I said. At the look in her eyes, I added, "Tony didn't know."

She held my eyes with hers, searched my face. I couldn't tell what she found, but finally she nodded, released me.

I left soon after. Leo ran excited circles around us on the driveway as Eve and I walked the short distance to where she'd put my car. It was very cold now, as day edged reluctantly into night. Thick clouds rode the wind. Eve asked, "Will you go back to the city soon?"

"Lydia will be able to leave the hospital in a day or two," I said. "I'll wait and take her home."

She was silent again. The wind gusted icily; there seemed nothing more to say. I opened the car door. "When you come back," she said suddenly, "will you come see me?"

"It might be a long time, Eve."

She took my hand. In the depths of her eyes I thought I saw the jewels sparkle, but I couldn't be sure. She said, "I'll be here."

I held her close again, this time briefly. Then we separated. I slipped into my car, started it up, began to move slowly down the drive, away from the house. My headlights caught the trunks of the chestnut trees; I heard Eve, behind me, calling Leo.

I drove back south through a fast-fading twilight. I passed Antonelli's, lit now, cars on the gravel, the tin sign dancing in the gusting wind. Fallen leaves skidded ahead of me across the blacktop as the wind changed direction. My lights picked out what was in front of me; everything else was hidden.

By the time I reached the road down to my cabin, it had started to snow.

Turn the page for an excerpt from
S. J. Rozan's next book

REFLECTING THE SKY

Available in hardcover from
St. Martin's Minotaur

Damp, soupy heat washed over me as I pushed out through the revolving door. The bright morning glare was already hazed up by the shimmering exhaust of a river of cars, buses, and trucks. I looked left, looked right, got my bearings, and headed briskly down the sidewalk.

"Come *on*!" I turned to yell to my partner, Bill Smith, who still stood, looking a little groggy, his hands in his pockets, just gazing around. "Relive your misspent youth some other time! I don't want to be late."

With muttered words I was just as happy not to hear, he lurched down the sidewalk after me. Jostling, rushing pedestrians, many of them yelling into their cell phones, hurried past in both directions, making me feel like I had to work to keep my footing or I'd be tossed on their tide and swept away. Bill caught up to me as I stopped at the first corner, waiting with a crowd eight deep for the light to change.

"Late is extremely unlikely," he grumbled, taking advantage of the momentary halt in our forward charge to light a cigarette. "Impolitely early, maybe. We're twenty-five minutes ahead of even your obsessive-compulsive schedule. Will you slow down? And how do you know where you're going? I thought I was supposed to be your native guide."

"I don't know what you're supposed to be doing," I said

as the light turned green and the crowd surged forward, "but it can't be guiding me around a place you haven't been in for twenty years."

A horn blasted as the last stragglers from our pedestrian stream leaped up onto the curb to avoid being mashed by a bus. The hiss and rumble of tires, the squeal of bus brakes, and the endless rattle of jackhammers from nearby construction made conversation difficult, but I was too keyed up to talk, anyway. The wind shifted, stirring the smells of diesel fuel and salt water into the scents of softened asphalt and frying pork already thick in the air. They were exciting smells, and it was an exciting morning, all the rushing, rumbling, surging, and yelling in the brightness. Though I didn't see, really, why I should be so affected by it. I've spent my entire life negotiating traffic, noise, glare, and sidewalks. I'm Lydia Chin, born and raised in Chinatown, a genuine native New Yorker.

Of course, this wasn't New York. This was Hong Kong, City of Life.

Life, pork, exhaust, and pedestrians. Bill matched his pace to mine and we hurried down the sidewalk in the sticky heat. Being from Chinatown, I was better at this business of threading through dense, moving crowds of Chinese people than he was, though the streams on the sidewalks of home had never flowed this fast. We kept being separated, coming together, getting pushed apart again. But we both knew where we were going—he because he had been here before, on R and R leaves in the navy; me because I had been studying maps for a week— and we ended up together and exactly where we wanted to be, at the turnstiles of the Star Ferry.

At which point I glanced at my watch, and then, because I know my watch, at his. "Wait," I said. "As you so accurately, although crabbily, pointed out, we're still early. The ferries run every eight minutes. Let's take the next one. I want to see."

He raised his eyebrows and sighed theatrically, but I didn't care. Leaving him to follow, I zipped past the

English-language bookstore, the Japanese snack shop, the newspaper vendors and the public bathrooms. The ferry terminal buildings gave way to an open promenade with a railing, and suddenly there was the Hong Kong skyline shining across the harbor.

It was as though someone had unrolled New York, slapped it with dozens of huge, neon brand-name signs visible even in the hazy sunshine, and spread it against a backdrop of mountains along a waterfront so long I had to turn my head way to the left and then way to the right to see the ends of it. Water sparkled in the sun, lapping against the seawall we were standing on. The frothy wakes churned up by barges, fishing boats, great white yachts, and tiny green sampans heading both ways through the harbor crisscrossed the trails of ferries plowing back and forth across it, from Hong Kong Island, where we were going, to the tip of the Kowloon Peninsula, where we were. The ferry we'd almost taken tooted its horn as it nosed out of its berth, and from way off to the right came a much deeper sound, some other horn saying something in the universal language of ships.

"Close your mouth," Bill said. "People will know you're a tourist."

"I'm not a tourist. We're here on business. And why didn't you tell me it was this *huge*?"

He gazed across the harbor. "When I was here, it ended about there." He pointed with both hands at the limits of a much shorter waterfront. "And none of the biggest skyscrapers were there, and neither was that." *That* was a low, swoopy building, all metallic curves and wings, shining in the sun, right in the center, right on the water. "But the impression was the same. I stood there with my mouth open, too."

"My mouth is not open. I'm Lydia Chin. Stuff like this doesn't impress me," I said, unable to take my eyes from the view across the water.

"I know," Bill said. "That's one of your best characteristics, how hard you are to impress." He looked at his watch.

"Now we're right on schedule. We'd better go, or we actually will be late, and you'll blame me."

"Well, it'll be your fault," I said, tearing myself away from the skyline, turning to hurry back to the ferry. "You're the one with the good watch."

"Maybe that's why I'm here," Bill said as we dropped our ridged coins in the ferry turnstile and headed with the rest of the crowd up the stairs. "Because I have a watch that works."

"That's an expensive timekeeper." I trotted down the wooden ramp onto the boat and took a seat at the very front so I could see us sail across the harbor. "A business-class ticket and a week in a fancy hotel? It would have been cheaper for Grandfather Gao to buy me a Rolex."

"Or he could have put me in the same hotel room as you. That would have saved him a bundle. In fact, maybe we have a fiduciary duty to our client—"

I gave his fiduciary duty a dirty look and turned back to the opposite shore; we had started to move.

As the harbor breeze blew my hair around, I watched the edges of the skyline sharpen out of the haze. The buildings grew larger and Bill sat silent beside me, watching them too. It really wasn't clear to either of us why he was here. It wasn't, actually, clear to me why either of us was here.

What had seemed clear a week ago when I'd first heard this idea was that I was probably hallucinating and had lost my mind. Either that, or Grandfather Gao had lost his; but even suggesting that idea to myself made me so queasy from guilt that I had to calm myself with another sip of his tea.

I still couldn't believe it, though. "You want me to go to Hong Kong?" We were sitting at the low, lion-footed table in Grandfather Gao's Chinatown herb shop, surrounded by the dark wood cabinets with their small drawers, the brass urns and ceramic jars, the mingled smells of sweet incense and dried herbs that were as familiar to me as the flowered upholstery, family pictures, and spicy aroma of my mother's cooking in the Chinatown apartment where I grew up.

"With your partner," Grandfather Gao replied. His voice was its usual calm, somber self, but even in the shop's peaceful shadows I could see him smile at the excited squeak in my voice. He used to smile that same smile when I was seven, when I made that same excited squeak.

I tried to control myself and act dignified. I liked to think I'd changed in the years since I used to come bouncing into the shop, interrupting Grandfather Gao in the middle of weighing out herbs for a customer or reading his Chinese newspaper, to tell him about some event or idea of enormous importance to a grade-school child. After all, I'm twenty-eight, a PI with her own practice, a licensed professional. Even if my license is in a profession my entire family abhors.

So I sipped my tea calmly and regarded my prospective client professionally. He wore a dark suit and tie, with a gloriously starched white shirt, as always. His thin black hair was combed straight back from his high forehead. He reached an age-spotted hand to the teapot and poured for me, and it suddenly occurred to me that maybe I'd changed in all these years, but Grandfather Gao hadn't, not one bit.

"I hope this is a convenient time for this journey, Ling Wan-Ju," he went on, as though this were a normal conversation. Because we spoke in Cantonese, as we always did, he used my Chinese name, as he always had. "Your partner also, I hope he is free?"

By my partner, he meant Bill Smith. Although, unlike my family, Grandfather Gao does not regard Bill as the human equivalent of the primrose path to hell, it was still a shock to hear him suggest that Bill accompany me to the other side of the world.

Nevertheless, resolving to regain my cool professional demeanor, as befits a private investigator about to be sent overseas, I said, "Grandfather, of course I'll do anything you ask. But you know I've never traveled. I may not be the right choice to perform this task for you, whatever it is." It was killing me to say this, since I was already seeing myself in a window seat on the New York–Hong Kong flight, but it was always best to come clean with Grandfather Gao.

"Your partner has traveled," he answered, unperturbed. "I have considered this carefully, Ling Wan-Ju. A stream undisturbed flows easily to the sea, but a stream can be diverted, set on another course. You are a person in whose ability to find the correct course I have a great deal of confidence."

I blushed from my toes to the roots of my hair. Grandfather Gao did nothing but sit in his chair and sip tea. I sipped tea, too, and tried to act as though people who meant to me what Grandfather Gao did said things to me like he'd just said every day of the week. When I found my voice, I said, "Thank you, Grandfather. What is the task?"

He didn't speak right away, but looked into the shadows of his shop. Behind him, tendrils of smoke wandered into the air from the three sticks of incense burning at General Gung's shrine, high on the wall.

"When I was a boy in China," he said, bringing his eyes back to me, "two other boys in the village were as close to me as brothers. We were constant companions, inseparable. One of those boys was your grandfather."

I knew that. That was why, when my parents came to America, Grandfather Gao had looked out for them, finding them the apartment my mother and I still lived in, getting my mother her first sewing job, arranging for English lessons for my oldest brother, Ted, who, along with my next-oldest brother, Elliot, had been born in Hong Kong. That was why, along with lots of other Chinatown kids whose families had been split apart when some came to America and some stayed behind, though he wasn't really ours, we had always called him "Grandfather."

As though he were reading my mind—a sense I had with disconcerting frequency—Grandfather Gao said, "When we were fourteen, I left China in the company of Wei Yao-

Shi, the third companion of our boyhood days. Your grandfather remained in the village. We never saw him again."

"My father always said grandfather couldn't bear the thought of living anywhere but where his family had always' lived."

Grandfather Gao nodded. He paused, looking not at me and not, I thought, at the dark wood or the parchment scroll his eyes seemed to rest on. "I came immediately to America," he said. "Wei Yao-Shi remained in Hong Kong for some years. He brought his younger brother, Ang-Ran, out of China. The two established an import-export firm." Now he looked at me. "When your parents left China, it was Wei Yao-Shi who sponsored them in Hong Kong."

He stopped speaking; I waited, wondering about the slight note of worry I thought I heard behind his calm, decisive voice.

"When the Wei brothers' firm began to do business in America," he began again, "Wei Yao-Shi came here. He opened an office. He married. He did not live in Chinatown, but bought a house in Westchester. Though he continued to spend a good part of each year in Hong Kong, he became . . . quite American. When you were small, Ling Wan-Ju, you met my old friend Wei Yao-Shi. He, like I, followed the progress of your family, for the sake of our friend, your grandfather."

This was news to me. Seeing my expression, Grandfather Gao smiled. "His reports to your grandfather were quite satisfactory."

Well, good, I thought, not sure I was quite comfortable with being watched and reported on, even if the reports were satisfactory.

"Your grandfather died many years ago in China," Grandfather Gao said. "Now Wei Yao-Shi has died here in New York."

At General Gung's shrine the incense smoke seemed to shudder, as though a breeze had found a way into the shop's cool recesses. "I'm sorry, Grandfather."

"Thank you, Ling Wan-Ju. He was, of course, as I am, an old man."

I didn't at all like what that implied. "Grandfather—"

He silenced me with a look. "The seasons will change, Ling Wan-Ju. The leaves will fall."

I knew better than to get involved when the nature metaphors began. I sat in silence, waiting for him to go on.

"Wei Yao-Shi left me with a task to accomplish. A letter to be given to his brother in Hong Kong. A keepsake to be delivered to his young grandson, also there. His own ashes, to be taken home for burial. I would like you, with your partner, to do these things for me."

We sat for some time in the quiet of the shop, drinking tea, as Grandfather Gao explained to me the specifics of the situation. The more I heard, the more I understood his thought that things were not simple. What was involved, though, still didn't seem like things you'd need a PI to accomplish, much less two, but I had voiced my opinion and Grandfather Gao seemed set on this path. I saw no reason to argue further.

When we were done I went home, took a deep breath, and explained my client's request to my mother.

"To Hong Kong?" She sat on our living room couch, me beside her. The sun poured in the window, sparkling off my father's collection of mud figures in their glass cabinet. The expression on my mother's face was the same as it would have been if I'd told her Grandfather Gao wanted me to fly up to heaven and bring him back one of the peaches of immortality. "Gao Mian-Liang wants you to go to Hong Kong? He has chosen you for this important task?"

"With Bill," I said. "He said Bill needs to come along."

I was as astounded as she was: she at what I had said, I because I had never before seen my mother at a loss for words.

I could understand her dilemma, though. On the one hand, she couldn't imagine I could go all the way to Hong Kong, a place on the other side of the world I knew nothing about—and where almost everyone is Chinese, a state of being that according to my mother I, an American born and raised, also knew nothing about—and not screw this up. On the other hand, there was no way she could contradict Grandfather Gao's decision in this or any other matter. And on the third hand, Bill was supposed to be going, too.

This last became her point of departure. "If you went alone," she said, "alone, with no distraction, possibly you could accomplish this task. Or—" her whole face brightened with inspiration and relief; she had found an answer, "—or, Ling Wan-Ju, if I were to go with you, I could guide you. I could help you. I could make sure you did not fail in this undertaking, so important to Grandfather Gao."

Oh boy, I thought. But I didn't stop her as she grabbed the red kitchen phone ("Red, most likely to bring good news") and dialed the number at Grandfather Gao's shop.

After that conversation, I called Bill.

"I'm coming over."

"Good," he said. "Why?"

"Just wait till you hear."

It took me, adrenaline filled as I was, about six minutes to get from the apartment to his place above the bar on Laight Street. Generally, it's a ten-minute walk, but that's if you walk.

Bill was waiting for me at the top of the stairs, a fresh cup of coffee in his hand. He poured hot water into a teapot as I paced the living room, outlining the job we'd been offered.

"Grandfather Gao?" Bill said. "Can I call him that? And will you please sit down?"

"Yes. And no. I can't."

Neatly sidestepping me, he moved to the couch safely out of my path and put his coffee on the table beside him. "Your tea's ready. You want it to go?" I glared. He grinned. "Boy, I've never seen you like this."

"Grandfather Gao!" I said, striding by. "Grandfather Gao wants to hire *me*! Do you know who he is in Chinatown?

Do you know what he's been in my life? Do you know what he is in the eyes of my *mother*?"

Bill did know, and I knew he did, but he asked, "What?"

"Respectability itself! The Man Who! Even my mother can't object to my working for Grandfather Gao. I mean, she does on principle because she hates this profession. But she's secretly thrilled that *Grandfather Gao* thinks a worthless girl like me can be some use to him."

"If it's a secret how do you know?"

"She's my mother. And Grandfather Gao—" I turned and strode the other way, "Grandfather Gao could get anybody he wanted to work for him! But he thinks *I'm* the one who can help him out. Me! Little Ling Wan-Ju. That tomboy. That misguided problem child. And—!"

Bill waited, patience itself. Finally, after I'd done another lap, he said, "And what?"

"*And* he wants to send us to Hong Kong! The other side of the *planet*! Ted and Elliot were born there. My parents used to live there."

"And Suzie Wong."

"Hong Kong! It's almost China."

"It is China, now."

"You know what I mean! I've hardly ever been anywhere in my whole life, and now I have a client offering me business-class tickets and a week in a hotel in Hong Kong. How can you just sit there like that?"

He picked up his coffee. "Okay, tell me again."

"Thursday," I said, telling him the important part. "Can you do it? Can you come?"

"He really wants me to? Why?"

I stopped pacing and just stood for a moment, looking at him. "I don't know," I confessed. "What he wants us to do seems pretty simple, not something a paying client might think he needs two people for. But it was his idea. He said, 'Neither the little bird nor the water buffalo, different though they are, can do its work alone.' "

"And I suppose you would be the little bird?"

I didn't answer, because it seemed obvious. Bill sipped

his coffee. "You know, of course, that the bird sits up there on the water buffalo's rump and eats his fleas?"

I detoured into the kitchen and picked up the tea he'd fixed for me. "If you have fleas, you're sitting in coach."

The tea was jasmine, one of my favorite kinds, and I had to admit that over the four or so years we'd known each other Bill had learned to make a not bad cup of tea. But all I could think as I sipped it was, I wonder if they drink jasmine tea in Hong Kong.

"And what are we supposed to do in Hong Kong?" Bill asked.

"Bring a bequest to a seven year old boy."

"Any particular seven-year-old boy, or do we get to choose?"

"Harry," I said impatiently, starting to pace again. "The grandson of Wei Yao-Shi. Didn't I tell you that already?"

"You haven't actually said anything coherent since you got here. I think it would help if you sat down."

"It wouldn't. I told you, I can't." He was following me with his head as though I were a one-woman tennis match. "Now listen: This little boy—his Chinese name is Wei Hao-Han, by the way—his grandfather, Wei Yao-Shi, just died. Mr. Wei and *my* grandfather and Grandfather Gao were inseparable buddies in the home village in China."

"Used to hang out on street corners together, whistle at girls, stuff like that?"

"Certainly not. The home village didn't have streets, just dirt paths. Can you hang out on a dirt path corner?"

"Depends on whether that's where the girls go by."

"Oh, of course. Anyway, my grandfather stayed there, but Mr. Wei and Grandfather Gao left to come to America when they were fourteen."

"Looking for street corners."

"No doubt."

I told Bill about Mr. Wei's younger brother, the import-export firm, the office Mr. Wei came to New York to establish, his marriage, his traveling back and forth, and the house in the suburbs.

"Now," I said, "a month ago Mr. Wei died and left this thing with Grandfather Gao with instructions to give it to his grandson Harry and a letter to his brother at the same time and Grandfather Gao wants you and me to go to Hong Kong to deliver them. How hard is that?"

"To understand, or to do? Or to say in one breath the way you did? Because I don't think I could do that."

"You could if you didn't smoke."

"You pace. I smoke." He struck a match and lit a cigarette, maybe to illustrate the point. I picked up pacing speed, to keep up my side.

"I understand it," he said, dropping the match in an ashtray. "Mostly. But I do have one question. No, two."

"Shoot."

"You say Mr. Wei came here and married. How come he has a seven-year-old grandson in Hong Kong? Did his kids move back there?"

"Ah. I was afraid you'd ask that."

Bill raised his eyebrows and I prepared to tell him the rest of the situation, the part that made the thing not simple. "Mr. Wei's American son, Franklin, lives here in New York. But apparently about a year after Mr. Wei got married here he got married in Hong Kong."

"Hmmm. Short-lived marriage, the one here."

"Actually, no."

"Say what?"

I took a defensive sip of tea. "Now don't go getting all superior and moral. It's the traditional Chinese way. A man is entitled to as many wives as he can support."

"He is? You mean still? Today? They still do that?"

"Well, no," I conceded. "By my parents' time they'd pretty much stopped, and of course Mao stamped that sort of thing right out. But men of Mr. Wei's generation—well, it happened."

"It happened." He was grinning. No one could ever say Bill was a handsome man, but when he grins this particular grin I sometimes have trouble staying as dignified as I like to be. "You mean, like an accident? Stumble into the church, wedding going on, you find out it's yours? Had one already, but what the hell?"

"We don't get married in church."

"You're grasping at straws. And you approve of that kind of behavior?"

"I can see certain merits," I said airily. "The more wives there are, the less time each one has to spend with the husband."

"A good point. I'll remember that after you marry me. Did Mr. Wei's wives approve?"

"At least you'll have something to remember. They didn't know."

Bill pulled on his cigarette. "Now that's not a sign of a man with a clear conscience. When did they find out?"

"The wives? Both dead, long since, and it seems they never did know. The people who were surprised were the sons, on both sides of the planet, when the will was read. Grandfather Gao knew all along, and the younger brother in Hong Kong, but no one else did."

"How many sons? And did Grandfather Gao approve?"

"Two: one here, one there. And when did you get to be such a puritan?"

"Hey, you're the one who doesn't drink, smoke, or swear. Who'd have thought that when it came right down to it you were as twisted as the next guy? Wei was supporting both families the whole time?"

"Better," I said, leaving the next guy out of it. "He was living with both. According to Grandfather Gao, each family thought it was just an unfortunate necessity of business that he had to keep going back and forth to the other side of the world."

"This is great. But what if they needed to talk to him when he was on the other side of the world? Wouldn't the jig be up as soon as someone made a phone call?"

"He told both families he was staying in hotels and to contact him at work if they needed to. In Hong Kong that was the firm's office. That's why the brother had to know.

In New York he used Grandfather Gao's number at the shop."

"And that worked all these years?"

"Seems to have."

Bill finished his coffee and set his mug down. "Okay. Intriguing as Mr. Wei's lifestyle is, let me ask my other question. Why us? This seems like a fairly straightforward job, delivering a legacy to a kid. You don't need an investigator to do this. What is it, by the way?"

"Jade. Some valuable piece, something Mr. Wei got in China on one of his buying trips and used to wear around his neck."

"Oh-ho, so he made buying trips to China? How do we know he hasn't got another three dozen wives over there?"

"Why do I get the feeling you're not taking this seriously?"

He gave me a look over his coffee that almost made me laugh. But someone around here needed to act like a grown-up, and neither Bill nor, I had to admit. Old Mr. Wei seemed willing to play that role.

"Anyway," I said professionally, "he didn't go there that often. It was usually the brother who did the China trips. And to answer your question—assuming you still care about the answer—"

"Oh, I do, deeply."

"—Grandfather Gao says he's hiring us because he wants someone he can depend on, partly because of the other piece."

"The other piece of jade?"

"The other piece of the job. Delivering the bequest and the letter is only half of it. We also have to deliver Mr. Wei."

"You're kidding."

"He wants—wanted—to be buried in Hong Kong. Next to his second wife. In a mausoleum in Sha Tin on a windy mountain with a view of the hills and the water—" I broke off and looked at Bill, who was grinning yet again. "*What*?"

"You mean we're taking the old two-timer with us?

Carrying his cheatin' heart home? Laying dem double-crossing bones to rest?"

"Ashes. And show some respect."

"You misread me. I have nothing but respect for your Mr. Wei. What a guy. Maybe just by being in the presence of his mortal remains, I can learn something."

"You," I said with all the dignity I could collect, "will never learn anything. Anyway, the ceremony should be interesting. The half-brother will be there."

"What, from New York?"

"Dr. Franklin Wei. He's an orthopedist, in case you get your foot stuck in your mouth. Grandfather Gao says he's planning to go to the funeral."

"This is getting better and better. Why doesn't he take the jade? And the letter? And the ashes?"

"According to Grandfather Gao he's a little irresponsible. Married and divorced three times. Sequentially, not simultaneously."

"I was about to ask."

"I know you were. A wild and crazy guy."

"Me?"

"Dr. Franklin Wei. New girlfriend every six weeks. Known at all the best clubs and hot spots. Cancels office hours to go to the ball game. May or may not actually show up in Hong Kong. Grandfather Gao didn't want to risk it. Besides, it seems a little weird for him to be the one responsible for taking his father's jade to the son of his father's other son, under these circumstances."

"I think this whole thing is a going to be a little weird."

"Are you telling me you're coming?"

He pulled on the cigarette again. "You remember, of course, that the last time we left town together you got hurt?"

"So did you."

"Not as badly as you."

"Whose fault was that?"

"Mine, no doubt."

"If that's an apology," I said, "I accept."

"I just wanted you to know what you're getting into."

"I'll sign a waiver. So you'll come?"

"Well, I'd still like to know why he wants me to. Besides the water buffalo thing."

I gave him a look a little more serious than the ones I'd been giving him. "You're thinking he's expecting some kind of trouble?"

"The thought had crossed my mind."

"Mine, too," I said. "I tried to ask him. I said whatever small skills you and I might have, we were honored to put them at his disposal. I said we would exercise all our powers to accomplish the task he was setting us, and I was sure we could be most successful on his behalf if he were to tell us about any special concerns he had so we could prepare ourselves to meet them."

"Elegant, setting aside the *small*. And?"

I shook my head. "He said, 'Ling Wan-ju, storm clouds often pass without rain, just as a dam can fail and flood a village on a clear, fine day.'"

"Well, that clears that up."

"You know Grandfather Gao never actually says everything he means. He thinks it works better if people find things out for themselves. And when he does talk," I admitted, "half the time it's in nature metaphors like that that I never understand."

"And that's why you're so crazy about him?"

"I'm crazy about him, as you so delicately put it, because he's wise, and kind, and fair. And he's a wonderful herbalist, and he makes great tea, and he never treated me like a dumb kid, even when I was one. And you," I told him, "should consider this: He's the only Chinese person of my acquaintance, with the possible exceptions of my brother Andrew and my best and oldest friend Mary, who would consider giving you the time of day."

"Well, you said he was wise." He squashed his cigarette out. "You don't think he could be setting us up?"

I was appalled. "Absolutely not! Grandfather Gao would never do anything to hurt me! If he's expecting trouble, and he wants to hire us, it's because he thinks we can handle whatever it's going to be. Which is another reason I *have* to take this job. I can't let him down if he's thinking like that."

Bill met my eyes and held them without speaking for almost longer than I could stand it. Then he looked back down and did some more cigarette-squashing. "When does he want us to leave?"

"Thursday! Thursday Thursday Thursday! *Well?*"

"What does your mother have to say? Not about the job, but about me going?"

"My mother?" I was surprised at the question, but I answered it with the truth. "You can't expect her to feel anything but pure horror at the idea of me flying to the other side of the world with you."

"I suppose not."

"On the other hand, like I told you, she secretly thinks working for Grandfather Gao will keep me out of trouble for a while, and she's always wanted me to go to Hong Kong. She says if I saw Hong Kong maybe I would understand better."

"Understand what?"

"She never says. But I'm sure it has something to do with my shortcomings as a Chinese daughter."

"So she approves?"

"She would walk off a cliff if Grandfather Gao suggested it, especially if it was for the good of her children. But she still doesn't like the idea of me going alone with you. She had a solution."

"Which was?"

"For her to come."

I enjoyed the expression on his face when I said that almost as much as I like his grin.

"Oh, my God. What did you say?"

"What could I say? She's my mother. But luckily Grandfather Gao said no."

"You said yes?"

"She's my mother."

He stared. "And I thought I knew you. My God, a guy's friends can turn on him."

"Besides, I wasn't sure you were coming."

"I'm not sure I should. You might be lying. We'll get to the airport, and there'll be your mother, with her shopping bags and that flowered umbrella to hit me over the head with—"

"I'm going to hit you over the head myself unless you tell me whether you're coming."

I stopped pacing and stood in front of him, resisting the urge to stamp my foot.

"Well," he said at last, "it's certainly tempting. The other side of the world on someone's else's nickel? A chance to spend a week in a hotel with you?"

"Separate rooms."

"A city where everyone smokes, where the weather's tropical, where I can relive some of the high points of my misspent youth?"

"On separate floors."

"Where the girls in the tight cheongsams sip mai-tais in booths in dim smoky bars until the Mama-sans call them over for you?"

"Separate hotels."

"Where the Tsingtao flows like water and every other basement's an opium den?"

"Separate land masses. Me on the Hong Kong side, you in Kowloon."

"Well, when you put it that way," he said, "how could I possibly turn it down?"